PRAISE FOR GRIMM, GRIT, AND GASOLINE

"Magic mixes with grease and jazz in this fantastic new anthology that brims with strong heroines, diverse settings, and a heaping helping of Nazi-punching."

—Nebula Award-nominated Beth Cato,
author of *Breath of Earth*

"These unfailingly clever tales are impressive and page-turning, helping to correct the dearth of speculative fiction set in the interwar era. There is also a frequent and welcome spotlight on heroic women. Any reader who enjoys early-20th-century history or retold fairy tales will find these familiar but new, with well-played wonder in every story."

—Publishers Weekly

GRIMM, GRIT, AND GASOLINE

DIESELPUNK & DECOPUNK FAIRY TALES

A Punked Up Fairy Tales Anthology

Edited by Rhonda Parrish

World Weaver Press

GRIMM, GRIT, AND GASOLINE

This is a work of fiction; characters and events are either fictitious or used fictitiously.

Published by World Weaver Press, LLC
Albuquerque, NM
www.WorldWeaverPress.com

Cover layout and design by Sarena Ulibarri.
Cover images used under license from Shutterstock.com.

*

First edition: September 2019
ISBN-13:978-0998702247

Also available as an ebook

GRIMM, GRIT, AND GASOLINE

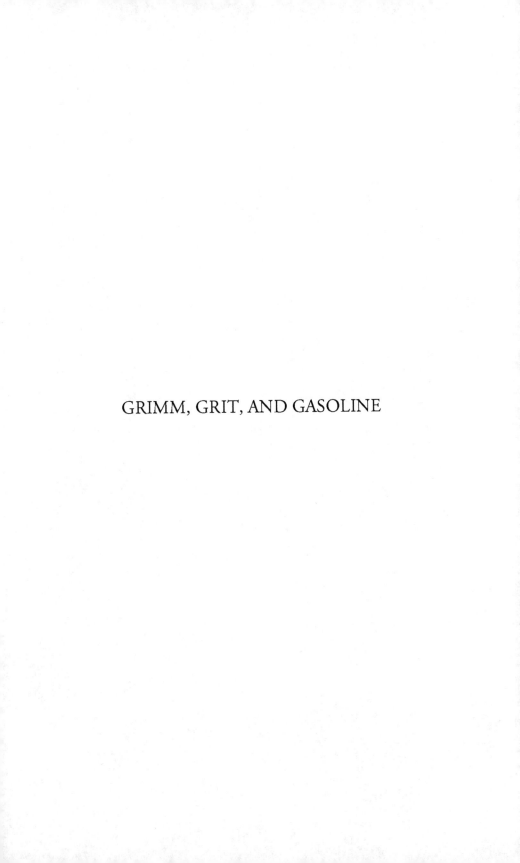

CONTENTS

INTRODUCTION

Rhonda Parrish

Inevitably when someone attempts to describe or define dieselpunk or decopunk they begin with, "It's like steampunk, except..." and I really wanted to avoid doing that, mostly to be different. But the thing is, steampunk is a genre that speculative fiction readers generally have a pretty good grasp of, so it actually does make the perfect jumping off point when explaining dieselpunk and decopunk. So I will ask you to forgive me for this, but...

Dieselpunk is like steampunk, except that where steampunk draws its aesthetics from Victorian and Edwardian times and features steam-powered technology, dieselpunk pulls from a later time period and is much more about the roar of massive engines than bustles and parasols. Steampunk is brass and glass, dieselpunk is iron and grease. And I like to think of decopunk as dieselpunk's flapper sister. Similar time period, but all dolled up and ready for a night out on the town.

I've noticed a bit of wiggle room when it comes to the time period that defines dieselpunk, but mostly it seems to be the interwar period—the years between the first and second World Wars. For this anthology, though, I stretched that and asked for stories set between the start of WWI and the end of WWII... and then I blatantly broke my own rule and included a story from the Korean War.

I actually broke a couple rules, not just of dieselpunk and decopunk, but of fairy tales. Some of these fairy tales, you will find, are not actually fairy tales. They are fairy tale-ish. Or folkloric.

And there might be a couple 'dustpunk' stories (alternate histories from the dust bowl days of the dirty thirties) in here too, so there's another rule bent.

But I'm not losing sleep over bending or breaking those rules, and the anthology is stronger for it.

I feel like, in some ways, this anthology has been inevitable. At the very least it is my childhood meshing together with my middle-age in a glorious storytastic way. I spent a great deal of my childhood and several years of my adult life living in Nanton, Alberta. Nanton is a small town that is best known for being home to a Lancaster bomber—one of only seventeen remaining in the world.

The bomber is now securely housed inside a museum there in Nanton, but when I was a kid it was just sort of parked outside right by a playground, and I spent a lot of time in that playground. My brother, cousins and I used to climb around the plane's wheels as much as we did the monkeybars. And then they one day there was a chain link fence around the bomber. And then a building…

But one day, one magical day before the building or the fence, someone with some authority let us go through the Bomber. He'd pulled up a set of stairs to a door near the tail for some reason or another, and he gave us a quick and dirty tour through it. I don't know if this was a community event or if we just happened to be at the right place at the right time—my memory of that is fuzzy—but the inside of that bomber left a very definite impression on me.

I think that might be where this anthology started. All those years ago when I was crawling through the belly of the bomber trying not to bump my head or catch myself on anything, and imagining how it must have been for the men who'd flown in it.

After that I had a low-key but persistent interest in WWI and

WWII—in fact, interesting side note, the first ever time I made money writing was when I won second place in an essay contest about Remembrance Day that was sponsored by our local Legion (at that time I was living in Vulcan, Alberta so that was the Royal Canadian Legion Branch #21)—but that interest really came to head a few years ago when I transcribed my grandmother's autobiography.

Reading about my grandmother's experiences. About her father who fought during the Great War with the 50th Battalion, and eventually died from injuries sustained during a gas attack, and how profoundly and personally that affected her. Reading about her brothers who went on to fight in WWII. Seeing her bitterness spilled across the page that after her father sacrificed so much in the 'war to end all wars' there was another war before the memory of the first had even lost its rough edges… well it personalized it for me in a way that nothing else had before, and re-ignited my interest in it.

And then I discovered dieselpunk and I was like, "Are you kidding me?" It was awesome. And then dieselpunk introduced me to decopunk and I knew I wanted to create something within those genres. Combining them with another lifelong fascination of mine—fairy tales and their retellings—just seemed like a perfect fit. And the timing couldn't be better.

I proposed this anthology to my publisher, Sarena, right about the same time as the white supremacist rally in Charlottesville, Virginia. A time when it seemed like the world could possibly benefit from a reminder that Nazis are bad and fascism must be stopped wherever it may be found.

And now we're releasing it in 2019—the perfect time for the Nazi-fighting of dieselpunk, the subversive spirit of decopunk, and the hope and happily ever afters of fairy tales.

Rhonda Parrish
Edmonton
2/2/2019

CIRCLES AND SALT

Sara Cleto

"When therefore the time was over, and the day came when the Evil-one was to fetch her, she washed herself clean, and made a circle round herself with chalk. The devil appeared quite early, but he could not come near to her."

— *Jacob and Wilhelm Grimm*

Before I leave my room each morning, I slide my silver gloves into place. I used to worry that people would notice them and ask questions. The only other gloves I'd seen before arriving in the city were the tough leather gloves that I sometimes wore on the farm when I needed to protect my skin from splinters and briars. These gloves, my silver gloves, are light as cobwebs before dewdrops weight their strands.

But here in the city, all the women wear gloves, and no one gives mine a second glance. Their fingers are wrapped in velvet and lace or netting and beads. Sometimes, they pull them off and let them rest on the table next to their drinks. When I bring round the pitcher of water, I see opals and emeralds gleaming on their fingers as they tap the table in time with the music. I never take mine off, not when I'm carrying a tray of drinks or tilting the microphone down to my lips.

In my gloves, I could be anyone. I could be Elodie of the empty glasses, Elodie of the syncopated notes, Elodie from upstate or overseas or a dream. Without them, the narrative possibilities narrow to one, and I refuse to live in only one song and not of my making.

Besides, my hands have been cold for years.

I've been working at the Pear Tree for almost two months now. I was lucky to get the job at all—two boys had quit, one after the other, the day I wandered in, brushing snow off my coat and grimacing when the flakes melted into my gloves. My request for a whiskey was met by a harried look from the woman behind the bar. "You can have two whiskies on the house if you'll clear those tables for me," she said, sliding me a glass with one hand and gesturing towards a cluster of tables crowned with dirty glasses. I'd stayed all night, tossing back drinks and a bowl of thick vegetable stew between table-runs. The bartender must have liked the quickness of my feet—I didn't sit down once—and she offered the room upstairs and more of the same if I'd come back the next day.

I've been here ever since.

The bartender—her name was Rona, I'd learned that the first night—decided she liked having an employee who didn't mind taking orders from a woman, and gave me room, board, and seven dollars a week for helping her run the Pear Tree. She tried to make me sit down occasionally during my shifts, but I tugged at the wrists of my gloves and kept moving.

I don't stand still, not for long. Rona thinks it's because I'm young, full of spunk and life, dancing from sunup to sundown. It's much simpler to let her think that I move for the sake of the music that always fills the club, for the sensation of my short curls brushing my neck. I can't imagine trying to tell her the truth, so I smile and shiver and keep moving.

The truth is that I've been dancing, moving, running since I was fourteen. Before that, I was a dreamier creature altogether, a girl who could sink into stillness like a bucket into a well. I loved reading. I loved the slow, methodical way soup came together in a pot if I stood beside it and stirred. I loved watching the leaves fall from the apple tree outside my window. My father called me lazy, though I tended all the animals on his farm and made three meals for us each day. The way I could stand still and look steadily at anything made him uncomfortable.

He says he didn't mean to do it, and I do my best to believe him, but at night when I lay in bed, careful to keep my arms and legs tucked carefully into my body, I am quite sure he did.

Everyone knows not to trust strangers in the wood. But when a man with a black hat and cold, cruel smile told him he'd pay half a million dollars for whatever stood in his backyard, he agreed.

"Well of course I thought it was nothing but the apple tree," he told me later. "How was I to know you were out there, staring at nothing? You should have been busy making dinner by then."

I looked at him in the steady way he hated for a long moment. Then I moved.

Always, the Pear Tree hummed with conversation, music punctuated with the scrape of chairs against the floor and the clink of glasses against each other and the round cocktail tables scattered across the large room. Small beaded lamps provided the only light, concealing nearly as much as they revealed. Sequins flashed on gowns and headbands, and teeth gleamed behind red lipstick as patrons moved between pools of light.

Tonight, the club positively brimmed with people, silk and the scents of leather and gin. The room was a perfect, unchoreographed dance, and I, at its center, was safe. I felt my muscles relax, my spine unstiffen as I went to stand behind my microphone.

Every day, when I arrived at work, the first thing I did was to lift the small burgundy rug and check the ring of chalk I had drawn there, on the ground beneath the microphone. Once I was sure the circle was perfect and whole, I could step inside and be still.

The band, brassy and sweet as always, brought their song to a close. The pianist shot me a toothy grin before launching fingers across the keys in the first bars of my opening song, a sinuous rendition of "My Blue Heaven." I felt my way back into stillness as I sang, letting my feet plant themselves against the floor. At first, I swayed with the music as words poured from my throat, but soon I let myself rest until all that moved was my mouth around the words and my eyes around the room.

Rona's daughter was here again tonight. Though we hadn't been introduced, the tight curl of her hair and the dimples in her cheeks were unmistakably her mother's. Her gloves were short and dazzlingly white against her brown skin, and her back and her gaze were straight as an arrow. She seemed at home with herself in a way that I could almost remember feeling, and I could almost imagine feeling that way again when I looked at her. Almost.

She found me behind the bar after my set.

"A gin rickey, please," she said. Her voice was soft and smooth, as if she'd been drinking bee's knees full of honey rather than water, which is all she'd had since she came in the door an hour ago.

I nodded at her and pulled a highball glass off the shelf and added a few lumps of ice.

"Your voice is extraordinary," she said. "Where did you learn to sing like that?"

Squeezing a lime over the glass, I looked up at her. She wasn't leaning against or over the bar but standing up straight on the other side, her head cocked a little to the side as if waiting for my answer.

"Nowhere, really." When she didn't press for more but waited quietly for her drink, I added, "My mother sang when I was little. I guess I learned to love it from her." Gin, then soda joined the lime in the glass.

The girl nodded. "It reminds me of a voice in a story I read once."

I slid her the glass, smooth and quick, so the soda fizzed against the gin but didn't splash over the top. "What's your name?"

She smiled. "June."

"I'm Elodie. What story?"

She laughed. "It was a in book of fairy tales. The story was about a mermaid who wanted to be on land. She wanted it so much that she gave up her voice, the source of her power and magic. She did it for a prince" — here she made a face, and I laughed out loud — "which all seemed like rather a pity, and she died in the end."

"I remind you of a ninny-mermaid?" I asked.

"No, no, just your voice. It sounds like something magic."

"That sounds dangerous," I said mildly. "You're Rona's daughter?"

"Yes. I'm between jobs, so I'm home for a visit," June said. "I play the trumpet. You ever sing in a band?"

"Me? No, I just sing here sometimes, on nights they need me to fill in."

"You should think about it. I know it pays better—I've worked here, too!" She dropped a few coins on the counter and slipped into the kitchen.

I realized I'd been standing still since I'd finished pouring June's drink. Scolding myself, I whirled back into motion, wiping down the bar, carrying around the water pitcher, clearing glasses, clearing my mind of anything past tomorrow.

The devil came for me the same day my father made his bargain.

Bags stuffed with crisp bills, bags brimming with bright coins spilled their bounty in our kitchen. My father sank his fingers into them and smiled.

I did the only thing I knew to do—I drew a circle round me with chalk, like a heroine from the fairy tales my mother used to tell me.

When the devil appeared, the circle was almost closed. He saw me, saw my hand guiding the chalk across the floor, and he extended his fingers and hissed a word that seared my ears and my flesh. A black mark bloomed across the pale skin of my hand, and I could feel his grip on me. I screamed in rage and pain, but I didn't stop moving my hand, not for an instant, and before he could fasten his hold on me, the circle was closed.

"You are mine," he told me. His skin was the bluish white of deep winter ice, and his smile was a string of icicles.

"I am my own."

"You are your father's. You are his flesh and blood, and he has given you to me. You are mine."

"I am my own, and you have no claim on me."

"Ah, but you are wrong, my beauty. You have but to look at yourself to know that I will never release you."

I refused to look down at my hand, but I could feel his mark settling into my skin, swirling around my palm and up my fingers, arcane and bruise-deep.

"No. I will stay in this circle forever if I have to, or I'll run for the rest of my life, but you will not take me."

He laughed, each icicle-tooth gleaming in the wet maw of his mouth. "A challenge! How delightful!" He grinned, teeth grinding together, snapping and spawning new spires as I watched. My stomach heaved but I swallowed, and met his gaze. "Well, my rabbit, let's see you run. I'll make a new bargain. Stay within a circle or run, run, run, and you'll be safe. But the moment you stop, the second you rest, I will take you."

The devil vanished from my kitchen. The stove, the teacups, and all the coins were covered in a thick layer of frost.

That night, the devil sat in the chair at the foot of my bed. I felt him come in with a blast of cold like a punch to the chest.

"You stood still, little Elodie," he murmured, his fingers tracing frosted obscenities across my bedroom mirror. "Not for long, just a moment, but it was just enough to let me find you. Why did you do it, my rabbit? Did you see a prince and fall in love?"

My bed was circled in rings and rings of chalk, so he could not reach me, not here, not yet. I turned my back to him and curled around my pillow. "You have some very outdated ideas about how modern ladies run their lives," I said in a reasonable approximation of my normal voice.

"Then what was it, Elodie? Tell me, and I'll go away until tomorrow night."

I was silent for a moment. His footsteps cracked against the floorboards like an ax into wood as he circled my narrow bed.

"I wanted to talk to someone. I wanted a friend."

"A friend?" said the devil, his voice incredulous. "You'd risk everything because you wanted a *friend*? Oh, Elodie, you delightful, foolish girl."

He vanished. When I sat up, I saw that the floor gleamed with a thick sheet of ice.

I packed chalk, bread, and my mother's best silver gloves. My father tried to offer me a handful of his shiny new bills, but I spat on them. And then on him.

"How dare you disrespect me! I am your father!" he raged.

"How dare you disrespect me! I am your daughter! May this money bring you nothing but misery and the devil's cold embrace."

I slammed the door behind me, threw my pack over my shoulder, and ran down the road that led to the big city.

When I bit into my bread that night from within the safety of a fresh chalk circle drawn in the dirt, I remembered that my father had never made a meal for himself, that he didn't know how to use the heavy kitchen stove. I chewed, swallowed, and smiled a very small smile.

June found me crying into the soup pot the next morning.

"Elodie! What's wrong?" She unhitched her trumpet case from her shoulder and ran across the kitchen.

"It's nothing," I croaked between sobs.

"Well, that's nonsense." She tentatively lifted her arms and when I stumbled forward, she enfolded me in a hug. I let myself cry into her blouse for a few heartbeats, then disentangled myself, darting around the room to catch up new ingredients and toss them in the soup. "Elodie, sit down. Let me get you a glass of water, and you can tell me what's wrong?"

"I can't," I said, manically sprinkling pepper over the pot and rushing back to the spice rack.

"Of course you can!"

"No, really. I can't." I looked up to see her looking at me, bemused. "I could tell you, I suppose, but I can't stop moving."

"Well, let's start there." June set her trumpet case on the long kitchen table and pulled out a chair. "Tell me."

Her eyes were so kind. "Well. The devil's after me."

June laughed a little. "He's after us all, isn't he?"

I don't know what came over me—the desire to be believed? Or maybe just the desire to sit down in a damned chair without fear?—but I ripped off my silver glove. His brand pulsed darkly against my skin and seemed to wind itself tighter around my fingers. The pads of my fingers had gone the sickly blue-white of milk.

"Circles of chalk and constant motion keep him from taking me. But I was careless. I stood still too long yesterday, and he came for me last night, and he says he's coming again tonight, and I don't know how I can stand this much longer."

Slowly, June stood up, and even more slowly, she took my hand carefully in both of hers to inspect the mark.

She looked up at me and said, "I believe you."

My breath went out in a rush.

"And if you believe in me, then I think we can fix him good."

I slept behind rubbish bins, under bridges and trees. I ate what scraps I could find or beg. Once, I climbed over high garden walls and ate apples and pears until the groundskeeper chased me away. I took work, when I could find it, washing, building, cleaning—anything that kept me on my feet and in motion. When I ran low on chalk, I'd buy more, or steal it. I never stayed anywhere long. Rest or comfort would draw the devil to me all the faster. And in this way, days, months, and then two years passed. By the time I wandered into The Pear Tree, I was too exhausted to run further, but my anger burned brighter than my father's coins.

"This is a terrible idea," I muttered as the sun melted into the horizon, leaving only a dim golden glow in its wake. We needed space and privacy to enact June's plan, and with only a few hours before night fell, we'd gone to the park in the center of the city.

June glowered at me over her trumpet but continued tuning it.

"You should leave. There's no reason for you to be dragged into this with me."

Lifting her lips from the mouthpiece, she said, "Just remember what I told you, and we'll be fine."

"*Fine?*" I demanded. "The devil is coming, but *it's fine?*"

"He's probably a minor demon who gets his jollies terrorizing humans. Personally, I'm not convinced there's a singular "Devil," just a bunch of bad numbers with too much magic and too little sense to stay wherever it is they come from." The sunset dimmed as true night fell. "Now, hush. It's time."

June lifted the trumpet to her lips, and a strand of notes, bright and sparkling as jewels, tumbled out. I stepped back into the cover of the trees—not hiding, that would only make me more enticing, but far enough away to let June and her trumpet shine under the glow of the nearest streetlamp. Her music was like nothing I'd heard before, lush and bright, full of motion and movement and dancing, and, as I listened, I knew the devil would like it.

I knew when he arrived, not by his voice, but by the sudden cold that ate my bones and made my brand swell like new ice.

"Elodie," he began, but he stopped, his head swiveling towards the music. "What's this?" he murmured, taking a step closer to June.

June didn't falter, though frost formed on the ends of her curls, climbing higher up the strands as he crept towards her. Her music surged, honey and brass and summer sunlight distilled in her tune.

"How wonderful," he murmured. "I think I'll take you, too."

As the music played on, I darted forward, my feet silent and sure from years of unceasing speed and motion. I reached deep into my pockets. Gathering fistfuls of salt, I poured a stream of white grains in an arc behind him. A perfect curve, a gibbous crescent, curled round his feet.

But it was only that, a curve, and I needed a circle, or I would be running until I died or he took me somewhere I had no intention of going. So I stepped back, took a quick, choked breath, and opened my mouth. I *sang* at him, a scrap of an old song I remember from my mother.

Well met, well met, said he
I have just returned from the salt, salt sea
And it's all for the sake of thee

The devil laughed, as well he might, and took a step toward me, his hand outstretched. His fingers were tipped in claws of ice. But when his boot touched the salt, it began to smoke. He turned, seeking a clear path, but June had already closed the circle with salt from her own pocket.

He was encased in his own perfect circle.

June blew a single, steady note on her trumpet as she reached for more salt, and I kept singing. He screamed until he sizzled and ebbed at our feet. Together, we threw salt, and more salt, and until the devil was naught but a steaming pool of water and a few pieces of gold. I took off my gloves. The brand was still there, would always be a mark of what my father and the devil had done to me, but it was my hand, and there was no one left to claim me but myself.

June tucked her trumpet back into its case and offered me her arm. I took it gratefully, and we followed the road out of the park and toward The Pear Tree.

For a time, we walked in silence.

"We should start a new band, our own band," June said thoughtfully. "If we can snare a devil with our music, surely we can charm a few drunk lads downtown."

I stopped in the middle of the road, because I could, and June stopped with me. "We could be the City Salters."

"No," said June, grinning. "The Ninny Mermaids."

The Pear Tree was full that night, as always, but after I sang, accompanied by June on her trumpet, and cleared the tables, I found a chair where I could drink a whiskey and do nothing at all.

Dr. Sara Cleto is a folklorist, author, and teacher. She recently completed her PhD in English and Folklore, and she is a co-founder of The Carterhaugh School of Folklore and the Fantastic where she teaches courses on fairy tales, creative writing, mythic adaptation, and more. Her poetry and fiction can be found in Uncanny Magazine, Faerie Magazine, Liminality, Mythic Delirium, Goblin Fruit, and others. Her story in this collection, "Circles and Salt," is a response to the gruesome but fascinating Grimms' fairy tale "The Girl Without Hands." She lives in liminal space with her husband and their cats. She can be found at saracleto.com and carterhaughschool.com.

SALVAGE

A.A. Medina

The small village was home to fewer than a hundred souls and tucked away in the middle of the Italian hinterlands. No one, not even Geppetto, thought their quiet community would see the war and yet the battle had ripped through the town, leaving loss and suffering in its wake. The countryside was once a peaceful place; blue skies, rolling hills, singing birds, and frolicking children. Now, pillars of smoke rose from the fires that pockmarked the fields, ash and remains—of both man and machine—littered the landscape.

Geppetto gazed out across the scorched earth. The zeppelins were faint dots in the distance. However, if he listened intently, he could still hear the percussion of the bombs resonate through the atmosphere.

His grandfather used to tell him, "*There is always a gold nugget in the heap of dung, put in the work and find it, or get out.*" Unfortunately, for Geppetto, there was no getting out.

He trekked through the aftermath, searching for metals and goods with minimal damage. Geppetto owned a small metal workshop where he forged and fixed tools, farming equipment, and even dabbled in décor. In the path of destruction, the armies left behind military-grade iron, bronze, and steel—he'd need it to rebuild and restore what was left of his village.

"Jiminy, whoa." Geppetto dug his heels into the side of his aging mule and dismounted. Searching the general area, he tossed small gears, nuts, bolts, sheet metal—anything he could lift and carry on his own—into the open carriage. It would take many days and many trips to scavenge just the little stuff and, if there were any able-bodied men left, he'd have to enlist them to retrieve the bigger scraps.

The thought brought pain to Geppetto. A sense of guilt weighed on him. Back at the village, grieving mothers wailed over the brutalized bodies of their dead sons. The few of the militia that survived wandered, shell-shocked among the ruins. When the horns had blared, and the denizens took up arms, determined to defend their homes knowing full well the attempt would be feeble, Geppetto had hidden like a coward. His every attempt to conjure courage stifled by the sound of the bombardments.

With tears in his eyes, Geppetto continued his search. *Those boys deserve honor,* he thought. *They cannot be lost to history, they fought and died for all they had—and for us. They deserve to be immortalized.*

Then he heard it. A groan, a moan, a cough. Geppetto spotted an arm jutting out from under a large piece of armor-plating and scurried over.

"Hey! Hey!" Geppetto fell to his stomach, trying to get a glimpse at the unfortunate being. A young boy and, from what he could see through the wreckage, he wasn't wearing a uniform. "Boy, are you okay?"

"Please… Help…"

"Hang on!"

Geppetto jumped to his feet, rushed over to Jiminy and unlatched the ropes from the carriage. "Let's go!" He pulled on Jiminy's bridle, leading him toward the boy. With haste, Geppetto tied, wrapped, and looped, the ropes to any jagged corner or holes he could find in the hunk of steel. "I'm gonna get you out of there, boy! Just hold on!" With one end of the rope secured to Jiminy's harness, Geppetto wrapped the other end around his waist and tied it tight. He smacked Jiminy hard on the behind, stinging his palm.

"Get! Get!" Both man and mule pulled. Every muscle in Geppetto's body strained. His heels dug into the ground and just when he thought his plan was futile, the mass of metal budged. "Get! Get!" Inch by inch, the slab slid away until Geppetto could see most of the boy's body. "Whoa!"

Geppetto untied the rope from his waist and scurried to the boy. He looked lifeless save the blinking of his eyes. His legs were a mangled mess, his farmer's clothes torn, shredded, and stained with crimson and mud. Geppetto wasn't sure if he wanted to cry or vomit. He looked away and collected himself.

"Okay, let's get you out of here." Geppetto knelt and scooped up the body. The boy screamed and writhed in pain, almost causing Geppetto to drop him. Then he fainted.

Tears left Geppetto's dirty cheeks bedraggled as he marched the limp, mangled body back to the carriage.

Geppetto brought the boy back to his cottage, cleaned his body, dressed his wounds, and placed him in a makeshift cot by the fireplace. The poor boy was still unconscious; his breathing short and stuttered. Geppetto knew there was a slim chance he'd still be alive when the sun rose the next morning.

He sat by the boy for hours, but his sympathy, his helplessness, his guilt, became unbearable. *This boy,* he thought, *this boy was no older than thirteen, yet he took up arms and fought. You will be remembered, boy.*

Geppetto stepped outside to his forge. He retrieved gears and bolts and nuts and scrap from the carriage and tossed them onto the burning coals. Throughout the night, he hammered away, manipulating the glowing steel and iron. Thin pipes for the legs and arms. A collection of forge-wielded cannisters for the torso. Carefully, with a ball peen hammer, Geppetto formed and shaped a face into a piece of sheet metal. He used nuts for the eyes and a giant bolt for the nose.

Hours and hours had passed before Geppetto was done. He dropped his hammer and sat against the stone half wall. His face flushed red and sweat streamed down it to soak his tunic. The strange metal sculpture, resembling a boy, only stood two feet tall, but Geppetto knew what he had to do to honor the fallen. *This is my prototype*, he thought. *Tomorrow, I'll begin work on the big one, the one I will erect in the village center as a reminder to what they sacrificed and to what we lost.*

Geppetto thought of the boy inside his cottage. He wondered if he were still alive. He looked up into the night, the glow of the rising sun had started to redden the horizon, and a shooting star streaked across the sky. "Please, let the boy live on..." he said to the universe. "Please." Geppetto climbed to his feet and returned to his cottage.

Inside, the boy was still. Geppetto approached and fell to his knees, clasping the small, cold hand between both of his, he placed his weary head on the boy's quivering chest and wept. The boy inhaled...

...Then exhaled, for the last time.

Outside, the morning sun gleamed off the metal sculpture and its iron arm creaked as it rose, shielding the glaring light from its eyes.

A. A. Medina is the co-owner and editor of *Aphotic Realm Magazine* and author of the transgressive-horror novella, *Siphon*. When he is not melting in the Arizona sun or rewriting the same three chapters of his next book, Medina writes short stories. One in particular may be inspired by the first World War's nine martyr villages of Verdun and his favorite childhood tale about a magical boy named Pinocchio.

THE LOCH

Zannier Alejandra

PART 1. HOME-PATROL

Home-patrol is the absolute worst assignment; any pilot worth his salt would tell you as much. Nights are long and lonely, flying circles over the channel, with little to no chance of seeing action. The road to glory is not paved with home-patrol shifts.

Previously, these thankless assignments were reserved for new recruits, and semi-retired captains; however, with the rise in German crows' sightings, we've all been dragged into the rotation.

There was a time when warfare was all about ships, aircrafts and the occasional mechanical walker; but we underestimated Hitler's fascination with the occult. It took us months to realize the inky birds tracking our troops' movements were in fact Nazi shapeshifting witches—the worst kind of spies.

We didn't take any chances after that. The second a black bird was spotted flying across the Dover skies the best aviators were dispatched. With more sightings in Brighton and even as far as London, even the best of us were stuck with home-patrol at least once every month.

This time, I wasn't particularly bothered by my home-patrol shift.

I was due for London in two days, anyway, so the timing worked out for me. And, I could use a night of calm before I had to face her Ladyship, the Countess of Woolton, also known as my mother.

The silence of the tranquil night was broken by a gruff voice that made the entire cockpit reverberate. "So, what's it gonna be, Sig?"

"Whatever do you mean, Reggie?" I asked, honestly clueless, but already knowing I wouldn't like the answer.

"Fat and rich, or pretty and dumb?"

Reggie was referring to the two choices of wife my mother had been pushing on me since the war started.

Her top candidates were Miss Haddock, a sweet, physically substantial heiress from America and Miss Chatterley, a beautiful and idle socialite from London. Or, as Reggie liked to call them: Miss Plump and Miss Airhead.

"Miss Chatterley is also rich," I reminded Reggie.

"So, pretty, dumb and rich, seems like Airhead has the advantage!"

"You're forgetting impossibly spoiled and shallow."

"Perhaps you should give them a test ride before you decide. If you know what I mean."

"Now, now, Reggie. Don't be crass, behave like a gentleman."

"Come on Sig," he protested. "I live vicariously through you. What I would give for a night with a lass… any lass, I would even gladly take the rotund one! Maybe you can invite the Ladies on a night flight and—"

"Reggie! Have some decency," I cut him off. The cheeky bastard…

You see, Reggie is my plane.

Reginald McGregor was a respected Captain during the Great War but he got into an unfortunate bit of trouble after returning home. I'm not entirely sure what he did, Reggie doesn't like to talk about it, but the words bootlegging and illegal gambling have been floated around.

Back in the 30s, magical justice was still commonplace in England

and Reggie was sentenced to spend a century as an object of his choosing. He had always dreamed of becoming a pilot, so he chose a fighter aircraft—a top of the line Supermarine Spitfire with a two-stage Rolls-Royce Centaur engine, powered by high cetane diesel.

I'm not sure where they found a wizard powerful enough to manage that metamorphosis, but the sentence was carried out scarcely two months prior to the British witch exodus of '36. To think that at one point we thought banning magic was the solution to our problems. All it did was leave us vulnerable. But I digress...

Everyone thought me demented when I agreed to become Reggie's pilot, but we were in the middle of war, and with no magical citizens left on British soil, we were at a terrible disadvantage. We couldn't afford to waste such a fine Spitfire, and someone had to fly him. Might as well be me.

In fact, having a sentient plane isn't all that bad. Reggie can be moody at times, and constantly gets up in my business, but he's an otherwise good egg. He's kept me safe so far and I appreciate the company during long haul flights.

"You're no fun, Skip," Reggie complained. "Would it kill you to share your exploits every once in a while?"

I sighed. Reggie believes I go gallivanting around like Casanova whenever I'm not flying him. In reality, I spend my free time smoking cigars and reading books on aerodynamics, but I would hate to disappoint him.

I searched for a story that would keep Reggie entertained. "Did I ever tell you about the time my plane, my previous plane, went down in the middle of the jungle?"

"No, but I don't feel like hearing about it, not unless it involves a woman. Don't you try to distract me, Sig."

"Well, Reggie, as a matter of fact, there was a woman."

Reggie perked up, or, in his case, jerked in the air.

"It was the spring of 1941," I started. "I was taking a new aircraft for a spin—"

"What type of plane?" Reggie interrupted.

"Hawker fury."

He snorted. "No wonder it went down."

"It was not the plane's fault. There was a storm, as a matter of fact. I lost control of the plane, must have hit my head at some point and lost consciousness."

"So, obviously, that piece of junk crashed."

"Not all planes can be as smart as you Reggie; so, yes, it crashed."

The memory of that day still haunted me, and not because of my brush with death.

"Were you hurt?" Reggie asked after my prolonged silence.

"I was. I was in and out of it for days."

My recollections from the time after the crash came in the form of feverish flashes. The seatbelt strap burning the skin of my neck as someone pulled me out, the wet soil under my back, the hollow echo of water drops inside a cave, soft hands peeling off my blood-soiled clothes.

"When I came to, she was there," I said still lost in thought.

"Who was she?"

"An angel," I said, and I wasn't talking in the metaphorical sense, not entirely; I couldn't think of a better way to describe my savior. "I hit the windshield when I crashed. My goggles smashed against my eyes. My vision was tinted red, but, for the briefest moment, I saw her ethereal figure."

Reggie flew ahead without talking.

"She bandaged my eyes and remained quiet for the longest time, but when she finally spoke, her voice felt like lemon juice and honey against a sore throat."

"I've never heard you speak like this, Skip. What did you talk about?" Reggie asked.

"I told her about my childhood, the good and the bad, like the time I got to ride my first horse; or the time I spent Christmas alone because Lord and Lady Woolton had engagements overseas. I knew she was just trying to distract me from the pain... but it felt good, it felt real. Ironic, considering—"

"Considering what?"

I chuckled with embarrassment. "You see, Reggie, I'm not entirely sure she was there."

"What do you mean, Sig?"

"After a couple of weeks when I was finally healed she went away to gather some water and fresh fruit. At least that's what she told me. I had made up my mind. I was going to ask her to come back with me, but... she never returned.

"I removed the bandages myself, and noticed they were made of leaves. I was alone inside a cave, and there was no sign of her. I looked around in the woods and there was nothing there either, no villages, no campsites, no sign of human life for miles. Eventually, I accepted that she was a figment of my imagination. A mirage my mind fabricated to keep me alive."

Reggie flew in thoughtful silence for a while. "Perhaps she *was* an angel then."

"Perhaps she was."

I didn't have time to regret oversharing with my aircraft, because fluttering movement in the horizon caught my eye.

Even with the recent measures against the crows, no one had been able to capture one. I would be lying if I said I didn't feel a certain exhilaration when I spotted the German flier—I could almost taste the glory of returning home with such a prize.

Reggie must have felt the same way because he propelled us forward at maximum velocity.

The bird, having noticed our presence, folded its wings and plunged down in a free fall. Reggie didn't hesitate to follow with a bold nose-dive, accompanied by a screeching battle cry. However, I could tell our attack maneuver was not sustainable.

The feathered bastard was plummeting towards the water in a sharp angle, waiting until the very last second to reverse the descent.

Our superior size prevented us from doing the same; so, we could either crash into the sea or overshoot. I could already tell we would do the latter.

As predicted, Reggie was forced to pull out of the dive earlier than the bird, the resulting arc placed us in front of our target and we lost our offensive position, but our disadvantage was momentary.

When you've been flying with a partner for as long as Reggie and I have, unspoken decisions are made in a matter of milliseconds. I pulled back on the stick, giving Reggie the reduced angle he needed for a High Yo-Yo maneuver. We rolled into a steep inverted turn, correcting our overshoot and regaining our position behind the bird.

We were much closer this time. I braced my finger on the trigger, but the bird was flying away erratically, making it hard to get a clean shot.

The crow's feathers were gleaming under the moonlight, taking on a silver almost white hue. I was considering how bizarre this was, when Reggie lurched unexpectedly.

"I hit something," he declared.

I still had our target in my line of vision, which meant we were dealing with more than one bandit. Reggie rose a few cherubs and, suddenly, we could see them all—a dozen birds, at least. An entire bank, and they were definitely not crows. Not unless crows had suddenly turned white and regal.

"What in God's name—" Reggie muttered.

"Swans," I said, finally getting a close enough view. I couldn't understand why the German witches would shape-shift into swans instead of crows. They were not fast enough, and their snow-white feathers made them easy targets at night.

"We can still catch one!" Reggie was not ready to give up. "Get ready for a hover, Skipper."

Regular Spitfires don't hover, but mine does. Reggie had mastered this skill through stubborn practice. He just wanted a cool party trick, but it ended up being one of our most effective combat maneuvers.

However, it is very taxing on Reggie. He can only hold a hover for a few seconds and usually no more than once per flight which is why he warned me, so I was ready and wouldn't waste his efforts.

Reggie selected a target, a swan that was flying slower than the rest. Judging from the blood soaking up its right wing, I concluded it was the one we'd hit.

As we got closer, we reduced our altitude, and for a moment we were flying lower than the wounded swan. I gave Reggie a signal, and he rolled upside down, flying in an inverted position for a few seconds. Next, we climbed back up, drawing a semicircle that placed us directly in the path of the swan. And there, he hovered.

The bird was right in front of us, all I had to do was pull the trigger.

My finger twitched in anticipation but stopped when I looked into the swan's eyes. Those were human eyes, no question about it, and they were also completely devoid of evil.

"Now, Sig!" Reggie screamed, but I was frozen.

Finally, unable to hold the hover any longer, Reggie let himself fall. I held on to the juddering stick, aware, on some level, that Reggie wouldn't be able to stabilize himself without my assistance.

"What happened?!" Reggie demanded with a mix of disappointment and contained rage. "We had him… or her, or whatever, we had it, Sig!"

"That was no spy," I simply replied and convinced a defeated Reggie to fly us back to Biggin Hill.

PART 2. THE TINKER YARD

We landed past midnight. The aerodrome was relatively quiet, with lights out on most of the Nissen huts and only a couple of latecomers having supper in the mess hall.

I took Reggie to the tinker yard for a tune-up before retiring. A couple of mechanics were working on a decommissioned German battle-walker, but the yard was otherwise empty.

Reggie and I stared up at the metallic beast in awe. The biped tank stood twenty feet tall, with a control cabin big enough for three soldiers, a rocket launcher on top, and two sub-machine guns strapped to each side of its 'head'. It puffed clouds of diesel smoke as the mechanics attempted to reignite its motors—no doubt they were hoping to reverse-engineer the technology.

Everyone knew the Empire was far superior in sea and sky, but we were lagging when it came to ground technology. Having a squadron of walkers would go a long way for us, but that was for Infantry to worry about.

I turned my attention back to my plane. Thankfully, Reggie's wing had only sustained minor damage when he hit the swan. What worried me most was that he hadn't said a word since we landed. A silent Reggie was a scary thing.

"Don't you think you're taking it a bit too hard?" I finally said, unable to withstand the silent treatment any longer. "You win some, you lose some, mate."

"This one, we could have won." Reggie sounded genuinely upset. "Getting that bird would have been a great coup."

"War is not about glory," I said, even though I had indulged those vain thoughts earlier myself.

"I know that," Reggie grunted. "But do you realize how good a heroic act like that would have looked on my record? Good enough to reduce my sentence, perhaps."

I must confess, I had not considered Reggie's stakes in all of this. Catching a German spy would have won me a medal; for Reggie, it could have meant regaining his humanity.

"I'm truly sorry, Reg. I've been a self-centered idiot." I knew nothing I said would fix my mistake, but I hoped a dose of self-deprecation would gain me some sympathy.

Reggie mumbled something along the lines of "Fine, I'll get over it," but I knew I had a long way to go until I was fully forgiven.

"I'll make it up to you, I swear." Inviting some ladies on a night-flight suddenly became a serious consideration. Anything to make Reggie happy. "Now, let's get you inside, Reg." I was still hoping to get a few hours of sleep, even though dawn was approaching. I climbed into the cockpit and drove Reggie to the nearest hangar.

"Why did you let it go, Sig?" he suddenly asked. "The swan."

"I don't know. There was something about it. The way it looked at me… as if it were asking for help."

The nose of the plane wiggled from left to right, and I realized Reggie was shaking his head.

My talking plane thinks I've lost my marbles. Great.

I was about to say something, but Reggie and I were stunned into silence when we entered the hangar and found a white swan in the middle of it.

To make the scene even more dramatic, our entrance was perfectly timed with sunrise. In a matter of seconds, the space was inundated with the light of dawn. My eyes took a moment to adjust to the light and, for a while, all I could see were shadows.

In this partial blindness, I watched as the white swan spread its wings and elongated its shape, metamorphosing into a beautiful woman in front of my eyes.

I glided out of the plane, careful not to make any sudden movements, shielding my eyes with the back of my hand. Once my pupils adjusted to the brightness, the woman in front of me became a picture of perfection. Her wavy hair cascaded over her creamy skin; and her cerulean eyes were so bright they looked like pieces of glass reflecting the sea.

A flash of recognition flashed across her face when she saw me. "It's you," she said, and I knew who she was in return.

I could have never forgotten that voice.

When I finally regained my wits, I grabbed a blanket from the corner of the room and draped it around her shoulders. I escorted her to an adjacent radio room that hadn't been used in years. Reggie wasn't too happy to be left out of the action.

"Hey, hey, Sig! Where are you taking her? You know I can't fit in there, come back out!" he called out as I closed the door behind us.

The woman sat on a chair by the window, her long legs tucked to the side, mimicking the lines of a marble statue from an ancient Greek temple. I did my best not to stare, but it was close to impossible.

I cleared my throat. "I thought I'd never see you again."

"I thought so as well, but I was hoping I would." Her words made my heart swell, but, to be honest, anything she said with that voice would have been enough to send me to the moon.

"You never came back to the caves," I started, careful not to make it sound like an accusation. "I waited as long as I could, but eventually I had to leave. It was not safe for me there."

"I tried to come back, but… I was held back." Her eyes drifted to the right, glinting with unshed tears.

I decided not to press her on the subject; instead, I asked something else. "You're a shape-shifter?"

She gave me a shy nod. "Is that why you went after us last night? I understand the British outlawed magic, but I didn't realize the army—"

"We were looking for German crows."

She stared at me blankly.

"Spies," I explained.

"You thought my flock… you thought I was a spy." Her beautiful face deformed with alarm. "Do you still think that?"

"No!" I said immediately. "That's why I didn't pull the trigger."

I reached for her hand, aiming to be reassuring. "You have nothing to fear. We're at war but we're not persecuting witches unless they pose a threat."

"I'm not a witch."

"Then… how?"

"A curse," she said. "But I suppose my curse was also my deliverance."

That's when I noticed something on her otherwise unblemished skin—a serial number, tattooed on her forearm.

"Auschwitz," she said.

I met her eyes and, though the word had no meaning to me, I could see the remains of unimaginable sorrow.

"There was a woman there," she said. "A Romani witch. She claimed she put a shapeshifting curse on a man before, turned him into a pig." She smiled. "When she offered to turn us, I thought she was crazy, but I accepted, mostly to humor her.

"We waited for the full moon. She took our blood and made us stand in a circle. There was smoke, but no fire, and she drew a pentagram on the ground. Next thing I knew, I was no longer myself, I was something else, and I was flying West. There were twelve of us, only ten escaped, nine remain," she finished with tears running down her face. "I don't cry only for the past," she surprised me by saying. "I escaped an awful fate but my life is no longer my own. My memories are fading, the person I was feels more like a ghost with each passing day. I'm cursed to this change every night and I cannot stop it. I'm alive, but I do not have a life. I am not free."

I wanted to hold her tight, drive the pain away, but a sense of propriety stopped me.

She shifted in her seat and the blanket she was clutching slid off her right shoulder, reminding me she had been hurt while still in swan form. However, in place of a bleeding wound, there was a small scar.

"I heal," she explained, noticing the direction of my eyes. "When I turn human, I heal."

My hand moved of its own accord, pulled towards her damaged skin. I traced the outline of the scar with a mixture of guilt and relief.

So hypnotized was I by her, I didn't realize my lack of decorum until it was too late.

"I must go," she said, shrinking away from me. "My sisters will wonder where I am."

I nodded. "Will I see you again?"

"Where will you be tomorrow?" she asked.

Anywhere you want me to be, I wanted to say. But then I remembered the party. The stupid, vapid party my mother was throwing in my honor. There was no way I could miss it. I cursed my luck, but told her where to find me, just in case.

She promised she would try to come to me, but I had no delusions. In my mind she was an angel, a spirit, not meant to walk among mortals.

She stood up and walked away.

"You never told me your name," I called out before she reached the door.

"Odette."

PART 3. SIG'S PARTY

"...And said she used to travel to Cornwall by train! Can you imagine? By land?!" Miss Chatterley finally paused to draw in some breath after what felt like a twenty-minute-long piece of nonsensical gossip.

"As a matter of fact," I started. "Even before the war, train travel was considered the safest, though perhaps not the most glamorous, mode of transport."

"Steam-powered locomotives," Miss Chatterley continued, oblivious to my comment. "I say! What are we? Peasants?"

The rest of our group burst into laughter.

I wished, not for the first time, that I could bring Reggie to these events; he was certainly better company than any of the people there.

As Miss Chatterley moved on to discuss unsuitable headgear for travel, I glanced around the room. Mother had outdone herself. The theme of the party was White & Gold—white for peace and gold... for money, I suppose. White tablecloths contrasted with golden center pieces that stood two-feet high, ivory feathers decorated the backs of the chairs and shiny lanterns hung from the ceiling, giving the space a glamorous glitz. There were several champagne towers and even a (white) chocolate fountain in the middle of the room. It was all so… much.

My mother spotted me from across the room and raised her glass in silent approval of my conversation companions. This tipped me off the edge. I downed my drink and walked away, without offering any apologies to Miss Airhead-Chatterley.

"Careful with the frowning, Captain," someone said as I stomped off. "One might think you're not enjoying the party."

I turned around. "Miss Haddock, I didn't see you there."

"Really?" She gestured to her generous frame. "But there's so much of me." She laughed, completely unabashed.

As a gentleman, I tried not to laugh, but I couldn't suppress a smile. "Of course I'm enjoying the party," I lied. "It's in my honor."

"Oh, is it?" She gave me a knowing look. "Your mother is throwing this party for the same reasons mine insisted I come."

I chuckled and felt relaxed for the first time all evening. The more I got to know Miss Haddock, the more I liked her—but as a friend, not a potential wife. Something told me she felt the same way about me.

"Fine," I admitted. "This party is so dreadful, it's making me long for the war."

Miss Haddock shrugged. "The chocolate fountain was worth the trip for me." She punctuated her comment by dipping a strawberry in the cascading goo and popping it whole into her mouth.

I was about to do the same when a new arrival caught my attention. It was her. Odette.

She was an otherworldly vision in tight black lace that clung to her every curve. The waves of her silky hair were draped over her scarred shoulder, and her lips were a hypnotizing shade of red.

I moved without thinking, pulled towards her by a magnetic force.

When I finally reached her side, she leaned up and pressed her crimson lips against mine.

There was something different about her, an edge of darkness, but I didn't care. I kissed her with abandon, so dazed by the elation of the moment that I failed to see what was right in front of me.

The rest of the evening passed in a spellbinding blur. The orchestra played in the background as I danced with Odette for hours, only half-aware of the whispers surrounding us. I could only imagine what my mother was thinking after seeing me devote all my attentions to an unknown lady. Miss Haddock, on the other hand, gave me an approving nod as she exited the salon with a cigar in her hand.

I was painfully conscious of the time; every minute brought us closer to midnight and to her unavoidable transformation. I led Odette to the balcony, so we could have a private moment. I realized then that no word had passed her lips since she arrived. Silently beholding her beauty was a joy, but I longed, more than anything, to hear her voice.

"I am glad you came," I tentatively started.

She smiled but didn't say a word. A strange tingling went up my spine. It was the same feeling I experienced whenever I sensed an enemy before seeing it.

"Odette, I've been meaning to ask you," I said. "Did you ever find a way to break the curse?"

She returned my gaze with icy eyes. There was a distant caw, but I didn't pay it any mind. I was too busy regretting the stupid question. If she knew how to break the curse, she would have broken it.

However, she surprised me by answering, "Yes. It took me a long time and a great deal of sacrifice, but I finally found the answer." Her voice didn't have the soothing effect it used to have on me; instead, that uncomfortable feeling, announcing impending doom, intensified.

The clock struck twelve, and the first chime was met by a louder cawing cry, somewhere in the garden.

"How? How do you break the curse," I asked, eager to get an answer before she was forced to fly away.

She walked towards me until our bodies were flushed against each other. The cawing sounds grew louder, and I finally recognized their origin—crows. I glanced up and saw them swarming towards us, looking more like a hive than a flock.

I could feel Odette's warm breath, as she whispered in my ear, "The only way to break the curse is with the heart of a good and honest man." As she finished speaking, I felt cold steel penetrate my chest.

As I collapsed to the ground, I finally understood. "You're not Odette."

"No," the woman looming over me said. "My name is Odile, and unlike my sister I'm not waiting to be rescued. I will free myself. Whatever it takes."

My mind had covered her with a veil of perfection, but now I saw the truth. She was an almost perfect ringer for Odette, but her eyes were tainted by malice.

She pulled back her hand, bracing herself for the death blow. At the same time, I saw the crows viciously plummeting in our direction, but both the birds and Odile stopped when a gun shot rang out. I twisted my head towards the garden and spotted Miss Haddock with a half-smoked cigar in one hand and a Colt revolver in the other. There was someone standing next to her, but it was too dark to make out who it was.

It was a shot in the air, but the distraction saved my life. The clock chimed for the twelfth time and Odile's entire body shook, making her let go of the knife. Her hands twisted and deformed, her bones cracked, and her silhouette shrank until she became a bundle underneath a puddle of lace.

She emerged as a black swan, her wicked, murderous eyes still fixed on me.

I was weak and losing a lot of blood, I doubted I could defend myself, even against such a small creature.

However, Odile didn't come at me. She turned her head sideways, reacting to a sound my human ears could not yet perceive. Moments later, a white swan vaulted towards her, savagely driving her away.

They flew directly above me, across the expanse of the starry sky. I drifted off amid a flutter of feathers and ferocious hissing sounds.

PART 4. THE HUNT

I woke up to rhythmic—not so gentle—undulating movement. I was lying down on soft leather, like a sofa, but I was certainly in motion. A train perhaps?

I blinked a few times to clear my eyes. I could see inverted buildings through the window above my head. Not a train then.

"You're awake, I was starting to worry."

"Miss Haddock?" I mumbled. She was in the front seat, behind the wheel of what I initially assumed was an automobile.

I brought my hand to my ribs and found the wound properly dressed.

"You'll be fine," Miss Haddock said. "The wound wasn't all that bad. She didn't hit anything of importance, and the blade didn't go in too deep. I think you just fainted of the shock, but I patched you up good."

"I thought you were an engineer," I replied, still dazed.

"I recently trained as a nurse, thought it might come in handy, with the war and all."

"You never cease to amaze me, Miss Haddock." I sat up, there was some pain, but nothing I couldn't handle. For the first time since I woke, I became aware of the situation and panic set in. "Where are you taking me? I need to go back, I need to—"

"—You need to find your girl, I get it."

I shook my head. "The woman at the party, she was not—"

"Your girl? I gathered; the stabbing tipped me off. I meant Odette."

"Odette was at the party?!"

"I was in the garden, smoking my cigar, when a lady in white appeared out of nowhere. She was frantic, talking about witches and falcons, or was it eagles? Don't know, some bird of prey or another."

"Crows," I said.

She snapped her fingers, "Yes, that was it. Anyway, she was desperate to find you. I thought she was a nutjob, but then I noticed she looked a lot like the woman you were with and then, well, things got weird. You got stabbed, and your attacker turned into a swan and then, the lady in white turned into a swan! I mean, clearly, I'm missing a few pieces of the puzzle here, Sig."

"Your warning shot saved my life," I said, not wanting to explain the curse. "What else did she say? Odette."

"Something about her sister, sorry, I can't remember much. You must understand, I was a bit shocked by the whole situation."

I let out a frustrated groan.

"But!" Miss Haddock said, handing me a piece of paper. "She had a letter for you. She left it behind when she… erm, *birdified.*"

I unfolded the paper and read:

My dearest Sig,

Only a life or death situation would have prevented me from returning to you, and that's exactly what happened that day in the caves. My sister was captured by the crows. Or so we thought. Years later, we discovered that she had joined them willingly. I can only assume they promised her something in return. A way to be free. And I believe it has something to do with you, I am afraid of what she might do.

Odette

"I need to find her!" I said, becoming more agitated. "Where are we going? And, Samantha," I said forgetting proper address, "what in God's name are you driving?" It looked like an elongated Rolls

Royce, but felt like it was skating over ice, rather than rolling across London.

"I heard some officers talking," she replied. "There was a sighting of crows near Rookery Lake, in Bromley. I'm guessing your girl was also headed there, and I'm afraid they will shoot anything with a beak. You must hurry."

"I need to get to Biggin Hill first. But we'll never make it in time, not on this thing."

"This thing," Miss Haddock sounded offended, "is my hovercar."

A hover what? I leaned over the window to glance down and noticed we were not touching the ground. The car was suspended a foot above the street, using some sort of propulsion mechanism.

"It might not be as fancy as that Spitfire tin-can you fly," she continued, "but let me tell you one thing, nothing can beat my Betsy when it comes to overcoming London traffic."

"Betsy? Your car's name is Betsy?" I managed to say, right before Miss Haddock pulled down a lever, making the car rise above the aforementioned traffic. We flew over the streets, oscillating from side to side, perilously avoiding the tallest buildings, but, true to her word, we were out of the city in no time and headed to Biggin Hill.

I jumped off the vehicle as soon as Miss Haddock landed—parked, or whatever it is you do with a hovercar. Reggie had caught wind of the attack and was waiting impatiently next to the runway.

"I nearly took off without you Sig," he said as I climbed into the cockpit. "But you know I can't shoot… or land on my own. Even then, I was about to risk it."

"I'm glad you waited for me you old Maverick," I said. "Let's go!"

Reggie had gathered as much information as he could while waiting. The crows were spotted north of Rookery lake, five Spitfires had been dispatched with shoot to kill orders. I needed to get there before they got to Odette and pray neither the crows nor Odile had managed to harm her.

"Are you sure we're going the right way?" I asked, starting to doubt Reggie's intel.

The legion of crows that aggressively smashed against our windshield gave me my answer.

We lost all visibility and spiraled down, out of control. Just when I thought we were goners, the birds dissipated, giving way to a friendly coming from my rear.

I managed to regain control of the plane, while the other pilot levelled up with me. I recognized Wing Commander Lennox, a dear friend and top-notch aviator.

"Skipper," Reggie said. "I think that's her."

Reggie's sight was better than mine—don't ask me how that works, it simply does—but I could just about discern white and black feathers in the horizon.

I turned to our neighboring Spitfire and saw Lennox getting ready to thrust ahead. I went for my radio, but all I got was static. A second later, Lennox's plane erupted at maximum speed, no doubt heading for the swans.

I trailed after Lennox, swishing from left to right in a futile attempt to overtake him. Luckily, he noticed my erratic behavior and slowed down. My radio made a cracking sound. "What the bloody hell are you doing, old boy?" came Lennox's voice.

"The swan!" I yelled, afraid of the radio malfunctioning again. "The white swan is a friendly, do not shoot. Repeat, do not shoot!"

There was a long pause, but finally Lennox replied, "Roger, I'll pass it alo—"

He never finished the sentence. His plane went up in flames, not shot down, but rather engulfed in a sudden blanket of fire.

Reggie reeled back. I searched the sky for the source of the attack, expecting a Messerschmitt or a similar enemy aircraft, but there were none. I was starting to entertain the ridiculous notion of the Nazis coming up with invisible vessels, when the attackers revealed themselves—the crows.

One of them flew towards us, its crimson eyes discharging a string of flaming light in our direction. The impact on Reggie's right flank shook us with more potency than any regular bullet.

I swerved to the left in a sharp angle, avoiding the second shot from the murderous crow. My new position gave me a good view of Odette. She was still fighting her sister and neither had the clear advantage. At least the crows seemed uninterested in them.

Another red-eyed crow threatened from the left, but this time we were ready. Reggie veered right and changed our geometric plane. The crow's fire blaze missed us, but a second shot came, almost immediately, from the opposite side. This one got much closer. I was almost certain there would be a third bird coming from the rear. The bastards were aiming for the engine, set on turning us into a fireball like they did to poor Lennox.

I hate to be the type of pilot who flees a dogfight, but our only hope at that point was our speed. I accelerated the plane to the max and sighed with relief when the black birds were left behind.

Reggie adjusted our angle, so we were flying straight towards Odette and Odile. He gradually reduced our speed, and I knew what was coming.

"It's now or never, Skip," he said, coming to a sudden hover.

I was still in the air, with Odile right in front of the bullseye. My finger was ready on the trigger, and, this time, I knew the right thing would be to shoot. But I made a mistake. I glanced past Odile, to Odette and I could not find the approval I was seeking in her eyes. She simply looked scared. This was not what she wanted, this was not how she wanted it to end.

Instead of shooting, my finger reached for another control on the opposite side of the dashboard. The hunting net. But it was too late, my moment of hesitation gave the crows a chance to catch up, and before I could trap Odile, we were hit again. Multiple times.

I'd always thought Reggie couldn't feel pain, not in the human sense at least, but the terrifying scream he let out when the shooting blaze hit us made me rethink that.

We rolled away, erratically flying down in a forced descent. What was even worse, I saw a crow diving after us, positioning itself for another shot—a fatal one.

The next few seconds felt like hours. The crow's eyes brightened, and two red torrents of light were hurled towards us. I had a fleeting moment of panic, followed by acceptance. And then… an angel intercepted the shot, only, it wasn't an immortal being coming to my rescue, it was Odette.

She absorbed the worst of the crow's discharge and smashed against Reggie. Her inert body slid down the fuselage, disappearing into the sea of clouds.

I landed Reggie on the lake's grassy shore. It's a miracle we survived such a ludicrous landing, but, to Reggie's credit, and my eternal gratitude, he didn't try to stop me.

At that moment, my own survival was secondary. All I cared about was Odette.

I found Odile first. Dead on top of a rock bank. So, my mercy had been for nothing. And then I spotted Odette's alabaster figure laying still on the gravel. I dashed to her side and fell to my knees, cradling her heaving body in my arms. She was still alive, but not for long.

"Just hold on," I whispered.

When I'm human, I heal, she had said. She would be all right if she survived until sunrise. But dawn was still hours away.

A tear ran down my face as I went from a state of denial to anger. Why? She was going to die because of me. Because she was trying to protect me. All she had done in our brief acquaintance was save my life, and I could not even return the favor.

"The only way to break the curse is with the heart of a good and honest man," I repeated Odile's words. She had found a way to break the curse and used my infatuation with her sister to get close to me. It was my foolishness that would cost Odette her life.

The irony was that I would have willingly ripped out my own heart if it would save Odette's life. I gave it some serious thought, but I concluded I would die before I could get it out.

Odette's breaths were becoming sparser. I couldn't bear it. "I'm sorry," I muttered, unable to find something more meaningful to say. "Your sister tried to take my heart, but it is you who possess it. Since the first time we met. I—"

I was blinded by an intense glow that enveloped the swan in my arms. She floated away, moved by an invisible force and I was left staring in awe as her body transformed in the air. Unlike the first time I saw her change, this was a smooth, seemingly painless metamorphosis behind a glowing curtain.

When the light subsided, Odette's human figure emerged and touched ground a few feet in front of me. She closed the gap between us and threw her arms around my neck. Her creamy skin was, once again, unblemished.

"Thank you," she whispered in my ear.

"What for?"

"Giving me your heart."

Zannier Alejandra grew up in Cochabamba, Bolivia, land of coffee and eternal sunshine. After university, she set out to travel the world and ended up living in London, where both coffee and sun seem to be in short supply. In a past life, Zannier was a credit analyst at an international bank, but traded in her spreadsheets for more creative pursuits. Nowadays, she spends most of her time writing short fiction, watching movies and analyzing TV. She even gets paid for two out of those things on a regular basis.

Her story, *The Loch,* was inspired by the ballet *Swan Lake.*

EVENING CHORUS

Lizz Donnelly

The Nattergalen was lit up every night with the glow of neons and the hum of chatter from the City's most elegant citizens. Martinis flowed freely and the occasional guest spilled drunkenly into the street. Of all the bars in the city, the Nattergalen was the place to be and be seen. It was owned by a man known only as The Emperor; no one alive remembered him by any other name.

The Nattergalen was famous for being, and owning, the best: every surface gleamed with gold and chrome. The flowers were always real, and rare, the liquor was top shelf, and the cigars were always Cuban, even after the country itself was gone. Still, the thing the Nattergalen was most famous for was the floor show. The Emperor brought in top talent from around the world. The most beautiful songbirds and highest caliber entertainers took the main stage seven nights a week.

One day, a talent scout for The Emperor appeared in his office. "I've found her," the scout said. "I've found the best damn singer this lousy city has to offer."

"When does she start?" The Emperor barely looked up from his paperwork. His hat sat low on his head and his cigarette—Turkish, naturally—was burning in the ashtray, untouched.

The scout hesitated. "That's the problem, boss. She doesn't want to work here."

The Emperor looked up slowly. It had been a long time since someone had told him no. He took a puff of his cigarette, stubbed it out, and stood. "Bring me to her."

The car that pulled around could hold a small army but only The Emperor and the scout climbed inside. It rumbled, the low diesel mantra of tubers—potato, potato, potato—and shone in the lights of the city. It was a Vanderbuilt Dreamliner, a luxury whale of a car that was already a classic, even though it was brand new. They cruised downtown, across the electromagnetic monorail tracks, the scout giving directions as needed, since no one drove this car except The Emperor himself. The Emperor pushed the button for the mechanical arms to raise the top of the convertible over them. The streets on this side of town were hungrier.

When they finally arrived at the pub, The Emperor nearly missed it. It was an almost literal hole in the wall, iron bars in the windows snaking like vines of a great tree, and dwarfed by the buildings that climbed several stories higher on either side. It looked like it had the weight of the world bearing down on it but still stood firm, short, but strong.

The Emperor sneered as he pulled the car over to the curb. "She sings here?" The scout nodded. "Not for long."

It was cool and dark in the pub. A dull roar of noise filled the room; the chatter of patrons came in chirps and growls, the clink of glasses and the trickle of taps. The Emperor eased himself into a seat at the bar. He was pleasantly surprised to find that it wasn't sticky, and in the low light of the pub, no one recognized him. It wasn't long before he had a drink in his hand and a dim, wobbly spotlight lit up the stage.

She wasn't much to look at, The Emperor thought. She was a plain woman, with dusty brown hair and dark eyes. Her dress was drab too, a russet brown that she'd clearly been wearing all day while she waited tables and cleaned the kitchen. But when she sang, The Emperor was spellbound. Her voice was clear and sweet; it lilted and whirled through the pub in a melody that he'd never encountered in all his years of entertainment. It was, without a doubt, the finest song he'd ever heard.

The Emperor waited until the pub was closing for the night before he approached the woman. She was putting up the chairs so she could let the VacuBot roam free, so The Emperor strolled across the room and lent a hand.

"I'm not interested," she said, after glancing up at him.

"You don't even know what I'm offering." A smirk tugged at his lips. She was stubborn, he liked that.

"You're The Emperor," she said. "I don't need to know what you're offering to know that I'm not interested."

"You have me at a disadvantage then, because I don't know anything about you."

The woman sighed and stuck out a tired hand. "Luscinia Meg Arhynchos. Most people just call me Luz. It's easier."

The Emperor didn't need to be told twice. "Luz, you sing beautifully. I don't need to tell you that."

"And yet, here you are," Luz said. "Even after I told your man the other night that I wasn't interested. I have a pub to run, Emperor, and I don't have time for fairy tales."

"Surely the owners can manage without you for a few nights. A two-week, limited run. Give the people what they want and then take it away; it's the best possible business plan. Leaves them clamoring for more every time."

"The owners can't manage without me," Luz said. "This is my pub."

"I see," The Emperor said, wheels turning in his head. Luz eyed him suspiciously. "I have a better deal. A one week engagement. I'll send someone out here for you to train to run the pub in your absence. You'll come and sing for a week. At the end, you're free to go, or stay. Your choice."

Luz laughed. "I don't really have a choice here, do I, Emperor?"

He smiled the smile of a man used to getting his way. The deal was set.

A week later found Luz backstage at The Nattergalen. She didn't have anything remotely suitable to wear to an establishment like The Emperor's so she had gone in her plain brown dress. The costumer took one look at her and sighed, but there had been no time to find her anything else. She was due onstage.

There was a twitter of laughter from the audience when Luz stepped onto the stage. She nearly disappeared into the shadows at the edges of the spotlight and had none of the glitter and pizzazz they'd come to expect.

Silence reigned as soon as she opened her mouth to sing. The audience sat, stunned, by her song. When she was finished, the applause went off like a bomb. The Nattergalen roared for more, and Luz obliged them with an encore.

News of her amazing voice spread like a gas leak through the city and The Emperor's establishment was filled to capacity every night. On the last night, Luz was considering The Emperor's offer of staying on another week, at twice the pay, when a large box was delivered to the backstage.

"What's in the box, boss?" Someone shouted down the hall and the Emperor's best talent scout, the one who had 'discovered' Luz, materialized at his side.

"You're going to love this. I had it imported special," the scout said. Luz watched from the edge of the stage as The Emperor and the scout tore into the box. When the packing material had been cleared away, there was a beautiful woman standing before them. Her skin was a shining, polished chrome, and she wore a tiara encrusted with the rarest of gemstones: sapphires, rubies and emeralds, all real, not synthesized by machines. She stood as tall as Luz, and was dressed in the finest French clothes. Luz felt drab by comparison, but her curiosity got the better of her and she took a few steps closer.

"What am I looking at?" The Emperor asked.

"She's called a Jenny," the scout said. "She's a one of a kind, custom order from the best automaton makers in the world. She sings, boss. All you have to do is wind her up."

The Emperor walked a slow circle around the Jenny. She was beautiful, all shimmer and shine, an ostentatious elegance that fit into his establishment perfectly. He reached out towards the key in her back, wanting to know if her voice matched her exterior. A shadow caught his eye. Luz stood in the corner, watching the automaton curiously. The Emperor grinned. He had a brilliant idea.

He beckoned Luz closer, a spark of fire in his eye and his lips twisted into a smile that made her want to run away. He turned the key in the automaton's back. "Tonight, we'll have a duet."

The machine woman sprang to life. Her eyes opened to reveal dazzling sapphires at their core, and her silk dress swished against the floor with the barest hint of a whisper. Everyone standing around her, except The Emperor, took a step back.

The Jenny followed Luz onstage that night. The Emperor watched from the wings as the audience took in the sight. A few people in the front of the room gasped, and someone in the back whistled. "Ladies and Gentlemen," the emcee's voice reverberated through the club. "We have a special treat for you. Fresh from Paris, the latest in artificial intelligence technology, may we introduce you to Jenny, a songbird like no other."

The audience applauded, eager to hear the machine sing. "For her first trick, a duet with our very own special guest, Luz!"

The lights dimmed. Two incandescent spotlights danced across the stage until they settled on the Jenny and Luz. The Jenny sparkled in the light, while Luz looked washed out and plain beside her. The audience rumbled in anticipation. The Emperor strode onstage, to a smattering of applause, and gave the Jenny one last wind up with her key. Then he flipped the switch and she began to sing.

There was nothing mechanical about her voice. It soared through the club, sweet and clear, with complicated runs and quick little grace notes. Her song was original, and beautiful. The audience was spellbound. Luz stood motionless in her spotlight, watching the Jenny with the same astonishment as the others in the room. After a few moments The Emperor hissed at Luz from offstage.

"Sing!"

She looked at him, startled. He gestured towards her. "Sing."

Luz didn't know what she was doing, but she sang. She usually performed alone at the pub, and she did her best to listen to the automaton, but the Jenny was on a set course, a pre-programmed spectacle, and Luz was at a loss. Her harmonies fell flat; she was off key, and out of tempo. The Emperor watched the audience recoil as the song came to a close. Someone in the back booed. Another voice called for a solo from the Jenny.

The Emperor strode onstage again, hands extended, palms out, in a gesture of peace towards the audience. He moved towards the Jenny and began to wind her up again. The audience cheered. When he was finished, he flipped the switch and left the stage, bringing Luz with him. The crowd settled as the Jenny sprang to life again and soon her tune filled the room. It was the same one as before, but the audience didn't seem to care, or even notice. They were enraptured.

The Emperor turned to Luz and reached into his pocket. He produced an envelope and handed it to her. "Your wages for the week. I think we both know that your services are no longer needed."

Luz took the envelope of cash without a word and disappeared into the shadows of the club. As the door shut behind her, Luz swore that she would never set foot in The Nattergalen again. The Emperor returned his attention to the Jenny. He'd felt a pang watching Luz disappear, but he quickly shrugged it off.

The Nattergalen's popularity exploded. If it had been difficult to get into the club before the Jenny arrived, it was absolutely impossible to get in after. The automaton was the talk of the town and even if patrons had seen her before, they were clamoring to see her again. She had only one song, but that didn't make a difference to the audiences, or The Emperor's pockets. Every night, after her show, the cries for encore were deafening. The Jenny headlined The Nattergalen night after night, and Luz returned happily to her obscurity, running her pub and singing a song or two most evenings. Her pockets weren't overflowing, but she had enough, and she preferred her cozy pub to the glitz and pretension of The Nattergalen.

Some years later, backstage at The Nattergalen, The Emperor stood opposite the Jenny. Time had been less than kind to both of them. Under his hat, his hair was a dusty gray, and the lines around his eyes were pronounced. He'd had to retire his beloved Dreamliner the year before. Despite meticulous maintenance, the old thing had simply worn out. The same was true of the Jenny. Her chrome, no matter how much it was polished, had lost some of its shine and the jewels in her hair were scratched and no longer gleamed. A few had even been stolen over the years, and The Emperor had had to replace them with copies. Excellent forgeries, to be sure, but fakes nonetheless. Her eyes were closed, because she hadn't been wound for the night, and The Emperor patted her shoulder gently as he passed her, knowing she felt nothing.

That night, when he wound her up in front of a packed house, the Jenny coughed and sputtered. Her song came out slow, with the eerie bent notes of a music box that is worn out. The crowd recoiled in horror and her song stuttered to a stop before it reached its conclusion. The audience grumbled loudly.

The Emperor stumbled out of the wings and onto the stage, barely catching himself on his newly acquired cane, in his haste to reach the Jenny. The crowd was restless, some of them were getting up to leave already. He hastily wound the automaton again. Her voice came out a terrible, grating screech, before she ground to a halt. The Jenny had reached the end of her career.

The audience was on its feet now, booing and demanding refunds. The Emperor's employees descended on him in a panic once he was backstage. He wiped a hand tiredly across his face and in a resigned voice told them to give the people what they wanted, since he couldn't. His employees were stunned. All the fight had gone out of The Emperor. He looked frail, and old. In the main room the audience was growing rowdy.

"Go," The Emperor said, with the last bit of authority that he could muster. "Give them their money before they tear the place down."

His employees did as they were told. Alone backstage, The Emperor stared sadly at the Jenny. Her eyes were open, but her face was void of emotion, as it always had been. She was cool, chrome and collected, and completely finished as a performer or anything other than an obscenely large paperweight. The Emperor could barely remember the entertainers he'd hired before the Jenny. Her single song had filled his head for years and pushed out everything else. He'd been a fool to rely solely on her for so long, and now, it seemed, his folly would be the death of his business. The Emperor, like the Jenny, was obsolete.

The crowd was noticeably smaller the next night, and smaller still the night after. Word spread faster than a bullet monorail and by the end of the week, The Emperor had laid off the bulk of his staff. Only his faithful scout and costumer remained. They drank top shelf liquor long into the night. Finally, The Emperor stood. He shook their hands, gave them the best severance package he could put together, and said his goodbyes. He watched them leave The Nattergalen for the last time, and he locked the door behind them. He knew, from the solemn looks on both their faces, and their reluctance to leave him alone, that they didn't expect him to last until morning.

The Emperor picked up his cane and set off, slowly, down the street. He caught the last monorail across town for the night, not sure where he was going, but content to wander. His expensive clothes made him a target, but he couldn't bring himself to care. His old feet traced a path that he'd only traveled once before, by car. When The Emperor found himself outside a plain old pub, half hidden by the other buildings, he wasn't surprised. There were lights on. He let himself in and headed towards the bar.

There were a handful of other patrons in the pub, and none of them looked up as The Emperor settled himself on a stool. Only Luz, standing behind the bar, looked startled to see him. After a moment, she came to stand in front of him.

"I'm not coming back, so don't even ask," she said. "Can I pour you a drink?"

The Emperor nodded, and pointed toward a whiskey. Luz bit her lip to contain her surprise at how old and sick the powerful man looked. She set the drink in front of him, and poured one for herself.

"The Nattergalen is dead," The Emperor said.

"I'm sorry." She'd heard whispers about the breakdown of the Jenny, but her customers weren't frequently found in the same circles as The Nattergalen's clientele, so she hadn't known the extent of it.

A man at the end of the bar called for another drink. "One more," he said. "Sing us a song, Luz."

"I'm busy," she replied. She poured the man his drink and returned to The Emperor.

"One song?" The Emperor raised his face toward her. "Humor an old man?"

Her lips lifted in a sad smile. "All right," she agreed. "One song."

The years had been kinder to Luz, The Emperor thought as she stepped onto the small dark stage. She hadn't changed nearly as much as he had, except her dress was a plain dark green now. "One last song for the night," she said, her voice effortlessly filling the small room. The patrons quieted immediately, eager to hear her song.

Her voice was exactly as he remembered it—clear, beautiful, and full of emotion, so unlike the cold metallic voice of the Jenny. The Emperor didn't know why he'd ever let Luz walk away. He turned on his stool to face her, as if soaking up the sun. The corners of his mouth lifted into a genuine smile, and a glimmer of hope returned to his eyes. When her song was over The Emperor stood to applaud. His cane dropped to the floor beside him and he left it where it fell when he walked out the door of the pub. He felt better than he had in years.

Lizz Donnelly is a writer, knitter, cat lady and baking enthusiast. She spent several years as a cocktail waitress in a four star resort; a job which leant some inspiration to her retelling of Hans Christian Andersen's "The Nightingale." Her writing has recently appeared in *Speculative City*, *Non Binary Review* and *Drabble Harvest*, among others. You can find her on Twitter @LizzDonnelly and on Patreon, where she writes a monthly Science Fiction blog series called Canon Blast!

TO GO WEST

Laura VanArendonk Baugh

Uncle Edgar died yesterday afternoon. Ellie died last night.

Uncle Edgar died of the dust pneumonia. I didn't mind so much as I should have. Aunt Ruby used to say that a man got to doing things when he was deep in hurt so he could still feel like a man, and we shouldn't hold what he did against him. Mama would say back that we were all in the hurt together, him and us three women, and that didn't justify the wrong he did, that hardship only showed the real material of a man the same way dust and sand showed the real material of a house or car when they scoured the paint off. Then Mama got suffocated outside in a storm and Aunt Ruby left on a rope over the kitchen rafter, and it was just Uncle Edgar and me, and it didn't matter why he was the way he was.

Ellie died of despair, I guess. It wasn't even a storm, so she didn't suffocate the way all the birds and small creatures did when the dusters blew. She was the last chicken left, only laying when she felt up to it, and I guess she felt the same as Aunt Ruby.

Looking down at her feathered body, I felt everything I should have felt when Uncle Edgar had stopped wheezing, that I'd felt when Aunt Ruby had given up on us, when Mama lost her way back to the house. I'd had to be strong then, helping the others left with me and without any time to grieve before the next duster, or the next lost cow, or the next neighbor's illness. But now that they were all gone, family and cows and neighbors, now I had no responsibility to anyone and no time but my own, it all caught up to me at once, and I cried for that silly chicken as if she were my sister.

I laid her body on the bed with Uncle Edgar, and I went out of the house and I started walking south.

I don't know why I went south. Town was east, and since the phone company had been out of business for two years and we hadn't been able to buy gas for the farm truck for eight months, I would have to walk in to get someone about Uncle Edgar, and just hope the cemetery wasn't still so deep in dust they couldn't find the headstones or dig a new grave. But instead I wanted to just keep walking away and let the dust drift up over the house and bury him and Ellie together. So I walked south, south to where Route 66 cut through the overturned plains and led west, west toward California and rain and fruit-growers and jobs and money.

I guess I went south because it was toward the Road of Flight.

I walked through the night, and the stars were visible. I folded my arms against my body, lean with stretching provisions, and imagined in the dark there were rainclouds above me and any moment I would feel the cold kiss of water against my dry, abraded skin.

But the world is full of sin, as the preacher said when I made it into church a few weeks ago, and we had sowed the wind and were reaping the whirlwind.

Dawn came, and I did not know exactly how far I'd gone. I walked on 'til I came to a crossroads where the road sign was lying down in the dirt. I stopped and stood at the crossroads, and I wondered if it mattered at all which way I went.

After a moment, I went to brush the dirt off the road sign to read it, and a spark jumped four inches from the metal sign to my outstretched fingers like snakebite.

Oh, no, not now, not so far from home… I turned and saw the mountains crawling toward me.

They weren't mountains, of course, only that's what the mind tries to make of a wall of dirt two miles high and stretching as far as you can see to the ends of the earth, twisting over itself faster than a truck can drive. There's no sight like a black blizzard coming at you.

I spun and looked for shelter, any shelter. I spotted an abandoned farm about a half-mile up the new road, and I ran.

There were others running to the old farmhouse, too, coming from the east, a figure on a laboring horse and three men running alongside.

I heard someone else shout behind me. "Can we shelter with you?"

I looked over my shoulder and saw a young man carrying a child, running as fast as he could with the weight of her. "It's an abandoned house," I called back. "We can share."

It was a poor house, a dugout with a roof and a single ground level room at one end. I made for the sunken door, hoping the previous tenants had done the right thing and left it unlocked for others in need. They had. I pulled the door back against its little drift of dirt and waved the man inside.

I didn't know him. He was nice-looking, I guess, with yellow hair and a good jaw, covered in dust but that wasn't unusual even when there wasn't a duster closing in. The girl, maybe four years old, had a flour-sack dress and hair to match his.

"Thanks," he said. "I'm Robert. Bobby to friends, which includes anyone who shares shelter."

"Tilly," I said, and I didn't put out my hand because of the coming storm's static electricity. "I'm not from here, I just saw the storm."

He nodded. "Nor us either. We're headed down toward 66, to hitch west."

West.

Could be he was easing the burden on his family, one less mouth to feed and maybe a paycheck in California to send home. No one needed extra hands when there was no farming to do. But that wouldn't explain the girl. "You lost family?" I ventured.

His lips thinned. "Nope, I've still got Peggy here. She and I are family."

Peggy clung to his neck, her wide, dull eyes assessing me, and I knew the words were for her as much as me. "That's good," I said, and didn't mention I'd lost the last of mine the day before.

The room we stood in was still furnished with a few chairs, a table, a bureau, and an empty shelf. There was a door to the left, probably to the bedroom, and to the right a short set of steep steps, nearly a ladder, to the ground-level room. There were a couple of high windows, but they wouldn't be any good in a few minutes. "Let's find some lights, if we can."

Bobby lowered Peggy to the ground and began to prowl the sparse room with me. The door to the bedroom swung open and a woman stepped through. "You're not the ones!" she said, a little angry.

I jumped half out of my skin. "I'm sorry! We thought the place was empty. The yard is so—we thought it was abandoned."

"It was," the woman said. "We came. You're not the ones."

I didn't know what to make of this. "We just need shelter from the storm." Surely no one would deny us that.

A second woman came from behind the first, resting a hand on her shoulder. "Don't worry, sister," she soothed. "They will come, and these will be no trouble, only an extra treat. Be patient."

The first nodded, her eyes on us. "But don't be any trouble."

"No trouble," I assured her. "No trouble at all, just waiting out the duster."

The windows began to rattle, and the familiar hiss of dust against the glass began like a chill against the spine. The second woman carried out two oil lamps, lighting both and setting one on the table and the other on the bureau. Peggy sat on the floor, her back to the earthen wall.

The door opened again. "Hello!" called a man, ducking to enter. "Give us shelter, if you please!"

He was an ugly man, with an upturned nose and ears too large for his face, and he carried a farm rake inside with him. As he stepped inside, someone opened the outer door to the upstairs room and led the horse in. It was covered in dirty sweat, streaked with muddy rivulets, but I could see it was grey beneath the grime. It looked like all the stock now, lean and hungry.

"Is there any water?" called down the bald man with the horse.

The first looked at us, and I shook my head. "We've only just come in."

"There's a tank outside," said the first woman, still standing in the doorway. "In the storm."

The man beside the horse sighed. "I suppose it can wait," he said, and he put a hand on the horse's lowered neck. The horse sighed with weariness and looked at me, and I had the awful feeling it was judging me as a person would. I wiped my dirty hands on my dirty dress.

Two more men came in through the low main door, arguing. "It is no ordinary storm," said the shorter of the two. He did not remove his hat.

"Dust storms are hardly unusual," returned the taller, slighter man. His voice was soft and cultivated, like one of the movie stars I used to see at the Artcraft in town.

"Come in, come in," muttered the first woman, still in the bedroom doorway, and I could not tell whether she meant to welcome us or resented our intrusion.

The light abruptly fell as if the windows had been blocked with boards, and the storm struck in full fury. The room darkened to midnight hues, with only the two lamps shedding rings of fragile light.

Peggy put her hands to her ears as the wind howled and whistled about the corners of the house. The dirt made it louder. The man with the eastern accent stooped slightly toward her. "It's all right."

Bobby shook his head. "Sorry, she's just not much for strangers."

"Hello, hello," said the first newcomer, settling next to me. I didn't like him, which was uncharitable of me in such a situation, but it was true. He reminded me of Uncle Edgar, half-drunk and impressed with himself. "Hello. We're not strangers, no. That's Trip, there, and that's Rocky."

Trip was a slight man, almost feminine in figure and prettiness, but with an air of authority in the little group I could already catch. Rocky was ugly and short, with a simian grin that looked like it should have manure stains. He was picking his teeth with a tiny red toothpick. Who bothered to paint a toothpick?

"And that's Sandy."

The man beside the horse raised a hand and started down the steep steps. Bobby grinned. "We're all sandy these days. I'm Bobby, that's Tilly and Peggy."

"And you can call me Tumbleweed." The man with the upturned nose beamed at me and leaned to bump me with his shoulder. I resisted a shudder. His eyes traveled over me like they might leave a greasy trail. Then he looked at the women who had come from the bedroom. "And who are you ladies?"

"Charlotte," said the first. "I'm Charlotte."

"Jessica," said the second. She smiled, showing teeth.

"Nice to meet you," I said, at least half for an excuse to look away from the man who had called himself Tumbleweed. "Thank you for letting us share your home. I'm sorry I thought it was abandoned."

"That's quite all right," answered Charlotte, but she did not smile, nor even look at me. Her eyes were on Trip.

Trip did not notice. He was looking up at the weary horse, which gave a loud groan. Its knees folded as if it wanted to collapse where it stood.

"He needs water," Trip announced. "You too, Sandy."

Sandy nodded.

"But that storm is brutal," Rocky protested. "Black Wind Demon is looking for you."

I stared at Rocky, who had seemed sane enough a moment before. But then, how could I argue? I had seen the winds and the vanishing earth drive folk to madness, and whether the wind had made Rocky believe in demons, or whether the wind was a demon to destroy our lives, who was I to say?

"Here's water," Sandy said, bending over a small lidded barrel in the corner. "It's nearly full."

Charlotte let out her breath in something almost like a hiss.

Sandy set aside the lid and dipped water. He drank the first dipper in one long motion, smacking his lips at the end. The second dipper he poured over his head, laughing, and shook the droplets free.

"You're a mess," complained Tumbleweed.

"You're a pig," answered Sandy without looking. "Leave the lady alone."

Tumbleweed harrumphed and looked away from me, but he did not look repentant.

Sandy bent and lifted the barrel of water, grunting slightly with the effort. "Tilly, will you help me with Yulong?"

I stood. "Is that the horse?"

"Yes." He carried the water up the steps, and I followed. I expected him to pour water into a bucket for the horse, but I did not expect him to half-fill a second bucket and wet two rags in it. "The storm could last for hours," I said. "We might need the water before it's over."

"He needs it now," Sandy said, and he began wiping the dirt from the horse's sweaty coat.

I thought it a waste of water—surely the horse could remain dirty like the rest of us for the duration of the storm—but the bucket was already wasted, so I went ahead, dunking a rag and starting at the crest of the horse's neck, rubbing so that water ran in rivulets through the dust.

The horse clearly enjoyed it, sighing with pleasure. I dunked the rag and rubbed again, and it seemed to skitter over the neck. I pulled back the rag and probed with my free hand, and instead of slick wet hair I felt smooth scales, like on the snakes we used to hunt before the mice died.

I jumped back, startled, and stared. The horse turned to glance at me with one eye, and the place I'd cleaned shone with brief iridescence in the lamplight. Then the horse shook his head wearily and relaxed again, and it was only a dirty horse with a clean spot standing beside a confused woman who had lost her last family and last chicken and had not eaten or slept.

The wind beat at the dugout. Trip pulled feed sack rags from the top drawer of the bureau and began passing them around. Bobby spread the first over Peggy's head, and she tugged it down around her face. Rocky and Tumbleweed accepted rags and tied them about their faces.

Bobby and Trip, their own masks in place, began tucking rags into the gaps and chinks of the walls above ground, slowing the puffs of fine grit into the house. Sandy and I rinsed the horse until we'd emptied the water he'd allotted, and then I descended again to the main room and took a seat at the table. I looked at Peggy, with her knees to her chest below the hanging rag. She knew how to wait out a duster. She had never known a time without dusters.

Tumbleweed touched my hand. I got up and went to sit beside Charlotte, settling on a bench by the wall. "It's a nice house," I said in desperation.

"Isn't he a pretty boy?" she murmured.

I followed her eyes to Trip. "Yes," I agreed.

"So fine," murmured Jessica from my other side.

I nodded awkwardly, glad their voices wouldn't carry over the dirt scraping the walls. "Yes."

"Don't you just want to eat him up?" asked Charlotte, and she licked her lips.

"Um." This was more than I was comfortable with. I raised my voice. "Say, this is quite a storm, right?"

No one answered, for dusters were familiar monsters by now, but the storm was indeed one of the fiercer ones I'd seen. The dugout's sturdy position meant we had only a fine spray of dust pushing through cracks, but the black blizzard pushed at us like a dog clawing at a dune where a rabbit's hid.

"He's looking," Jessica complained.

"Looking for what's ours," Charlotte agreed.

I felt uncomfortable beside the women. It wasn't kind of me; there were plenty who had gone half-mad with the wind and the dust and the hunger and the hopelessness. More than a few had done the same as Aunt Ruby, and I should have been glad Charlotte and Jessica were only odd. But sitting by them felt eerily like sitting beside Tumbleweed. I got up and helped to push rags into the high walls.

"I tell you, this is no ordinary storm," Rocky was saying again to Trip. "He's looking."

Startled by the echo, I looked from Rocky to the two women. Rocky glanced at me as I looked back at him. His eyes were gold—not yellow, not hazel, but gold, and faintly burning like embers. The room rocked around me.

I tore my eyes away and looked back at the women, staring hungrily at Trip across the room. "Soon, sister?" asked Charlotte.

Rocky followed my gaze, and then his golden eyes popped wide and he pointed. "Spiders!"

I jumped at the sudden shout and then caught back a laugh. I'd never seen a grown man, even a short fellow like Rocky, screech at sighting a spider. It was a laugh we needed, trapped in—

"Spiders!" he repeated, and he leapt toward the women like a cat at a mouse.

"No!" shouted Trip.

But Rocky was midair and spinning his toothpick between his fingers, and it grew as it spun into a staff as long as his height, red with golden caps at each end. He gripped it with two hands and smashed it onto Jessica's head with a sickening crunch that made my stomach twist and drop. Jessica folded to the dirt floor like a discarded rag doll.

"No!" repeated Trip, and this time it was a wail of despair.

Bobby lunged for Peggy, pulling her close with the rag still over her face. Sandy and Tumbleweed stood in quiet surprise, mouths slightly open. Charlotte folded and stared at her fallen sister, shocked into immobility.

Trip brought his hands together, palm to palm at his chest, and closed his eyes. As I stared in mute amazement, he began to chant something low and fast, words which tumbled like the wind outside and blew past my ears.

Rocky shrieked and dropped his red and gold staff, squeezing his golden eyes shut and clutching at his hat. He dropped to his knees and tore at the hat as if it were burning him, but it clung to his head. "I saved you!" he cried, twisting to look at Trip. "I saved you!"

Trip opened his eyes. "You killed a woman!"

"Look at them! Really look at them!"

Bobby clutched Peggy close, backing to the dirt wall. "What's going on?"

And then Charlotte turned on us, pulling her mouth unnaturally wide in a hideous shriek to expose black fangs. She flung out her arms, and there were too many of them. She sprang at Rocky with hissing rage.

Rocky rolled, releasing his hat, and everyone scrambled backward in the too-small room. Tumbleweed reached for the rake he'd left against the wall, and Sandy took a protective step closer to Trip.

"I'm sorry," gasped Trip.

"You never listen to me!" snapped Rocky, and he surged upward to punch Charlotte under the jaw. Her head snapped backward, but three of her arms caught him. Her body swelled as she bent forward, a dark carapaced torso tearing out of her calico dress.

Tumbleweed stepped forward and swung his rake in a great horizontal sweep, clipping Charlotte as she ducked. She snarled and snapped her fangs at him, raising two limbs. Rocky wriggled one arm from her distracted grip and reached for his red staff. He planted one end in the floor beneath Charlotte and shouted. The staff burst upward, extending from the ground and punching through the chitinous body to the dusty ceiling. Charlotte shrieked and thrashed.

I couldn't breathe. An arm pulled me close, and I realized I'd backed into Bobby and Peggy. We stared as the spider-woman shivered and then went limp, sliding down the pole like a demonic carousel figure.

The wind howled as we all stood still for a moment.

"What was that?" I asked, my voice trembling. "What are they?"

Rocky pulled free of the misshapen woman and stepped onto the body, gripping the staff with one hand. He spoke a word, and it drew in each end, shrinking into a rod in his hand.

Trip looked at us, and his expression melted into sympathy. "I'm sorry," he said. "I'm sorry you saw that. I'm sorry you were caught up in our troubles. I'm sorry."

Rocky coughed and folded his arms across his chest.

"And I'm sorry I used the headache chant," Trip added to him. "I'm sorry I didn't believe you."

I forced my voice above his. "What are you?"

Trip stopped, looked at us, sighed. "We are on a journey west."

"Lots of people going to California," I said. "Most of 'em not fighting giant spider-women."

"True enough," he answered. "We're on a mission from heaven. Not everyone wants us to complete our journey."

Bobby had to try twice to ask. "So they are—demons?"

"Not the demons you mean, but yes, something inhuman."

"So you killed them?"

I answered before Trip could. "They said they wanted to eat you."

To my surprise, Trip only nodded solemnly. "If they devour my flesh, it will render them immortal."

Bobby laughed, a high, nervous sound.

Trip smiled patiently and turned back to the dead women, or what had been women. "Should we put out the bodies?"

Tumbleweed leaned his rake against the wall again. "I suppose we can chuck them out the door. A moment of wind and dirt is better than staring at them for the next few hours."

Bobby opened his mouth as if to protest and then hesitated. I understood. It seemed wrong to toss a body into the storm without dignity or ceremony; even Uncle Edgar had been left in order on the bed. But one was a great spider, almost too large to fit through the door, and the other allegedly the same, and they'd come to this abandoned farm to devour the soft-spoken Trip. It was surreal.

Tumbleweed pulled a couple of pincer-arms over his shoulder and dragged Charlotte to the door, where Sandy unlatched it and caught it against the wind. Bobby shielded Peggy while they worked the great corpse outside. Rocky tossed Jessica out after, and they pushed the door against the wind.

For a long moment, we sat in silence.

"I saw the spider," I said at last, "and I know what they wanted, so I'm not going to call you murderers. But tell me if Bobby and Peggy and I are safe."

Trip smiled sadly. "You are safe from us, child."

"I'm not a child. I've run our farm, what there is of it, since Mama died."

"I did not mean to belittle you. You have a strong spirit to have endured here."

I snorted despite myself. *Endured.* It was that we did not have a choice. We could die, or we could wait to die.

Or we could go to California.

I looked at Bobby, still holding little Peggy, and I wished someone would hold me as protectively. To have just a moment where I could not fear the wind or the bank or Uncle Edgar.... What were spider-women, after years of fear?

Peggy lifted her rag and looked at Rocky. "You could see them."

He nodded and popped his golden eyes wide in a silly monkey face. "I can see evil." He resumed his normal expression and glanced at Trip. "But not everyone believes me."

"Can you see who's outside?" Peggy asked.

We spun together and looked toward the high windows, dark with the midnight of the storm. If someone were there, it was impossible to see, magical golden eyes or no.

Bobby bounced Peggy in his arms and squeezed her. "There's no one outside, baby girl. Just the storm."

Rocky looked at Trip. "I told you, it's his storm."

I had no idea what they were talking about, but the black blizzard outside made the words plausible, and I shivered.

Peggy tugged the rag over her face. "I saw someone. At the window."

You couldn't see a train outside. She had imagined it. I sat down at the table and faced the far end of the room, drawing a calming breath through my protective rag.

Something banged into the side of the house.

It should have been nothing, less than nothing. Things blew around all the time during a storm. It was only that it came on the heels of Peggy's words, and that I'd just seen a spider-woman try to crush Rocky so it could eat Trip.

I turned my head to catch a glimpse of the others, and they were staring at each other in the kind of trepidation where no one wants to speak it first.

"Someone's outside," I said, "right?"

"It could be someone else needing shelter," Bobby said. "Like us."

Or it could be another spider-woman.

But I thought of Mama, lost in the storm and unable to find

shelter, until she suffocated and died. If there were someone outside—

"We have to look," I said. "We have to see if someone's out there."

Sandy reached for a spade left in a corner. "I will look."

But at that moment we saw it, a blackness against the dark, pressing outside the window. It scraped the glass, a texture rubbing against the dust, and I had the terrible sense it was probing. And then it moved on and we could not see it.

But it had not gone.

"Oh, God, please," whispered Bobby.

I looked at him, and then at Trip, the leader, the one the monsters wanted to eat. "What's that?"

He sighed and looked at Rocky, who answered, "Black Wind Demon."

I was confused. "The storm?"

"He is a person," Rocky said, "but he is also the storm. In a way." He shrugged.

"This is why Yulong has been suffering," Sandy said with a sympathetic glance at the horse. "Since we came to this place, with the drought and the storms of dust. He came ahead to wait."

"The storms came years ago," I said bitterly.

"We've been traveling this way for years," Tumbleweed said with a shrug.

"And he wants you?"

"All of us," Trip said, "but mostly me."

"So he can eat you and be immortal." I fought fear with skepticism. "Does that mean you're immortal?"

Trip laughed. "Of course not."

"Of course not," I repeated, as if it made perfect sense in a black blizzard tearing apart the very ground around two dead spider-women.

"What if it gets in?" Bobby's voice was tight, his eyes on the window.

"He hasn't found a way in yet," Sandy answered, tracing the perimeter of the house with his gaze.

"What are we going to do about him?" The question was expectant, and I turned to Bobby with fresh respect. He set Peggy down. "That door won't hold against someone who really wants it down."

"Black Wind Demon has waited years for us," Rocky said. "He will take his time now."

Something crashed into the outside of the house, and the boards and packed earth shook visibly.

Rocky's gold eyes narrowed and he glared at the wall.

"Find rope," Trip said.

Why had I set off from home without so much as a handkerchief? I had a pocketknife and twelve cents in my dress. I had walked straight into a duster with nothing. Foolish, idiotic, stupid.

But Bobby found a short coil of rope in the bottom drawer of the bureau beside two dead mice. "What are we going to do?"

"I hope nothing," Trip answered.

It struck the wall again. Sandy reached for his spade and Tumbleweed his rake.

Peggy lifted her rag. "I'm scared."

Bobby scooped her up. "Hold on to me, baby girl."

The wall shook again, and sprays of dust pushed through fresh cracks. Trip stood, and Rocky stepped in front of him.

"We can't stay here," Tumbleweed said quickly. "We have to get out. Go out the back while he's trying this side."

"He'll see us," Sandy protested.

"Even he won't see anything in this storm. If we stay here, we're sitting ducks."

"There's a barn behind us," Bobby said grimly. "About a hundred feet. I saw it when we were running here. Will he follow us?"

Trip shook his head slowly. "I don't know."

"He can't see us when he's the storm," Rocky said. "He's got to sniff us out himself. He probably found this house following the spiders."

The wall cracked and the air began to cloud.

"The rear window," Tumbleweed said.

"What about Yulong?" asked Sandy.

"Leave him!" barked Tumbleweed, already starting for the window.

Sandy looked distressed. Bobby caught my arm. "Here."

I tied the rope about my waist and tried not to think of Mama caught against a barbed wire fence. Bobby tied on next and pushed Peggy's hands against the rag over her head. "You hold that tight," he cautioned her. "Really tight."

Tumbleweed boosted himself to the window's height with a chair and levered it open with his rake. The storm rushed in like a torrent of angry bees. He shielded his eyes and, with a wet rag over his nose and mouth, crawled outside.

"You know where the barn is?" shouted Trip.

Bobby nodded.

"Then you two next."

I held Peggy while Bobby climbed out the window and then passed her to him. She curled like an infant against the wind but it was too loud to hear if she whimpered or cried. I followed them.

The grit slapped into my face like sandpaper, and I bent my head away from the blast, hiding as best I could behind my shoulder. My bare legs screamed with the sting of the storm. I ducked behind Tumbleweed, leaning against the wind. Bobby pointed and Tumbleweed started into the dark.

The barn was a hundred feet, Bobby had said. I don't know how far we had gone—distance is a hard thing in a storm—when Tumbleweed stopped suddenly. I heard his curse even through the howl of the wind and then he bolted back toward the house, quick as his namesake.

I did not understand, half-turning to squint after him. Had he given up on finding the barn? Bobby pushed into me from behind and shouted. "Keep going?"

I took six steps before I saw the bear.

It was a huge bear, with dark fur rippling in the duster winds and claws that extended a hand's-breath from its dinner-plate paws. I could not imagine a bear so large outside of nightmares, much less in the stricken panhandle where even rabbits died for lack of food. I stood still, paralyzed with confusion and fear.

The bear rose on hind legs and swung its head around as if to search the lot, heedless of the wind and flying dirt that blinded me. It roared through the howl of the wind, and it seemed to me there were words in the sound. *Tang Sanzang!*

Some folk, when things were getting desperate, had said they'd seen the face of Jesus or Satan in the black rolling clouds.

I groped for Bobby's arm. I knew when he saw it by the way he went rigid in my grip. That meant I was not imagining it.

"Help," I said, though it was not possible anyone could hear me. "Bear."

But then there was a rush of motion beside us, and I saw Rocky. His golden eyes burned in the dusty dark and he did not shrink from the wind. He pulled his toothpick from his bared teeth and it grew into a staff as long as his height, red with golden caps at each end.

"Come back!" shouted Bobby. "I've got Trip!"

I stumbled, trying to squint through the storm at Rocky rushing the bear. I kept going in what I prayed was a straight line, one arm over my eyes and one hand outstretched, reaching, hoping, grasping for—

The house.

I kept my hand on the wall and crept alongside, searching for the broken window. Something grasped my ankle, and I gulped a mouthful of dust to scream before I realized it was Sandy. He helped me inside and turned to the others.

We all crowded away from the gaping window, a dirtfall choking the air, and Sandy put a protective arm around Trip. "Are you all right?"

Trip nodded, choking and spitting black mud like the rest of us. "Where's Tumbleweed?"

"That pig," growled Sandy. "He's probably hiding somewhere."

"What about Rocky?" I asked, coughing.

"He'll be all right," Trip said, but he looked worried.

Sandy closed the window, leaving Rocky and Tumbleweed on their own. Dirt and wind still sprayed through the damaged front wall.

"That is a bear," Bobby said, pointing in the direction we'd come. "A *bear*."

"That is not a bear," Trip corrected him quietly, or as quietly as possible over the wind. "Or not only a bear. Rocky said he would lead him away and kill him."

"Why not kill him now?" asked Bobby, and I saw his face change when he realized the answer for himself. Rocky couldn't be sure of killing him, so he had to lead him away first.

The horse Yulong nickered nervously.

Peggy started sweeping dust off the chairs and table. It was almost cute, had it not been so hopeless.

Hopeless. I turned into the bedroom and dropped on a crude stool, hopelessness sapping my energy.

"Tilly." Trip came and squatted in front of me. He took my hand, but it was not oppressive or leering as when Tumbleweed did. He held it firmly but gently, as if comforting a child. "I am so sorry you have been caught up in this."

I shook my head. "The storms come to everyone."

"Not this storm, it seems." He cast a worried glance at the ceiling.

"The land is full of sin," I said without thinking. "You said heaven sent you on this journey. The world is being scoured clean, imperfections sanded away."

"Oh, child," he said quickly, and his voice brimmed with sympathy and concern, "you are right and you are wrong. The world is full of sin, indeed, and it is sin which causes suffering, often even that suffering which appears to be from nature and from heaven. It was not greed which brought the wind, but it was greed which stripped the land to be carried away."

I nodded. The new soil conservation men had explained the mistake of turning the sod and destroying the bison grass.

"But whether heaven sends the wind or the rain, it is not the end. There is more to understand than the price of a bushel of wheat. Sometimes we must lose what we think matters to find what does matter."

Anger rose in my chest. "You talk in pretty riddles just to hear your own cleverness. We've lost everything, even the things that matter. My uncle died yesterday, and he was the last of my family. The farm is wasted and gone. The fields are empty, the stock long dead. There is nothing left that matters."

Trip looked down. "I am truly sorry."

"I want to go west," I said, surprising myself. "I want to go to California, where there's water and work. Where there's money."

He squeezed my hand. "Treasure a handful of dirt from your home, but love not foreign gold."

"Oh, I've got more than a handful of dirt just in my pockets," I snapped.

Trip released me and stood. He turned, sighing, and took a stack of baskets from atop another stool. He hooked a foot and dragged it nearer, sitting on it with the three baskets on his lap.

"What will you find in California?" he asked gently.

I rested my face in my hands, elbows on my knees. "I don't know. A job. People." I choked. "Hope."

"What if you found hope here?"

I didn't have the energy to laugh derisively or the tears to cry. I had used those all up, that well dry with the dust that was burying us.

Peggy pushed through the half-open door. “What’s in the baskets?” she asked.

Trip glanced down. “It’s hard to guess,” he said. “What do you think is in the baskets?”

Peggy grinned, a child amusing herself in the middle of futility. “In the first basket is…a ruler! For measuring things!”

Trip made a show of tipping the basket to look. “What do you know? Look at this.” He drew out a playing card, the nine of hearts. “This is exactly three and a half inches long, so now you can measure anything.” He handed the card to her.

She clutched it like a prize. “What’s in the second basket? I think it’s a…treasure!”

Trip drew out the reveal, making me smile a little too. “You are correct! Here is a diamond!” He handed her the ace of diamonds from a half dozen cards, all that remained of the deck.

“The third basket has a map!”

Trip looked inside and made a comically large frown before inverting the basket. “I think a pirate stole the map!”

There was a ferocious crash against the roof and Peggy jumped, dropping her cards. Trip rose and scooped her into his arms in one motion, retreating to the main room. Sandy had the spade in hand, looking up. Bobby, without a weapon—who would have thought to need one against the storm?—reached to take Peggy from Trip.

The window shattered inward and Rocky sailed in on a cloud of dust, which dissipated as he tumbled to the floor. He was badly beaten, with bruising and blood on his face beneath his indestructible hat. “He’s coming,” he gasped, spitting dirt. “He knows you’re here, he wouldn’t follow me. Get out, I’ll hold him here.”

But the bear was already at the window, roaring with the wind and clawing into the dugout with streams of dirt. He was the bear and the storm, and we could not outrun him even if we could get out of the house.

Bobby turned and shielded screaming Peggy. Sandy rushed

forward with the spade and hacked at the reaching forelimb, slowing but not stopping it. There was a terrible sound from the horse in the attached room. The bear pushed through the window, collapsing the dugout upon itself, and a tumble of support stones fell upon Rocky, pinning him and throwing his red rod to the back wall. He screeched in pain and rage. The bear crawled forward, jaws wide like no normal bear, pushing toward us as we scrabbled backward.

The bear ignored Sandy and Bobby for Trip and me. Trip tried to push me down and behind him but there was little room to maneuver in the fallen dugout for us or the bear. It pressed forward, snarling a pleased grin, and stretched a forelimb for Trip, dirty claws extended like scythes to hook and harvest. Trip straightened and closed his eyes, pressing his palms together at his chest.

I snatched the short red rod flung from the stony tumble and jammed it against the ground, stepping across the end to hold it in place. "Rocky!"

Rocky snapped a word. The red staff kicked against my instep like a shotgun and extended, stabbing deep into the hollow exposed by the reaching arm. The bear screamed and recoiled, but the staff did not break with the motion. The bear thrashed and choked blood and threw back its head, raging, and then it folded to the ground and faded to dark dust.

We stared, except for Rocky, who was swearing at the rocks and wriggling free, somehow unharmed. Trip put a hand on my shoulder where I still crouched to hold the staff and shield myself from the bear's convulsions. "Are you all right?"

His voice was too loud. I could hear Rocky's swearing clearly, and even Peggy's crying in the far corner. The wind was slowing—still there, still blowing, but without the same ferocity.

"I'm okay," I said through the dirt in my mouth.

Rocky crawled free and took the hand Sandy offered to stand.

"Where is Tumbleweed?" Trip asked.

We spilled out of the house by its several new routes, careful of loose stones and nails. Our feet pushed through loose dirt, making deep prints. Sandy went to a drift against the side wall and stabbed it roughly with his spade. A squeal came from within, and Tumbleweed roused himself and uncovered his head as dirt streamed off the tarp he'd made of his coat. "Is he gone?" he asked, looking only a little ashamed.

"Dead," Rocky confirmed with a smug grin. He did not so much as glance at me, but Trip and Bobby gave me meaningful smiles.

An angry whinny came from inside and the wooden planks of the upper room bowed as Yulong kicked the wall. The wood splintered with the next kick, and I saw a glimpse of hooves. Then Yulong turned and leaped through the opening he'd made.

We stepped back as the horse jumped free, and he ran about the lot in the fading wind, kicking at the lightening sky as if to punish the storm in his freedom. Sandy ran for the windmill now visible near the barn we had not reached. "The tank!" Sandy shouted. "Open the tank!"

Rocky dashed with him and the two of them pulled back the heavy cover which shielded the enormous water tank, though nothing escaped a duster. Yulong galloped toward the wide circular tank, thirsty like all of us after the storm. But he did not slow to drop his head to the windmill's water—he jumped the side of the tank, plunging into the water and making Sandy and Rocky turn away from the splash. Peggy shrieked a laugh and clapped her hands as he disappeared to wallow in the tank.

I chuckled and followed the horse, more than ready for water myself, to bathe my eyes and nose and mouth clean.

Something surged upward from the water. It was not a horse. It streamed into the sky like an enormous snake tearing free, the tank walls its old skin. My jaw dropped as I looked up, up into the yellow-gray sky and saw a serpentine dragon twisting through the remaining ribbons of dust, playing in the clouds as the horse had played on the ground. It gleamed white and iridescent, fish scales in the sun.

Sandy punched a fist into the sky. "Yulong!" Then, grinning, he sat on the wall of the tank and threw himself backward into the water.

I half-expected him to emerge as something else, too, but he sat up as himself, laughing joyfully. He splashed Rocky, who splashed him back, and muddy water went everywhere.

I gaped at the sky again, looked at Bobby staring just as stupidly upward, looked at Trip who had folded his arms over his chest and was laughing. I decided that as long as I was going to be confused, I might as well feel better, and I started for the water tank.

Trip caught my upper arm. "Wait. I think, now that Black Wind Demon no longer holds this land and he has had water, Yulong is feeling better."

I did not know what that meant. Yulong executed a neat convoluted loop in the sky and soared upward, and as I craned my head up to watch, a drop struck me in the cheek.

A water drop, from the sky.

Rain.

No, it was merely the dragon shedding the tank's water, of course. I took a step toward the tank, and another drop struck me. I looked up as Yulong twisted and dove.

The sky opened, and water fell.

"Rain!" I cried before I could help myself. "It's raining!"

Yulong wove his dance through the sky and falling water pelted the last of the airborne dirt to the ground. I clapped my hands and spun in place and danced in the rain, just as Bobby and Peggy were doing beside me.

I spun and hugged Trip. "It's raining!" I laughed and rubbed filthy water from my face.

Bobby rushed to join us, and the thin mud running down his cheeks was the most beautiful thing. "Rain! Will it stay?"

"Black Wind Demon is gone." Trip put his arms about us, pulling us close. "Treasure the dirt of your home," he said.

Bobby nodded. "If there will be rain again…."

"I don't want to go to California," I said. "I want to stay here. I have a farm." With Uncle Edgar's death, I was the heir.

Bobby nodded and his joy faded a bit. "Bank's got what we had. I still need to go west."

I was one person, I realized. Not enough to run a farm. "I need a hired hand," I said. "And maybe a girl to help in the house while the hand and I replant. There's a lot of dust to sweep out."

Bobby grabbed my hand and pumped it. "You're a champ, Miss Tilly."

"As happy as I am for the both of you, we *do* have to go west." Trip raised his hands to his mouth. "Yulong! We have a journey!"

The dragon twisted and plunged to the ground, streaking through the rain. It pulled up just before the ground, writhed into itself, and landed as…gosh almighty. It was a Duesenberg, long and sleek and straight out of a movie. Its paint gleamed white—no, not merely white, iridescent, a flash of dragon scale.

Trip laughed his approval and then called, "Rocky! Sandy! Tumbleweed! Let's go!"

They came, laughing at the car, and piled into its roomy interior without regard for how their wet and dirt spread across the creamy seats. Peggy ran up and rubbed the fender in open-mouthed awe, and Yulong gave a friendly snort which made her leap back and then giggle.

Trip gave us a wave. "Take care. Thank you for your help." He pointed toward where 66 waited to carry them away to California. "To the west!"

The Duesenberg purred like the largest lion ever invented and leaped forward, spraying dust behind.

Bobby, Peggy, and I watched until they disappeared—it did not take long with that horsepower—and then we turned to the road ourselves. We had a farm to return to.

Laura VanArendonk Baugh loves writing with all kinds of folklore and so appreciated the chance to engage with the world's best-known folk tale (if less familiar in the Americas), of the Monkey King and the Journey to the West. Bringing it to the Dust Bowl was a play on the westward journey she thinks Xuanzang/Tripitaka and his friends might have appreciated. She can often be found writing tales of *youkai* or weaving epic fantasy or eating dark chocolate. You can find more of her award-winning folklore-based and original fiction at www.LauraVAB.com.

BONNE CHANCE CONFIDENTIAL

Jack Bates

Out along Long Island Sound, separated by Manhasset Bay, are the cities of Nottingham to the east and Fitzgerald Park to the west. A narrow peninsula neither community wants to claim pushes out into the bay like a gnarled pinky finger. Fitzgerald Park folks call the land Rumple's Pinky while Nottinghammers refer to it with a much more vulgar name for an appendage. Those of us who lived there called it by its actual name.

Rumple's Crossing.

At one time Rumple's Crossing was a very pastoral place. The land was lush and the wildlife plenty. Then mansions went up to the west and east and the people living in these Edwardian castles needed a place to dump their trash. The mayor at the time took bribes from both our neighbors. Doesn't take long for garbage to pile up. We either burned it or dumped it in Manhasset Bay.

There used to be a two-mile stretch of dirt road full of potholes and washboard ripples everyone called Rumple Gap Road. The Queensborough Line train tracks both crossed and ran parallel to Rumple Gap Road. One mile to the east and one mile to the west the paved roads of Nottingham and Fitzgerald Park began (or ended) and smack dab in the middle was Rumple's Crossing.

It was the kind of community where everyone knew one another's business without having to gossip or pry.

Or so we thought.

Quaint little burg for an otherwise unpleasant peninsula. Home to fewer than a thousand year-round residents. There was a market, a filling station, the train depot.

My office.

And Rumple Castle.

Rumple Castle was just that, a castle. Rectangular foundation with four turret towers. Built by industrialist Ephraim Rumple in 1895 at the end of the devil's gnarled pinky. Rumple married a much younger woman and planned to raise a family in his castle. Six years later, he and his younger wife had one child, a daughter, who mysteriously went missing on the night of her tenth birthday, taken from her room in the southernmost tower. The only clues in her abduction were a sharply tapered spindle from a spinning wheel and a ransom note the spindle pinned to a goose down pillow. The note suggested the girl would be returned if the young wife revealed the kidnapper's name. The wife, Lydia Rumple, claimed to have no idea what the kidnapper meant, though many in Rumple's Crossing believed she was lying. She had a reputation for entertaining men while her husband traveled the country selling his steel.

I guess we did gossip a bit after all.

Days became weeks became months. The daughter never returned. Rumple Steel collapsed. Ephraim Rumple went mad. A rumor persisted he had converted all his money to gold ingots he buried on his grounds. Would be treasure hunters found Ephraim living alone in his castle, surviving on small game he trapped and ate. Bones piled high in the wine cellar where Rumple lived.

Lydia Rumple, like her daughter, was never found.

Rumple Castle sat empty for many years until Duke Diamond, a self-made millionaire who had fought in the First World War, bought Rumple Castle for a song. Diamond's arrival was grist for the rumor mill. War vet. Lots of money. Living in the castle. A curse, like history, is doomed to repeat itself.

The summer Duke Diamond moved into the castle was a hot, sticky mess. Unrelenting heat. Humidity so thick it became damn near impossible to breathe. I felt like I was walking under the waters of the Long Island Sound. I wasn't alone. My neighbors in Rumple's Crossing complained of the same. It didn't help that a trash fire burned almost continually just outside town in a place we called Little Hell from the first of May to the first of November.

All of August that summer of 1925, Little Hell brimmed and burned. The smoke billowed thick and black. Five days a week Rumple's Crossing existed in a perpetual fog, as if someone had scooped up our tiny town and put it in a glass globe filled with dirty water and soot. Tip it over, give it a shake, and abracadippity, Rumple's Crossing disappeared.

But not Rumple Castle.

On summer weekends, Rumple Castle came alive with lavish parties. Duke Diamond hired locals to work for him and let them bag leftover food to take home to their families. It wasn't long before Rumple Castle became known as The Duke's Palace.

I didn't immediately jump on the Duke Diamond bandwagon. Not that I wasn't invited. The door to the castle was always open. I'd sit in my office over the train station watching revelers shoot past along Rumple Gap Road and make the breakneck turn over the railroad tracks, pass through Little Hell on their way to the Duke's Palace at the end of Devil's Pinky Point where the air was pure and the sky as clear as the water from a wishing well. Some claimed the cooler air off the Sound kept the soot and smoke away, others said it was a spell.

On Friday nights I would open my window to hear an orchestra playing syncopated jazz. By the end of the night, fireworks exploded over Manhasset Bay. Often the last car left at sunrise and I would pass the late-leaver on my way into my office.

Towards the end of August, there was a horrible accident after one of Duke Diamond's parties. Rumple's Crossing didn't have a police force or a fire department—the closest Rumple's Crossing came to law enforcement was me and I was just a private detective. Otherwise, Fitzgerald Park sent the fire truck and Nottingham sent its sheriff, John Small who was there when I came upon the grisly scene.

A poorly placed tarp barely covered the body of a young woman sprawled in the middle of Rumple Gap Road. The lifeless, fish belly white of her eyes stared up at the morning sun and a large shard of glass protruded from her forehead.

Sheriff Small pushed his wide-brimmed hat back off of his eyebrows. "Hell of a way to start the morning, eh, Miriam?"

"For me or the dead girl, Sheriff Small?"

"All of us."

"Any idea who she is?"

"Aurora Knightly."

"Arthur Knightly's daughter. He owns that big place on Nottingham Beach."

"Right. I don't suppose you were in your office last night?"

"Not when this happened. Who identified her?"

"Sam Farrow said she came into the market just before it happened to buy cigarette papers and a tin of tobacco, charged both to her old man's account. Sam could tell she'd been drinking. Says he told her to watch for cars tearing off of Castle Lane and warned her about the incoming midnight express he could feel shaking the floorboards."

"Guess she didn't heed his warning."

"Well, she *had* been to the castle."

"Oh, come on, John. You don't believe in the Rumple Curse, do you?"

"Kidnapping. Missing wife. Former millionaire living in squalor. Now this. What do you call it, Miriam?"

"Coincidence. Besides, Duke Diamond has been having parties every Friday and Saturday night all summer long. This is the first bit of bad trouble to happen."

"Is it?"

I studied Sheriff Small's face. "That I'm aware of," I said. "Has there been trouble out there?"

"You tell me. You've got the watchful eye."

He meant the painting on my office window overlooking the town. A single eye inside a larger-than-life magnifying glass. Sheriff Small was right about one thing. The eye was watching. It just wasn't watching the town.

"When did this happen?" I asked.

"Just before midnight."

"Midnight? It's almost eight in the morning. Why isn't she in the morgue?"

"No one can find the coroner. I can't release her to the morgue boys over there until Doc White examines the scene."

"Does her family know?"

"Sent one of my deputies to the Knightly spread a few minutes ago."

"You couldn't do it?"

Sheriff Small shook his head. "I hate delivering the bad news."

A black sedan pulled up from the Fitzgerald Park side of Rumple Gap Road. A short man with a stout belly and stubby, little arms hobbled out of the car. His round, metal frame glasses stayed perched on his snout-like nose. The thick, white beard on his face made him look more like Santa Claus than county coroner.

"About time, Doc," Sheriff Small said.

"I was playing squash with some of the old gang. Saturday tradition."

Doc White walked with a pronounced limp—how he played squash was beyond me. He leaned on a cane as he knelt next to the body. He didn't stay down long.

"Yep. She's dead. The glass in her forehead didn't break bone. The impact of the car that it came from more than likely caused internal injuries that killed her. How long she been out here?"

"About eight hours." Sheriff Small did not sound pleased. It felt good to know I wasn't the only one to disappoint a peer or a superior. Not that I did it intentionally, I just had my way of doing things.

Doc White nodded. "Consistent with body temp and muscle rigidity." He waved his cane at the two men from the morgue. One of the men flicked away his cigarette while the other kept his dangling in his lips. The two put the body on a stretcher and put the stretcher in the back of the hearse.

"Where's the car?" Doc asked.

"Hit and run. Sam Farrow said the gal driving it tried to beat the midnight express but hit the tracks too fast and spun out of control. He thought the train dragged the car north but we didn't find anything except a flattened penny on the track."

"Kids." Doc White pointed at my office with is cane. "Looks like you've got company, Mir."

Duke Diamond stood at the window behind my desk. The single eye hovering inside the oversized magnifying glass seemed to be staring inside at him instead of peering down at the crime scene. He pointed at me and waved me up to my office. He was still at the window when I entered.

Diamond held a white Panama hat that matched his white suit and his orange sherbet Oxford shirt matched the band on his hat. A heavy slick of hair tonic held his sandy blonde locks out of his eyes.

"Miss Fee?" he asked.

"That's the name on my door."

"It's an interesting name."

"It's French for 'fairy'."

"I'm—"

"I know who you are, Mr. Diamond. If you're here about the dead girl in the middle of the intersection, you should talk to John Small, the sheriff from Nottingham."

"I'm not here about the dead girl."

"I'm surprised. She'd been at your party."

"A lot of people come to my parties. In fact, that's the reason I came here. I need you to find a young lady who was in attendance last night."

I stepped behind my desk. He looked at me like I was an enemy advancing on him. I could read the uncertainty in his eyes. His hand moved inside his white jacket.

"Relax, Mr. Diamond. I just want to sit down."

"Oh. Of course. Pardon me." He pulled out a white, linen handkerchief and dabbed his forehead. "It's awfully warm. Makes me want to go to the city and drink gin."

"Why not drink it here?"

"I guess—I guess I never thought about it that way. Sometimes it's just better to be somewhere other than where you are."

Rich folks. Always finding something to be miserable about.

I sat down. Diamond stayed at my window, standing behind the painted eye and magnifying glass as if it allowed him to see the world in a different perspective.

Diamond looked at me. He stepped away from the window. "I need you to find a young woman. Bobbed hair. Platinum blonde. Mysterious gray eyes."

"She have a name?"

"If I knew that I wouldn't have need of your services, Miss Fee."

"Do you know how many blonde haired princesses there are in the borough of Queens alone?"

"I'm pretty confident only one has the match to this."

Dangling off the end of his finger was a glass slipper earring the size of a half dollar.

Diamond continued his story. "She wore them to the party. I never spoke to her. She arrived in an Essex touring coach the color of freshly minted copper pennies. I remember seeing it pull up in front of the house from one of the turrets that overlooks the entrance drive. The evening sun made the slippers on her ears sparkle."

"She arrive alone?"

"She had a driver. Her chauffer couldn't have been much older than her, though the white hair under his cap aged him."

"So you want me to return this slipper to her?"

"I want you to find her and bring her to me. Something happened that frightened her and I want to know what it was."

"Maybe she saw the ghost of Lydia Rumple."

"Who?"

"Lydia Rumple? Wife of Ephraim Rumple? Their daughter was kidnapped. Lydia Rumple disappeared. Ephraim Rumple went mad. You *do* know your castle is cursed and haunted, don't you?"

"Folklore, Miss Fee. Nothing more."

"What time did this woman leave?"

"Just before midnight. What? Did I say something troubling?"

"A witness to the crime said the accident they're cleaning up out there occurred a little before midnight."

"Did the witness get a look at the coach?"

"I'll have to ask him."

"So you'll find the young woman and bring her to me?"

"Hundred dollar retainer. Fifty dollars a day plus expenses. I'll need to hold onto the glass slipper earring."

"Fair enough. Oh, and just so you know, it's not glass. It's Windsor crystal from London. That one shoe is worth a small fortune."

Diamond paid me my retainer before he left.

I went into the small washroom on the second floor, stood in front of the mirror and dangled the crystal slipper next to my left ear. It would have made Lon Chaney's Phantom of the Opera look good. Back in my office I emptied a matchbox and lined it with a tissue. I put the earring inside the box and then put the box in the drawstring carpetbag I hung on my belt. The bag was small, more of a pouch, but it held everything I put in it.

A tiny bell chimed on the inside of the screen door as I entered Farrow's Market. It was midmorning and no one else was in the store. Sam Farrow sat in a rocker next to a table made out of half of a pickle barrel. On top was a chessboard with a game in progress. A hand-rolled cigarette smoldered between his lips and he looked up when he heard the bell.

"You here about the dead girl?" He took the cigarette out of his mouth and cupped it in his hand.

"Why would you think that?"

"I saw the Duke of Diamonds up in your office standing behind that magnifying glass. Gives me the creeps."

"Duke Diamond?"

"No. That eye peering through that magnifying glass. Like it's inspecting me."

"Guilty conscious?"

"Hardly. What can I do ya for, Mir?"

"You see the car that hit Aurora Knightly?"

Sam Farrow laughed and sat forward in his rocker. "Damn me if I didn't know you were going to ask about what happened. Diamond thinks it's the curse of the castle, don't he?"

"He doesn't believe in the curse."

"How do you know?"

"He told me. Now you tell me about the car that hit Aurora Knightly." I made sure no one else was around and when I was certain no one was visiting the outdoor plumbing, I snapped my fingers three times and said, "Verite!"

Simple spell casting. Stand in front of the person who has the information, snap fingers thrice, and say 'truth!' In French, of course.

I wasn't yet a veteran fairy godmother. I still had green wings. The Charm, the name of the Council of Fairies, had yet to grant me all of my powers. They were a tricky bunch and the Grand Fairy held some reservations about me. The eye in my window giving Sam Farrow the willies wasn't there to watch him. It was there to literally keep an eye on me. Until I could prove myself, atone for some past faux pas, I was merely an apprentice, which was one step up from Tooth Fairy.

Sam Farrow fell into a consciousness stream unaware of what he was telling me.

"Like I told Sheriff Small, I knew it was Aurora Knightly—"

I snapped my fingers. "Dis-moi la verite sur la voiture!" I said. 'Tell me the truth about the car.'

"First I saw the lamps on the front. The car was far off but it was coming up fast. When it passed under those lights over there at Waterston's Full Service Garage that car was the color of a sunset over Long Island Sound. Something odd about it, though. Steering wheel was on the opposite side like a car from Great Britain. Never saw it until last night."

"Who was driving it?"

"Some young gal. She looked angry and wild at the same time. Like she had to be somewhere else."

Rich folks. Better to be there than here.

"You're certain it wasn't a man driving it?" I asked.

"No. It was a young woman."

"Young guy with white hair at the wheel." I said testing his memory and my spell casting. Sometimes I get that sense my abilities may feel like they're at full strength only to find out I was a little more spent than I thought.

"I'm telling you the truth, Miriam. It was a young woman with bobbed hair. Platinum blonde. Like Carole Lombard. Only—prettier."

"Prettier than Carole Lombard? Ever see her before?"

"I only got a glimpse of her."

"But…?"

"Damned if my first thought wasn't, 'Is that Jacqueline Rumple?' Crazy, I know."

"Crazy on account of Jacqueline Rumple was kidnapped in 1911 when she was ten years old. If that was Jackie Rumple driving that car, she'd be alive and twenty-four. You think it was her?"

"She and her mother used to walk down here when Stilts Weaver owned this market and I was just a clerk. I remember thinking how much she already looked like her mother, who maybe looked a little like Carole Lombard herself. Her mother would buy her a dollar's worth of penny candy and tell her to sit on the stoop and count trains while she and Mr. Weaver discussed the grocery bill. Stilts would tell me to keep an eye on the girl."

"Where did Stilts Weaver live back then?"

"Ambrose Hills over there by Nottingham. Not quite the upper crust but close. Stilts married Dorothea Hixson who inherited her first husband's pastry and pie company after he drowned in Manhasset Bay. Dorothea and her kids come in here once after Stilts died. She come to tell me Stilts deeded the market to me with the understanding I sold Hixson Desserts I kept in the cooler. Her daughters were two of the orneriest young girls I'd ever seen. And what brats they were. Eating everything they saw. The son, though, he just sat on the stoop watching the trains."

"The son?"

"Yeah. Stilts had a child from his first marriage to Loretta Gabradino. She was the one that stepped in front of the train. No one knew why. She just slipped out of the house and waited out there by the depot. When the train come, off she went. Anyhow, I only saw the boy from the back. Dirty white undershirt and a pair of denim overalls. Towhead kid."

"Where is Dorothea Hixson now?"

"I imagine she still lives out over to Ambrose Hills. At least her girls do. Neither ever married far as I know. If you met them, you'd know why."

The tinkling of the bell above the door ended the spell as I left the market.

"Next time buy somethin'," Sam Farrow said from behind the screen.

Outside in the street, Arthur Knightly roared like a revival preacher, delivering his version of fire and brimstone to a congregation of Sheriff Small and Doc White. He wasn't too happy with the way the two men had handled the death of his daughter. I would have cast 'Calm' but I had to save my spell charges just in case. Knightly saw me and changed his mood on his own.

"You Miriam Fee?" Knightly asked.

"I am."

"I'm Arthur Knightly. I'd like to hire you to find who killed my daughter."

"I'm confident Sheriff Small will find your daughter's killer."

"The sheriff is an incompetent boob who took seven hours to notify me and even then all he did was send a flunky out to do his job for him."

"I ain't no flunky," the deputy said taking a step forward.

Sheriff Small stopped him. "It's okay, Red. The man is grieving is all."

Deputy Will Redmond cooled down, a near impossibility in that August heat.

Arthur Knightly pressed harder to hire me. "Seriously, Miss Fee. Whatever the cost. I need your help in finding my daughter's killer. Name your price."

"It's seventy-five a day plus expenses. Two hundred dollar retainer."

He peeled off three one hundred dollar bills from the wad of money held in place by a fourteen-karat gold money clip. Guys with money didn't pussyfoot around and neither did I.

"That's how it's done, sheriff," Art Knightly said. "Miss Fee, I'd like a daily report on your progress."

"Is that what the extra hundred was for?"

Knightly's driver held the door for him. The driver darted his eyes away from mine.

"Excuse me, Mr. Knightly."

Knightly stopped at the open door. "Not changing your mind, are you, Miss Fee?"

"No, sir. I was wondering if I could ask your driver a couple of questions?"

"Charles? He doesn't know anything."

"He might."

Knightly looked at his driver and nodded. Charles turned to me. He straightened his back and tucked his hat under his arm. "Miss?"

"Did you drive Aurora Knightly out to the Duke's Castle last evening?"

"I drove her there but she told me she'd get a ride home and I shouldn't wait about for her like an overprotective nanny."

"Did you see an Essex touring coach the color of shiny pennies while you were there?"

"I passed one such car on Castle Lane. At first I didn't think it was going to move out of my path. The driver didn't appear to fully understand the rules of the road."

"Did you get a good look at the driver?"

"Younger man. Shocking white hair."

"And his passengers?"

"Only one. She sat alone in the back."

"After you dropped off Miss Knightly, where did you go?"

"I returned to the Knightly estate. I wish I had stayed like an overprotective nanny. Mr. Knightly, I am sorry."

"You have nothing to be sorry for, Charles. Miss Fee, if you don't mind, I have to go into the city to make arrangements for Aurora."

Knightly got in the car. Charles closed the door. He pinched the bill of his chauffer's cap and nodded his head at me. I had no doubts that Charles told the truth. His condolences to Arthur Knightly were sincere.

I took the train to the Ambrose Hill station. Like I said, my wings were still green. Besides, it wasn't a good idea to fly during the day.

A few taxis waited outside the terminal. A valet whistled the next in the line to the curb. A black and white checkered one from Bridgeview Cabs. The driver put down his paper and pulled forward. I got in the back.

"Where to, miss?"

"Looking for the Hixson house."

"Petunia Hixson's house or Daisy Hixson's house?"

"Actually, I was looking for Dorothea Hixson's house."

"That would be Petunia's house now. After their mother died, Petunia and Daisy had a falling out of sorts."

"Guy troubles?"

The cabbie snorted, scratched at the gruff of hair on his narrow, pointed chin. "Those two? Hardly. Although, the step-brother does live next door with Daisy so maybe there's something we don't know about."

"Next door? Great Mother Goose. If I had a falling out with my sister I wouldn't move next door to her."

"It's actually a guest house on the same piece of land. An in-law's suite I think they call it."

"Thanks for the tip."

"Look at that. Me. A cabbie. Handing out tips!" His laugh was more of a bray. "Maybe you can give me one."

"Can you break a dollar?"

He pointed at his newspaper. "I meant about the horses. I don't beg for my fares."

I looked at the paper. "Easy. Second Fiddle. Third race. Belmont. Bet it to Show."

"Show? You think coming in second is a win?"

"Look at what it pays. Here's a dollar. Bet it for me."

"How do you know I'll pay it to you?"

I snapped my fingers three times. "Honnetete!" French for 'honesty'. I looked at his cabbie's license. "I know your name, Billy

Gruffman. I'll find you when I'm ready to leave."

"I bet you will." He winked at me.

Twenty minutes later he dropped me at the Hixson's Victorian manor. I opened the wrought iron gate and proceeded up the stone steps of an elevated yard to the smaller of the two houses I could see and I knocked on its screen door. A petite maid stood in the doorway.

"It's okay, Jeanine," a male voice said. "I've got it."

I couldn't see who'd spoken. The maid looked over her shoulder into the kitchen.

"As you wish, Mr. Ashley."

"Jeanine. Are you ever going to stop calling me Mr. Ashley? It's just Ash."

"As you wish—Ash." Jeanine giggled and returned to the kitchen as the man calling himself Ash came out to greet me.

"Is she the cutest?" Mr. Ashley said. He stood on his side of the screen, his arms folded over his chest. He wore camel trousers, a striped Oxford, and a pair of penny loafers but only one shoe held a copper coin in its tongue band. A yellow tennis sweater was tied around his neck and covered his shoulders. His thick, blonde hair hung down over his left brow and he occasionally pulled it back behind his ear.

"I'm sorry," he said. "You are?"

"Miriam Fee, Mr. Ashley."

He scoffed. "Why does everyone insist on calling me 'mister'?"

"Well, you *are* a man."

"Yes, well, some things are out of our hands, aren't they? How may I help you, Miss Fee?"

"I'm looking for someone and I thought maybe your sisters—"

"Stepsisters."

"Of course."

"They made up and live together next door in the bigger house."

"Are they home?"

"They rarely leave but they do take in a party now and then." He raised his voice as if he thought they might hear him from across the yard. "Not that they would ever tell me..." He looked at me. "I'm not their 'real' sibling so they treat me like I'm an interloper. Who are you looking for again?"

"Whoever has the match to this." I opened the matchbox and showed him the crystal slipper. He pushed open the screen door and joined me on the porch.

"Where did you find that?" he asked, his voice barely a whisper.

"Do you know the young woman who has the match to this?" I asked.

Ash Hixson frowned. "Young woman?"

"The man who gave me this asked me to find the young woman who wore these earrings last night to his party. He said he saw her arrive and intended to speak to her but when he finally had the opportunity, she'd left abruptly."

"Some girls can't wait all night for their prince to arrive, can they?" He gave me back the box. "The slippers belonged to my mother."

"Your stepmother?"

"Right. Of course. Either way they belonged to her."

Jeanine the maid floated back into the room. Her skirt was so long she seemed to glide over the marble floor and I thought I picked up the gentle whir and flap of moth wings.

"Mr. Ashley—Ash—it's almost time for your one o'clock salon appointment. Should I have the car brought around from your sisters' house?"

"No. I'll walk. Thank you, Jeanie."

Jeanine laughed and glided back into the kitchen.

"I just adore her," Ash Hixson said. "If you'll excuse me..."

"Just one thing."

"Hmm?"

"What happened to the penny in your right shoe?"

"Spent it on some candy, of course."

Ash Hixson went down the steps and through the gate whistling Bessie Smith's 'Second Fiddle' on his way. It made me think of the wager I had Billy Gruffman place for me. Perhaps it was a sign, an omen, but I wondered how the Charm would feel knowing I had used my abilities to cast for profit.

"Oh," a woman said. "Who are you?"

I looked down to see a plus-sized woman standing at the gate. She wore a yellow dress that came up high around her neck and rivulets of sweat trickled along her temples from the mound of brown hair on top of her head. She made her way up onto the porch. The first step groaned a bit under her step.

"Easy, Daisy I have you..."

I hadn't realized another woman was standing behind the first until the second woman put her hand on the first woman's back to steady her.

"I'm fine, Petunia," the woman in the yellow dress said.

"Of course, Daisy," the second woman said. She was shorter with a bit of an overbite and whistled slightly on 's' sounds.

I blinked. I must have been in a daze. I hadn't seen the two women approach the house. On top of that, standing next to me was Jeanine, the maid, and I couldn't recall her coming out of the kitchen let alone onto the porch.

"This is Miss Miriam Fee, Miss Daisy. Miss Petunia," Jeanine said. "She's a private detective."

"Private detective? Oh, it's much too hot for inconsistencies such as these. Jeanine, please go and make a pitcher of gin blossoms for us, if you would."

Jeanine smiled at me. It wasn't pleasant. It was a snarl. A warning.

"Yes, Miss Daisy." Back into the house went Jeanine with a slam of the screen door behind her. Daisy Hixson yipped.

"This heat is positively murder on my nerves." She sat down on a wicker settee that, like the lower porch step, groaned. "Please do sit.

Your standing is apt to give my heart palpitations."

I sat in a fan back rattan chair on Daisy Hixson's right.

"Now why has a private detective come to my house?"

"Our house, Daisy." Petunia said with that slight whistle.

Daisy smiled patiently. "The last thing we Hixsons crave is scandal."

"If it involves us." Petunia continued to whistle.

"I came to inquire about the match to this earring." I showed the crystal slipper to the Hixson sisters.

"Never saw it before," Daisy Hixson said.

"Never saw it before?" I was flummoxed. "Your brother said the earrings belonged to your mother."

"Oh. So today he is our brother, Ash, and not our sister, Ashlee."

"That's with two Es at the end," whistled Petunia.

"I'm afraid I don't understand."

"Our stepsibling views gender as an option, Miss Fee," Petunia said. "One day he'll be Ash and a few days later he'll proclaim to be Ashlee."

"Whole lot of nonsense," Daisy said.

"When our mother married his father, we knew him as Ashley," Petunia explained. "That's with an l-e-y. Then one day he came to dinner in a dress and announced he was Ashlee—"

"With two Es," I said.

"I blame his father," Daisy said. "He came from that place they call Little Hell. Married our mother for her fortune. I don't know what she saw in him. It was as if she'd been enchanted. Ah, good, the gin blossoms."

Jeanine stood behind Petunia's chair holding a silver tray with a glass pitcher and three tumblers. I hadn't seen or heard her come out and I was facing the door, so that was something. Jeanine set the tray on a small wicker table, poured two drinks, and handed them to the Hixson sisters. Before they could take a sip, Jeanine snapped her fingers three times and said, "Se faner!"

French for 'fade'.

"They can't hear or see us," Jeanine said. "I've faded us from their consciousness."

"Are you part of the Charm?" I asked, surprised. "I didn't know there was another apprentice in the area."

"I'm more of a free agent. I know why you are here, Miss Fee. It's about the woman killed after the party last night, isn't it?"

"I actually came about this crystal slipper earring. The man who hired me wants me to find its owner and bring them to him."

"Yes, well, I think I need to explain what happened. You see, I've been with Mr. Ashley—Ash—for a very long time. From the day he was born his mother—his real mother, that is—began to notice things about her son she feared would upset her older husband. When the father was away on business, Ash's mother allowed her son to play dress-up and that was how he came to be known as Jacqueline even though his Christian name was Jackson. But the father traveled less as the child got older and one night the mother took her child into the forest to hide him from his father who had found him dressed as a girl. The mother made a desperate wish upon a star for help and I materialized."

"So you weren't sent. You were summoned."

"Something like that. I told the mother her wishes would be granted and took the child. The mother came up with a ruse about kidnapping."

"How did Jack Rumple become Ash-slash-Ashlee Hixson?"

"I needed someplace to hide him so I delivered him to Stilts Weaver who I knew had been friends with the mother and said I would help Mr. Weaver find another wife if he promised to raise the boy as his own. He agreed."

"But what of the boy's birth mother? What became of her?"

Jeanine paled. She wrung her hands together. "I screwed up. Ephraim Rumple believed the rumors his wife knew the kidnapper. Said she plotted with him to use the child as a pawn to take his fortune. They argued and, in a fit of drunken rage, he beat her to within an inch of her life and sealed her inside the wall of his wine cellar."

I was aghast. Appalled. "Why didn't you rescue her?"

"I know. I know. But Lydia Rumple had wished me to protect her son, not her."

"The Charm would have approved."

"I told you. I'm not with the Charm."

I understood why. Rogue fairies like Jeanine made the rules up as they went along. Sometimes they got lucky. Most of the time they screwed up in notably disastrous ways.

Jeanine continued. "Ash was older so I thought telling him what happened and giving him the earrings would appease him. I was wrong. He became obsessed with returning them to her. I tried 'forget' and 'ignore' spells but Ash is persistent. So we made a deal. He wanted to go to a party at the castle as a woman—a real woman like he told his real mother he always wanted to be. I said he could go to the party and told him where to look to find her, but he mustn't, under any circumstance, tell anyone why he was there. And he had to be home by midnight because that was the extent of the magic I had in me for the day. Masking these two really takes it out of me."

"Masking? Why?"

"I'm cursed! Their mother served me red valerian tea!"

"She trapped you. How long are you held?"

"With these two it could be quite some time. It was their mother's wish a man must fall in love with the person within them and not how they looked."

"How do they look?"

Jeanine dropped the mask spell. Daisy still had curves and Petunia still could use some orthodontic work, but they were attractive. They looked at one another as if seeing a stranger and Jeanine quickly replaced the spell.

"We must be drunk," Petunia said.

Daisy nodded. "I know. For a minute there you looked pretty."

They laughed and went back to drinking gin blossoms. I was pretty certain Jeanine was in need of one herself. She would have never been in the predicament had she been in the Charm.

"What happened at the party?"

Jeanine sighed. "Ashlee panicked. There were too many people and men kept approaching her. Before she knew it, midnight was close at hand. That's when she saw Duke Diamond coming towards her. She ran from the castle, dropping the earrings on her way. She got to her car but the chauffer had already dematerialized. She just wanted to get away before she, too, reverted to her natural state and in her haste to escape, she lost control of the car and hit that young woman."

"Where did you get the chauffer? The car?"

"I couldn't use the Hixson's actual driver or car. I portal-jumped into Manhattan, found an old man sleeping in Central Park and brought him back in a bag of infinite holding. I promised him youth and food for the night. The car I winged. I popped what I thought was a penny out of Ash's loafer only it was a British tuppence he had acquired from a soldier he met. When I conjured the car, it gave us a British car. I should have ended it then."

"Why didn't you?"

"He was so happy to be Ashlee. Completely Ashlee and not pretending to be Ashlee. It had been so long since I'd seen him like that I couldn't take it away from him. I've watched over him for so long it's like he's my son. And I will do anything to protect him."

She snapped her fingers three times and cried, "Oblier!"

French for 'forget'.

I counter cast. "Reorienter!" and sent the spell back at her.

"Oh, Jeanie," I said. "Your power is too weak right now, to cast 'forget' on me. You've got 'fade' and 'mask' and who knows what else going on."

The fade spell faded. The mask spell dissolved. I quietly walked down the sidewalk to the wrought iron gate.

"Goodbye," Daisy Hixson said.

"Thanks for stopping bye," Petunia Hixson said without whistling.

Jeanine just stood there staring at the street. Her spell had been quite strong after all. She must have forgotten who she was when I redirected it back at her.

I walked back to the Ambrose Hills depot. Halfway there Billy Gruffman pulled up next me.

"I thought you were going to find me, lady. I got your payout. Forty-six bucks."

"Keep it."

"Naw. That's too much."

"My union won't let me profit from games of chance while I'm on a job."

"The union won't know."

"Yeah. This one will."

"Well, you want a ride?"

"No, thanks. I'm in no hurry. I'll walk."

"Okay. Thanks again, Toots!"

I rode the first passenger train to arrive back to Rumple's Crossing. My thoughts were muddled. How could I tell Duke Diamond the woman he found so alluring was a phantasm? How could I explain to Arthur Knightly his daughter Aurora was killed by that phantom in a car that didn't exist?

The bigger concern was how would I tell the Charm I had wiped clean the thoughts of Jeanie? I was still on probation for misuse of magic. This would tip the scales against me.

For a gangster, Duke Diamond took it easier than I thought he would.

"Did you find her?" he asked.

"I did but she asked to remain anonymous."

"Married, I guess. Or engaged."

I left it at that. “Here’s the glass slipper.”

“I would have thought she’d want it back.” He took it.

“And your money.”

“No, you keep it. You did your job. You earned it.”

Arthur Knightly snatched the money out of my hand when I offered it to him. “I was wrong about you, Fee. I’ll go to Manhattan. Get someone who knows what *he’s* doing. You country bumpkins are a sad lot.”

I thought about transmogrifying him, but frogs were the whole reason there was that whole probation thing already hanging over my head. Turn one bad date into a frog and leave him that way until he’s kissed by a virgin and everyone gets pissed.

As for the Charm, I will present the story as I have here. What I did to Jeanine was out of self-preservation not maliciousness. Still, it is doubtful her powers will be restored or that I will become a full fledged fairy godmother.

But it is no longer in my hands. It is in theirs.

What’s French for ‘good luck’?

Jack Bates is a three-time finalist for a Derringer Award from the Short Mystery Fiction Society. In 2007 he co-wrote WHITE OUT, a horror screenplay that had its option picked up twice by Triboro Films in New York. His stories have appeared at crime sites such as *Near to the Knuckle, Shotgun Honey, Beat to a Pulp* and many others. He has also appeared twice before in *Mystery Weekly*. Most recently his short, ‘The Fakahatchee Goonch’ was included in the Bouchercon 2018 anthology, FLORIDA HAPPENS.

Drawing on his experience as an educator, Bates sets his Cinderella based story in the Hudson Bay region of New York. The homage to F. Scott Fitzgerald’s *The Great Gatsby* is not accidental. After deconstructing both stories, certain tropes and themes align. Reinventing self is a major component of each story. Both characters yearn to be free of their poverty level lives. One takes matters into his own hands while the other has a chance encounter. Either way, fate has a way of putting a twist on the final outcome.

늑대 - THE NEUGDAE

Juliet Harper

In the burnt out edges of the bombed and gassed villages of South Korea, a little girl was handed a bundle in the early fog of morning by her mother. "Chae-Won," she said, "take this to your Auntie. Tell her it's all we can spare." In the bundle were rations—dry, tasteless foods handed out by the soldiers in place of the crops they had spent so long tending, only to see them ruined just before harvest. Chae-Won fastened her Saekdongot hanbok, her favorite due to its bright color, the stripes of vibrant shades of red, like a patchwork flower, and prepared for the long walk. She had to go, rather than her parents or older sister, because she was the only one still too small to work in the fields or do odd jobs for the army camps. "Tell your Auntie she will need to evacuate soon, or be bombed too," her mother called after her, already on her own way down the road, in the opposite direction.

The road was long and dusty back to the farm where her Auntie lived, barely making a living on what little was still left after the bomb had turned her fields, cow shed, and husband into one big crater. But she refused to leave it. Chae-Won admired her Auntie's tenacity, her refusal to let the war break her, even if her mother said it was bullheaded and sure to end in the old woman's death. But Auntie did not listen, and so neither did Chae-Won, nor did she mind the long walk. She enjoyed the breeze that wafted away the burnt, sulfur stink of the bombarded land, the pong of unwashed bodies and the shit of the last few remaining cows. Bundle in one hand, Chae-Won broke off a branch from a low-lying shrub brush, swinging it back and forth in the other.

When she passed the wreck of a bombed jeep, the once green sides now singed black and dusted with dull brown dirt, the tires melted flat and slumping into the earth, seats nothing but bare springs and oil stains, she banged her stick against its metal side and listened to sound as it echoed back from the foothills. When she passed the makeshift altar to a family that had died, their graves still faintly visible as truncated lumps, she bowed her head and let her swinging stick fall still. When she passed a flowering bush, she dropped her stick in exchange for a few blooms, thinking her Auntie might like them. When she passed the beastly tank silent at the side of the road,the closest she had ever been to one of the great behemoths, she expected it, too, to be dead, the hulking shell cool to the touch. But the scent of diesel was still ripe, the oil still thick and warm in its leg joints. She did not expect that, nor did she expect the man.

Hopping down from the top of the turret far over Chae-Won's head, the man was undressed from the waist up, with dark hair covering his chest like a forest. Sweat gleamed on him like rain. He wiped his oil blackened hands on a white cloth, staining it. "Hello, little sister," he said in accented Korean. An American. Chae-Won nodded to him politely, eyes averted, but kept walking. "Where are you going that way?" the American asked, again in rough Korean. "The road gets dangerous." He gestured to his tank, toward its insect-like multitude of mechanical legs. That gave Chae-Won pause. The road had not been dangerous before.

"I am going to see my Auntie, on the other side of the old village," she answered, "to take her rations. How is the road dangerous?"

"Have you been this way by yourself before?" he asked instead.

Chae-Won nodded. "Many times."

The American tsked. "Must have been a while since the last time," he said, moving in closer to Chae-Won. "There have been reports of deserters, hiding out in these foothills. Attacking civilians and army units when they pass too close." He reached out to stroke Chae-Won's hair, fingers dragging lightly over her Baetssi, which matched her hanbok. Chae-Won did not like him touching her with his oily hands, but she remained still. Americans were there to help them, her mother had said.

"Is your Auntie old?" the American asked, leaving Chae-Won fighting not to giggle at his clumsy pronunciation of the word old. She nodded respectfully instead.

"She refuses to leave what is left of her home and farm," she answered.

"But you and your family must still take care of her," he said, like a statement not a question, pointing to Chae-Won's bundle of rations. She nodded again. The American kneeled, fishing something out of his pocket. "Do you see this?" He held up a glint of metal between his thumb and grease-stained forefinger. It looked like a flat flower, a little like the sundew plants her older sister had shown her once, its petals brassy and golden in the sunlight. "It's a flower your family would be happy to see you picking. It's a spent bullet casing," he explained, twisting the metal a little in his fingers before engulfing it in his fist, pointing to the field behind his tank. "There's tons of them, and other shrapnel, out in that field. I bet if you collect enough, your family could sell it for scrap, help to pay for providing for you and your Auntie."

Chae-Won turned her head to follow the American's finger. They had never been wealthy, but with everything gone now she often heard her parents and sister worrying about food. It would be good to help them. Help her Auntie too, if she could find enough scrap.

Noting her interest, the American continued. "Why don't you go pick the field over, while I go make sure the road ahead is clear, hmm?" Chae-Won turned back to him, bowing deeply, murmuring her thanks. As he stood, she stepped off the road, placing her bundle and flowers down on a flattish rock, and gathered up a section of her Chima like a basket to collect the metal pieces in.

The American watched as the girl moved out into the field, her steps light enough she might not even set off the landmines he knew were buried there. As she walked, eyes glued to the ground and back hunched looking for scrap, he swiped his shirt off the muzzle of the tank's main gun. He pulled it on, followed by his coat, dish-shaped helmet and gas mask. Flicking up the furred collar of his coat, he picked up his gun and the little girl's bundle of rations, and set off down the road, whistling to himself. The rubber and valving of the gasmask turned the sound into a haunting tune.

He had not gotten very far when he heard the explosion, a light rain of dirt clods falling down around him. *A pity*, he thought. He wouldn't have minded her surviving; she probably would have been fun to play with. But he consoled himself with the thought of bigger, older fish to fry.

It didn't take the American long to find the farm the girl had spoken of, a ramshackle little house perched on the edge of a shallow blast crater, now mostly filled in with junk and garbage. He sauntered up to the door, knocking casually on the frame, low down, like a child might. Inside he could hear movement, then the door swung open. The Auntie stood expectant, looking down about little girl height, her face crinkled only at the edges of her eyes, the fullness of her cheeks burnt rosy from working in the sun. Registering that she was looking at coat-covered legs, her head jerked up. Panic crossed her face, her eyebrows flying upward as her mouth dropped open in a short cry. She slapped at the door, to slam it in his face, bolting backward. But the American caught the door with his boot, watching as the woman ran from him. He could now see why she didn't work outside her farm, even if she didn't look very old. Her gait was wrong, something bad at the hips, leaving her hobbling as she screamed.

It took almost no effort for the American to catch the woman; she was an easy chase. Gripping her by the arm, he slapped her hard across the face. Her shouts cut off at the impact, red flushing across the cheekbone, crystal tears brimming in her eyes. "Oh, yes," he said, yanking her into his chest, voice distorted by the gas mask, "cry for me."

The American slaked his hungers on the woman, beating her black and blue, and leaving her bloody and used on the rough floor. It was always better when he didn't have to pay a madam first. He gorged himself on the meager rations, tubers, and kimchi the woman had left, satiating those hungers as well, then collapsed on the low cot to sleep.

Back in the field, the little girl stood up. She looked around her, at the crater and metal shards which circled her feet. A landmine. She should have known better, her parents had warned her away from scavenging in open land like some of the children whose parents had died, searching for landmines for the army to reclaim.

She looked at the fragments of body parts upon which she stood. The shreds of red hanbok, the strands of long black hair still attached to a scalp laying like a discarded cap.

She looked at her hands, ghostly pale in the sun's light. So pale she could almost see through them.

She looked at her feet, which she could not see.

Turning in a slow circle, Chae-Won glowered at the tank parked on the side of the dusty road. At its valves and iron sides. At the flatish rock she had left the bundle for her Auntie on, now empty.

Turning her head, peering through her now loose hair, she stared toward the horizon, in the direction of her Auntie's farm. The American.

Hot coals burning in her stomach, Chae-Won screamed, the

piercing noise echoing off the foothills until it was the only thing in the world. Ignoring the pull she felt toward the earth, toward the underground world of the dead, she moved back to the road. She glared at the tank, feeling the burn in her chest bubble up, until the tank was on fire, its fuel chamber starting to groan, the metal pinging. Turning her hot gaze back to the road, Chae-Won followed the American.

If someone had possessed the ability to ask Chae-Won how she had gotten to her Auntie's house, how she had come to be standing in the doorway, she would not have been able to answer. But stand there she did, the fire inside her burning ever hotter as she stared down at her Auntie, curled up and weeping on the floor. At the American sleeping in her Auntie's bed, still in his coat and gas mask, helmet cocked by the cot cushions. At his pants low and unzipped, crumbs dusting their seams. The fire pulsed through her veins, pulling her forward. "What big eyes you have," she hissed, "what a big mouth you have, what a big appetite you have." Vision running red, Chae-Won lunged at the American.

Translucent body plunging into the American's sweaty flesh, Chae-Won took hold. Blazing claws hooking into red meat, Chae-Won filled his bones and limbs. Eyeballs springing open, the American screamed. Fire threaded his veins, insects squirming in his belly. Blinded by the pain, he pawed at his abdomen. Shoving away his coat skirt panels and popping the buttons from his shirt, the American bared his softly rounded stomach. He could feel his insides writhing, burning. He scratched wildly at the exposed skin, eyes bulging as he saw it distend and shift, as if pregnant with a parasite. Pocket knife suddenly in hand, he stabbed down, trying to pin the thing moving inside him. He tore and cut and sawed, stabbing over and over and over, his throat going raw and bloody behind the valve of his gas mask, his belly going red and slick. With his free hand he grasped and pulled, ripping the ragged skin and squeezing at the elusive eels of his intestines. Something popped, beneath the flailing of his knife, and a surge of fluid, of bile, spilled from the open cavity of his belly, chunks of flesh, half-digested food washing out onto the already soiled bed clothes.

At the American's frantic screaming, the Auntie had woken, dimly resurfacing back into consciousness. She watched now as he tore at himself, cut himself open, eviscerating himself. She clapped her swollen hands to her ears, trying to block out the sounds of his crazy, panicked screeching and burbling. The stink of his bile and excrement hit her split and blood-clotted nostrils, but she did not look away. She watched as he gutted himself, searching within himself with weakening hands. She watched as he dropped the pocket knife from limp fingers, losing it in the blood and waste. She watched as the wolf leapt, finally, from within the ruin of red.

It was a Mongolian Wolf, dark hair and fair skin melted together to tawny fur and pale feet. Burning fire eyes stared hard at her.

Chae-Won stared at her Auntie.

The Auntie made eye contact with the wolf, a bloom of recognition forming within her, a soothing balm to her hurt. She nodded in respect. "Gwisin," she whispered, the wolf's true name held back.

The wolf nodded in return, and watched as her Auntie stood stiffly, and, hobbling, began to pack a bundle of her belongings. She would evacuate with the family after all. Satisfied, the wolf turned back to the corpse of the American, still warm and steaming, and began to slake her hungers.

Juliet Harper is a queer witch and horror writer who hails from well off the path through the forest, residing among the wolves and flowers. Her love for all things wild, transcendental, and horrific often inspires her writing, resulting in such other stories as "To See the Light," published in *Mad Scientist Journal*, and "Beast," published on the Mills College art museum blog. She enjoys exploring the odder side of mundane, bringing horror, or magic, to the everyday, seeking to paint the ultimate gory but delicious scene for her readers.

Harper possesses a B.S. in Forensic Psychology and is currently working toward attaining her Masters in Creative Writing at Mills College in Oakland, CA.

THE RESCUE OF TRESSES MALONE

Alena Van Arendonk

Inspector Rex Regent paused in the sheltered doorway of a shabby warehouse to light a cigarette. The flare of a wooden match briefly illuminated his face—more youthful than others in his line of work, but marred by a livid scar down one cheek—and sputtered out, leaving only the cigarette's red tip to interrupt the darkness.

Regent extended his arm and held the conspicuous cigarette as far from his body as possible as he advanced into the dark alley. Every few steps he flicked the stub to knock ash free and keep the tip glowing bright, so it would be clearly visible to anyone waiting at the end of the alley. At this range, the only way to make certain a gunman missed was to trick him into aiming three feet off center mass.

Rex reached the end of the alley without incident and stubbed out the cigarette on a garbage bin. The next street was awash in neon twilight, and he allowed his eyes to adjust and probe every corner between his location and the yawning entrance of the Dark Horse Inn. By design, the area was pockmarked with hiding places; every two-bit bookie and cheap floozy in town had a working address along this block. Each of them paid tribute to Johnny Malone, and not one would shed a tear over a lone officer of the law.

Rex had never set foot inside the Dark Horse itself, but he'd stormed enough of the dive's cousins to know exactly what he'd find inside: A handful of thugs, some pinstriped hoodlums, a couple of mafiosos, and a half-dozen tawdry hostesses wearing cheap perfume and little else would decorate the bar. Another doorway—probably concealed behind a tobacco-stained velvet curtain—would lead to a back room where a a single green-shaded chandelier would illuminate a high-stakes poker game.

Upon entering, Rex noted the two-bit thugs had been upgraded to half-dollar heavies for the occasion of his visit. One or two recognized him and shifted uncomfortably, but no one pulled a gun. Rex was glad of that; while he didn't shy from a fight when necessary, the six rounds in his Colt Official Police .38 were useless against a dozen armed men.

Rex exchanged a glance with the bartender, who nodded at a door at the far end of the smoky room where the velvet curtain had been tied to one side. Before he could knock, the door swung inward, revealing a small, balding man with a mustache and wire-rimmed spectacles.

"Come in, inspector," simpered the little man. "You are expected."

Rex shouldered past him and fixed his eyes on the room's only other occupant, seated at the poker table. "I got your invitation, Malone. No game tonight? I'm disappointed."

Johnny Malone chuckled, but the sound quickly turned into a wracking cough. The bespectacled man hurried back to his employer's side and rummaged in a bag strapped to the chair. The chair slid forward, and Rex realized it was a wheelchair. That was new.

Malone swallowed the pill pressed on him by the little man, then waved him away. "Wait outside," he rasped.

The assistant's eyes boggled behind his glasses. "But boss—" His gaze shifted meaningfully to Regent.

Rex rolled his eyes. "What, you think I'm going to collar your boss and drag him off downtown? All by my lonesome, past all your friends out there?" He jerked a thumb toward the bar. "Relax, sunshine. I like this coat, and I don't want to see it turned into cheesecloth."

"Go on, Benson, scram. Wait, bring the wine first." Benson placed a pair of tumblers and a bottle of wine on the baize tabletop, then Malone shooed him out. Benson gave Rex a final glare before closing the door behind him.

Malone gave a little sigh and wheeled himself closer to the table. "Sit down, Regent."

Rex didn't move. "You wanna tell me why I'm here?"

Malone grinned. "This was the only one of my joints low enough for you to take my invitation seriously. Besides—" He glanced around the dim room. "—I wanted to see how far I've come. This is where I got my start, you know."

Rex followed his gaze. "You certainly have come up in the world. But you didn't call me here for a nostalgic romp down memory lane."

"More of a roll, now," Malone replied dryly. "Don't pretend you ain't noticed." He patted the wheel of his chair.

"I was trying not to stare."

"You always was a polite kid." Malone settled back in the chair. "I'm dying, Regent."

"Tough break." Rex frowned. "Is that why you called me here? To bid farewell to your bosom… enemy?"

"Not exactly. I need a favor."

"Something tells me it's not accepting your many confessions so you can pass on with a clear conscience."

Malone rasped another laugh. "I'd see you in hell first, kid. No, I want you to do something for me."

Rex squinted at him. "You sure you called the right Regent?"

"Shut up and listen. There's this… this young lady, see. She needs your help. She's… sorta been kidnapped."

"Sorta?"

"It's a long story. What matters is, the moment I kick the bucket, her life is gonna be in danger. I want your word you'll rescue her."

"Hold on," Rex broke in. "Who is this sorta-kidnapped girl? Why would she be in danger if you die?"

Malone sighed. "She's my daughter. She don't know about my business," he added hastily. "I always tried to protect her from this life. Maybe that was my mistake." He coughed. "You know the Martinellis?"

"Do you mean the Martinellis who run the little fruit stand over on Euclid Avenue, or the Martinellis who own the East Side and are your syndicate's most bitter rivals?"

"If you had half as much brains as you got mouth, kid, there'd be no crime left in this city," Malone scowled. "A while back, see, the Martinellis found out about Teresa. We'd had a… disagreement over the whiskey trade, and we'd just nabbed Giacomo Martinelli's grandkid, Giovanni. To make sure nothing happened to him, they took my girl. We couldn't come to terms to exchange, so we agreed to leave things as they was. Each family would keep the other's kid as a kind of insurance. We agreed that if there was a change in the head of either family, we'd swap the kid out for someone in the next head's family. Figured that was good insurance against anybody in our own organizations getting too ambitious, too."

"Every time I think you guys couldn't get more ruthless…" Rex shook his head. "So what's the problem? If you die, won't they just let your daughter go?"

Malone shook his head. "See, a few months back, Giovanni up and died. Doc said it was a burst appendix. Of course we didn't tell the Martinellis, on account of they'd blame us. But Fast Frank—my second—he don't have no kids, so when he takes over it's only fair that the Martinellis are gonna want Giovanni back, since they got no insurance on Frank. Only when they find out their kid's dead…"

"They might take it out on Teresa." Rex considered Malone

thoughtfully. "What I don't get is why you're talking to me. You've got a whole organization of tough guys who do whatever you tell them. Why not have your own men go after your daughter?"

"Three reasons," Malone rasped, holding up the appropriate number of fingers. "One... You and I have spent a lot of years duking it out, and even with all those tough guys weighing in on my side, the best we've come to is a draw. So I figure if I have to trust Teresa's safety to one man, you give the best odds. Two, Teresa's an innocent bystander in all this. And I know you well enough to know you wouldn't let an innocent girl get hurt, even if she is my kid. And three..." Malone grinned. "Because there's something in it for you."

Rex crossed his arms. "You know I don't take bribes, Malone—"

"Winnie the Witch Doctor."

Rex blinked once, then leaned forward over the table. "Dr. Winifred Gothel? Martinelli's chemical specialist?"

Malone's smile turned smug. He gestured to the scar marring Regent's left cheek. "I know you want her."

Rex's mouth twitched reflexively, and the still-healing wound across his cheek twinged. "You're telling me you can deliver her?"

Malone shook his head. "You'll get her when you free Teresa. Rather, that's *how* you'll get her. According to my sources, Teresa's being kept in the old Tower Hotel. That's where the Witch Doctor has her laboratory."

Rex let out a low whistle. "That's inside Giacomo Martinelli's private estate. Practically a secure compound."

"As I said, I have my sources. I can give you the layout. Teresa's witnessed a lot, living in the Witch Doctor's attic. With her testimony, you'll have enough to put Winnie away for good—maybe even send her to the chair." Malone rummaged in the bag behind his wheelchair and produced a leather document wallet. "All the information you need to rescue her is in here," he said, slapping the wallet on the table. "I asked for your word, Regent. Do I have it?"

Rex hesitated, but his department had been after Gothel for years.

If Malone's information were genuine, it could save a lot of lives. "You do," he said at last.

"Good." Malone pushed the folder across the table. "Pour the wine and we'll drink on it."

"I'm on duty," Rex pointed out.

"What, you think I'm gonna tell your boss?" Malone chuckled, but stopped when it threatened to trigger another fit of coughing. "You know how I do things, Regent. No toast, no deal."

The bottle had already been opened, presumably by Benson, so Rex splashed some of the expensive Cabernet into each glass. Malone stared into it meditatively. "There's something you need to know about Teresa before you meet her." He paused to cough, but the rattle in his breathing grew worse as he hacked. Soon he was wheezing, and he reached feebly for the bag behind him. "Pills," he gasped.

Rex hurried around the table and dug through the bag until he found a glass pill bottle. He shook a few tablets out onto the table, where Malone's trembling fingers grasped two of them and pushed them into his mouth. He managed to stop coughing long enough to wash them down with a generous mouthful of wine, but it was another minute before the coughing subsided.

Finally Malone fell back against the chair, panting. His face was flushed red, and the glass shook in his hand. "Teresa," he gasped. "She's—"

The tumbler slipped from his fingers then, splashing dark wine across the rug, and Rex watched in horror as life drained out of the man in the wheelchair. He seized Malone's wrist, but no pulse beat beneath the flushed skin.

Rex used a handkerchief to lift his own glass, still untasted, to his nose. The distinctive bitter-almond odor was not quite covered by the rich fragrance of the wine. *Cyanide.* Someone had wanted both men dead—someone who not only knew Regent would be coming here tonight, but knew how Malone traditionally closed his deals. A traitor in Malone's organization?

Rex went to the door, but hesitated. If the men outside were loyal to Malone, Rex doubted they'd wait for an explanation before avenging their boss's apparent murder by his long-time police rival. If they were working for whoever had poisoned the wine, he still wouldn't be allowed to leave the building alive. Rex quietly slid the bolt home, thankful for once the poker room was designed to repel police raids, and looked around. Though windowless and single-doored, these rooms *always* had an escape hatch somewhere.

He had examined half of the room's wainscoting for secret panels when Malone's thugs discovered the locked door and began battering against it. He didn't have long before they started shooting, and while the bolt was strong, he doubted the door was bulletproof. He turned back to the wall and saw it—a tiny knothole in the floorboard, no bigger than a mouse hole. Pulling back the rug, he found a long seam in the boards a few feet from the wall. He scanned the walls and ceiling until he spotted a long metal rod with one hooked end in a gap above the crown molding.

Rex pushed Malone and his wheelchair out of the way—"Sorry, Johnny"—and climbed onto the table. He caught the knothole with the hooked end of the pole and a four-foot-square section of boards lifted on a hinge, revealing a narrow packed-dirt tunnel.

Rex dropped into the tunnel just as the first shot splintered the door behind him. He took the hooked pole with him into the passage and sealed the panel over his head. It wouldn't stop his pursuers, but lacking the proper tool to open the wide trap door might slow them down.

It took half a box of matches to light his way through the tunnel to the exit, which turned out to be a slimy stormwater drain that emptied along the waterfront. Rex hastened back to his apartment, keeping to bright, regularly-patrolled streets in case Malone's men were inclined to pursue him, and used the pay phone in the lobby of his building to call his captain at home.

"I'll send the coroner's van to the Dark Horse, then call Judge Harper about a warrant on the Martinelli place," Captain Axford said. "He won't be happy about being awakened at this hour, but if anyone overheard Malone say that the girl is willing to testify, her life could be in immediate danger."

Rex agreed. "Get men there as soon as you can, so they're ready to go in as soon as you get the warrant. With any luck, the flock of black-and-whites on their doorstep will distract the Martinellis from the girl for a while. I'll head over myself as soon as I get into some dry clothes."

"Regent," the captain warned, "don't do anything stupid. You of all people know how dangerous Gothel and her inventions are."

Rex grinned into the receiver. "When was the last time I did anything stupid?"

"What day is it again?"

"Very funny. See you at the Martinelli place."

While he changed out of his mud-caked clothing, Rex perused the documents Malone had provided. In addition to a photograph of a fair-haired child of ten or eleven, an odd collection of papers outlined his mission: A sketch of Martinelli's compound was accompanied by a note warning of traps set on every door of the former Tower Hotel. An ink-stained cocktail napkin detailed guard rotations. The most curious item was a sheet of notepaper with the words "fire escape" scrawled across it. A strip of adhesive tape anchored a lock of wheat-colored hair to the paper.

Once dressed, Rex donned his shoulder holster and checked that both snap pouches were loaded with extra ammunition. He hoped it wouldn't come to a shootout. If Judge Harper came through with the warrant in time, they could remove the girl safely and legally from the Martinelli property. Even so, he knew Axford had been right: Once Malone's traitor reported back to Martinelli, Teresa Malone's life wouldn't be worth the paper her photograph was printed on.

Rex only hoped he wasn't too late already.

"Inspector?" called a uniformed officer, waving at Rex. "Captain's on the radio, asking for you."

Rex abandoned the trench he was wearing into the ground and hurried around the patrol car. When he'd arrived, Martinelli's goons and the police were already ensconced on their respective sides of the drive gate, trading meaningless threats through the bars. Until the warrant arrived, Rex could do nothing but pace the street and wait.

He hated waiting.

"How's that warrant coming, captain?" he asked, taking the handset from the officer.

"Not quickly," came the reply. "Judge Harper's dragging his feet. I don't think he wants to ruffle any Martinelli feathers this close to election season."

Rex stifled a growl. "Have you told the judge a child's life may be in danger? Looks pretty bad to voters when you get a kid killed this close to election season."

"I have. And he told me—strictly off the record—that a child of such criminal parentage was of no particular concern to the voters of this city."

Rex stared at the handset in disbelief. "Well, he just lost *this* voter's support," he snapped when he'd found his voice again. "And you can tell him that, *on* the record."

"I'll keep working on him," Axford sighed. "But it doesn't look good."

"What would it take to—" Rex broke off and swore under his breath as a sleek automobile pulled up to the line of police cars. The driver laid on the horn.

"What's wrong?" Axford demanded.

Rex left the handset in the seat and jogged to the new vehicle, where an officer was examining the driver's license. "Out of the car, Bernard," Rex ordered. "Keep your hands where I can see them."

The driver blinked with exaggerated innocence. "Bernard? I'm afraid you've mistaken me for someone else, officer. My name is Thackeray. Morris P. Thackeray." He pointed to the license in the policeman's hand.

"It seems to be in order," the officer told Rex doubtfully. "Gives this as his home address."

Rex leaned an arm on the roof of the car. "Tell me, Mr.—Thackeray, was it?—where were you, say, two hours ago?"

"Why, I was at the cinema with Mrs. Thackeray." The balding man turned to the passenger seat, where a woman waved cheerfully. "We saw the new Cagney film. Even have the ticket stubs to prove it."

"Sir?" The officer glanced from Rex to the driver. "Should I let them through?"

"You have insufficient cause to make an arrest, inspector," Thackeray added, grinning.

"An arrest, probably not. But it just so happens that you match the description of a murder suspect." Rex opened the car door. "Morris P. Thackeray, I'm detaining you for questioning. Watkins, take him in."

The constable escorted Thackeray to a patrol car, and Mrs. Thackeray slid over behind the wheel. "What an unfortunate misunderstanding," she sighed. "Well, I'm sure it'll all be cleared up in the morning. Good night, inspector."

"Hold on." Rex propped an elbow on the wing mirror. "Just where do you think you're going?"

"Home." Mrs. Thackeray pointed through the Martinelli estate's gate. "Unless I look like a murder suspect, too?" She smiled engagingly.

She had him over a barrel, and they both knew it. Rex gritted his teeth, smiled, and patted the roof of the car. "Have a lovely evening, Mrs. Thackeray."

Rex returned to the radio. "We just ran out of time," he told Axford. "Bernard—or whatever his name is—just pulled up, minus the mustache and glasses. I've detained him, but he had a woman with him, and I had no cause for holding her. She's going in now. Please tell me we have a warrant."

"We don't." Axford sounded battle-weary. "I'm beginning to think Harper is on Martinelli's payroll."

Rex scrubbed a hand over his face. "Well, that means there's only one thing to be done."

"What's that?"

"Something stupid."

Sneaking into the Martinelli estate proved easier than Rex had imagined. The compound was surrounded by a high stone fence, which—according to the cocktail napkin—was ordinarily patrolled by armed guards. But the police presence had drawn all the guards to the front gate, allowing Rex to simply climb the fence with the help of some overgrown shrubs, then drop to the ground inside.

Of course, getting out was going to be trickier than getting in, especially encumbered with a child, but he'd think of something. Provided he didn't get himself killed first.

Locating the former Tower Hotel didn't require the map in his pocket, either. The structure loomed heavy and black against the night sky, rising ten stories above the surrounding gardens. The nearly-full moon cast a long shadow behind the tower, and Rex stayed in the strip of darkness until he could hug the brick. Most of the windows were dark, but lights burned in a few ground-level rooms, as well as one at the top of the tower.

He crept carefully around the perimeter of the building until he spotted the fire escape, a rickety structure of ladders and platforms clinging precariously to the brick wall. The lowest rung of the lowest ladder was more than eight feet off the ground, and his fingers scarcely brushed it when he stretched up on his toes.

He gathered himself and leaped. His hands closed on the metal bar of the bottom rung, but the impact sent a shower of rust cascading over his face. He hissed in pain as flakes of metal struck his eyes, and had to drop to the ground and blink them clear. He brushed the grit gingerly from his face with a handkerchief before attempting the jump again—this time, with his eyes closed.

The climb was slow and harrowing; under Rex's body weight, bolts shifted, rungs broke loose, and at one point an entire section of ladder dislodged from the wall, threatening to drop him more than thirty feet to the ground. *If I make it up there alive,* he thought, clinging to the platform with shaking arms, *I'm going to have to find some other way down. There's no way I can make this descent carrying a child.*

At last he reached the highest platform and looked around for the window or door that connected to the fire escape, but all he found was a series of stripped bolts above him on the wall: Someone had cut away the final ladder and platform.

Rex looked down at eighty feet of rickety, broken steel beneath him and swore aloud.

"Who's there?"

Rex whipped around and flattened himself against the brick. The voice had been a woman's, and more curious than threatening.

"Sam?" the voice called again, softer this time. "Is that you?"

Rex eased away from the wall and looked up. He could just make out a human silhouette leaning out the window one floor above him. "Hello?" he whispered.

The silhouette reoriented toward the sound of his voice. "Hello," the woman called. "You're not Sam. Who are you?"

"I'm… not Sam," Rex confirmed. "Would you mind keeping your voice down?"

"Oh," she whispered back. "You don't want the guards to hear, right?"

"Right." Rex squinted at the figure. "I don't suppose you could help me get up to your window? I seem to be stuck down here."

She sighed. "Aunt Winnie had the fire escape removed years ago. Here, use this." The silhouette disappeared for a moment, and a thick rope swung over the sill and flopped against the bricks.

Rex had to stretch to reach it, but once his fingers sank into the dense braid, he was able to pull himself up relatively easily. He'd climbed several feet when he realized what he was hanging from. "Is this... *hair*?"

There was a laugh from above him. "You know, Sam said the same thing. Is it that surprising? Nobody's bothered to give me a haircut in ten years."

Rex finished climbing and tumbled awkwardly over the sill. His rescuer was occupied in unwinding her thick braid from the tension crank which had borne the weight of his body. Her hair was the color of wheat, like the lock taped to the notepaper in Malone's folder, and now that he could see her face there was no doubt that she was—had once been—the little girl in the photograph.

"Did you say *ten years*?" Rex sputtered.

She nodded, but didn't look at him. "Probably closer to eleven, now."

"You're Teresa Malone." Rex slumped against the wall. He'd expected to rescue a kidnapped child, and instead found a woman in her twenties. A *beautiful* woman. "Yes." Teresa tilted her head curiously, but her eyes were still turned in the direction of the window. "Isn't that why you're here? Sam is the only one who ever came up the fire escape. Didn't he tell you about it?"

"Possibly. Did Sam write these?" Rex opened the document folder to show her the notes that had guided him.

Teresa stretched out a hand and patted it over the pages until she encountered the lock of hair, which she rubbed between her fingers. "Is that mine? Sam asked if he could cut a bit. He said he was going to take it to Daddy."

Rex's mouth fell open as he watched her pale blue eyes rove sightlessly across the space between them. "You're..." He stopped himself just short of blurting it out.

"Blind?" Teresa cocked her head again. "Sam didn't tell you? Or did someone else send you?"

"Johnny Malone sent me. I'm guessing Sam was the 'source' he mentioned." Rex pushed himself to his feet and glanced around. They were at the end of a hallway, dimly lit by a single bare bulb mobbed with moths. Wallpaper peeled from crumbling plaster on either side. Numbered doors opened off the hall, their paint in various stages of shred. The Tower had once been a fine hotel, but Rex had seen condemned buildings with better decor than it currently exhibited. "We have to get out of here, Miss Malone. Your father—" He paused, unsure how to break the news of her father's death, then decided it could wait. "We have reason to believe you're in danger. My name is Rex Regent. I'm with the police. I'm going to get you to safety."

"Sam said someone would come for me, but I didn't expect the police." She frowned. "Are you *sure* my father sent you?"

"He certainly did."

"Only… I thought he was, you know, a major criminal. If you're with the police, why are you working for him?"

Rex hesitated. "He told me you didn't know about his… line of work."

Teresa scowled. "I'm blind, but not deaf. Everyone here talks." Her expression grew thoughtful. "If you're really a policeman, you must have a badge." Rex produced the metal emblem, and she traced her fingers over the raised lettering. "You're an inspector," she noted with surprise.

"I am. Will you come with me?"

She stood and tied a knot in her braid, shortening it to knee length. "I sure will. I've wanted to get out of here for years."

Rex started to lead the way toward the stairs, but Teresa pulled him back. "No, not that way. The stairs are trapped." She steered him toward a yawning set of elevator doors at the far end of the hall.

"This way."

"But—"

"Trust me, I know every inch of this building."

Rex was ready to pull her back from the dangerous opening, but Teresa felt along the wall, then crabbed around the corner without hesitation. Rex leaned around to see her clinging to the shaft's access ladder.

"This is the only safe way to go between floors," she whispered. "Aunt Winnie planted bombs in all the stairwells. And be as quiet as you can; the sound carries."

Rex swung around to the ladder, his arms screaming in protest after the exhausting ordeal of the fire escape, and followed Teresa down several floors, until their path was blocked by the elevator car. As easily as stepping off a streetcar, Teresa swung out through the open doors. When Rex followed, she pulled him into an alcove that had once been a private seating area, but which was now filled with trash and a mouse-chewed chair frame.

"We're directly above the laboratory," she whispered. "It's the old hotel kitchen. There's a door to the outside there, but it's only unlocked when Winnie is in the lab. Guards patrol that floor to make sure none of the prisoners escape."

"Prisoners?" Rex echoed.

"Members of rival gangs, I think. Winnie experiments on them." Teresa shivered. "I don't know what she does, exactly, but their screams carry right up the elevator shaft."

"Charming. Where are they?"

"They're locked up in the basement. Do we rescue them, too?"

Rex saw the innocent, hopeful look on her face and hated that he couldn't satisfy it. "Later. I have officers waiting just outside the gates. Once you're safe, your testimony will give us enough to come back in with a warrant."

She nodded. "We still need to get down the stairs to get out. But they're trapped."

Rex glanced around the corner. "Too bad the elevator doesn't work."

"It does; that's how they bring my meals up. But the controls are inside the car."

"Which is also down a level." Rex thought for a moment. "How many guards are there?"

"Not more than three, usually."

"Do they patrol this floor?"

"Only if there's a reason to. Why?"

"We need the elevator up here, don't we?" Rex leaned around the corner to push the call button.

Teresa brightened. "You want me to create a diversion while you take him out?"

Rex raised an eyebrow at her suggestion. "I don't want to put you in any danger."

"Oh, I won't be. They have orders not to touch me."

They settled into silence while they waited for the elevator car to arrive, but soon Teresa turned toward him. "Say, inspector…"

"You can call me Rex if you like."

"Rex, I don't know what you look like." She extended her hands tentatively toward his face. "May I?"

"Sure." Rex held still, scarcely remembering to breathe, as her fingertips traced his features.

"Seems like a nice face." Her fingers lightly brushed the scar. "What happened here? Cut yourself shaving?"

He smiled wryly. "A little souvenir from Aunt Winnie."

"Ah. You, too?" Her rueful smile matched his.

"What do you mean?"

Teresa waved a hand toward her own face. "My eyes were just fine when I came here, you know. Aunt Winnie—she insists I call her that—she put me in a room, and told me I wasn't to leave it, or I'd regret it. Well, tell any ten-year-old that, and honestly, what would you expect? I stumbled into one of her traps. The explosion burned my eyes and ruptured both eardrums. My hearing came back, but my sight never did."

"That's…" He couldn't find words to express his horror. "I'm so sorry."

"I've learned to live with it." She gave a humorless laugh. "Though Winnie said it was my own fault for disobeying."

Rex gave a low whistle. "Sounds like a real mother of the year."

"A regular Mama Mussolini."

"You know about Mussolini?"

"I'm not completely cut off from the outside world." Teresa laughed, a musical sound. "I have a radio upstairs. I listen to it every day. Not much else to do around here." Her voice took on an edge of almost childish excitement. "Have you heard that new program, *Gang Busters*?"

"I have." Rex didn't add that the absurd dramatizations were nothing at all like his department's real-life investigations. He didn't want to extinguish the enthusiasm lighting her face.

The elevator whirred to life just then, and before Rex could speak, Teresa slipped out of the alcove and was down the hall. Rex flattened himself against the wall.

Soon Rex heard the squeal of the elevator gate, and a red-haired man came into view. The man sighed when he saw Teresa and holstered his pistol. "Tresses, you know she don't like you comin' down here."

"Is that you, Red?" Teresa called innocently.

Red didn't have the chance to answer, as the butt of Rex's revolver came down hard at the base of his skull, and he sank to the floor unconscious. Rex cuffed him and crammed the man's necktie into his mouth.

"That'll keep him quiet for a few minutes." Rex glanced up as Teresa approached. "Tresses?"

"It's a nickname the boys gave me when I was a kid. First it was Tessa, then when my hair got longer…" She swished her braid.

"Tresses."

Rex took her arm. "Well, Tresses, care to join me for an elevator ride?"

"Well I ain't stayin' inside, copper," she rejoined in a perfect radio-gangster accent. Rex laughed, despite the danger of their situation.

The elevator controls were archaic, but Rex was able to operate them well enough to reach the lower floor. "Where to from here?" he asked when he'd guided Teresa out of the car.

Teresa paused and listened, tilting her head. Presently she pointed to the left. "That way. I can hear the machines humming."

They crept down a corridor and through what had once been a restaurant, now filled with shelves of chemicals, powders, and rolls of fuse. "Don't sneeze," he murmured, eying a canister marked *nitroglycerin.* "This whole place could explode."

"Oh, it's rigged to. Aunt Winnie built a time-delay bomb under the floor, in case of a raid. She calls it her 'police trap.'"

Rex thought of the thirty officers outside the gate, and was suddenly thankful the warrant hadn't come through.

They passed through another set of doors into what had once been the kitchen. Along one wall, a bank of equipment emitted a steady hum as machines rocked, sifted or mixed chemical components. Work tables housed a collection of beakers and distillation equipment. "This is unquestionably the laboratory," Rex said. "Which means the exit should be…"

"Straight ahead, through that door," announced a woman's voice, alarmingly loud. Rex spun to see Mrs. Thackeray standing in the doorway behind them. She had changed from her evening dress into a white lab coat and jodhpurs. A bandolier of metal canisters was slung across her torso, and a pair of goggles crowned her head.

"Aunt Winnie!" gasped Teresa. Her fingers dug into Rex's arm.

Rex stared at the erstwhile Mrs. Thackeray in surprise. "Dr. Gothel? My, you've changed."

Gothel smiled. "I change faces like some women change hairstyles, inspector. It's useful in my line. Otherwise, you might really have had cause to detain me outside."

"I've more than enough to detain you now." He flashed a charming smile. "Would you mind coming down to the station to answer some questions?"

"I would mind, very much." She slipped the tinted goggles down over her eyes. "It's a shame you didn't sample my little cocktail at the Dark Horse."

"Cyanide doesn't really agree with me."

"Fortunately, it didn't agree with Johnny Malone, either. The coroner was just arriving when we left." Gothel shrugged. "Eliminating you at the same time would have been a bonus, but that's easily done now."

Teresa had gone rigid at the word *coroner*. "Daddy is… dead?"

"And long past due. Now I can finally get rid of you, dearie." Gothel unclipped a canister from her bandolier. "I'm afraid the sudden police interest in this property has just forced me to destroy the last of my test subjects—eliminating the evidence, you see—but I have plenty of time to finish you both off in a suitably unpleasant manner. That search warrant won't come through before morning, and the incinerator is already hot.

"Smile for the camera, inspector." She tossed the grenade at his feet.

Rex's pistol had scarcely cleared the holster before the flash bomb ignited. The blast of heat across his face vanished beneath the pain that lanced through his eyes, searing his vision in unbearable flares of red and white. Rex cried out and threw up his hands to protect himself, but the damage was done. He crumpled to the floor.

Through the ringing in his ears he dimly became aware of voices, then felt strong hands lifting his arms, half-dragging him down a flight of stairs. He knew instinctively that he must resist, but the pain in his head was staggering, and he couldn't see *anything*. Just endless fire, burning where his view of the world should have been.

From the cotton wool surrounding him, Gothel was speaking. "Whitey, go find the girl."

"She won't get far without someone to guide her," the man holding Rex's left arm grumbled, but released his grip.

Just then, a heavy *click* sounded from overhead, followed by the descending whir of machinery winding down. "Hey!" cried the man on Rex's right. "Who turned out the lights?"

Gothel swore. "Someone's switched the power off at the main. Cangey, go fix it. Kill anyone you find."

"How?" protested the guard. "It's pitch black in here! I can't see a thing!"

"It's just in the next room!" snapped Gothel. "Feel your way there!"

The pressure on Rex's arms released, and a trail of cursing and falling objects wound through the room. Rex slumped against a wall, still dazed from the explosion. He had to use this opportunity to escape… but how?

A gentle touch grazed his arm, and he felt Teresa's small hand lock into his. "Follow me," she whispered in his ear.

"I can't see," Rex protested.

"Neither can they. And I don't need to."

She towed him along at a rapid pace. He stumbled behind as best he could, certain he would trip and fall with every step. Teresa guided him up the stairs and through a door, and his burned skin stung anew as a wave of cool night air struck his face. "Hurry," she said. "We need to get as far away from this building as possible."

"Why?" Behind him, Rex heard the mechanical click and whine of the power being restored. It was followed by outraged shouts, then feet pounding on stairs.

"Just go! Quickly!" Teresa bolted forward, pulling him across the grass.

He heard the explosion an instant before the wave of heat and pressure threw him to the ground. The pursuant sounds of shouting and sirens faded beneath the buzzing in his ears, until he was claimed by blessed silence.

Rex squinted against the light that burst painfully across his retinas as the layers of bandage were peeled back. His vision was badly blurred, but as he blinked, he thought he could make out a few figures standing nearby.

"Not bad," said the day nurse. He recognized her voice; she'd been there when he'd awakened in the hospital. "The burns on your face are nearly healed, and your corneas look much clearer."

"I think I'll just crawl back under my rock, thanks," Rex rasped. He closed his eyes, a faint sting across his eyelids a mild reminder of the searing pain he'd experienced a few days before.

The nurse patted his arm. "You can visit with your friends until the doctor comes to check on you."

One of the figures settled into a chair beside the bed. "You look like hell, Regent," declared the strident voice of Captain Axford.

"I feel like hell. How long was I out?"

"Not long, though you've been on morphine for a few days, for the pain. But the doc says you'll make a full recovery."

Rex hadn't realized how much he'd feared the worst until relief swept over him. Then he tensed again, remembering. "Teresa—is she all right?"

Axford chuckled. "Ask her yourself."

"I'm just fine, Rex." A familiar hand brushed over his, seeking, then grasped his fingers. "It's funny, isn't it? I'm so used to being the one who can't see, I never thought about someone else not being able to see me."

"I'm glad you're safe." Rex squeezed her hand, then turned back to Axford. "My memory's a blank. How'd you get us out of Martinelli's place?"

"That was Miss Malone's doing." The captain stood. "I'll let her fill you in; I have to get back to the station. Oh, and Regent—you're suspended."

"I'm *what?*"

"Conducting a search without a warrant. Judge Harper insisted. So I don't want to see you back at your desk for a full *two weeks.*" He clapped Rex on the shoulder. "Of course, to simplify things, I've scheduled your suspension during your mandatory medical leave. But if the judge should ask, you were properly chastised." Axford whistled cheerfully as he walked away.

Rex tried to focus his eyes on the other form beside his bed, but soon abandoned the effort. He could feel Teresa's touch, even if he couldn't see her properly. "What did he mean, about you getting us out?"

"Well, you had said there were police waiting nearby. I knew they couldn't enter without probable cause, so after I switched off the power, I triggered Aunt Win—" she caught herself. "Dr. Gothel's time-delay bomb. A warrant isn't required in emergency situations, so once the building was on fire, your men came right in and found us."

Rex shook his head in wonder. "How do you know so much about warrant law?"

Teresa laughed. "I told you, I listen to the radio. *G-Men, Police Headquarters, Gang Busters*... Besides, I've spent my entire life surrounded by criminals who exploit legal loopholes. Do you really think there's anything about the law I don't know? I might as well be a gangster myself." She tossed her long braid over her shoulder and turned in a very credible imitation of James Cagney: "The name's Tresses Malone, see?"

Alena Van Arendonk inhabits a virtual creative pentathalon, shuffling the hats of writer, actor, artist, seamstress, and costume designer. Her hair is long enough that she has received her fair share of Rapunzel jokes, but she insists that in no way influenced her choice of fairy tale.

DAUGHTERS OF EARTH AND AIR

Robert E. Vardeman

The ground shook so hard that Dorianya awoke from her slumber. Extending tiny hairlike tendrils, she sampled the sweet earth around her and cringed at the nitrate bitterness which had entered the soil. Pulling in her appendages and willing her body into a streamlined shape, she glided through the dirt around her, letting it flow and arouse her senses until she tingled with anticipation. She passed through the solid rock just under the surface but recoiled as she touched an outcropping of iron pyrite. It burned. Her usual chore would have been to remove it by encapsulating it with her body and slowly dissolving it, but today the quakes sending bitter nitrates into her domain had to be dealt with first.

Dorianya broke through the hard, crusty earth shell, coming to the surface and rising to her full seven-foot height, a column of amorphous mud and dripping stone. She turned slowly. Lacking ears did not keep her from "hearing" distant thunder. She remembered years earlier how this shrine had lit up with foxfire during a lightning storm. She had seen the outlines of the Daughters of the Air as they cast down their electrical discharges in some obscure celebration. But this lightning came not from the air but from a distance along the horizon. Flash after flash to the west was followed by the ground shaking. Moving carefully, her earthen appendages mimicking legs, Dorianya circled the standing stones worn by wind, rain and unthinkable eons. Her light touch left mud streaks. Even as part of her body vanished, she felt renewed through her feet so firmly in touch with the damp soil.

She considered the flashing lights and the quaking ground to be related, but she could not understand how until an artillery shell landed at the edge of the shrine. It blasted away a marble plinth and caused the column below to shatter into a thousand pieces. One bit of shrapnel cut through her body, an even more unpleasant sensation than passing through the iron pyrite beneath the shrine. Dorianya shrank, absorbing the rocky projectile. As she did, movement caught her attention. Two similarly dressed men dived for cover at the far side of the shrine and pointed their weapons westward, toward the flashing lights.

Dorianya sank into the earth, keeping only her head above the surface. One man jerked and fell forward. The other began firing his rifle until it broke, then he picked up his fallen comrade's and used it until it, too, broke. In the distance Dorianya saw a dozen men, dressed differently than the one taking cover behind the earth shrine. They advanced methodically on the single man. This must be a battle. Part of the war raging across the land.

"You won't take this land, this shrine! You killed my mate but you won't kill me. You won't!"

The man's words came to her muffled by the earth, but Dorianya understood. This man defended the shrine. Dorianya sank deeper and moved close to him, rising a few inches immediately behind him. He bled from a dozen wounds but still he refused to give way.

She slipped back into the welcoming earth but did not return to the depths.

"Earth Mother, what should I do?" Her question sank deep into the ground and was answered almost immediately.

"Do not permit yourself to feel for this human."

"He is so brave. He fights for our shrine, his friend's life, his honor."

"Do you find him handsome?"

The stern question caused Dorianya to quake. To answer was to betray her innermost emotions.

"You are young, Dorianya, hardly more than a hundred years old. You have much to learn about our world—and the surface."

"I can help him, and he will never know." She flowed up, becoming a mound in front of him.

She winced as lead pellets drove through her. Rising, adding more mud beneath her body, she enlarged the mound and caused the soldier to roll away. It worked, but too slowly, so she began digging a cavity in front of the soldier and adding that to the rising wave of dirt. Mimicking her sisters in the sea, she rose and sank, rose and sank, moving the soldier constantly away from the shrine as if caught on a wave. The muddy terrain turned rocky, causing her to slow. When she hit a patch too hard to lift, she sank down and let the man struggle about.

"Whippet," he grated out. "Whippets! Rescue him. Get him."

She had no idea what he meant, but his excitement was contagious. He sat up and waved. Dorianya followed his gaze and saw mechanical devices with big rifles mounted on top clanking along at a breakneck pace. They bypassed the shrine. A shower of dirt rose into the air and fell down on the soldier.

"There's one. Fetch him, mates."

Dorianya flowed around the rock to stand guard over the soldier as another vehicle with a cross painted on its side drove up. Two men with identical crosses on their helmets jumped down and hurried to the soldier's side. They didn't seem aggressive so she let them pass.

"You're in good hands, me lad. You with the First Canadian Division?"

"Under General Sir Arthur Currie."

"You with him at Passchendale?"

"Missed the gas attack. I arrived from Halifax a week after. Got an instant promotion, Lieutenant Campbell, Alvin Campbell. That's me." He let out a low moan of anguish as an artillery shell rocked the world twenty yards away.

"Bloody awful business, that phosgene. Ought to be outlawed. We have to avoid the Bosch's artillery right now, and that'll kill us dead. Ready? Up you go, Lieutenant Campbell."

The soldier groaned as the two men hoisted him. They started for the vehicle, Campbell bumping along between them. Dorianya shivered as the toes of his boots dragged over her subterranean body. The sensation combined horror and sensuality in a way she failed to understand. She sank lower into the earth, watching as the soldier's comrades wrestled him into the back of the truck.

"There's another man, back there in the woods, by the shrine." Campbell tried to turn and point.

"Sergeant Guthrie checked. He's a goner, Lieutenant."

"Guthrie?"

"He's our driver. He's a crackerjack man behind the wheel, as crazy as Barney Oldfield."

Alvin Campbell let out another squawk and almost tumbled from the rear of the ambulance as it shot away, kicking up a spray of mud and stone. Dorianya rose to her full height and reveled in the dirty storm from the ambulance's tires. The soil felt good splashing against her, and it reminded her of the soldier.

Alvin Campbell. And he was not simply a soldier but a lieutenant. Whatever that meant, it had to be something special.

She sank back into the ground, her thoughts chaotic. Somehow, they had become more ordered when she slipped past an ore deposit and came to where the Earth Mother spread out over an immense portion of land ruptured by the human fighting, doing her best to heal it.

"You are not here to aid me, are you, Daughter?" the Earth

Mother confronted Dorianya.

"I have seen nobility unlike others in the above world," Dorianya said. She expelled a long gout of mud and slid after it. "He needs me. I should go to him."

"There is more, isn't there, sister? You have fallen in love with him."

"That is not… true." Dorianya considered what that meant, compared what she had experienced with Alvin Campbell and how she anguished with him and rejoiced in his safe escape. "No, that is true. You see clearly, Earth Mother."

The ground shook as the elder daughter of the earth sighed.

"You are young and have not truly experienced life underground. Your sisters show nobility."

"Not like Alvin Campbell!"

"Such passion," the Earth Mother said sadly. "You would join him?"

"I have heard of such a thing. Is it true? Can I become human and… and human?"

"You mean experience love in all its human manifestations?" Again the ground shook with the sigh, this time less of sadness and more of resignation. "It is true, but you must know the penalties."

"Anything! I helped him once already but I can do so much more for him."

"You speak of helping him, but there is a selfishness to your wish, isn't there, Dorianya?"

"What if there is? Can life on the surface be so bad? They can see our sisters in the air and sea, as well as we who are under their feet. And Alvin Campbell…"

"If you turn away from your sisters of the earth, you can never return."

"I'll have him."

"And," the Earth Mother continued, "your love must be pure."

"It is!"

"And his for you must be shown."

"I am sure he will love me as I do him."

"Youth," Earth Mother said. "So be it. At the shrine you will be reborn as a woman. You are permitted one wish."

"To be the most beautiful human woman ever! How can he not love me then?"

"So it will be, but you can never speak of your love for him until he speaks of his for you first. Do so and you will die a terrible death."

Dorianya agreed. Alvin Campbell would see her love, even without words, and return it a hundredfold. How could he not if she were truly the most beautiful woman in the world?

"There is another condition. If he does not love you—"

"He will, he will! I know it!"

The Earth Mother enfolded her youngest daughter and compressed until Dorianya cried in pain at the transition. Even after she was taken to the surface, to the shrine, and left there naked but for a thick blanket of mud, the pain did not subside.

"But I am human," Dorianya said, running long, slender fingers over her new body, experiencing thrills of sensation and marveling at all she had missed as an earth elemental. The world flooded her with fierce colors, sounds of distant fighting hammered her ears and the pungent scents of life and death made her nostrils flare. She threw her arms wide and tried to take it all in at once.

Then she looked down and saw the dead soldier, the one her Alvin Campbell had tried to rescue. Kneeling, she rolled him over. The ambulance driver had not been wrong. This unknown soldier had died long since. Humans buried their dead. She had come across many of their cemeteries, more since their war had begun, as she cruised about underground.

Using her fingers to dig out a grave in the sacred shrine proved impossible. Where once she'd burrowed and excavated with ease, this body permitted none of that. Giving up, she lifted the curiously light body, slung it over her shoulder, and began walking back toward the human city where Alvin Campbell's comrades had assembled for this fight.

Through the night and into the next day she walked, getting to know her body and learning to ignore the constant pain it gave her. At sunset the next day, naked and covered in mud, she was hailed by a sentry for the First Canadian Division.

Lieutenant Alvin Campbell's unit!

"He *will* be here, won't he?" Dorianya flicked ash off her cigarette and looked anxiously toward the door. The ballroom was so crowded with revelers that her view often disappeared. She ran her free hand over her curvaceous body. The pale beige dress clung to her every contour, reminding her of the way the earth had once pressed into her elemental body, but this dress gave different sensations, so many different ones! It caressed and flowed, cooled and added to her enjoyment of being among the humans. They all watched her move across the ballroom floor—the men hardly holding their desires in check and the women uniformly hating her. Dorianya reveled in the reactions. Among the elementals, all had been equal physically and clothing such as this gown, the beguiling pearls dangling around her swanlike throat or the flashing diamond earrings in perfect shell-like ears were superfluous.

She half turned when she realized the hand on her posterior belonged to the man edging closer to her by the minute.

In the month since she had become human, she had learned so much. A step as graceful as any ballet dancer moved her away so that the man seeking her attention found his hand groping emptiness rather than her waist. She thrust out her cigarette in such a way that if he approached her again, she would burn a hole in his tuxedo. He got the message. She enjoyed the movement of exotic smoke through her lungs, the surge of energy it gave her, but in this social setting the cigarette served primarily to keep the unwanted at a distance.

"What does Lieutenant Campbell have that I don't? You haven't even met him—he only got out of the hospital this morning." The man's pleading turned into a whine that displeased her. If she hadn't been so intent on meeting this gala's guest of honor again, she would have been wroth. Even that thought amused her. Anger was not an earth elemental emotion.

Nor was love.

"He's quite dashing," she said, looking down her nose with a combination of disdain and amused disinterest. "And heroic."

A murmur passed through the room. She caught her breath when the man she had come to love made a grand entrance. She took in his full height, his strength, the sharp, clean lines of his face only marred here and there with small bandages that reminded her of his battlefield condition—small imperfections that enhanced his appeal.

Her would-be beau moved to block her view of Alvin Campbell. With a fluid move, she sidestepped to keep Lieutenant Campbell in sight as he crossed the ballroom to great deserved acclaim.

"I've heard that you are something of a heroine, yourself," persisted the man she could not brush off. "Something about carrying a body back to his command post."

She had created quite the sensation as she dropped Corporal Yarrow's corpse at the sentry's feet. Realizing the truth would never be believed she had feigned shell shock, something those along the Allied salient understood, and slowly added to her story as she learned what gained her the most approbation. Alvin Campbell had been taken to a better equipped hospital in Paris, and her new heart hammered with emotion when she wheedled her way onto a train going to the capital a few days later.

The train had been a revelation to her. The huge engine stood thirty feet tall, was streamlined gleaming steel and blasted along spewing diesel fumes and shuddering with barely suppressed power. She had wanted to explore it, but it had been crowded with soldiers from a half dozen different countries she had never heard of on their way back to the Allied headquarters.

Instead, she had listened and soon fit in with the men. Her physical beauty was a boon, as much as the constant pain she felt in every joint of her body. The doctors and corpsmen fussed over her because of the honest and obvious agony she experienced, but only the most dedicated remained once it became obvious her pain was nothing they could ease.

The train station was a huge cavern of steel girders, filled with a dozen trains bringing troops back from the front lines. The war was winding down and the time had come to wait for armistice and celebration. In no time the urban swirl caught her up but her notoriety kept her in the public eye. She adapted quickly and within a week might have been mistaken as a Parisienne by birth though more than once she had eyed the gardens and patches of bare earth, yearning for the life she had left behind beneath the paved streets bustling with powerful machines. Then the thought of the man she had rescued on the battlefield rose and convinced her this human life had been the right choice.

Even if her joints threatened to collapse at any moment.

"That's a jaunty tune," the man before her said above the party's din. He reached out, waiting.

Dorianya hesitated, flicked away her cigarette, put the holder in her beaded clutch purse, and then slipped into his arms, her body stiff. They spun about onto the floor in a quick foxtrot. The man was a decent dancer, and she fell into the rhythm, letting it possess her. Music was another thing that the subterranean world lacked. Oh, there were sounds of the earth moving, continents grinding together and sliding apart and the occasional roar as a volcano erupted, but nothing rhythmic like this. Her new body responded well and as she danced with increasing grace and fluidity, the pain wracking her disappeared. Without seeming to do so, she guided them to the center of the floor amid the other couples losing themselves in the music.

"See? I knew you'd—" The man grabbed for her as she seemed to stumble.

Dorianya's grace was put to the test with her deliberate move. One toe of her slipper touched the heel of the other. Arms windmilling, she twisted around. For a heart stopping moment, she thought her ploy had failed.

Alvin Campbell moved with all the speed she expected. His arms circled her waist and pulled her upright, letting her put her arms around his neck for support. For an instant their faces were inches apart. Dorianya resisted the urge to move closer and kiss him, but oh, how she loved every wrinkle and imperfection of his strong face!

They hung frozen in the moment, then she straightened, unsure if so boldly kissing him would violate the precept of declaring her love for him before he spoke of it to her.

"You are so strong, and I am so clumsy. Pardon me." She spoke softly. She should have averted her eyes, playing coy as she had seen so many other women do, but taking her eyes off him proved impossible. Not only was he handsome, but she worried he might vanish like a will-o'-the-wisp if she looked away for even an instant.

"I'm glad I had the strength to catch you."

"Oh? Why is that?" Dorianya moved to block her former dance partner from annoying her with questions about her condition. To forestall any more interruption, she stepped up and pressed against Alvin Campbell's body, the warmth erasing any return of aches from her condition as a human. A quick whirl and they melted into the crowd of dancers, leaving the lieutenant's partner with Dorianya's discarded one.

"I was released from the hospital today," he said. "I hardly recognized myself when I looked in the mirror."

She lifted a laced glove to touch the scar on his face. "It makes you look distinguished and distinctive. You're just not another pretty face." She saw a tiny smile creeping onto his lips at her words. Humor won his heart!

"You dance divinely," Alvin Campbell said, spinning Dorianya around as the music begged for a lively two-step. "I apologize about how clumsy I am."

Dorianya kept from wincing as her joints creaked. She worried they drowned out the music.

"It is easier with a partner so handsome," she said. Though the other couples tended to dance a sedate hands width apart Dorianya pressed closer. She couldn't help herself. She had forsaken a life underground for this moment.

"You're too kind."

He stopped suddenly and looked at her, as if for the first time.

"I know you!"

Her heart skipped a beat. He remembered who had saved him out in the battlefield.

"And I know you, too."

"You're the woman who brought back the corporal's body. I tried to save him but couldn't. Then…"

"Then?" she prompted.

"Then someone saved me. I don't know who, but you succeeded where I failed. They gave me a medal. Did you get one, also?" Alvin Campbell touched the gold medal dangling from the varicolored ribbon on his chest.

"The corporal wasn't the only one I saved. I—" Before Dorianya said any more, she worried that she would blurt out her love for him which would mean disaster. The Earth Mother had warned her and losing Alvin Campbell now, when he was so close, would devastate her.

"I have been so lucky," he went on, not hearing her. "I was rescued from the Bosch and found the love of my life."

Dorianya started to speak, but the words jumbled in her throat. He had spoken of his love for her first. It was now permitted that she speak of it to him. That made the transition from immortality in the underworld to upper world mortality worthwhile.

"There she is."

"What?" Dorianya blinked in confusion. "What do you mean? I'm right here."

"My nurse. The one who brought me back to health. Excuse me." Alvin Campbell bowed slightly. Then Dorianya found herself alone on the dance floor, surrounded by whirling, loving couples as Alvin Campbell nimbly crossed the room to a woman dressed, not in a ball gown or other finery, but a plain nurses' uniform. He circled her waist with his arm and drew her close for a kiss.

"No," Dorianya gasped. Tears welled and she dabbed at them.

Alvin Campbell had found his love and it was not her. It was a nurse who had bewitched him. When he had awakened, she must have been hovering over him, an angel of mercy, healing him and giving him what Dorianya could not. Not then.

But she could now. She could win him away from the nurse and get Alvin Campbell to proclaim his love, unleashing the torrential outpouring of emotion she felt for him.

From the way they pressed against each other, Dorianya had no time to waste. She went after Alvin Campbell, but the dancers caused her to bounce about and by the time she reached the far side of the ballroom, Alvin Campbell had climbed atop a chair and held up his hand to get everyone's attention. The band discordantly slowed and stopped, further focusing the attention on the soldier.

"I have an announcement!"

Cheers went up, cries from many of his comrades about Alvin Campbell's heroism. That her love was so well thought of by his men warmed Dorianya, but his next words chilled her to her new bones. Her new aching bones. The ones she had accepted because she loved him so.

"I have asked the lovely Bertha Benedict for her hand in marriage and she accepted! Nurse Benedict and I are to be married tomorrow evening!"

A cheer went up. Dorianya's legs buckled under her, and she

sagged into a pile on the floor. Again came the tears. This time she made no effort to stop them. Someone helped her to her feet, and then even he rushed away to congratulate Alvin and Bertha.

Dorianya had never felt so alone.

Dorianya knelt in the garden, her knees touching bare earth. After fleeing the soiree and Alvin Campbell's chilling news, she had wandered aimlessly, her face to the setting sun until she found this small contact with her old life. Soil. Damp and fragrant, though as an elemental she had never thought of it as anything more than a highway for her subterranean movements. How different she saw the world through human senses!

She bent forward, placed her palms on the dirt and closed her eyes. She felt distant tremors and knew the Earth Mother came for her. She bowed her head, and after a few minutes, felt filled with a presence. A Presence.

"I want to return to the earth," Dorianya said in a choked voice. "I was wrong to think I could win his love."

"You cannot return. That is not allowed."

Dorianya sensed more in the Earth Morher's words. Somehow, being human allowed her to better understand emotions, even as she endured constant pain in her new, mortal, body. Along with the heightened senses, the smells and vivid colors and wondrous music that filled the human world, she felt a deeper understanding.

"The mortals live short lives, but full ones crowded with sensory onslaughts we cannot share."

"And emotions," Dorianya said. "Never have I experienced such swings of joy and sadness."

"You have learned, Daughter."

"Let me return. Never again will I make such a mistake," she begged, though she already knew what the Earth Mother would say. Youthful foolishness had betrayed her.

"You cannot return. And there is more." Softly, an earth's whisper, "You will die."

"I never said to him that I loved him. There is a chance I can win his love. I need to—"

"If he marries another, you will die at that exact instant."

"Then I must stop him!"

"You can never return to the earth…"

"Wait, I need to know more," Dorianya protested, but fell silent as the Presence faded away. And for her, in that moment, she realized what had been was irretrievably past. Only her actions now would win Alvin Campbell's love and prevent her own sorrowful death.

All else had failed. Every time she had tried to speak with Alvin Campbell, he rebuffed her, he ignored her, he even had the soldiers with him remove her as they enjoyed his bachelor's party.

If Alvin Campbell married, she died.

She had to tell him of her love, what she had done for him, but if she did, she died.

Any way she turned, she died.

She wandered the brightly lit Paris streets, aimlessly. A soft rain left mist on her face and turned her hair into a sparkling net of diamonds which shone as she moved through the lights from nightclubs and stores. The roar of powerful engines sent mighty automobiles past her, some throwing up sheets of water and mud from puddles. She closed her eyes to the indignity and walked on, lost in her sorrow for what she had given up as an elemental.

"Self-pity," she whispered into the night. "I know it. What shall I do?" Dorianya considered rushing up to Alvin Campbell as he entered the church and proclaiming her love. How dramatic it would be to die in his arms, slain by her love. Even as she imagined the scene, she knew she could never do it. She loved him. Blighting his marriage with death at the altar proved nothing of her love for him, only her love for herself.

But she loved him with her heart and soul. He could love her, too, if only circumstances had been different. Saving him won his love—only Bertha Benedict had been the one he had seen as his eyes first opened after leaving the battlefield. If it had been her smiling face, her perfectly lovely face radiant with love for him, she would be the bride and not the nurse.

Above in the cloudy sky roared a new aeroplane, one outfitted with twin propellers and a tail-mounted jet that left its flaming scar against the night. It headed westward, taking soldiers home to Canada. She had heard Alvin Campbell's friends talking. Alvin Campbell and his new wife would be aboard such a conveyance after their honeymoon. But what did Dorianya care? She would be dead.

The mist hardened into battering cold raindrops. She walked with her head down, only stopping when a half dozen women in nurses' uniforms went past her, chattering. Dorianya almost screamed. They were gossiping about their companion, about her catch, about Alvin and Bertha's wedding. In a daze, she followed them to a three-story building decorated with steel gargoyles on the cornices. Staring at the hideous creatures hardened something within her. She took the steps to the front door slowly, then hurried to trail the nurses past a sleeping sentry just inside the lobby door.

She let the nurses lead her to the third floor, where she fell behind, letting them vanish into rooms lining a corridor.

She crept through the quiet dormitories where the nurses slept. Dorianya picked up a sharp-edged letter opener from a desk at the door and slowly walked down the rows of bunks. One or two nurses stirred, but none awakened. She came to the last cot where Bertha Benedict tossed and turned.

"Do you dream of your wedding tomorrow?" Dorianya asked softly.

The nurse rolled onto her back, as if responding. A gentle smile came to her lips. No doubt she was dreaming precious dreams of life with Alvin Campbell and all Dorianya had were nightmares. Dorianya would die even as Alvin Campbell and the nurse started their new life. She stepped to the side of the bunk and held the letter opener in a shaking hand.

She lifted the blade and held it poised over the sleeping woman's breast. It had to be this way. If the nurse married, Dorianya died. She deserved to die. All she had done was nurse Alvin Campbell back to health. She hadn't saved him out on the battlefield.

Dorianya lifted the weapon higher for a solid stroke. Her hand cramped. Her elbow snapped. Her joint pain fed her resolution.

At the top of the stroke, she stopped and stared at Bertha. A chance reflection of light off the silvered blade bathed her face, her sleeping, content, happy face. Dorianya grasped the knife in both hands. She closed her eyes, tensed and… and turned away.

Tears filled her eyes, those damnable human tears driven by damned human emotion. She hurried from the dormitory into the cold night. Wind whipped off the Seine and created new tears, but these were of a different sort. Dorianya endured these as she made her way to Sainte-Genevieve hill. Several times she had passed by the hill crested with the Pantheon. Making her way past the church, she went to the base of the dome and stared upward. The massive colonnaded dome beckoned to her. She took the stairs steadily, her joints protesting. She ignored the agony. What clutched at her heart was worse.

She reached the top and stepped out onto the balcony overlooking the city. All of Paris beckoned to her.

A storm rose in the north, lightning too far away to be seen clearly lit the clouds from behind. The recently built Eiffel Tower filtered the lightning, giving it a surreal appearance. Away from it she saw Notre Dame. Was this where Alvin Campbell would marry? He was a war hero and deserving of such ceremony but she didn't know. She had never heard the location of the wedding.

She took a deep breath and appreciated her human senses one last time. She could wait for her death the instant Alvin Campbell said "I do" or she would pass on now, at her own hand, on her own time, choosing how to go.

This place seemed appropriate. So much of what made humanity great was visible. She even imagined she saw the quarters where Alvin Campbell stayed this final night as a bachelor. She lifted the letter opener she still carried and stared at it, then cast it aside. It spun over and over before clattering on the pavement below. A knife was not a fitting way to die, but she knew one that was. She stepped forward into emptiness and began the stories-long fall. The wind clutched at her, buoyed her—and held her gently.

Dorianya fought for a moment and then stopped struggling, trying instead to understand why she no longer plummeted to her death.

"Do you truly wish to exist no more, Daughter?" A softness touched her, entered her and made her new form quiver in a sensual resonance. Wind interacted with wind, and she responded instinctively.

"Earth Mother?" Her heart rebelled. "I thought—"

"I am a daughter of the air. You did not think there were only elementals of the earth and water and fire?"

"Why are you keeping me from death as a human?"

"We have watched you and wondered why you chose to leave the earth." A soft airy sigh. "You chose to preserve human life rather than take it, though it meant your own nonexistence."

"I was foolish."

"Young and foolish and you made bad decisions, but your reluctance to take life and your choice to save lives, drew our attention. Do you wish to perish?"

"No." Dorianya felt herself choked with human emotion. "But I have no other choice."

"You can neither return to the earth nor remain a human, but you can join us in the air. We would welcome your kindness and empathy. Come, soar with us, free on the winds, rising to the sun and sinking to the valleys to whip along the earth and live in the sky!"

Her decision came quickly. Her human body fell as her airy spirit soared upward, joining the other elemental, twisting through the storm she had seen and rising even higher to touch the moon and wait for the warming sun.

Writing is a lonely profession, as **Robert E. Vardeman** knows well after more than 40 years at it. The sense of otherness and pain and rejection in "The Little Mermaid" speaks volumes to him. But his crazy optimism offsets even such sorrow. There should be hope in the world, and his current short short story takes that tale a little farther to soar into a realm above loss and the guns of The Great War.

EASY AS EATING PIE

Amanda C. Davis

Eddie stood in front of the basement shelves in his undershirt, fists on his hips and suspenders slipping down over his shoulders. There were rings in the dust marking where jars of food had once stood. He swiped the empty shelf in disgust.

"My own fault," he muttered. "'Come live with me,' I says. 'You married my dead sister, you're like family.' What do I get? Big dumb deadweight name of Chuck that snores and eats my food when I ain't looking. Some family. This ain't exactly a land a' plenty, you know. Folks is starving to death in Oklahoma." He raised his voice in the direction of the basement stairs. "Hear that, Chuck? Starving!"

He grabbed a quart jar of green beans and plodded upstairs. In point of fact, the Depression hadn't hit Eddie very hard at all—not the way it would have if he'd ever had money. His garden still produced, his apple trees thrived, and he knew how to cook a groundhog until the tough flesh grew soft and sweet. It helped that his old mother had died with a cellar full of canned food. And that he had no particular ambitions. Eddie was on friendlier terms with idleness than he was with Chuck.

He was at the top of the stairs when Chuck burst through the kitchen door with a child's collar clutched in each hand and, beneath each collar, a dirty-faced fair-haired child.

Eddie leapt back so far he nearly fell into the basement again. "Geez a'mighty, Chuck! Where'd you get those?"

"Out back," said Chuck. "I told you it wasn't me eating all them apples."

The children did not look like they'd had their fill of apples in a long time. The boy, the smaller, stood limp in Chuck's grip, with his eyes down. The girl, however, wouldn't stop struggling.

"Let us go!" she said, her eyes bright with hate. She couldn't have been older than nine. "We don't want your rotten apples."

Eddie settled himself onto the corner of the kitchen table. "We let you go, two days later you'll be back robbin' us of the hard-earned fruits of our labor."

Chuck grew uncertain. "What else we supposed to do with 'em?"

"I dunno," said Eddie thoughtfully. "I mean, look at 'em. Ain't a hundred pounds between 'em. If they was horses you couldn't sell 'em for glue."

The boy went rigid with fear. The girl raised her chin. "You can't do that!"

"Like I said. Nobody'd take you."

"We can do tricks," whispered the boy.

The girl hissed sharply, but Eddie perked up. "Yeah?" he said. "What kinda tricks?"

"Magic tricks."

Eddie looked from one small, dirty face to the other. "Okay," he said. "I like magic. Show me what you've got, and maybe you can stay for dinner."

Chuck let go of their collars, and the children flew at each other like magnets. Clutching her brother, the girl said, "We need a cigarette."

Eddie's eyebrows flew sky-high. "At your age?"

"For the trick."

"Hehn." Eddie pulled his papers and tobacco from his back pocket and made a big show of rolling a thin cigarette. "Good enough?" he asked, presenting it to the girl. "Or you like 'em big as a cigar?"

She made no move to take it. "Hold it flat in your hand."

Eddie did so, winking at Chuck.

As one, the children turned toward Eddie and linked hands. Their hollow eyes fixed on the cigarette in his palm. The cigarette quivered like a washline sock in a light breeze. Then it rose from Eddie's palm, spun in the air for half a minute or more, and settled back into Eddie's palm.

Eddie's jaw dropped. He picked up the cigarette by one end and squinted at it. "That is some trick."

"Do it again," said Chuck.

They did. This time the cigarette stood on end and rotated like a dancing girl.

"Hot dog!" said Eddie. He rubbed his chin. "Chuck. C'mere a minute."

The two men withdrew across the kitchen.

"Listen," said Eddie, his voice low and quick. "I know this fella, owns a farm and a pair of mutts. Well, they whelp 'em, and one of the pups comes out with no front legs. Just stubs. But the pup doesn't die! It learns to hop around on its hind legs like a duck. The fella takes it all around the country. Everybody lines up to pay their two bits to see the armless dog. Fella made a real mint before the dog died. He paid off his farm. Got himself a tractor."

Chuck glanced uncertainly over his shoulder at the children. "Just what do you mean, Eddie?"

"I mean," said Eddie, "that these kids is our armless dog."

Chuck's dull eyes widened just a little. "Take 'em on the road?"

"All over America."

Chuck let out a single loud chuckle. "Oh, Eddie, that sure is something. Let's leave right away!"

Eddie slapped him on the arm. "Are you nuts? Skinny little scrappers looking half like to die? We got to feed these kids up before we take 'em anywhere. Train 'em too. I mean lifting a cigarette is something, but what if we could get 'em to do a book? Or a barrel? Or a person?"

"Hey," said Chuck. "That'd really be something."

"You got it now," said Eddie, patting him on the shoulder. He turned back to the children huddling hand-in-hand at the front door. "You kids got names?"

Again, the girl spoke for them. "I'm Gretchen. My brother is Hank."

Eddie made a face. "We'll come up with something better. Welcome to show business, kids. Now sit down. Uncle Eddie's gonna feed you till you split a seam."

Open, spontaneous joy broke over the boy's face. His sister's stayed fixed and wary.

He served them green beans and cold oatmeal. The children ate more than Eddie expected and then fell asleep in the threadbare armchair beside the radio, holding each other like a couple of dolls.

"I ain't so sure about this, Eddie," said Chuck. "Kids is a lot of work."

"Ah, it's easy as eatin' pie," said Eddie. "Just keep 'em fed is all. By that age they raise themselves. Say, take a bushel of apples into town and see if anyone'll swap 'em for an old dress. We can't show the girl around in them rags."

"How about the boy?"

"We'll worry about him later," said Eddie. "I got a feeling the girl is the horse to put money on."

The following morning it occurred to Eddie that kids were supposed to earn their keep. He sent the boy to the garden with Chuck and installed the girl at the kitchen sink. He and Chuck weren't much for washing dishes and he figured it might be nice to have them done while they had the chance. So she wouldn't cause any trouble, he sat at the table to pick his nails with a knife and watch her work.

"So," he said, once the wet dishes began to clink. "Where'd you two learn a trick like that, huh?"

The girl kept her eyes on her work and her hands in the sink.

Eddie shrugged. "All right, never mind. Just making conversation is all."

He grabbed an old newspaper from under the table and opened it to the funnies. They'd been funnier two months ago when they were fresh.

The day was warm and dry. Through the open window came the sounds of birdsong, of rustling trees, of Chuck explaining garden work in slow, patient words. Although the kitchen window was above the sink, the girl kept her face grimly lowered.

"They left us in the woods," she said.

Eddie tore himself away from Mutt and Jeff. "Hmm?"

"Mama said there wasn't enough food, and—"

"Sure, sure," said Eddie. "Same as everybody." His eyes drifted back down. "What do you think of the name 'Evelyn'? All right, it's common, but anything's better than 'Gretchen'."

The girl went silent again.

"Maybe 'Ginger'," said Eddie, studying the smeared frames of Barney Google. "I knew a Ginger. Classy from head to toe, a real firecracker—"

He broke off. While the girl scrubbed one of his crusted oatmeal pans, another one hovered beside her, drip-drying inches above the sink. At Eddie's silence, she looked up sharply. The floating pan lowered itself guiltily to the counter.

"Say!" said Eddie, putting the newspaper aside. "You did that all by yourself."

The girl met his stare with a glare. "So?"

"Can he do it too? Without you helping him?"

Her face went blank and hard as slate.

Eddie stood up. "Chuck!" he shouted. "Bring that kid in here!"

In moments the pair of them, earthy at the hands and knees, scuttled inside. Eddie beckoned to the boy. "You. See if you can lift that pan there."

The boy started toward the sink, but Eddie shot out a hand and stopped him. "Like your magic trick. Just yourself. Hold it, Ginger," he warned, as the girl tried to join them. "You stay out of this."

The boy looked helplessly from the cast iron pan to Eddie and then back again. His brow furrowed in concentration.

The pan didn't twitch.

Eddie patted the boy on the shoulder. "That's okay, kid. Go help your sister. Hey Chuck, let's take a walk out to the garden."

"But I was just—"

"You kids get them dishes clean now!" he added, in a cheery singsong. He and Chuck left them in the kitchen and headed around back.

Eddie burst out with it like an oil strike. "You shoulda seen it, Chuck. She lifted that thing like it was a feather. I bet she couldn't a' done it with her own skinny arms. But did you see the boy?"

"Eddie, he didn't do nothing."

"That's what I'm talking about! Kid eats like a horse but he can't even levitate a cigarette on his own."

"Neither can you," said Chuck.

"That ain't the point!" said Eddie. "I'm sayin' why feed two mouths when we can get the same act with just one?"

"You got a plan, don't you."

"Better believe I do. It's easy as eatin' pie. See, the girl won't leave without her brother, so we make like he ran away from her. We get the boy into the basement, knock him on the head, and lock him in there. Then we all get gone! By the time we get back, the boy's nobody's problem, and even if the girl raises a stink, we got her by the purse strings."

Chuck's eyebrows came together. "You mean kill him?"

"Nah, nah!" said Eddie, waving his hand. "Just smack him with a shovel, put his lights out a while. He'll be fine! Basement's full a' food! Anyway, a kid that can't take a shovel to the head wouldn't grow into no kind of man."

Chuck, who had taken many a shovel to the head, said, "Suppose you're right."

"Course I'm right. Now don't let on. We got to keep feeding 'em up 'til they're presentable. Don't skimp on the boy neither lest they figure we're up to something. Better to feed an extra mouth for a week, and not have to feed him at all after that."

Chuck said, "I thought you said he'd be okay and eat the food in the basement."

"Sure he will," said Eddie. "Don't you worry about it. From now on, Chuck, you better leave the thinking to me."

A week isn't long enough to fatten anybody, but by the end of it Eddie's patience ran out. He sent Chuck into the basement with the shovel. He handed the girl the dress Chuck had bartered for, and while she was in the back room putting it on, he called the boy to the top of the basement steps.

"Hey, kid. Run down and get me an onion."

The boy shook his head and stayed where he was.

"Come on!" said Eddie. "Whatsa matter with you?"

The boy stared at the floor. "There's witches down there."

"Witches!" barked Eddie. "Ain't no witches. Just Chuck."

"Hello," called Chuck jovially from below.

"And witches!" the boy insisted.

Eddie huffed out his impatience. He'd planned to be on the road by sunrise, but he and sunrise had a rocky relationship, and now it was almost noon—almost too late to do anything at all. "Okay. How about I go down there and show you."

The boy sucked his fingers uncertainly.

"Sure, I'll just go down—" Eddie trotted down the first two steps and stood there with his arms out like a swimmer vouching for the water temperature. "See? No witches here."

"They're at the bottom," whispered the boy.

"Oh, for crying—" Eddie caught sight of the little girl sidling up behind her brother, hard mistrust on her face. He raised his palms. "Okay, okay." He skipped down the last few steps until his shoes landed on the dirt floor. "Okay? Now be a good boy and come on down."

The door slammed shut.

"Hey!" Eddie barked. He scrambled up the stairs and threw himself against the basement door. It held fast. "Chuck! Get up here! Little so-and-so's locked us in!"

Chuck worked his way up the stairs and laid his shoulder against the door. "Feels like they got a piana blockin' the way," he grunted.

"We don't have a piana!" screamed Eddie. "They're gonna get away!"

Chuck stood back from the door. "You hear that?"

Eddie, with his shoulder to the door, stopped shoving and started paying attention. The clatter from outside turned into a kind of straining creak. The door, under no stress at all from Eddie's end, trembled against his arm. His legs began to wobble. He tried to recall what all he'd drunk that morning, until he realized that it was the wood beneath his feet doing the wobbling, and that it extended down the stairs and—now that he looked—to the narrow walls at the cellar door and the ceiling at the level of their ankles.

"Chuck," he said. "Get under the stairs."

Chuck raised his head. "Huh?"

Eddie, feeling his eyes grow wide in his head, gave Chuck a huge shove. "Get under the stairs!"

Chuck leapt the whole staircase at once and landed in a cloud of dust. Eddie scuttled afterward. And after them both, a rain of splinters, then sticks, then whole beams. They threw themselves into the shallow gap under the stairs as the house rumbled and every board in the ramshackle walls came apart from the others and filled the cellar from bottom to top.

And then it was dark.

And then it was quiet.

Eddie peeked out from under his elbows. Darkness. The air smelled of dust and mildew, old potatoes and onions gone to rot. He cocked his ear. Nothing sounded above but the soft, dry creak of wooden beams shifting very gently against one another. "Chuck?"

Chuck's voice was strong and not too far away. "Yeah, Eddie?"

"You still got that shovel?"

"Yeah."

They sat in contemplative silence for a moment, trying to work out in their minds just how much house lay scattered like kindling above them, and exactly how they were going to get through it.

"I thought of something, Eddie."

"Yeah?"

"Maybe we oughta not mess around with magic shows anymore."

"That's some real good thinking, Chuck. Real quick thinking. Maybe you ain't so dumb after all." Eddie spat out wood dust. "Say, you can dig us out of here, right?"

"Sure," said Chuck, although he didn't sound sure. "Easy as—"

"Don't you say it," Eddie warned. "Nothing's ever that easy, and if you hear me say it again, you just hit me in the mouth."

"Okay, Eddie."

"You know what's the matter with kids these days? They don't want to work. And they're ungrateful."

"I thought of something else, Eddie."

Eddie let out his breath from between his teeth in a long, resigned hiss. "What's that, Chuck?"

"Maybe from now on you better leave the thinking to me."

Amanda C. Davis likes fancy baking almost as much as she likes fairy-tale retellings, so Hansel and Gretel was a perfect choice. Her other dark, funny takes on fairy tales have appeared in *InterGalactic Medicine Show, Daily Science Fiction, Mirror Dance,* and others; in 2013 they were collected with pieces by her sister Megan Engelhardt in *Wolves and Witches: A Fairy Tale Collection.* You can read more on her website at http://www.amandacdavis.com or follow her tweets at @davisac1.

ACCIDENTS ARE NOT POSSIBLE

Sarah Van Goethem

Hot ashes rained down on our heads, father's, Emilie's, Earl's, and mine. Luna Park was on fire. People scrambled away from the blaze, workers led circus dogs and ponies to safety, and Emilie, extravagant Emilie, with her rose-leaf rouged cheeks and tight chignon, latched onto father's arm and had him swept into the deserting crowd before he remembered to look back, to look for us. When he did, it was too late.

Emilie kept him moving, leaving us behind.

My brother's palm was slick with sweat against mine. His eyes, usually a pale watery blue, now flashed orange. All day the park had deceived me into feeling more childlike, but now, the dejection in his eyes reminded me we had years behind us, sixteen of them. It often felt like more.

Smoke crept into my nostrils and down my throat. I knew they'd all think it had started in a bathroom, or a tool room, a short circuit, a malfunction. They'd probably blame electricity, the thing we all craved, the thing that was absent in the dim-outs and left the ocean, with the sparkling new white beach, dark at night. They'd say it caused the raging blaze that was currently wiping out concession stands and using the wooden rides as dried tinder.

They'd never know. That it wasn't an accident.

Earl squeezed my hand, hard enough to make me flinch. *He* knew. "Jeepers, Ellie."

He dragged me behind him. Father and Emilie had been swallowed whole, just the two of them in the horde. Earl tracked his way back, the way we'd come in earlier, for a family day, *a day to remember*, Father had said.

Outside, I dug in my heels and watched as cars exploded. A brisk breeze pulled strands of my hair from my scarf and fed the raging fire. The fire wasn't supposed to be this big; I hadn't counted on the wind.

Soldiers and sailors and unchaperoned girls younger than me, with warm cheeks and fire-lit eyes, stood with us and watched the black smoke cloak the park, until the old tower buckled and then collapsed.

One of the girls, probably no more than thirteen, rubbed herself against a man twice her age. She wore a cheery dress and bobbysox. She was intoxicated with the power of the fire, drunk on a world of war that touched us, yet didn't. The war was far away but the fire was here, something we were part of. She cupped the man's face and yanked him toward her, pressing her bright red lips against his.

Someone, somewhere, said, "The whole country is going to hell."

Earl led me back to our three-storey walk-up, and we climbed to the roof. Father and Emilie were waiting, drinking black tea in mismatched china cups, no sugar. Emilie was stingy with the food ration stamps and even more sparing of what Earl and I were allotted. She would regularly grumble, loud enough for Earl and me to hear, *too many mouths to feed.*

I lowered myself into a rotting French folding chair, one of the ones Emilie had brought with her when she'd married Father. Earl sat, too, crossing one long leg over the other. We'd been the same height all our lives and then two years ago, after our fourteenth birthday, he'd shot up, rising above me by a good five inches.

"Tea?" Emilie asked, pouring from her hand-painted enamel (also French) teapot.

I took it, surprised. It was unlike her to serve me anything. Next, she sliced us both a piece of Lazy Daisy cake, which had been hidden under a flour sack towel, and a cold spike of fear pierced my throat. I tried to swallow it down; I desperately wanted to eat the cake. I could smell the butter and vanilla and coconut and my mouth watered.

Father returned his own plate to the table with shaky hands, his cake half-finished. He wouldn't meet my eyes. Beside me, Earl was gobbling down his slice as if he hadn't eaten in years. He felt it too; the weight of anticipation.

I took my plate to the edge of the building and looked out over the ledge. The fire licked at the night sky, a brilliant ginger to match the sunset. No one except Earl could possibly know what I'd done.

And yet.

I wasn't surprised when I saw them below, headed straight for our building.

The Nazi Collectors.

They had a special affinity for twins. At first it had just been twins, but now the rumours said those who had mental abilities, who were clairvoyant or telekinetic or something unusual, were being sought out, as well. Both together was an intense blessing and a horrific curse.

Earl and I had discussed it, how we thought they would come for us, eventually.

But Father had known it would be today.

The amusement park. The cake. Farewell gifts.

I shoveled the cake into my mouth as fast as I could, but it stuck in my throat, hard to swallow, like Father's betrayal.

There were two people in charge aboard the airship—Herr Hoffmann and Frau Braun. They met us on the metal gangway the next day. They were dressed nicer than anyone I'd seen in a long time; him in a thinly-cut tweed suit with a tan felt fedora and her in a plaid A-line skirt and a white button-down blouse with a matching neckerchief. I could tell Earl was sorely disappointed; I knew he would've preferred to see them in uniform trousers and tunics, slate grey mixed with olive green, with patches and insignia to condemn themselves. But the only swastika was on the tail fin outside, at the end of the vast silver hull, and we couldn't see it from inside the belly of the ship. Herr Hoffman and Frau Braun, in every day clothes, were only people.

People who sauntered the corridors and stood in the feather-light doorway of our private cabin, scrutinizing us after they'd delivered us. Our bags had already been inspected prior to boarding; they'd taken Earl's lighter and asked if we had anything that could produce a spark or electric charge. They'd never had an accident with the hydrogen, and had been using the safer helium ever since they'd discovered the reserve in Tanzania, but still.

"Just a precaution," the porter had said, and I'd known then, for certain, no one knew I was responsible for Luna Park. If they did, they would've never let me board.

I'd giggled a bit at the absurdity. *You had better take my fingers,* I'd wanted to say, *and my mind.* But I remained silent under Earl's heavy gaze.

Now, it wasn't funny anymore.

As Frau Braun analyzed me, I half-wondered if she could read my mind, too. I was suddenly ashamed of my worn workwear: cotton overalls and a thin blouse.

"You will not wear pants," Frau Braun said, in English so sweet and perfect it made my teeth ache. Her eyes were focused only on me, as if Earl wasn't there.

She came forward and untied the old scarf that held my hair back, letting it fall around my shoulders. Then, she cupped my chin in her hand and inspected my skin and eyes. I knew she would find everything satisfactory; I'd heard about the master Aryan race plan, about the pale skin, blonde hair and blue eyes. I was all of it and more. It was the one thing I had that Emilie couldn't take from me—my fortuitous beauty. Nodding with approval, she finally turned to Earl.

She had to look up, and Earl straightened to make it even harder for her. "You're not as fair as your sister," she remarked, with a flick of her gloved hand. "But useful, nonetheless."

Useful for what? I wondered, and Earl's elbow knocked into my side.

As if I was going to say it out loud.

Frau Braun's eyes narrowed, but not cruelly, not like Emilie. "You may dress for dinner and meet us in the dining room. You will find new clothing in your closet."

She left us alone, then, and I surveyed the small berth: two bunks, a fold-down desk, a wash basin, fabric-covered light-blue walls, and a closet with the clothing we'd been promised. I gasped, fingering the vibrant dresses with the contrasting fabric belts. Three of them, enough for each day we would be on the Hindenburg LZ-132. And floral silk scarves and stockings. Three pairs of trousers and shirts and one sport coat hung on the other side, for Earl.

It felt like betrayal, slipping a new dress on while Earl turned his back. But it was also sweet, something I hadn't tasted in a long time. It felt like when Mother had made me new dresses and put satin bows in my hair, before she'd died and the war had come. It felt a little like love.

The tears were unexpected. I sat on the edge of the bed and tried to make them stop.

Earl's arm wound around my shoulders. "We'll find a way out of this," he said.

"Out of a flying balloon? I don't think so." I wiped my palm over my wet cheeks. "Why would he do it?"

Earl knew what I meant. *Father.* "He does whatever she says."

"She always wanted us gone." A jolt of heat ripped through me, turning my sadness to anger. I clenched my hands in my lap and Earl quickly wrapped his own around mine, subduing me.

"They would have found us, regardless," he said. His fingertips were cool. "Why did *you* do it—the fire?"

The truth hissed past my teeth. "I wanted to see if Father would save me."

In the lounge, I was captivated by the map of the world that took up an entire wall. I knew each Hindenburg had one; it'd been a tradition. Earl steered me to the long bank of windows and opened one. I leaned out and breathed the fresh ocean air, taking in a trans-Atlantic liner in the sparkly water below that would take far longer to reach their destination than we would. An airplane would be faster than this, but the Germans preferred the luxury of their airships and liked to flaunt them whenever possible.

"*Frau* Engel," said a voice behind me, and I whipped around. Frau Braun smiled. "The blue dress matches your eyes, yes?"

"Yes." I twisted my hands behind my back, and then remembered. "Thank you."

"Yes, thank you," Earl chimed in.

"You're welcome. Now, have you seen my pet bird?"

I shook my head.

Herr Hoffman appeared and addressed my brother. "Would you like to join me to meet Captain Werner Franz?"

Earl's eyes bulged. "*The* Werner Franz?" Everyone knew Werner Franz was the cabin boy from the original Hindenburg, the LZ-129, now turned First Captain. *Commander of the Graceful Giants,* he was called. A legend.

"I'll assume that's a yes." Herr Hoffman was waiting, but Earl hesitated.

"Go on," I encouraged him, forcing a smile. "I'll be fine."

Herr Hoffman led Earl away, and I was left with Frau Braun.

"Let's take a walk on the promenade," she said, slipping her arm easily through mine, as if we were old friends. We strolled half the length, nearly twenty-five feet, before she said anything else. Then, "you may call me Eva."

I inhaled sharply. Another E-name. I'd always thought Earl and I were special, because we were twins, because we were two of a kind, Earl and Eleanor. Emilie had ruined the effect of the E's for me, with her French airs and hostilities. And now this.

Eva.

I didn't know what to make of it.

"May I call you Eleanor?" she asked.

I nodded. Who was I to refuse?

"I want you to enjoy your time onboard," she said.

Like my father wanted me to enjoy my last day at home? I wondered, with a warm tingle in my fingertips.

Eva's arm tightened, and I looked straight ahead, forcing myself to think of something else. Abruptly, I pulled away from Eva and leaned over the built-in seats, staring through the downward-sloping windows. I needed to see the world again, the ocean and the air, to know that freedom was out there.

"You will be part of something you can only begin to imagine," Eva said quietly.

"Why?" I asked, my voice flat. "Because I'm of German descent? Because I was blessed with golden hair?" I raised my chin, feeling bold. "Because my eyes are the colour of the sea? Why, *Eva*? Because someone else shared the same womb as me?" My voice had risen, and when I looked over Eva's shoulder I was surprised to see four pale faces observing our exchange. Faces that had each had a match, two sets of identical twins. "Well," I said. "Looks like you've outdone yourself, *Frau Braun*."

"Enough," Eva said, fingernails biting into my arm. With a swift roundabout, she had us both facing the group of girls. "Eleanor Engel, this is Patsy and Pauline Schmidt, and Mary and Hazel

Becker."

The girls all had on dresses similar to mine, only theirs were paired, like cards in a game of concentration. "Hello," they said, their voices blending into one.

I couldn't make words. I should've known there would be others but I felt the need to hurt Eva; to bestow years of unresolved bitterness toward Emilie on her. "Was ist los?" I asked the girls casually. Triumph seeped through me as Eva's eyes widened. So, she didn't know everything.

"You speak German," she said, making a quick recovery. "How perfect."

I smiled sweetly, not telling her I only knew a few tidbits, only what Father had taught me before the French invasion. "Now, where's this bird you promised me?"

"In the dining room. Mary, I imagine you'd like to see the bird, too." Eva linked arms with Mary and added, quite casually, "Oh, and Eleanor, you'll be dining with the girls."

And just like that, she took from me the one thing I had left—Earl.

The cockatoo was white as snow, with a faint tracing of lemon peeking out from the underside of his tail and wings. He cocked his head and surveyed us with his beady black eyes.

Eva opened the door of the cage and held out an arm. "This is Hans," she said.

The five of us stood watching as the bird clung to her arm and made his way up to snuggle into her neck.

"He's cuddling you," Mary said with envy.

"He is. He's quite…" Eva's voice trailed off, as if she were searching for the English word. "Affectionate."

"May I?" Mary stretched out a hand.

Eva shook her head. "I'm afraid he's bonded to me, I'm not sure he'd let you. But if you'd like to get him some berries or nuts to eat, that would be wonderful."

The pairs scurried over to a table with a crisp white tablecloth, laden with fruit and flowers, and I used my opportunity wisely. "I'd prefer to dine with my brother," I said. "And not strangers."

Eva was unruffled, her gloved hand stroking the bird's neck. "You'll get to know them soon enough." She gently detached the cockatoo from her and placed him back in the cage. "He's perfect, yes?" she asked. "He bonded closely with me, imitates my speech, and best of all, was easily trained." She winked.

The girls returned with a plate of blueberries, orange slices and sunflower seeds, and after the food had been deposited in the cage, Eva announced it was time for us to eat.

I was reluctantly seated at a table with the look-alikes. Across the room, Earl was sitting with four boys, all of which had a matching face in the crowd, except him. An invisible chord of understanding flowed between us as he nodded to me; we were the only non-identical pair on the ship.

I turned my attention to the menu, ignoring the idle chatter of the girls. Their motions were marked with nervousness; the small frequent sips of their iced water and the constant readjusting of the giant linen napkins across their laps. After I'd decided on the venison, I looked over the top of my menu at Eva, seated at a table with Herr Hoffman. She was the epitome of sophistication, drinking red wine, seemingly amused by every word uttered from the man across from her. It struck me how similar she was to Emilie, all smiles, hair-flips, and cold calculations.

A uniformed steward brought us wine and took our orders. He promptly delivered three courses, one after another, making us feel like glamorous movie stars, the likes of which I knew frequented these ships. The only thing missing from the china-laden table was the candles. Had they been there, I could've lit them. Earl could've put them out.

Luna Park had been too much. Earl hadn't even tried.

Hazel (or Mary) was gawking at me, and I scowled at her.

An array of desserts was added to the fruit table, and all our jaws dropped. Sugar was like gold, and the frothing icings of the layered cakes and the gilded crusts of the fruit pies had us in a stupor. Hard stick candy and licorice sat at the edges in glass jars, and we nibbled and licked until we couldn't possibly eat another bite.

Drunk on sweets and wine, I whispered to Earl from the top bunk that night. "How was he? Werner, I mean…"

"He was most entertaining, quite the fella, brilliant of course."

I giggled. "No, he wasn't."

"Okay, he was—"

"Just a man."

Earl sighed, and I knew he wasn't too disappointed to discover his hero was only human. "Yes, Ellie, he really was *just a man*."

"And the boys?" I asked.

"Dreadful drips. The girls?"

"Lovely little lambs, eager little beavers for Eva."

"Swell." Earl yawned. "You'd do well to follow their lead."

We both knew that was unlikely.

I fell asleep easily, with Earl snoring softly below me. The sheets were like silk and I thought, in my dreamy haze, that perhaps, just this once, I could let myself believe things would be okay.

After a breakfast of pancakes and fruit, Eva separated us. Not just Earl and I this time, but everyone. One of each pair was instructed to move out of the shared cabins, and into their own room. I didn't try to fight it, it was only another two nights. Instead, I mimicked Eva's cool demeanour.

"Auf Wiedersehen, Earl," I said, standing on my tiptoes to kiss him on both cheeks.

His voice was raspy in my ear. "Be careful, Ellie."

After that, Eva took the girls to the lounge, making the cabin separations appear to be only for the benefit of Earl and I, as that left the identical pairs together during the day. It stung.

"Why?" I asked Eva, slinking close to her against the world map. "Why do you bother with my brother and I? Surely the identical ones are more interesting." I'd read everything I could get my hands on about twins, years ago. It fascinated me, having something most people didn't—a person that was made at the exact same time as me. But even I thought identical ones were the most interesting.

"What do you notice about this map?" Eva asked me.

The other girls came near and Eva repeated the question.

I may not have finished school, but I knew this. "The routes are of the famous explorers," I said. "So what?"

"They're all men." She waited, drawing her finger over one of the lines. "What do you think of that, girls?"

The other girls shifted uneasily.

I thought of Hitler, of the man Eva worked for. "It's dangerous to think of things, is it not, Eva?" My voice was cool, but heat sparked inside of me.

Eva's eyes bore into me. "Perhaps it is more dangerous to *not* think of them."

Her riddles made my head spin. I didn't relish being toyed with by the devil's advocate. I'd let my guard down last night.

"You collect us only for experimentation," I said, drawing my own finger over one of the routes. "Don't think you fool me. I've heard of your Doctor Mengele, of his genetic studies on twins." My voice had risen, and the girls gasped and covered their mouths, but I didn't care. They should all know what we were in for. I moved closer to Eva and she backed into the wall, the world around her head like a halo. Sparks flew within me, and my palms burned, but I couldn't stop. "Is your twin supply dwindling? Is that why you have to snatch us from across the ocean, now?"

"Enough!" Eva grabbed my hand, but immediately drew back as if she'd been burned. "That is not why you are here."

"Fire!" screamed Pauline (or Patsy), though I'd done nothing—yet.

"Sheisse," Eva said, then, "Eile, disen wag." *Hurry, this way.* She pulled me behind her, and I followed willingly, only because I couldn't control myself any longer. It felt the same as Luna Park, the anger that had cut through me when Father wouldn't ride the Ferris wheel with me. Emilie was afraid of heights and hadn't wanted to stand by herself, or with Earl. Only Father.

Eva shoved me past a steward and into a room, where a man stood, puffing on a cigarette. "Out. Now," Eva barked. He left the nub of his smoke in a tray and disappeared out the air-lock door.

I looked around wildly, the pressure too much to bear. In the middle of the room, a single lighter was chained in place. I released the imperceptible energy, and a single tiny flame sprung out of the lighter.

Small, but enough. Relief coursed through me.

Eva produced a pack of cigarettes and with shaky hands, slid one out and lit it before settling into an arm chair.

I collapsed into one myself.

"You could've taken down the entire ship." Eva inhaled.

"Yes." I let my shoulders slump, feeling drained. "I thought there was no smoking allowed…in case of accidents."

Eva exhaled, leaning forward. "Accidents," she assured me, "are not possible." She looked around. "Danke Gott, for this room. Fireproof floor and walls. Perhaps we should keep you here for the remainder of the trip."

There was no point in disagreeing. "Perhaps."

Her eyes found mine. "Or perhaps you should trust me."

"Why would I do that?" I asked.

"My choice of you was no accident."

I sighed. "You chose us because our stepmother…"

Eva put out her cigarette, though half was left. "No. I chose *you,* Eleanor. Because the time is coming."

"For what?" I asked. "A campfire?"

To my dismay, she laughed. "Is that what you call it? The inferno at Luna Park?" She patted my hand. "How about this? You trust me, and we'll let everyone believe your fire was an accident."

That night, Eva came to my room, where I now slept alone. "I tried to kill myself before," she said. "To get a man's attention." She was already shutting the door again, before I could even sit up. "I have discovered there are better ways."

The airship docked in Munich and we were taken to an apartment building. I breathed a sigh of relief; it wasn't a concentration camp. But less than an hour later, a familiar face entered, the face that scorched the front pages of newspapers everywhere. Heat soared through me, making even my ears burn, and I felt Earl's cool fingers on my shoulders, grounding me.

"Herr Hitler," Eva said, and though her voice was as smooth as always, I thought I heard something different, something new. A slight lilt that seemed to have one of the boys, Carl (or Uwe?), cocking his head to the side, letting me know he'd heard something, too.

"You've brought them," Hitler said. He twirled the dark moustache that hovered above his thin lips, but didn't come closer.

"Exactly as I told you." Eva bowed her head slightly.

"Excellent." Though seemingly awkward, when he began to speak, his voice was almost hypnotic. "You children are of a special breed. Not only do you have pure blood, you also carry the genes that invite multiple children. You have been brought home to begin our master race."

It took several moments for the horror to sink in, to find its way through the honeyed-words.

"You mean for us…to procreate?" one of the boys asked.

I raised a hand, but Earl gathered it, and my other, holding them down.

Hitler observed us with his grayish-blue eyes. "Get them started, immediately. If there are any problems, eliminate them." And with that, he turned and left the room. Eva slid out the door after him, wrapping her arm around his waist.

My shock sank in further as it dawned on me that Eva was not just working for Hitler—she was his mistress. I had no time to dwell on what that meant; Herr Hoffman was pairing us off, very different than the pairs we'd started with. Now, the numbers made sense. "Eleanor Engel, you're with Ben Mayer."

I didn't hear the drone that foretold the other pairings; I was too busy controlling my rage. "Don't even think about touching me," I hissed at Ben.

Herr Hoffman heard me and crossed his arms. "If you do not produce at least one child in the next year you will be deemed incompetent and therefore,"—he drew out the last word, slowly—"*unnecessary.*"

It was weeks before I saw Eva again. The days blended into each other, a monotonous mix of cooking, baking and cleaning. The marriages had taken place quickly, one after another, and we'd been settled into a routine. The boys were taken to do *men's work* during the day, but returned to us at night, to perform their most important mission. Always, the locks were bolted—from the outside. If it wasn't for that, and the bars on the windows that Hazel regularly clung to, crying, it was almost possible to imagine we were all newlyweds, living together in a honeymoon complex.

I lay beside Ben at night, refusing him contact.

"Eleanor, please," he pleaded with me. "It's preferable to death. Everyone else is…"

I didn't care if the others were or not, and it wasn't that I didn't like Ben. He was attractive, with high cheekbones and a dimple I rarely saw. One night, after a particularly lucid dream in which we'd consummated the marriage, I awoke sweaty, my nightgown clinging to me. I'd watched him in the moonlight, his broad chest rising and falling, and indeed, I'd even wanted to be in his arms, to have some comfort, but instead, I'd curled into myself, a tight ball of heat.

When Eva finally came, it was during the day. The other girls and I, minus Hazel, who'd taken to knitting baby blankets and rocking in the corner, were peeling potatoes and carrots and baking bread. Eva took us each, separately, for a walk, with two Scottish terriers she'd brought along.

Each time she brought one of the girls back, I wondered why they hadn't run.

My turn was last. The air was crisp and cool, and I was surprised to find autumn had come to Germany, with a blazing of red and orange that reminded me of the fire. I'd been soothing my own fire myself, without Earl, and I prided myself on the self-control I'd been exhibiting.

"Where have you been?" My tone was accusatory, but Eva didn't seem to notice.

"At the holiday house in Obersalzberg."

"On holiday?" Heat rippled under my new coat as I let Eva lead me around the block. "You're on vacation, while we are to be incubators?"

Eva barely flinched. "The time is coming, you must be patient."

"The time for what?" I asked. Eva's eyes shifted to a place on our left. I followed her gaze, and saw a man observing us from behind a newspaper.

"Keep your voice down and look straight ahead." Eva slipped her arm through mine. "Are you pregnant, yet?" she asked loudly.

I wanted to scream *no*, but Eva's nails dug into me. I could think only of one thing. "Accidents are not possible," I whispered.

There was a soft snort, before Eva said, "It is a great gift to be a mother of the master race." Then, as we rounded a corner, her voice dropped so low I almost couldn't hear. "Paris was liberated right after we brought you here. A defensive battle is brewing."

Her words were so quick and sharp, it took me an entire block to absorb the information, while she rattled on, loudly again, about eugenics and my privilege. It was all rehearsed, I realized. Eva was reciting her part.

I chose my words carefully. "I look forward to following your lead."

Eva didn't even flinch. "So do I."

By December, both Mary and Pauline were pregnant, and Eva informed me the Germans had been beaten back in Belgium. It'd been their last defense, and now both the Red Army and the Western Allies were advancing.

The time is coming, she repeated.

"Someone is coming," Carl said on Christmas Day, with an ear cocked to the door, and sure enough, Hitler arrived, with Eva, carrying a tiny frosted gingerbread house. Behind them, a doctor and the two terriers brought up the rear.

The doctor gave us all thorough inspections. Both Carl and Ben were declared too thin, and Hazel mentally unstable. My only infraction was not being pregnant (yet), but I did feel badly for Ben when he was taken aside, and I wondered what would come of it.

Earl and Mary, and Sam and Pauline, were given an assortment of sweets, cakes, fruits and nuts for their accomplishments, and I sat, twisting my skirt in my hands, as I watched my brother kiss Mary under a piece of mistletoe. It almost appeared as if he loved her.

Eva was watching them as well, green-eyed, while Hitler nursed a cup of tea in the corner furthest from Hazel. Hazel hadn't taken her eyes off Hitler and it seemed to unnerve us all, the way she looked at the space around us, and not at us.

Eva continued to watch Earl and Mary, and I thought she was jealous. I knew I was. My heart shattered into pieces at losing the last person that had been mine. Earl belonged to Mary now.

My heart was an open wound in my chest. I looked down, sure I must be leaking blood onto my white lace blouse. But there was nothing of the sort, only the shock of Ben's penetrating gaze.

I'd denied him too long.

Eva saw it, too, and met me by the punch bowl, with an almost undetectable piece of advice. "Your time has run out," she said, her lips barely moving.

I followed her lead and ladled myself a cup. "And whose fault is that?"

Eva broke a candy cane off the gingerbread house and offered it to me. Then, she moved to her left, blocking herself from Hitler's view, using me as a shield. "You'll have to…with Ben."

"But—"

"It's unavoidable." She meant pregnancy.

I loathed her. "Why have you stayed with him?" I asked. "What are you getting out of it?"

Eva grew stiff and set her cup on the lace tablecloth. "Appearances can be deceiving. The entire world believes him to be a celibate single man, dedicated entirely to his political mission." Her hand brushed over mine, and I was surprised to feel my own cool. "But what if—" Her voice was barely a breath on her lips. "—he was gone?"

"You intend to—"

"Quiet now."

Hitler and Eva left us after dinner, and I stayed up late, cleaning the apartment and licking peppermint. By the time I went to bed, Ben was already asleep.

Much of Germany was in ruins by January, and so was I. I wanted my husband. Not out of fear, but out of desire. I wanted someone of my own again, someone to cling to. Someone to love.

Ben hesitated. He rose above me, the whites of his eyes gleaming in the light that filtered through the window. Tears rolled off his cheeks falling onto my forehead.

"It's okay," I said, surrendering.

And it was.

It was a quick jolt, a sharp burn that swept upward through my belly and breasts, down through my elbows and into my fingers. I spread my arms like wings, my palms open to the frosted window at the head of the bed while he moved inside of me. A few more thrusts, and the streetlamps outside flickered across Ben's face, then exploded in a rain of glass that clattered in the street. All went dark, and then it was over with a rush of warmth, and Ben rolled off of me, spent.

He lay panting, while giggles erupted inside of me. I covered my mouth and shook silently, as Ben went to the window. "Three lamps are broken," he said.

With a swift change in direction, my giggles turned to an onslaught of tears. Ben was beside me in a flash, pulling me against his chest. He was hot, like an oven; I had given him my fire. But I'd given myself something, too—power.

Ben belonged to me, now.

He led me to the window, to show me the darkness outside. I pressed my cheek to the cool glass and scraped my fingers over the iron bars, afraid I would crack like Hazel. But instead, things seemed a little better. Without the lamps, I could see the stars.

The winter seemed never ending, a slow-moving frigid defeat. Eva would show herself from time to time with the doctor in tow, murmuring small pieces of information to me through chapped lips, *the Allies were crossing the Rhine,* and *the Soviets were coming from the East,* while the doctor examined Mary and Pauline's growing bellies. Patsy admitted to feeling nauseous and Eva took her for a walk in the snow, with an arm about her waist as if they were the best of friends. Hazel sat dutifully on the sofa, randomly staring at the spaces around our heads, her face pale. Whenever Pauline or Mary waddled past, Hazel's eyes latched onto their bellies with unreserved envy.

Eva observed us all with a motherly protectiveness that made my scalp tingle.

Just when I feared I'd burn us all alive, April swooped in with a thaw.

Eva appeared suddenly, with instructions to pack up. She barked orders to the other girls and whispered to me in my room as I threw clothing into a bag. "Roosevelt has died, but it has changed nothing." She folded my dresses meticulously, unseeing. "We're going to Berlin, to join him in the Führerbunker."

I finished with my clothing, and began on Ben's.

"That won't be necessary," Eva said.

I filled the tub with ice cold water and plunged my hands in until they turned blue. Then, we left.

It was dark when we reached the Reich Chancellery and I didn't see much before we were ushered underground. Mary had not stopped crying about the loss of Earl, and I felt strangely empty without Ben beside me.

"We must go through the Vorbunker," Eva told us, leading us into a shallow room below the cellar, which held a kitchen and a dining room. There had been no one around anywhere, almost as if everyone had been dismissed on our account. We were ghost girls.

The Vorbunker soon turned into the Führerbunker, a vast expanse of damp space with lavish décor. Eva secured a door behind us, once again protecting us from the world, or maybe the world from us, it was hard to know which. She then led us to a conference room, where mattresses had been placed along the floor. "No one will know you are, or ever were, here."

We didn't exist, but we were worth saving.

At dinner, the girls fidgeted, and Hazel gaped at me. Annoyance forced me to pace the room to relieve the burn in my belly throughout the entirety of the evening. My fire had, for months, proved useless. Any escape was impossible because always we were locked into a space that would only create an oven. Always, it was suicide.

Hazel cried, but Pauline held her hand, murmuring about babies and a cottage by a stream, a dreamworld that seemed far-fetched from where we were now.

"The Red Army has surrounded Berlin," Eva said, later. I had no idea how many days it'd been; the only math in my head was the months that had elapsed from the fire at Luna Park until now.

Nine.

It was time.

Eva woke us after midnight, to witness her marriage. We stood like soldiers in white nightgowns, watching the civil ceremony of the devil, who was really *only a man*, to the woman who'd stood silently behind him and his horrors.

I wasn't sure what the purpose of the wedding was, but I did notice the rare spark in Hitler's otherwise dead eyes as he said the words that made Eva his wife, and it made me think of the way Ben had looked at me on New Year's Day, the same way my father looked at Emilie, and Earl looked at Mary.

A wave of realization rolled over me, too late.

Eva was never on my side. Eva *controlled* the other side.

By the next afternoon, word reached us that Mussolini had been executed.

Hitler wanted Eva to leave. He never mentioned the five of us. We were never his idea—we were *hers.* I wondered what else had been her idea.

"No," she told him. "We avoid capture together." She opened her palm, displaying a capsule. "Cyanide," she said. Her weapon of choice.

When the Red Army was within two blocks, Eva locked us into the conference room.

Minutes of silence lapsed into memories that would haunt me my whole life. And then, a shot made us all jolt. Mary gasped, and Hazel vomited.

I wiped my sweaty palms on my dress, knowing it wasn't over. "Get up," I ordered the others, as the key turned in the lock. "And be ready."

The door creaked open.

"He committed suicide," Eva told us.

I ran my tongue over my dry lips. "He thought you were going to, as well."

Eva produced the unused capsule from her pocket. "I suppose he did." Then, she noticed my hands covering my abdomen. "Congratulations." She raised her chin to the other girls. "We will have a lovely family."

"Everything…all of it…was you." Fire raged inside of me, but Eva thought I was giving her a compliment.

"I told you, you could trust me." She took me to Hitler's body and patted my hand. "Use it to burn the evidence," she said. She'd chosen me long ago. For this. She'd spent months cultivating me, bonding me. For this. But I wasn't a cockatoo.

"Perhaps you should say goodbye," I suggested. The air was moist below ground and I wondered if my heat would be enough.

Eva considered what I said, hovering in the doorway.

I thought of my father. "Despite everything, you still love him." I knew it was true.

She did, too. Love was a funny thing, like an accident, a mishap you didn't see coming. Eva went to the bed, leaned over, and pressed her lips to his forehead.

Heat surged through me, stronger than ever, and energy sparked through the air, igniting the bedclothes and Hitler and Eva in a fury of flames.

I ran for the door, with Eva on my heels.

The other girls were already waiting in the Vorbunker, and they slammed the door shut behind me.

My last sight as I turned around was Eva rolling on the floor, her wedding dress a blaze around her.

I pressed my back to the door, until Eva quit screaming and the door grew too hot. Sounds seeped into the thundering in my ears; shells flying over the garden of the Chancellery.

In the midst of the war, no one was interested in the five of us as we slipped out of the bunker, breathless. *Double suicide,* I whispered to a guard, then in German, "tot." *Dead.* The fire licked at the surface and no one cared enough to try to stop us. No one knew who we were.

We'd been only an experiment of Eva's, a passing fancy of an unacknowledged woman.

By the time we reached Munich, word on the street was that Berlin had surrendered.

The apartment building was unguarded, but the boys had been left locked inside with little food. They were nearly starved when we freed them.

Ben clung to my hand in the dim living room, using his other to shove the cheese and bread we'd looted, into his mouth. I'd lit candles with my fingertips, and slowly the others had revealed their own undisclosed talents: Mary could hear the thoughts of animals, Hazel could read auras, Pauline could see the future, Patsy could read the past through items, Carl had the gift of clairaudience (hearing beyond normal human perception), Uwe was a master of locating people by touching an object that belonged to them, Sam could move objects with his mind, and Ben, my glorious husband I hadn't wanted, was a dream manipulator.

Ben's cheeks were red when he said, "I'm sorry. I only did it the once. Then, I promised myself I'd never do it again."

There was a long silence while we all absorbed each other.

"What now?" Earl asked. "Shall we find a way home?" He was asking the group, but his eyes were on me.

Did we have anything to go back to?

I could picture it in my mind, the relief etched on Father's face at our return. But overlapping it was a sharp clear memory, the vivid image of Eva returning to Hitler's side, kissing him goodbye. She'd made a mistake.

I wouldn't.

"Mary and Pauline are due soon," I said. "Travelling seems ill-advised."

"Especially in an airship," Pauline murmured, but didn't elaborate.

The others agreed, the consensus being that the cities were unsafe as well.

And so, we set out through the ravaged countryside, the weight of mourning heavy on our shoulders. We joined the ranks of other misplaced people, trudging quietly through a silent country.

In the end, we found an abandoned cottage in the Black Forest, just in time. I lit a fire in the hearth, and the boys went hunting. Rabbits and squirrels told Mary where there was a stream for water.

Mary's baby slid into the world at dusk, with a wisp of soft golden hair and dark blue eyes like the sea at night. She was perfect in every way, her only flaw being that there was only one of her.

Several months later, in the crisp autumn air, we watched over the colourful treetops as an airship went up in flames. It blazed bright like a giant paper lantern and crumpled to the earth.

I raised my hands in innocence. "It wasn't me."

I thought of Eva.

Did she know—that accidents *were* possible?

After all, were identical twins not just strange genetic accidents?

I walked to the cradle Earl had made, and looked at my different, sleeping babies. The only pair born in the group. They took after my mother, with ginger hair the colour of a sunset. Or a fire.

They were perfect.

Sarah Van Goethem is a Canadian author who resides in southwestern Ontario. She spent lazy childhood summers on the farm, reading on the old tire swing beneath the maple tree, believing in fairytales.

Her first YA novel was in PitchWars (2016), her second novel was longlisted for the Bath Children's Novel Award (2018), and she's busy working on her third. She's also won various awards for her short stories.

Sarah is a nature lover, a wanderer of dark forests, and a gatherer of vintage. You can find her at auctions, thrift stores, and trespassing at abandoned Gingerbread houses. But don't worry, she always leaves herself a breadcrumb (or pebble?) trail to find her way home.

A PRINCESS, A SPY, AND A DWARF WALKED INTO A BAR FULL OF NAZIS

Patrick Bollivar

It was a dimly lit country inn. Tendrils of smoke fogged the air, coupled with the stench of strong cologne. When a tall woman entered, her long legs showing under a short coat, she turned the heads of the soldiers. Wisps of blonde hair peaked out of the traveller's scarf that covered her head and neck as she surveyed the room, smiled, and removed her coat. Bare shoulders and a sleek sparkling dress were revealed. After dumping the coat into the arms of her dwarf companion she strode to the bar.

"The name's Jacqueline. Now who's buying me a drink?" she said in a husky voice. Multiple men competed for that honor.

No one paid any heed to the shorter woman or the dwarf who had accompanied Jacqueline. They were fine with that, and quietly made their way to a table in the corner.

After ordering the largest beers on offer, they scanned the bar, including the stairs up to rooms above. Not much of an establishment, just a stopping point from A to B. The only locals were some women from the nearby town who appeared unhappy to be there, their faces overly painted to hide the strain from years of war. All the men were soldiers, many wearing SS uniforms. Some glared at the dwarf, but most eyes were on his sparkling lady friend.

"So, what do you think, Turk?" said the woman. She wore a grey jumpsuit under a leather jacket, her black hair done up in a bun. In the eyes of the dwarf she seemed no more than a girl.

"This plan is stupid, which isn't a surprise, since it's Jack's idea." Turk removed his own leather jacket, revealing thick, hairy arms, corded with muscle. He lit a cigar, leaned back, and watched as Jack charmed the whole bar with smiles and laughs.

"Jack will get the job done. We need to be patient."

"Whatever you say, Princess."

"Call me that again and I'll shove my wrench up your arse."

Turk chuckled. "Sorry, Briar. Looks like Jack's hooked our man."

The man led Jack away from the others and together they spun out onto the dance floor while a phonograph behind the bar played Benny Goodman's 'Sing, Sing, Sing.' The Nazi officer led her in a classic ballroom dance style as they swept around the room. His stiff moves didn't match the song at all, but Jack humoured him by following along.

The SS officer in question was Oberleutnant Heinrich Spindle. Jack's connections in the resistance had led them straight to him. Spindle knew the secret route to the enchanted castle.

Briar and Turk ordered drink after drink while they watched Jack work. The cigarette smoke itched Briar's eyes and Turk's cigar wasn't helping so she grabbed it from his mouth and smashed it into the ashtray. Turk shrugged, quaffed his beer, and waved at the serving girl for another.

"Excuse me, Fraulein," said a young officer to Briar. He clicked his heels and gave a bow. "Might I have this dance?"

"No."

"You can have me, handsome," said Turk with a grin. He'd somehow lit another cigar without Briar noticing. The officer scowled at him and returned to his friends.

"Jack's done it," said Briar with a nod towards where Jack led Spindle up the stairs to one of the rooms while men hooted at them from below. "Let's go."

As they got up to leave, the young officer appeared with his friends in tow.

"Your little abomination was rude to me," he said, his eyes on Briar, as if Turk was her servant. "The midget will apologize."

"I ain't no midget," snarled Turk. "I'm a dwarf."

The young officer scoffed. "What's the difference?"

"A thousand years of protecting Princesses, and a fondness for axes," said Briar. "Now if you'll excuse us, we were just leaving."

"I think not," said one of the man's friends. He stopped Briar with a hand to her chest and grinned unpleasantly.

From under her jacket Briar produced a large wrench, the size of a club. Teeth flew out of the man's mouth as his head whipped sideways from her blow.

"Really?" said Turk before punching the young officer in the nuts. He lifted him into the air, and chucked him into the third man. "I thought we were trying to be subtle."

"Change of plans," said Briar as she punched another Nazi in the jaw, clubbed a fourth with her wrench, and dodged the groping arms of two more. "Now, we run." She saw the serving girl, hiding under a table. "Get the townsfolk out of here. It's going to get messy."

Turk acted as a bowling ball through the pile of converging Nazis. Those that didn't fly like pins out of his way met with Briar's wrench. The pair barrelled out of the bar into the cool night air and made it to the bar's dirt parking lot before lights from a vehicle stopped them in their tracks.

Dozens of rifle pins slid into place. German soldiers had disgorged from the nearby transport truck at the sound of the ruckus, and now had them in their sights. Briar dropped her wrench with a savage curse.

The young officer stepped outside, blood dripping from his chin.

He wiped it with a handkerchief. "What is the hurry, Fraulein? I believe we have a dance to finish."

"Sorry, honey," said Briar. "The only dancing I do is with my fists."

"Then we shall dance your way." He signalled for the soldiers to advance.

A body fell off the roof and landed with a thud at Turk's feet. Oberleutnant Spindle groaned where he lay. Everyone looked up to the open window above. Jack smiled and gave a weak wave.

"Would you believe he tripped?" Jack said.

Turk grabbed Spindle's ankle and hauled him backwards. "Let's go, Jack. We've got what we came for."

Jack threw high heeled shoes to the ground, ran down the roof, and leapt over the soldiers. His wig fell off as he tumbled back onto his feet, revealing the short brown hair of a very skinny man. The spy grinned at the Nazis and blew them a kiss.

"Kill them!" snarled the young officer.

Before the soldiers could move a flash lit up the forest's edge, followed by a boom. Something whistled past Briar's ear and hit the truck. It exploded and the soldiers cart wheeled away like leaves on the wind.

A Sherman tank rolled towards them, a great green beast, the words 'Grizzly One' painted along the side. Its 75mm gun pointed straight at the Nazis. Those left standing wore faces wide open with shock.

Turk and Jack hauled the Oberleutnant up the turret and threw him inside while Briar hopped up onto the tank's front. She smiled at the Nazis.

"May I introduce you to my friend, Lionel? He doesn't like it when Nazis threaten me. Isn't that right, Lionel?"

The tank's engine growled. It sounded distinctly human. A voice spoke from a speaker. "That's right," said Lionel. "Now say goodbye. Fire in my hole!" Briar plugged her ears as the 75mm lit with a flash and the bar exploded in a shower of splinters.

"Fire in my hole," laughed Jack for the twentieth time. "You're so dirty, Lionel."

"That's saying a lot, coming from you," said the tank as he drove them under a canopy of wild birch trees. "I don't see why he wore the dress and not you Briar."

"Because I look better in it," said Jack.

"He's right," said Briar from where she stood in the command chair, her head out of the cupola as she watched the night roll by. "Just because I'm descended from a long line of princesses doesn't mean I like to wear taffeta. There's nowhere to hide my wrench."

"How much further, Lionel?" asked Turk. He carefully watched their prisoner while sharpening his axe.

"Not much longer. We're in the deep dark wood now," said the tank. His voice spoke softly from the intercoms, as if afraid to be heard.

The forest of Urwald Sababurg had indeed grown darker. They smelled burnt cinder from recent fires as thick oaks and spindly beech trees drifted past, their shrivelled branches crooked claws that tried to reach out and grab Briar's hair. The moon slid out from behind the clouds. Eerie light showered a hill not far away, where old stones leaned against each other, like the bones of some great dead thing. Briar shivered and slipped back inside.

"This place feels evil," she said.

"It is," said Lionel. The growl of his engine sounded rough, as if something choked the gas line. "Up on that hill. That's where they shot me."

"Major Malice's men?"

"No, my own."

Turk and Briar glanced at each other. Briar crawled up to the driver's side of the tank. Electric sparks travelled past her along copper threads as she weaved her way between them. They extended from the tank's controls to the Mason jar strapped to the driver's seat. Inside the jar was the brain of Lieutenant Lionel Perkins, one time Commander of First Grizzly Battalion. She'd read his file at the department, before they shipped her overseas. A tough commander who'd cut his teeth in Italy with the First Canadian Armoured Brigade, he'd had more victories than anyone else in his division, but more casualties as well. She touched the Mason jar, and spoke directly to the glowing brain floating in the fluid.

"That wasn't in your report, Lionel. What happened?"

"We were travelling with the army towards the Netherlands to reinforce General Crerar when Jack recruited us to capture Sababurg Castle. I figured it would be an easy win, less difficult than clearing the banks of the Scheldt River, but we lost the fight before it even began. Our tanks broke down as we travelled through the Urwald and we couldn't fix them, no matter how hard we tried. It was like a dark magic had a steel grip on their pistons and wouldn't let go."

"Why did your men turn on you?"

"They didn't at first, not until they started to disappear, one by one. Wolves, fast, deadly, dragged them away. We climbed that hill to escape them. It gave us our first view of the castle. Its windows glowed like fairy lights, beckoning me forward. My men wanted to retreat. We argued. Smitty, my gunner, shot me. My battalion walked away, left me to die."

"And that's when Major Malice got you."

"The wolves did. They spoke, like humans were inside them. They dragged me to the castle, and, and did things to me. I woke up, transformed into the very tank I'd abandoned in the woods, just as my men had abandoned me."

"At least you managed to escape," said Briar.

"Being a tank ain't too bad," said Turk. "I knew a guy that got turned into a frog once."

"Did he get turned back?" asked Lionel.

"Nah. Unfortunately for him, this was in France, and they do love their grenouille."

"Turk!"

"Sorry."

The joke had offended Briar, but Lionel chuckled. They rolled on in silence, except for the sound of the tank's engine, which sounded closer to normal.

"Tell me, Briar," said Lionel after a while. "How did you become involved in this?"

Briar sighed. "Our family comes from here. Sababurg Castle used to belong to us. It's an old place, cursed with dark magic, or so my Gran said. She fled to Canada decades ago, to escape it. When Jack came searching for her he found me. My uncles and I were doing our part for the war, building Sherman tanks at a factory in Halifax."

"That must have been hard work."

"Nah. I grew up on a farm. My uncles taught me all about engines. By the time I was seven I could take a tractor apart and put it back together again. Tanks are easy."

"Only if you buy us a few drinks first," said Lionel. Briar frowned. "That was a joke."

"No, it wasn't."

The engine coughed. "So how does Jack think you can help?"

"I know the secret to getting into the castle," said Briar.

"Which is?"

Briar smiled. "Me, of course."

"We've got company," said Jack from the command post. Briar grabbed her submachine gun and opened the driver's hatch.

Briar shone a spotlight into the forest. Eyes glowed in the black depths. "Don't shoot, Jack. We don't want to alert any patrols."

"I'm not letting them drag me off," said Jack, his itchy trigger finger caressing the co-axial machine gun. "The Nazis don't like people like me, and they think they can fix my unnatural tendencies. I refuse to be made into some Nazi lab rat. I like me just the way I am, thank you very much. No offense, Lionel."

"I'll take care of them," said Turk. He squeezed past Jack and jumped off the tank. The dwarf's axe shone in the moonlight, as did his grin of pleasure. He marched off into the woods, alone.

"Is he crazy?" said Jack.

"My family deals with talking wolves all the time. He'll be fine."

"That's not normal you know."

"I know. Gran used to tell me bedtime stories about our crazy ancestors. How they'd get trapped in towers by evil usurpers, constantly fall asleep from a poison apple or some stupid spell, or get turned into one ungodly creature or another. We've always attracted strange shit. Like you, Lionel. When they introduced us, I didn't even blink an eye at the fact you were a tank."

"No, you didn't," said Lionel. "I did think it odd at the time."

"Odd is my middle name."

Howls sounded in the woods, followed by the bellow of a man. Then silence. When something rustled a nearby bush, Jack fired. Bullets bounced off the trees.

"Stop that, you idiot!" said Turk. He stepped out of the bush, his face covered in blood. Not his own. "Two got away."

Turk shoved Jack down the hole and took over at the machine gun. "Get our captive to talk, Jack. Lionel, let's move."

They rumbled through the woods at twice the speed. Down below, Jack removed the gag on Oberleutnant Spindle.

"I'll never talk, you pervert," spat the Nazi.

"Takes one to know one. Admit it, sugar, you liked our kiss." Jack pulled out a file, and began to sharpen his fingernails. Only then did Spindle notice how long and pointed they were. "I've heard of you, Oberleutnant."

Spindle spat in reply. "When you're captured, we shall fix you, and put down the midget like a rabid dog."

"Oh, torturing you is going to be so easy," said Jack. "Now then, shall we begin with a circumcision? I think my Jewish friends would appreciate the joke."

Briar climbed onto the front of the tank and left Jack to his business. After an hour they arrived at the edge of the woods. A grass slope descended into a valley. At the bottom, resting atop a hill, sat Castle Sababurg. The lights in the windows flickered, from sickly yellow to unearthly green.

The wind sighed, as if happy to show Briar her old home. She didn't feel happy at all. The sight of the place gave her knots in her stomach.

A thick nest of what Briar thought to be thorny vines surrounded the castle. Her binoculars however, revealed it to be endless coils of barbed wire, mounted one on top of the other. Mounds of it, rising a hundred feet high.

"There's a way through," said Lionel. "Inside is a maze of paths, peppered with landmines. I only managed to escape because of my thick hide. I can't remember the way back, but Spindle knows."

Briar cursed. "Turk, take a look." She handed him the binoculars and pointed.

Six Panzer tanks patrolled below, their guns pointed in every direction. "I guess we know where the entrance is at least," said Turk.

"How's Jack doing in there, Lionel?"

"The German's urine is staining my interior," said the tank. He didn't sound very upset by this. "I believe he'll soon be willing to help."

"Great, but how do we get through those tanks?"

"I'll handle them," said Lionel.

"You can't take on six tanks!" said Briar.

"I'll have to," growled Lionel. "Besides, it'll feel good to fight something my own size."

"You'll need a loader for the 75mm," said Turk. "I volunteer."

"Thank you," said Lionel. "I didn't wish to order anyone. I'm done forcing people to risk their lives for me."

Briar jumped off the tank and ran for the trees.

"What's gotten into her?" asked Lionel.

Turk patted the tank in sympathy and followed his niece.

He found her slumped against a tree as lightning flashed in the distance. "Storm's coming," Turk said.

"It always is," said Briar.

"True," said Turk as he lit a cigar. "How are you holding up, kid?"

"What do you think? Half my battalion wants to charge off to die."

"I thought this was Lionel's battalion."

"You know it isn't."

The uncle nodded agreement.

"Turk, did you ever think you'd end up in one of these damn fool stories?"

"I have six brothers as short as me, and a niece as fierce as she is beautiful. What do you think?"

She gave him a shove. "You old charmer, you. I never really cared for Gran's stories, you know. I was happy on the farm, fixing tractors."

"Me too, Briar, but if this Major Malice character manages to unlock Sababurg's secrets, it could change the tide of the war back to the Nazi's favour. People like me, people like Jack, won't be safe, anywhere. We need to end this."

"Bloody Nazis," said Briar, spitting. "I sure enjoyed punching them in the mouth."

"Well, you're about to get another chance." Turk nodded to Jack as he approached. "He talk?"

"Sang like a canary," said Jack as he wiped his fingernails with a handkerchief. "We'll need to take him with us though. The maze is changed every night, with secret signs showing the safe path. Too complicated to memorize in a night."

"That's fine. Didn't want a Nazi in the tank when I go to battle anyway."

Briar gave Turk a teary-eyed hug. "Good luck, Uncle."

"You too," said Turk. He mashed the end of his cigar into his palm. "I need to quit these things. Damn smoke waters my eyes."

"Ohhh!" said Jack. He gave Turk a hug too. "I love you too, you big softy."

Turk patted his back. "Alright, alright. Get off me, you pansy. Take care of her, Jack."

"I will." Jack went back to the tank to collect the Oberleutnant.

"So Uncle…" said Briar. "In most of Gran's stories, doesn't the princess end up marrying some stupid boy?"

"Yeah, but it won't be him, that's for sure."

Briar laughed. "Well, I'm not marrying a tank. Lionel is a little cold for my taste."

"He's a tank, Briar, what do you expect? Besides, it might not be him either. Sometimes the Prince doesn't show up until the very end."

"If he does I'll punch him in the mouth too."

"That's my girl."

Jack and Briar followed Lionel down the road towards the castle. Thunder boomed, and so did the guns of the enemy tanks. Dirt exploded around them. They crouched lower. Spindle stumbled. Jack hauled him up by his bound hands, and they carried on. Lionel responded with a crack of his 75mm. A Panzer died.

Almost there.

Acrid sulphur from gunpowder scorched their nostrils. A shell rocked the Sherman sideways, but Lionel didn't stop. He kept on charging, his gun firing again. Two more Panzers out of commission. Too late the enemy tanks realized he intended to ram them. Close quarters now. Turk riddled the hulls with the .50 Cal. Lionel pushed one Panzer down a ravine as his turret swivelled and fired another shot.

A shell hit Lionel in his right track. The Sherman rocked sideways just as Jack dragged Briar and Spindle into the barbed wire maze.

"We have to go back!" Briar said.

"We can't. Keep moving, sugar."

Into the silvery growth of spiked steel they went as bullets and explosions continued behind them. Briar tried hard not to think of her uncle, or Lionel, out there. Her left hand held her M3 submachine gun at the ready, while in her right she gripped her wrench.

"This way, no this way," said Spindle.

"You better not be lost, sugar."

"No, no. It's this way, I'm sure of it."

The sky had lost all its light. Only their flashlights guided them now. There were brightly coloured clothes hanging on the wire at each fork. Spindle took different colours in different directions.

They rounded a corner and came to a stop. Jack let his grip on the Oberleutnant's bindings go, raised his rifle. Before them sat a wolf on his haunches. He wore clothes, an SS officer's uniform. Jack laughed.

"My, what big eyes you have," Jack said.

"All the better to eat you with," said the wolf. "Where's your friend the lumberjack?"

"Back there. You're welcome to go visit him."

"I'll eat the midget later," said the wolf. "You look tasty enough for now."

"I like men, not dogs. Stop flirting with me," said Jack.

"I'm not! I wasn't—"

Jack fired at the wolf before he could answer. Missed. Another wolf leapt out of the barbed wire, but Briar was ready. She clocked it with her wrench, right in the snout. The wolf fell and rolled. She placed a bullet in its skull before it could rise again.

The SS wolf vanished into the barbed wire before Jack could get off another shot.

"This way," said Spindle, his voice shaken from the encounter.

The princess and the spy followed Spindle down the narrow trail.

The castle loomed closer, backlit by cracks of lightning and booming thunder. After many more turns they reached the exit, guarded by two men.

Jack used his lanky form to spider his way between the barbed wire, snuck up on them, and rendered them dead with a few choice stabs. They walked out of the maze, and stood under the castle's imposing shadow. "So what now?" said Jack.

"We go through the hidden door. I have the key," said Spindle. He withdrew it from a chain under his shirt and held it up.

The air stirred behind Briar and she jumped away as the SS wolf charged, but he hadn't been aiming for her. He chomped down on the Oberleutnant's hand. Spindle let out a scream.

A bullet from Jack's rifle killed the wolf, another shot silenced Spindle. "You okay, Briar?" he said.

Briar nodded, her eyes on the dead wolf. He looked so stupid, lying there in clothes. "I hate this place," she said.

"Yeah, me too. So what do we do now? Cut open the wolf and get the key?"

"We don't know where the hidden door is." Briar glanced up at an open window. "Can you climb?"

"Sugar, I dance and gather intel. Isn't that enough?"

"Fine. Hold my wrench." Briar climbed the wall of the castle, her strong fingers digging into the gaps in the stone. She slipped through the window, and soon after found the hidden door at the bottom of a set of stairs. A fake wall opened, and let Jack inside.

A passageway led them through abandoned stables into an empty courtyard.

"Where to now?" asked Jack. Briar pointed upwards, and he nodded.

They made their way up the next staircase, towards the topmost tower. Anything that ever happened, happened in the topmost tower.

No guards here, and a door half ajar. "Too easy," said Briar. She tucked her wrench behind her jacket again, and settled her M3 in both hands.

They slowly stepped inside.

A bed hidden behind a curtain took up most of the room. The air hung heavily with the smell of the flowers lining the walls. Lamplight flickered on sconces, the lightning outside close enough to affect the electric currents. Briar searched the shadowy corners of the room for any sign of hidden guards while Jack stepped up to the curtain and carefully drew it aside.

"Well hello, sleeping gorgeous," said Jack.

A man lay there, under glass, his dark hair draped over his brow, his hands crossed over his chest. He wore a white hospital gown, though in this setting it appeared more like the slip of a wedding dress. An icy cloud circulated inside his glass tank, fed by machines hidden on the other side of the bed.

"It's Lionel," said Jack. "But why would the Major keep his body preserved?"

"Because he was my first success, and as you said, he's quite gorgeous," said Major Malice.

She stood by the door in a white doctor's coat, beside two soldiers whose rifles were pointed at Briar and Jack. The princess and the spy dropped their weapons and raised their hands.

"I'll admit," said Jack. "I'd hoped Malice was a man."

"So you could try to seduce me with your perversions?" said the major. "Oh yes, I know all about you, Jack. I've watched your progress with great interest."

"How did you know we were coming?" asked Briar.

"The mirror in my office shows me all I wish to see in this land. I simply asked, 'Mirror, mirror, on the wall, who is the most dangerous of them all?' And lo and behold, your face appeared, Briar. You seem fond of Lieutenant Perkins, so I set his body here for you to find."

"A trap, eh? Well done. Tell me, are you even capable of putting back his brain?"

Malice laughed. "Of course not! I barely understand how it

worked in the first place. It's almost like magic, the stuff that happens in this castle. No, Lionel's body is quite dead, I'm afraid. Soon you will be too."

The soldiers gathered the weapons from off the floor and left with the major, locking the door behind them.

"I don't like the way she said that," said Briar. "Search the room."

They found the explosives hidden amongst the flowers. "That's a lot of dynamite," said Jack. "Timer gives us ten minutes."

Briar ran to the window. In the courtyard she could see vehicles being loaded with crates. "They're bugging out." She smashed the glass and tried the bars. No luck.

"Nine minutes," said Jack.

"Can you pick the lock?"

Jack examined the door. He tried his knife, but it bent. "Sorry, I don't carry picks for fifteenth century keyholes. I'd need a hammer to open this."

"How about a wrench?" said Briar.

Together they dismantled the door, removing the lock and all the hinges. After laying the door down, they stood and looked back at Lionel's body.

"I've got a crazy idea," said Briar.

They strapped the glass tank to the door, and climbed on top. "Hold tight," Jack said. He grabbed the frame of the entrance and pulled them forward.

They rode the door down the spiral staircase, kicking their way around corners and picking up speed. At the bottom they careened past a soldier, who Briar silenced with a whack from her wrench. Once in the courtyard they leapt off the door and rolled towards cover behind some crates. The door kept skidding until it came to a rest against the vehicles being loaded.

Briar tried to peak around the corner, only to have bullets riddle the dirt nearby.

"Quite imaginative, little girl," said the major. "Though I don't know why you're trying to save Lieutenant Perkins. I told you his body is useless. Your emotions have proven the better of you once again."

"Only time will tell," said Briar, and both her and Jack started giggling uncontrollably.

That's when Major Malice took a closer look at the glass tank, and saw that the body had been replaced with all her explosives.

The timer hit zero. Briar and Jack plugged their ears.

The princess and the spy returned to the topmost tower and retrieved the body. They wrapped it in the bed's silk sheets, and carried it down to the courtyard, just as a tank appeared through the smoke of the ruined vehicles.

Lionel had seen better days. His right track had lost its duckbill ends and was in danger of falling apart. His engine clanked. His chassis wobbled. The tank came to a stop in front of Briar.

"Is it done?" hissed Lionel, his voice like a steaming kettle. "Is she dead?"

"Yes," said Briar. "She's over there. And there. And I think a bit of her landed up there."

Lionel chuckled, and then groaned. "It turns out this body feels pain," he said. "Jack, is that me you carry?"

"It is, sir, but I'm afraid, that is, Malice said…"

"There's no hope for me, is there? Well, at least she can't do this to anyone else. Can I have it back please?" Jack carried the body into the tank, and laid it to rest underneath the man's brain. Jack came out and stood at Briar's side. "Thank you, Jack. Thank you Briar."

"You're welcome," said Briar. "I wish we could do more, truly. Where's my uncle?"

"Down the hill, sifting through the Panzer wreckage for working parts. He seems to think you can fix me."

"I can. Don't worry, you big lug. You'll be right as rain, sooner than you think." Briar gave him a pat and a kiss on his plating.

The lights of the castle suddenly brightened then began to flash in weird intervals.

"Uh oh," said Jack. "Briar, what did you do?"

"Nothing!" she said as all the lights sank into a quiet darkness.

A single flashlight bobbed up the hill, held by a dwarf carrying a satchel full of spare parts. Turk's light shone down, not on a Sherman tank, but on a body wrapped in silk bed sheets. It stirred to life. Lionel unwrapped himself from the sheets and stood up in amazement. He stared at his hands, felt his chest. Then he looked at Briar, and smiled.

"Don't think this means we're getting married or nothing," said Briar. "I barely know you."

"That can be remedied," Lionel said with a flash of a smile.

Briar rolled her eyes. "I liked you better as a tank."

"This is Lionel?" said Turk. "Nuts!" He threw down the satchel of parts. "Now we're going to have to walk home."

Patrick Bollivar has always enjoyed fairy tales involving princesses, especially the ones where heroes fight their way to the top of a tower. When not indulging his fantasies, Patrick works at the top of a tower at Vancouver Airport while his princess works from home, managing their two little dwarfs. You can read more of his short stories in *Pulp Literature Magazine, Tesseracts Nineteen: Superheroes Universe*, and *Alice Unbound: Beyond Wonderland.*

STEEL DRAGONS OF A LUMINOUS SKY

Brian Trent

Li Yan, Brigade Commander of the National Revolutionary Army and secret lieutenant of the Luminous Sky, spat into his goggles, wiped the lenses, and refitted them over his eyes to watch the qilin galloping up from the beach towards Qiantang River Bridge. Its red eyes burned holes in the choking smoke, and more red lay behind it: the crackling sampan villages and embers of Hangzhou Bay were like fireflies in the air.

The American pilot, Eva Eagels, tracked the galloping shape with her pistol. "I see it," she muttered. "That one of ours, Li?"

Li winced as another Japanese shell exploded overhead. "It's Chinese," he answered evasively.

"Well I hope it swallowed something useful," Eva said, lowering her weapon. "Otherwise we're in shitcreak without a paddle."

He regarded the chestnut-haired aviatrix beside him, her face streaked in soot, her knuckles white around her trusty M1911, and her alert gaze studying the hellfire rolling up from the beach. "That passes for a proverb in the West?" he asked.

She opened her mouth to reply when another explosion rocked the darkness, showering them with sand. Against the red fires, the giant robots descended like old gods returned. They resembled samurai. Blue-hot plumes of flame fanned from their boots, controlling their terrible descent towards the beach. Li supposed their construction had as much to do with Japanese tradition as with psychological warfare. Even as murky silhouettes they cut a nightmarish sight—twenty-foot-tall machines in the shape of men, overlapping steel scales cladding their frames, and the decorative *kabuto* they had for heads displaying curling horns like prehistoric monsters. Their appearance conjured not-quite-vestigial memories, too, of wood-block paintings Li had seen showing past invasions of China… the ruthless hordes of Genghis pouring through the Great Wall.

In the predawn gloom the Japanese navy had arrived and quickly reduced the defenders' junks to smoldering flotsam on the bay. Next the turrets had turned their attention on the beach defenses themselves. Only then had the actual invasion begun, not as troops from the sea or battalions from the land, but machines dropping down from the sky…

Li craned his neck to heavens. Stars and moon were lost behind the pall of diesel fires and gunpowder, but he wasn't interested in such lofty things anyway. His eyes scanned for the ominous shadow of Tengu Castle, floating high and terrible above Shanghai.

"Li!" Eva tugged at him. "Here it comes!"

He glanced back to the beach. The qilin was nearly at Qiantang River Bridge, weaving around what remained of the barbed wire and cointets. Its movements were gyroscopic, hips snapping fast adjustments as it avoided debris, bodies, and descending robots. Those flaring eyes spotted him where he crouched on the hilltop, and then the qilin leapt full onto the ancient bridge.

One of the hovering robots shot a spotlight onto the fleeing creature.

"Run, boy!" Eva cried.

The stuttering muzzle flash of Gatling-guns illuminated the

miasma.

Qiantang River Bridge had spanned the river for a hundred years; now it shredded into sawdust around the weaving, galloping qilin.

For an instant, Li thought the machine had been obliterated. Then his heart lifted as it darted out of the sawdust-haze and scrambled up the hill towards him. The hilltop was thumped by shrieking 50-caliber rounds, forcing Li and Eva to duck. The qilin leaped the hillcrest, soaring over Li's head; he had a view of its smooth steel chassis, the actuators and steel coils throbbing wildly. Then it landed nimbly in the reedy wetland below them, turning its vaguely lion-like head to regard Li expectantly.

Li tugged at the American. "We can leave now!"

She scrambled up and ran towards her Fiat CR.32, which waited where she'd landed hours ago like a patient bird on the high banks opposite them.

"Eva, no! Not that way!"

The pilot had taken two steps towards the embankment when suddenly a shell screamed past them and struck the plane. The detonation of fuel tanks blew her, Li, and the qilin backwards, and all went dark.

When Li came to, he was being dragged by his boot through the muddy banks of the bay. Flies swarmed around him, attracted by his sweat. The qilin, dutifully pulling him out of harm's way, left him by the water's edge and then eagerly sprinted back to fetch Eva; a moment later she came jogging alongside it, a dark expression on her face. The qilin's leonine countenance remained fixed in a serrated grin, its scarlet eyes swiveling in their rubber sockets to regard the Japanese navy filling the bay.

"Eva, you're alive!" Li said stupidly, and for a moment his eyes moistened. He thought he'd spent all tears at the loss of Shanghai's beach perimeter. The surge of emotion made him appreciate that the war wasn't over yet, even if Shanghai had fallen.

Don't let the war deaden you.

The words from his eldest brother Qimei came back to him. Growing up in a small household, Li had always idolized his brother, seeing in Qimei everything he wanted to be: Handsome, confident, courageous. It was hero worship as well as brotherly adoration, and Li's enlistment had as much to do with his brother's short-lived military career as with the need to defend China herself.

The night Li was to ship out to Shanghai, his brother embraced him on their bamboo porch and whispered the hard-earned advice: *I've seen how war can deaden a person, little brother. I've seen men transformed into shambling husks, as if the horrors of battle had killed their spirit. Promise me that won't happen to you, Li. Don't lose your smile, even if you must hide it at times.*

"You're alive," Li told Eva again, and he nodded. "I thought..."

If Eva noticed his tears, she pretended not to so he could save face. Against the clouds and fiery bay, she was as wild-eyed as the demon empress herself, black hair a tangled mass about her face. Another woodblock flashed into Li's mind: a female hungry ghost, escaped from one of the Eight Hells to feast on the living of *zhonguo*.

"They blew up my *Damsel!*" the American raged. "Just get me some replacement wings, Li, and I'll take back the skies, gun chattering like the doomed brothers in *Hell's Angels.*" She glared and jabbed a finger towards the qilin. "I hope this *thing* was worth it, goddamn it all!"

Li squatted in the mud. "Qilin, what did you find?"

The machine sat back on its haunches with a wheezing squeal like rusted door hinges. It bowed its head, jaws swiveling open, like a dog bringing back a bone. It disgorged something from its throat and then looked at them expectantly.

The qilin were designed for battlefield reconnaissance and delivery of supplies. While not combatants, they were designed to do whatever was necessary to obtain things their sensors deemed worthwhile.

Li blinked.

The thing the machine had disgorged was a young Chinese woman.

For perhaps half a minute, Li stared, trying to accept what he was seeing. He wondered if the qilin had gone berserk, abducting some poor peasant from the rice paddies.

Eva peered over his shoulder. "Who the hell is she?"

The woman was unconscious. She looked young, slender, almost frail, with delicate bone structure suggesting noble stock. She also wore a peculiar amulet tightly around her neck.

"Assist me, please," Li said, taking the sleeping woman by the arms.

"Why?"

"If we leave her here, she'll be taken as a comfort woman for the Japanese."

Together, they bore the mystery woman towards the water. "But why did the qilin grab *her?*"

It was a good question. Li mulled over the last orders he'd been given from his superiors: Find the qilin and recover its catch. It has something from the Luminous Sky for the war effort.

At the water's edge, Li fidgeted with his ring.

Something from the Luminous Sky for the war effort…

He checked his ring, made sure the jade dragon sigil was facing east. Then he held it over the girl's face and squeezed the ring.

Pale, fuzzy light sprang from the dragon and rippled over her face.

"It's a girl, Li," Eva chided. "You really need a flashlight to tell?"

Ignoring this, he directed the light to the unconscious woman's forehead. Golden calligraphy materialized under the beam, and Li gasped.

Luminous Sky!

She was Luminous Sky, just as he was!

For a moment he forgot about the invading robots and the loss of Shanghai's defenses along beach and bay. The Luminous Sky was *not* destroyed! There were others! Others besides *him*...

A top-secret agency, formed after the First Sino-Japanese War, the Luminous Sky was tasked with defending the Middle Kingdom. Even in a country torn apart by tribal loyalties—local warlords tangling with Nationalists, Communists, dieselmages and Manchus—the Luminous Sky represented something all could agree on: the nation must be defended against the rising specter of the Rising Sun. Its top agents were known as "steel dragons."

Li scooped the girl back into his arms and waded out into the bay, keeping her head safely above the debris-strewn water. Eva splashed in behind him.

"Where the hell are we going, Li? Gonna walk to Sidney?"

He halted at an unsightly pile of flotsam. Tangled beams, netting, and planks of ruined sampans floated unceremoniously on the water.

With his free hand, Li reached under one of the lacquered beams and found the secret knob. He twisted it.

Unseen pneumatic levers hissed. The water began to froth. The wreckage lifted up, like a weary animal, exposing a deep, dry gullet.

"Inside!" he said. "Quickly, Eva!"

Once within the secret, water-tight compartment, Li flicked the propeller switch, and the flotsam began drifting through the sizzling, fiery bay. Pushing out into the Sea of Japan.

Leaving China in flames behind us, he thought.

"I've heard of junks before," Eva said, hunkered down in the depths of the secret watercraft. "But this is ridiculous, Li."

The interior of the vessel was little better than a cramped, damp closet. Li hunched over the mystery woman, emptying some of his canteen onto a cloth and rubbing it over her lips. She came awake slowly. Li helped her drink, squeezing the cloth into her mouth. She sat up, wary of the low ceiling, and blinked dazedly in the gloom of the single wall-lantern.

"*You are safe for now,*" he told her, speaking in Mandarin.

She nodded dreamily.

"*I am Li Yan, Brigade Commander of the National Revolutionary Army,*" he said, and then, quieter even though the American couldn't speak a word of Chinese, he said, "*I am also a Steel Dragon lieutenant of the Luminous Sky.*"

There. Her eyes glimmered in reaction to this. She glanced to the qilin which sat obediently beside them, its red eyes attentive.

"*My name is Xin,*" she said at last.

She had a soft accent, vaguely Northern. Her skin, too, was ruddy, red-tinged; product of that cold country where even rice refused to grow and life was hard.

"Say," Eva interrupted, "You got a drink in this tub, Li? Hell, I'll even settle for some of that cheap local beer."

Ignoring this, Li helped Xin drink more from the canteen. The woman was fully awake now, and she drew herself into one cramped corner beside the qilin.

"*I was sent to recover you,*" Li explained, hoping she could shed some light on the next stage of the mission. "*The Luminous Sky also provided this craft…*"

The woman studied Li's face. She turned next to Eva. Now that she was awake, there was something harsh about her gaze—something dangerous and bright, like tempered steel in the gloom.

Finally, she said, "*The steel dragons were being sent to the front. Our cars were converging well out of range of the Japanese naval guns…*" Her eyes narrowed. "*Or so we thought. As the last car came around the bend there was an explosion. We had been fired on from above—those robots were already coming down from Tengu Castle. I pulled myself out of the flaming wreck, and the next thing I remember was the screeching whine of their .50-caliber bullets all around me, and then…*" She patted the qilin's metallic paw appreciatively.

"Glad to see we're all friends," Eva observed, pulling off her leather flying cap. She shook free her chestnut curls. "Li, you know I don't speak a lick of Chinese. Care to fill me in on what's going on?"

"She is Luminous Sky."

"Great! Except that *you're* Luminous Sky, too, and you didn't exactly save the day out there, you know?"

Li blinked. How did Eva know his secret allegiance? The American had never shown any indication that she understood Mandarin. Had the National Revolutionary Army seen fit to advise his Flying Tiger associate who he really was?

He was still wrestling with that when, in perfect English, Xin added her voice to the conversation. "The Japanese invasion is being controlled by Tengu Castle," she said.

Eva sighed. "Not exactly news, sister."

"The Luminous Sky was sending its steel dragons—its highest agents—to infiltrate the castle and end the invasion."

"*What?*"

But Li felt a smile twitch at his lips, a smile born of desperate hope. The mysterious Luminous Sky, always inventive, always operating in the shadows. He believed in them. While the in-fighting of China's political factions had left the land vulnerable to attack, the Luminous Sky always operated in the service of the Mandate of Heaven.

After all, what was the mantra of the Luminous Sky?

All Under Heaven.

It was the ancient dream of a unified world. A world in which peace was not a dream of poets but a daily, irrevocable reality. A world without borders. A world of one government, one law, one purpose.

Eva scoffed. "Tengu Castle is thousands of feet above us! Li, what's going on here? People say the Luminous Sky is crazy, and I'm starting to believe—"

Xin stood so swiftly, so suddenly, that Eva reached for her Colt. The Luminous Sky agent strode to a section of the wall and pried open a hatch Li hadn't known was there.

"The Luminous Sky wishes to reach Tengu Castle," Xin said. She reached into the hatch and suddenly, the junk began to rumble, exactly as if hidden engines were whirring to life. "Therefore, we shall reach Tengu Castle."

Li felt the junk lift up from the water. He and Eva exchanged an astonished look.

Outside, a black balloon had snapped open from hidden compartments. The core of the junk was listing into the air like a newborn cicada crawling out of its terrestrial shell and climbing into the night sky.

Xin smiled, and switching back to her vaguely-accented Mandarin, said, "*All Under Heaven, Li.*"

It was called the Lantern, Xin told them.

Eva grumbled. She drew open the junk's door, revealing a sea of clouds around them and the fires of China glowing far, far below. The wind immediately leapt in through the opening, biting them all with icy fangs.

They had ascended above the fog of war into the clouds themselves, until it seemed they were skating along on a wispy sea. The starry firmament turned this dreamlike horizon into quicksilver, and the Lantern—born aloft by its ebony-colored balloon—glistened like a sea creature peeking up from the depths to consider the wonder of the firmament.

Eva pointed across the sea of clouds to a distant black shape floating perhaps ten thousand yards off. It looked like the tip of an island jutting up from a misty sea.

"Is that the castle?" she asked.

Xin nodded.

Eva gave a savage grin. "Know what a balloon buster is, sister? Every flying ace worth her salt knows how to look for observation balloons and shoot them out of the sky. Its standard protocol: knock out the enemy's eyes. You think the Japs are any different? If we don't reach the castle before the sun comes up, we'll be a big black target hanging against the dawn sky."

"We will reach the castle," Xin said simply.

"By being at the mercy of the wind?"

"Are we?"

Li closed his eyes in the silence that followed and listened. Then he smiled for the second time that day. The Lantern was *not* beholden to the wind. He could hear the whir of propellers beneath them, pushing them straight towards the flying castle of their enemy.

But Eva slammed the hatch door shut and said, "Li, get that idiotic grin off your face! Have you ever met this dame before? How do you know she's not a spy for the enemy? Maybe this is their plan: scoop up the last Luminous Sky—*you*—and bring him to the castle on a silver platter?"

His smile slipped a little. "She has the Luminous Sky mark..."

"I have a skull tattoo on my arm. That doesn't make me a bone doctor. You're betting our lives on blind faith!"

The blind faith of his brother, Li thought. Qimei had spoken with unflinching worship of the Luminous Sky. He was a true believer, and therefore Li had been one too... enough of a believer to seek the group out and pledge himself to their cause.

Still, some of what the American was saying snuck through Li's certainty, and he gazed at Xin with a sudden flash of paranoia.

Come to think of it, she didn't look especially Chinese. Not a Han, at any rate...

"You are from the American regiment," Xin said to Eva.

"That's right," the aviatrix replied, not appreciating the subject change. "The Flying Tigers. We're not here in an official capacity, but our President knows it's only a matter of time before we get drawn into the war. Besides, can't have our Chinese brothers and sisters falling before the Jap war machine. So we get a paycheck and open license to fight."

"So you're mercenaries?"

Eva stiffened. "We get paid, sure, but that don't mean we don't believe in this. And no salad would make me work for the enemy."

Li sighed and, switching to Chinese, said to Xin, "*Salad, an American euphemism for—*"

"Greenbacks," Xin answered swiftly in English. "I spent a year studying in Chicago."

He was startled. "The Luminous Sky sent you to America?"

"And to Paris the year before. And Berlin in '34."

"You speak all those languages?"

Xin smiled politely. "My mother called me 'Bird of a Thousand Songs.'"

Eva said scornfully, "That's terrific, sister. But let's keep on target here: how does reaching Tengu Castle end the invasion? Is your intention to somehow take control of the robots by using the Jap transmission tower? That's crap. You'd need the security codes!"

"The Luminous Sky has figured out a way to bypass the codes." Before the aviatrix could retort, Xin continued: "Control radiates out from the castle's tower, yes. Your America uses the same technique to control its Minutemen robots, broadcasting control signals from the Statue of Liberty. Paris utilizes the Eiffel Tower to control her *soldats en acier*. Switzerland, Britain, Spain, they all follow this model. Even Mussolini has control towers jutting like needles from the Pantheon's dome." She went silent for a moment, losing herself in a faraway land of contemplation. "And of course, Japan prefers its own method of '*hakkō ichiu*' to be mobile and aerial: Tengu Castle. If we can wrest control of the tower, we control its robots. We end the war."

Eva made a disgusted sound. "American technicians have tried inventing an override signal for years. You're saying that your secret little band has done something no Western nation could manage?"

"Well we did invent paper before you," Xin replied softly.

Li choked back a laugh.

Eva didn't smile, but she began to clean her pistol, rubbing a rag across the brown grip and iron sights in loving strokes.

"Look, if you think you can override the robots, that's swell. Just tell me what you need me to do."

"We may encounter resistance once we're at the castle," Xin said. "I shall need you to watch my back."

By way of answering, Eva cocked the Colt's hammer and grinned.

The Lantern crossed the airy gulf to Tengu Castle and now, only a hundred meters away, Li saw what distance had hidden before: sleek black shapes moving around the castle like the sharks he'd once seen while pearl-diving; ominous shapes hanging above him in the murky water. These shapes were black, nearly invisible and betrayed only by the winking of starlight around them as they made their lofty patrols.

"It's a dragonboat fleet," he breathed, and he looked to Xin for signs that the Luminous Sky had anticipated this.

Or for signs of treachery in her face, he thought. The American's doubts were growing like a toxic seed in his own mind. What if this was all a trap?

Eva had donned her flying cap and scarf again, out of habit, perhaps, or a pilot's superstition that they had talismanic powers of protection beyond simply protecting her from the chilling wind. "If we'd *flown* up here…"

"Even the best flying ace would have attracted the Japanese dragonboats' attention," Li finished for her. "It looks like the entire invasion force, aside from what they sent to soften the beach and bay."

Soften, he thought bitterly. *Now I know I'm a military man. Thousands of my countrymen have been 'softened,' and in the summer heat their dead bodies will grow soft indeed.*

The Lantern tilted backwards slightly, like a rickshaw drawn by an over-eager driver. They were bearing down on Tengu Castle now, slipping silently past the dragonboats in the predawn darkness. Snow glittered on the curving tenchu-style castle roof.

Sure enough, a transmission tower stood out from the uppermost roof like a mighty acupuncture needle. Xin lifted a hatch and pulled out a length of black rope-ladder, which she dropped over the Lantern's side and let unroll below them. "I'll go first, with Li behind me. Eva, I'm switching the Lantern over to manual control. While we're down there, you steady her until I can plant the override device and get back."

"I'm a Flying Tiger," Eva snapped, "Not a glorified balloon mistress!"

"Since we're fresh out of glorified balloon mistresses," Xin said crisply, "You'll have to do."

Li helped her clamber down the rope ladder while the American went to the manual wall-controls. The shingled rooftop was only meters below them. He was relieved to see the absence of guards; the thin, cold air precluded them from being stationed outside.

He followed Xin down the twisting ladder. The Lantern's propeller chassis fought against the wind; Eva fought to steady them.

When Xin reached the rooftop, she slipped on the icy surface; Li caught and steadied her. Snow like confectioner's sugar spilled off the shingles and fell, in dream-like slowness, to the roiling ocean of clouds.

"All Under Heaven," he said with a smile.

He expected she might grin at the small joke. Instead, she peered into his face, as if trying to read lines on an oracle bone.

"Do you believe in it?" she asked pointedly.

"Of course," he said defensively.

"I wonder how many do? China has returned to the Warring States period; it is all chaos. The foreign devils merely compound an underlying fracture." She fingered her amulet and craned her neck to regard the transmission tower, the blinking lights reflected in her eyes.

She took a step towards the tower. Li watched her go.

It seemed that someone punched him from behind, a sharp blow to his kidney. The snow in front of him splashed red, resembling the Imperial Japanese flag with its streaks of crimson lines.

"Xin!" he screamed—tried to scream—but a second bullet slammed into him. He pitched forward, lost his footing on the ice, and rolled to the edge of the shingles. He stopped just short of tumbling off the rooftop altogether.

From this angle, he could see Xin climbing the tower like a cautious spider ascending a weathervane.

Then he heard snow crunching under boots. His body was suddenly sluggish, and he could feel numbness spreading along his limbs. He managed to lift his head, staring up into the eyes…

…of Eva.

For a moment, all he could do was stare uncomprehendingly. Above her, the Lantern spun in a neat circle, like a balloon caught in a strange combination of drafts so that it rotated around and around, listing dangerously but going nowhere.

"You…" he began. "You were… my friend!"

Eva clucked her tongue. "We've known each other a goddamn week. You set a low bar for friendship. Now…" She turned and aimed her Colt at Xin on the tower.

"No!" Li pleaded. "Please don't!"

"Don't what, Li?" Eva cooed. "Don't conclude my deal with Hirohito and be made a rich lady with a fleet of planes under my command and my own palace in the Orient?"

Xin was a tiny figure now, a delicate creature, only two-thirds of the way up now.

So close…

"You're not with the Americans?" Li asked Eva, trying to stall her.

"Remember what Odysseus told the Cyclops? 'I am Noman.' Same with Captain Nemo, whose very name means 'no man,' beholden to no country, no people. Well, that's me!" The woman flashed a smile that was so warm, so brilliant and full of charm, that for an instant Li was half-convinced this was all some sort of joke: the blood on his back, the pain he felt, the spreading numbness, this was some silly prank, and all would be well, Xin *would* reach the top of the tower… she was only *six meters* from the zenith now!

"But no one can be that selfish!" Li whispered. "Why would you betray all of us?"

"Salad," Eva replied, laughing. She had removed her leather flying cap while in the Lantern, and now her chestnut curls flailed wildly around her head. "You're a Nationalist, Li. But there are other factions in China who were willing to parley with the Japanese, just to see your side defeated. They struck a deal with the emperor and prime minister. The best part? I get paid in triplicate. China, America, and Japan."

Li began to mount another stalling effort, but Eva shushed him.

"Want to see me slay a Steel Dragon?" the aviatrix purred, and she inched the pistol's sights higher, turned the barrel slightly into the wind, and fired at Xin.

She missed! he thought, hoped, prayed.

But she hadn't missed.

Xin was only two meters from the top of the needle, now, but something was wrong. She was no longer climbing. She was clutching the steel rungs as if she had fallen asleep there. A dark stain began to spread from the center of her back.

"What was that thing she kept saying?" Eva asked, aiming the muzzle a fraction of an inch higher. "What was it, Li?"

Li squinted at the Lantern spinning above them. "All…"

"All Under Heaven!" Eva laughed. "Watch me send your Luminous Sky friend straight to hell."

She closed one eye and steadied her aim. For a moment, it seemed to Li that she actually *was* summoning hell itself, for the aviatrix was suddenly aglow in fierce, crimson light from no discernable source.

Then Li saw that something was leaping out of the Lantern's hatch, dropping down upon them. Something with burning red eyes…

The qilin landed against Eva and knocked her sprawling. Whatever else she was—traitor, villain, spy—she was also as agile as a cat; she rolled over backwards, avoided a lunge from the beast's steel jaws, and fired point-blank into one of its eyes.

Sparks exploded, wires hissed like a nest of vipers. The qilin lunged again, head-butting her and driving the wind from her lungs. With only one scarlet eye functioning, it clamped its jaws down on her pistol-hand. Eva' eyes bulged and her mouth stretched into a howling scream as she squeezed off more rounds into the creature's metal throat.

Then the qilin wrenched its head sideways. Eva's hand came away.

Li pulled himself to his feet. He looked towards Xin. She was barely hanging onto the tower's rungs. Her tunic was sodden with blood, yet he watched her pull herself up another rung.

One meter from the top now.

The qilin lunged again. Even wounded, Eva proved her agility; she nimbly sidestepped the beast, drew a smaller, concealed pistol from her jacket with her left hand, and aimed. The beast slid on the icy roof, turned to face her.

She fired into its other eye.

The qilin shook its head, wires dangling, smoke gushing from its ruined sockets. Still, it lunged for her, striking out at the last place it had seen her.

"To the right!" Li cried—but his voice wouldn't come. He collapsed, the strength leeching out of his limbs. He fell to his knees in the snow.

Eva tossed her last pistol to the roof's edge. The qilin leaped at the sound, lost its footing, and slid to within an inch of the last row of shingles. The aviatrix hurled herself into it, giving the needed push to send it rolling off into the endless sky. She laughed as it fell out of view.

Summoning his very last vestige of strength, Li held up his hand, palm-out to Eva. The hand with the ring from the Luminous Sky. The dragon sigil was still facing east.

He rotated it so it was gazing north.

In that same moment, Eva turned to face him.

Li squeezed the ring.

Light sprang from the sigil, only it wasn't the soft revealing beam he'd used to identify Xin. This was a golden lance that shot forward, hitting Eva squarely in her face. She shrieked wildly, and suddenly the air stank of burning flesh.

When the light went out, Eva was a half-melted, blinded thing. She flailed in a tight dance of agony, arms lashing out for him. Her boots slipped on the ice. She tumbled away, cursing wordlessly, and vanished after the qilin.

Li let out a satisfied sigh. His arm fell to his side. He tried to turn his head to see how Xin was progressing, but now his sight was failing, graying at the edges, and finally, turning dark.

In that private darkness, he heard his eldest brother's voice:

Don't lose your smile, Li, even if you must hide it at times.

Li smiled, and with that smile, he died.

Xin pulled the medallion off her neck and, with the last of her strength, she slapped it against the tower antenna. The wind bit and shook her. Her hands were numb.

Below her, the rooftop door flung open, and the first of seemingly endless Japanese troops scrambled onto the snow like ants emerging for war. They fanned out, found Li's body. One soldier spotted her, and every rifle swung in her direction.

In the howling gale, she never heard the bullets.

Bloodied, entwined into the antenna like a crumpled flag, she grinned much as Li's corpse was grinning below her.

All Under Heaven, she thought.

It was a Chinese concept that world peace was only possible when the divided countries of the world were united under a single banner. But China had failed miserably. War-torn Europe had failed. The Middle East, the Americas… all were squabbling barbarian states. None of them were deserving of the Mandate. None of *them* could bring about a unified world.

Only one empire had come close, *so close*, to achieving the global conquest. To achieving peace.

Xin fell from the tower, hitting the rooftop with a sickening collapse of bones. Her body slid along the shingles; a soldier reached for her but missed, and a moment later she was tumbling down from the sky and into the clouds.

The tower began broadcasting its secret signal, freezing the Japanese robots on the shore, yes, but also rippling out, nabbing every other communication tower from the Eiffel to the Statue of Liberty, bringing all under one control, one command…

Xin tumbled down to the ocean, weeping in joy.

One world, united, *under the Yassa of a resurrected Mongolian Empire.*

Love live the Great Khan, she thought, and even as she died, robotic feet all across the world marched to a new pulse.

Brian Trent is the author of the sci-fi novel *Ten Thousand Thunders* (published in 2018 by Flame Tree Press), and the *Rahotep* dark fantasy series. His contribution to *Grimm, Grit and Gasoline* is an original tale that explores dieselpunk in a deliberately non-western setting, mixing in fairy tale elements from ancient Chinese and Japanese traditions. His short fiction regularly appears in the world's top markets, including *Analog, Fantasy & Science Fiction, Orson Scott Card's Intergalactic Medicine Show, Terraform, Daily Science Fiction, The Year's Best Military and Adventure SF,*

Escape Pod, Pseudopod, Galaxy's Edge, Nature, and more. A Writers of the Future winner and contributing author to Baen Books anthologies, Trent lives in a foggy mountaintop town in New England. His website is www.briantrent.com.

RAMPS AND ROCKET

Alicia K. Anderson

When the lunch whistle screamed through the factory air, everyone grabbed silver lunchboxes and thermoses, and found a spot in the shade outside. There, they waited for the weaver to cut off her machine, belching diesel fumes and rattling to a halt. The machines were dirty, heavy, and ugly. But the fluttering parachute fabric on the weave was as light and strong as spider silk.

Weaver settled into place, using her black and red bandana to wipe the sweat from between the deep wrinkles on her forehead, the wrinkles like vertical slashes down her cheeks. Everyone passed some bit of their lunch to the weaver, as payment for the story.

"Have you ever heard the story of Rampion?" the weaver said, taking a quarter of an apple from the person beside her.

"Like the salad?" Bertel asked as someone passed a chocolate chip cookie around the circle toward the storyteller.

The old woman's laugh sounded like rusted gears in the back of her throat. "Like the salad, but this is a story about a girl named Rampion."

You see, when her ma was wide and heavy with the baby, she got cravings. Cravings so bad her pa couldn't do anything about them.

She wanted rocket. She wanted rampion roots. She wanted spicy, tasty leaves without the dressing. This lady was hungry for the best salad. The most expensive salad. And the thing is, her husband worked in a place like this one. He couldn't afford rocket or ramps—he could barely afford a carrot.

But you know how cravings go. You know how hard they hurt, and how much that baby twists up a mama's belly wanting that thing that will make them healthy and strong.

They lived in a tiny apartment way up on the ninth floor. And no elevators in that building. No air conditioning. The ma would sit out on her fire escape, nine stories above the world, and she watched an old lady tend a garden in the vacant lot next door. The lady—name of Gothel—slipped under broken fence slats and kept the garden hidden from the neighbors, but it was there. And nine stories up, the woman could tell that the old lady grew salad greens that made her baby twist and kick.

"Go steal me some of Gothel's greens," the ma told the pa, pulling him out onto the fire escape. "Just pick a little bit from each plant, she'll never notice."

The pa hemmed and hawed and he shuffled his toes. Finally, he gave in, because he didn't love anything as much as he loved that woman. So down he went, down nine flights of stairs in the pitch black of night. He slid through the broken fence slat, and he filled up his hat with greens.

That lady made the biggest salad of ramps and rocket you've ever seen. She munched and crunched and ate 'til the baby fell asleep inside her. But the baby wasn't done with those salads. The next night, the baby twisted and kicked, and the ma asked pa to go back down to Gothel's garden. He didn't even fight her that time, those greens had made her so happy. He went down the nine flights of stairs and slipped through the broken fence, and he stole another hatful of rampion.

You know this happened a third time. And you know that the

man did it even though he knew that the third time is always when you get caught. And sure enough, there was Gothel with a revolver and a mean look waiting for him to come fill up his hat with her greens.

While he stood with his hands in the air, his wife shouted out the window nine floors above. Her water had broke. She could feel the baby rushing out, ready to breathe the air.

"I'll do anything to make it up to you!" he cried, looking back and forth between the window nine stories up and the gleaming silver tip of the gun pointed at his chest.

"Give me the baby, then," the old woman said, gesturing with the revolver. "I'll help her deliver, and I get the child." Afraid for his life, the man agreed.

Ma thought Gothel was just a midwife, not a thief come to steal her baby as payment for a few hats of salad. She beat at her husband's shoulders and chest as he held her when the old lady walked out with her baby girl.

Gothel named the baby Rampion. Now, that old lady didn't live anywhere near that vacant lot where she kept her garden. She had them all over town, secret and tempting the poor people in the area, making them owe her favors. Some called her a witch but nobody really knows for sure. We do know she owned a tall, smoky factory that made the bits and knobs used on dashboards of automobiles and airplanes.

Baby Rampion didn't stay a baby forever, she became a girl, then a young lady, and then a full-grown woman, all under the careful, glittering black eyes of old Gothel. Weird thing was, Rampion grew up while old lady Gothel didn't age a day. She should have been dust—older than me to begin with, you see?

Rampion had pretty, gold-blond hair like her ma, and a tall, athletic build like her pa, and she didn't know anything of the outside world without it going through Gothel first. Rampion wore that hair up in a tight knot—so tight it pulled her eyelids open a bit.

And she only ever let it down for Gothel to brush it right before bedtime. Her cleaning lady told the barkeep at the tavern down the way that Gothel never threw Rampion's hair away—not a single strand of it. She had a whole drawer full of the soft gold stuff that she hoarded like a secret. Maybe it was what kept her from aging. Nobody knows.

Rampion was a good foreman on the floor of Gothel's factory. The people making knobs and dials all respected her, and worked to make her happy. It was like a bonus paycheck to make her nod in approval at their work and they poured blistering hot celluloid, blew glass and stoked fires, all for the hope of seeing her smile.

On the twenty-first of June—oh about forty, fifty years ago this was—on the hottest, longest day of the summer, the roar of a new kind of engine filled the air in the parking lot below the factory windows. Rampion peered through the smoke-tinted glass as a strange, long kind of motorcycle roared up to the door at the docks. She pressed her cheek against the pane to watch as the rider pulled long levers and turned a heavy knob. The driver gave a mighty heave one of one final lever and the wheel at the front of the motorcycle drew back to beside the seat, and the seat itself twisted to the side. Where before the driver had straddled the bike, the seat was now a bench, and most of the engine rumbled between its wide rubber wheels. Smaller front wheels poked out and the motor relaxed to a dull putter as the black-jacketed rider steered what had become a wheelchair up the ramp and into the hiring office on the ground floor.

Day after day Rampion watched this transformation until she knew the sound of the rapid-fire of the twin exhaust pipes, the purr and hum of the motorbike becoming a chair and even the wavy head of black-brown hair that hid beneath a leather helmet. She even knew exactly which department had hired on the rider, because the chair's unique hum could be heard alongside the familiar sounds of the welder's end of the metallurgy floor.

If the supervisor on the metallurgy floor noticed that Rampion was spending more time in his unit, he didn't say it. If anyone *had* mentioned it, Rampion would not be able to say what it was that fascinated her about the woman. She would be able to describe her cheekbones under the goggles, or the way her gloved hands handled the tools. But she had no idea what she felt. She had no words for it.

There were good, strong elevators running up and down the spine of the factory. The welder Rampion was so intrigued by was not the only one in a pneumatic chair. There were ramps and lifts all over the place for people who had good brains and strong hands. But that welder was the only one who didn't wheel in off the city bus. That welder was freer than anyone Rampion had ever met, and it scared and elated her to close her eyes and imagine straddling the back of that motorbike and going—somewhere. Anywhere.

Weeks went on. And no word passed between them. But it ended after those weeks when old Gothel was brushing Rampion's hair and caught the girl smiling.

"You are daydreaming again." The old lady pulled hard at the hair at Rampion's neck, and demanded every thought, every wish, every dream. Poor Rampion was a prisoner inside her own head just as much as she was inside the tower of the factory but watching that old motorcycle had made her sly and thinking about the wind in her face made her brave.

"Just thinking about the way the sunlight slants on the rows and rows of glass meter-shields early in the morning." The lie was bold. But the old lady swallowed it. "And the little green and red light-caps, how they glow when the light hits them just right."

Gothel cleaned the hair out of the brush, tucked it safe in her pocket—patting it a bit for safekeeping—and sent Rampion to bed as if she were still a child. Rampion laid quietly on her crisp white sheets and stared at the ceiling, floating on a sea of triumph. That was the very first time she had lied to Gothel, you see. She had kept a daydream to herself!

Spurred on by her success, Rampion ventured deeper onto the metallurgy floor the following morning. The supervisor was not there yet, but several smiths and welders had already punched their cards, including the one who rode the interesting motorbike. As she edged her way closer to the work area, the welder cut off the bright blue flame on the torch. Broad shoulders straightened up, and a gloved hand dropped down to bump the wheelchair away from the welds. The same hand lifted the googles.

Rampion gasped at the loveliness of the face that appeared before her. Wide, lash-lined hazel eyes blinked at her from over freckled cheeks carved by the grooved by the goggles.

"Good morning." The welder woman's voice was deeper than Rampion expected it to be, a little raspy, like it wasn't often used. Her smile was more like a wolf baring her straight, white teeth. The eyes were too wary to smile.

Rampion gazed at the woman in the welder's gear and listened to the hum of the wheelchair. "Good morning."

A handful of silent heartbeats passed between them. Blue eyes gazing into hazel full of questions and longing, and no words for either. Embarrassed by her stupidity, by her lack of words, Rampion turned on her heel and walked away. She spent the rest of the day pacing the glassworking floor. She was angry and impatient with herself, but she didn't have words for that, either.

"You're in a foul mood today," Gothel said as she untwisted the thick rope of Rampion's braid from the bun.

"I have a headache," Rampion lied. When the old woman left her chamber for the evening, Rampion took out a scrap of letterhead and a small stub of a pencil. She had no possessions, nothing of her own. Everything belonged to the factory or to Gothel, even her hairbrush.

She sat, trying to scratch something on that paper with that lead for five full minutes. Then she hid the page again, hid the pencil, and went to sleep.

The next morning, Rampion rehearsed what she would say as she waited for the welder to finish the piece she was working on.

"Good morning." Those eyes looked up at her again, searching, waiting.

"My name is Rampion." It was a foolish beginning. She was a foreman at the company, everyone knew who she was. Foolish, but at least it was a beginning. She stuck out her right hand.

"They call me Rocket." The welder bared her sweaty hand before holding it out. The warm, wet palm against hers gave Rampion the shivers.

"Pleased to meet you," she stammered. It's a wonder she could talk at all.

"Likewise." This time Rocket smiled for real, all the way up to her eyes. Rampion's breath panted out of her nose, and her skin flushed red and hot. "Do you need something?"

Rampion—poor Rampion—she wanted to ask for anything. Everything. Her emotions were loud inside her.

"There you are, Rampion!" Gothel shouted across metallurgy. "Finish writing up that welder. Let's go."

After that, Gothel kept Rampion busy. She kept her so busy Rampion couldn't visit metallurgy at all for weeks. Gothel poked at the young woman's daydreams and her thoughts every night, pulling them out of her like the tangles in her hair.

Rampion never gave the old lady one bit of Rocket. She grew bolder and bolder with her lies even though she didn't know why she felt she *had* to lie to her. She just felt it *must* remain her secret.

Finally, after months of waiting, one morning Rampion slipped out of the factory doors, and waited in the parking court for Rocket to arrive.

"Hi, Rampion," Rocket shouted over the motor. She smiled—a full, real smile—and released her dense, dark hair from its little leather helmet. Rampion nearly had to sit down with all the feelings that made her feel.

"Hi!" She waved a little in case she couldn't be heard over the sputtering engine and watched up close how the levers and gears of the motorbike were pulled and pushed to create the motorized chair. The steaming steel animal engine of the motorbike grew quieter and more lethargic as it turned into a chair, the roar dulling to a humming whirr.

"Can I… help you with something?"

"You're the freest person I've ever seen." Rampion smacked her hand over her mouth after she said it.

She kept her hand there to hold the rest of her feelings in, heaved open the heavy steel door and let it slam shut. It is mean to let a door close on someone in a chair like that, but she didn't dare stay, you see. And she couldn't ever go back to metallurgy after that.

One night, late at night, when there was a full moon, Rampion couldn't sleep. She paced her little room at the top of the factory tower. She pulled out her blank piece of letterhead and the nub of the pencil. She wrote "I love you" on the blank page. Those words just sat there, bold as you please, on that paper. She stared at it for most of the night. And when the sky turned purple she stuck the paper and the pencil both in the incinerator shaft.

"Did she cry?" Bertel asked, leaning forward. Bertel's sandwich was half flopped open in her hand, a bit of salami threatening to drop to the ground.

Weaver shook her head. "Poor Ramps didn't know how to cry yet. She didn't truly know how to smile yet, neither. Not 'til a bright afternoon a few weeks later. One of those sunny days where all the dust lights up in the sunbeams."

Rampion was inspecting the cafeteria, frowning over her clipboard. She nearly leapt out of her skin when someone rolled up behind her and spoke.

"Rampion, you've got to let your hair down sometime, you know."

Rampion spun around. She touched the tight braided bun at her neck. Rocket was relaxed in her chair, her hair matted with sweat. Rampion wanted to run her fingers through it. She had never felt bolder in her life.

"I'll let my hair down if you take me for a ride." Her face was expressionless because there was no way for the fireworks of her emotions to appear all at once.

The smile spread across Rocket's face. "Tonight?"

"Tonight," Rampion said.

She had no idea what she was doing, how she was going to get away, but sometimes a little bit of magic happens. Just before the end of the first shift, a pencil got jammed in the incinerator. A massive rumble shook the whole tower. Smoke poured from the lowest levels of the building. Production was called to a halt.

Rampion edged her way through the flow of people shuffling through the parking lots to bus stops and automobiles. She couldn't see Rocket over the heads of everyone around her, but she could hear a familiar whirring hum. And she heard the roar of the chair converting into motorbike, coming to life, across the parking lot. She had never wanted anything so badly in her life.

Rocket held out the little leather helmet as a slim offering of safety.

"You have to take the bun out to wear it," Rocket said.

With her belly doing flippety flops, Rampion started pulling out hairpins. At first, she tried to save them, holding onto them neatly for the next day's use, but there were too many, and she didn't want a pocket full of hair pins. The tiny pieces of metal glinted as they fell on the parking lot and stuck in the warm tar, twinkling in the late afternoon light.

Her thick, golden braid tumbled down over her shoulder and reached her waist.

"The braid, too," Rocket demanded, her voice was husky over the motorbike's purr.

Maybe there were people standing at the bus stop who had turned to watch the show of Rampion's hair coming down. Maybe not. Rampion only knew Rocket was watching. Rampion only knew Rocket looked hungry. Rampion's fingers teased apart the chunks of her braid and loosed her entire bright mane to the fading sun. They stared at each other for a moment before Rampion had to smack her hand over her mouth again—this time to hold in a shout of fright and joy.

She took the helmet and popped it snugly around her ears, and before she could think of another reason why she ought to pause, she threw her leg over the back of the motorbike.

Rocket lowered a pair of dark sunglasses onto her nose and twisted one wrist to make the engine roar. It sounded lopsided, somehow and one tailpipe was guttering smoke. Rocket fiddled with throttles and knobs until the black smoke was the same on both sides. Rampion wrapped her arms around the other woman's waist. She could feel Rocket's strength and the hardness of the muscles under her leather jacket.

She let all that noise and joy out of herself when the motorcycle leapt forward onto the road. "Whoooooooop!"

The wind whipped her hair behind her like a bright banner. The exhaust pipes rattled and shook so loud it sounded like they were tearing the world apart behind them. Her thighs pressed against Rocket's and she could feel every place where their bodies touched. Pretending fear, Rampion hugged closer. She had never felt so alive. So free.

They wound around curves and over hills, through town and out again. They traced the zig-zag path up the forested hill to the west, and curled around the little lake that glinted against the sunset. They rode together until the last of twilight surrendered to stars.

Rocket stopped the motorbike on Overlook Ridge. The factory's tower was visible at the bottom of the hill.

"Do you want to go back?" Rocket asked.

"I—I have to." Didn't she have to?

But that's not what Rocket had asked, she'd asked if Rampion *wanted* to. And that answer was no. Not yet.

Rampion could smell Rocket's sweet breath. She could feel her soft cheek against her own. She thought about the slip of paper and the pencil that had burned up in the factory incinerator. And she leaned forward and kissed Rocket full on the mouth.

Remember how that first handshake had made her all weak and crazy? Well, lord. You could light up the whole town with the electricity from that kiss.

They sat together on the grass up there on the ridge, and they kissed and touched and talked until the moon moved across the sky. Rampion had never felt so alive.

Rocket was finger-combing the tangles out of Rampion's hair when she said they needed to go back to the tower. Rampion said she'd rather run away together, but Rocket said they didn't have anyplace to go. Not yet, at least.

Their trip back to the tower did not go as well as their escape. Old Gothel was standing in the parking court, right over the puddle of glimmering metal hairpins, and she was spitting mad. She grabbed poor Rampion by the hair and hauled her to the elevator, yelling and hollering the whole way.

Shouting things like "How dare you!" and "How could you!" Gothel took thick steel shears—like the kind we use for oilcloth—and she hacked at Rampion's golden hair. She tore at it and chopped, creating a jagged, messy puff of short-cropped yellow hairs surrounding Rampion's face.

"You are *mine*!" the old lady shouted. She kept all of the hair—every last strand—and locked Rampion in her room at the top of the tower.

There were only two or three hairpins in Rampion's pocket, few enough that she regretted the pile she'd left on the ground outside, but she sat by the door and worked at picking the lock with what she had.

Gothel waited for Rocket to be working at her welding station before she struck. She stood behind her and draped the ponytail of Rampion's hair over Rocket's shoulder. Rocket lifted her welding goggles, and turned to look at her lover. As she turned, Gothel kicked the fuel cannister on her blow torch, causing the flames to flash bright and too hot, blasting over the metalwork and blinding and burning Rocket.

When Rampion made it to the metallurgy floor, determined to run away, she found Rocket's chair resting at her station, empty. The workers beside Rocket's station described the medics who had arrived and carried her away, abandoning her chair behind them. No one knew where Gothel had gone.

Rampion steered the chair out into the parking lot. She had watched the process of converting from chair to motorbike so many times, she knew what to pull and where to push but, once she had a motorbike firmly between her legs, she realized she had no idea how to operate it.

Rampion took one glance back at the tower before she pushed the motorcycle toward the road. She had no idea how far she would have to walk. But Rocket needed her chair, and Rampion needed Rocket.

Blisters grew in her boots and along the edges of her palms on the cycle's handlebars. Sweat ran in a river down her back. Rampion cried as she walked. She sobbed and then she grew angry. Then she sobbed again. Rocket had taught her how to smile. Now, she had learned how to cry, too.

Strangers pointed her to the hospital, twisting her hobbling, limping route down alleys and busy streets. The hospital staff were kind, but assured Rampion that there was no one among their patients that fit Rocket's description. They gave her directions to the other hospitals in town, and Rampion, without resting, turned to push the motorcycle down the street.

She would not sit on the bike again, no matter how badly her feet hurt her, or how those blisters bled. It belonged to Rocket, it was molded to Rocket's hips and legs. It was not something she could think of, sitting in the cycle she pushed ahead of her along the cracked sidewalks.

She tried the next hospital, and again, she had no luck. But remember, these things happen in threes.

The Hospital of the Desert Rose was across town, and through neighborhoods a woman had no business walking alone, let alone slowly and pushing a clunky motorcycle. But she made it just before the sun began to set and the nurses told her where she could find Rocket.

She walked into the room and Rocket turned her head, her eyes bandaged with thick white cushions of gauze, blind to the world.

Rampion ran to Rocket's side. She cried out and pulled at the bandages. She wailed and sobbed. Rocket shouted, but she didn't push Rampion away. Rampion sobbed some more. Tears poured from her eyes and dripped down her nose. The tears drenched Rocket's face, and she couldn't stop them from flowing.

"You all know how this story ends." The weaver took a sly bite of cheese while the whistle interrupted her.

"Tell us!" the workers cried as they stood up and stretched, but did not disperse. "Tell us the ending!"

"Rampion's tears healed Rocket's burns and blindness." The old weaver waved her hand like that was the only obvious answer. "And they rode away on Rocket's motorbike."

"What happened with the old witch?" Bertel asked as she put her thermos in her lunch pail.

"Nothing, that I know of." The weaver shrugged.

"What happened after that?" an older man asked the weaver. He stood up and strapped his toolbelt back into place without looking away from the storyteller.

The old weaver smiled and stood up, brushing crumbs off her lap. She winked at the man and said, "Well, I suppose you could say they lived happily ever after." She turned to go back to her station, and her long silver and gold braid swayed against her hips.

On nights and weekends, **Alicia K. Anderson** squeezes creative writing between the assignments for a Ph.D. program in Mythological Studies. During the weekdays, she is a freelance SEO consultant—which is a form of wizardry in its own right. Sometimes she wishes she were locked in a tower with only occasional headaches from visiting loved ones. Alas, her husband and stepson don't have to ask her to let her hair down to gain entry to her lair. At best, they sometimes knock.

AS THE SPINDLE BURNS

Nellie K. Neves

When the world perched on the brink of devastation, we turned to the scientists. Maybe that was our mistake. Too late to know now. Can't take the ship out of the proverbial bottle.

I suppose it might have been our destiny to watch the economy crumble. I can imagine the alternative world. Thousands looking for work, babies starving, people dying, but this place we've landed where science is God?

I'm not sure it's a decent alternative.

I swing down from the ladder and let my boots thump against the metal grate below. Crankshaft is working on the car, adding some new gadget or gizmo. She's a gear head, but unmodified. The clanking and cursing coming from where she's beating metal into submission is common place around here. The old hangar amplifies the sound, especially when the storm doors are closed.

They aren't closed to keep out the elements.

Today they're closed to keep in the secrets.

We have a mission.

"Crankshaft!" I shout over the steel bar I'm leaning on. "Come on! Commander wants a briefing."

A wrench clatters against the cement and a trail of cursing follows after it. I can't help the grin creeping over my cheeks. She's not a lady. None of us are. That's what makes us special.

"Oiy." Her brown eyes are set off by the grease on her cheeks. "Can't he wait a bloody minute? I nearly got the new engine mods in."

"You know how he gets," I say like it's an answer. It's enough and she tosses her tools in a bucket.

"They make better tools," I say as she falls into step beside me. "The advances in the last year alone could really speed up your work."

"Go'on." It's not a word but a noise to mean she thinks I'm crazy. "Now you're soundin' like Specs. Nobody's makin' any dohickie better'n a cold steel wrench."

"Speaking of Specs," I say as I start up the stairs that lead to the briefing room. I nod to our lead scientist staring down from the top. "You two make up yet?"

"Ehhh, more or less."

"I'm guessing more on the less side."

"She shouldn't touch my things," Crankshaft says like the crime is punishable by death. In her world it probably is.

"Cutting it close, aren't you?" Specs asks as we trounce the last stairs. She adjusts the glasses on her face and I can see the iridescent glow that means the technology in them is working. Tracking our heart rates, checking for broken bones, likely she's just messing around. Ethel "Specs" Rosenburg is not only our lead scientist, but our team doctor as well. Her love of technology leaves a few of us uneasy, because of what we've seen in the field.

A whole world gone mad with gear and gadgets.

"Tell 'im to keep 'is pants on. We'll get there when we get there."

"Are Jazz and Mouse already in there?" I speak before the two of them can get into it again.

Specs draws a tight breath in through her nose as if draining it of life first, but really she's likely considering whether or not to beam Crankshaft with her bionic arm.

"Yes," she says without looking away from Crank. "Just waiting on you two." She turns on a heel and walks away from us.

"Don't know why we put up with 'er," Crankshaft whispers.

"Yeah, well, it's your fault. Always gotta get her goat, don't you?"

She has nothing to say because she knows it's true. Specs would be more than willing to lose Crankshaft, but she's the only mechanically inclined member of the team. If the world has taught us anything, it's that the scientist can't get far without the mechs. But right now Science is racing like an Alpha Romeo and mechanics are flailing off the back end hoping to avoid a bruising.

Mouse has set up the projection. I can see the team emblem flickering on the screen. The loaded bow and arrow spins, white against the black background.

12 Huntsmen is written within the center.

Our name.

Our identity.

We're an elite group of agents created by what is left of the military departments as we knew them. Originally I suppose they meant for it to be men, but with the men on the front lines, the women are picking up the slack. Not all of us can be riveting the newest war machines on the scientist's assembly lines. Those of us who were selected for this were picked for a reason.

Mouse, AKA Nancy Wake, was married to a special agent. When he went missing after a trip home to see his dying father in Germany the government interrogated Mouse for days, suspicious she was a double agent. She never cracked, never said a word, no matter the abuse. It wasn't long before those in power determined she hadn't learned her special skills from her husband, but that she'd taught him everything he knew. Jack, her husband, was killed behind lines, a raid on his father's home, and Mouse has been cold steel ever since.

Jazz, AKA Josie Baker, was a singer and dancer in the city back when that sort of thing mattered. She started in espionage before the war, passing secrets overseas while she toured. Her dark cocoa skin works to her advantage, leaving her unnoticed when she chooses, and yet center of attention when necessary.

Specs is our only member handpicked by The Commander, top of her class and leading scientist on all things war. Ask her and she'll tell you she got stuck with The Huntsmen because the men couldn't stomach her out leading the charge, better to stick her in an abandoned airplane hangar where no one could see her superior skill. The arm is a story she won't tell. No point in asking.

There were more of us when it started, a full twelve. But war isn't for the weak and it has a way of gleaning back the chaff. Khan, executed after a double cross betrayed her. Kawashima, our decoder, killed while trying to save another huntsman who had been captured. Shakespeare, shot while delivering a message on the frontlines. There were more, most before my time.

I came in a wide-eyed nobody from Iowa with a special set of skills that got me into nothing but trouble in a small town. Men love me. It doesn't take much to wind them between my fingers and bend them to my will. Leave it to what's left of the government to want to exploit that. I was born Margaret Harrison, but as a huntsman I'm Hari, leader of what remains of the 12.

We're not normal, I know that, that's why we're here. The 12 Huntsmen do what no one else can, going behind lines, moving in shadows, working the back channels. While the rest of the women chant "we can do it" in their patriotic drones, the 12 Huntsmen whisper, "we already did."

The transmission crackles and chirps before Commander's face flickers into view on the screen. Specs is on the device, twisting gears, pulling wires and slapping Crankshaft's hand every time she tries to help. I rub my palm over my face and draw in a breath. It's this moment, the moment before the mission comes through where I question my choices—walking away from the farm, from the sunsets, from a life without bullets and corsets and fishnet stockings with a leather holster cinched to my thigh. But the image clears and Commander is speaking and those thoughts will have to wait.

"Agent Harrison, Huntsmen, we have a mission."

"Yes Commander, we're ready," I say as I square my shoulders and send a glare toward Specs and Crank.

There's no time wasted as Commander dives into the details. "Plans are rumored for a new weapon, *The Spindle,* developed by the Axis powers."

"What's the worry? They took up knitting?" Crankshaft asks, kicking her boots up on the table.

"I doubt it," Commander says. "If Intel is correct, one charge from The Spindle can wipe out an entire squad in seconds. That's the worry, Crank."

Her feet slip to the floor and slap the grate. A bright flash before oblivion, it's easy to picture it. If this war has taught us nothing, we've all learned there's no limit to the horrifying creations of man.

"Yeah, okay," Crankshaft says after a moment, "then what's the mish?"

"You'll go to Belgium where the plans are held. I'm transmitting the intel we have now about the facility. You'll steal the plans and bring them home."

"Then what?" I ask. "Why not destroy them? If this technology is dangerous, why should we allow it to survive?"

The quality of the picture on the screen isn't crystal clear, but I can still make out the way his jaw tenses and tightens in frustration. I bring it out in him, always the first to question authority.

"Agent Harrison, that isn't for you to decide. You have your orders." He looks at the rest of them. "Crankshaft, you're transport. Jazz, Mouse and Hari, you'll breech the facility. Specs, go along, but stay outside the walls to coordinate. Retrieve the plans, and destroy the base." He looks at me again to restate himself, "You have your orders."

My jaw clenches before I say, "Yes, sir."

The picture cuts out. My gut tells me there's more, something else he's left for the need to know, and I don't fill that bill.

"What is it?" Mouse asks in a voice that's only meant for the two of us.

I shake my head because I don't have enough yet, but my guard is up.

This mission is different.

I sleep most of the way to Belgium. Most of the team can't, not on this shaky bucket of bolts Crankshaft has welded together, but I've worked hard to develop the talent. It's not that the plane is without merit, quite to the contrary. With all the modifications Crank's made to it, it's a wonder there's still room for an engine or wings.

Mouse kicks my boot before she sinks next to me on the floor. Vibrations from the engines roll through me. "What are you thinking about, Hari?"

"Home," I lie. It's always an acceptable answer with the war on. I don't need to divulge my innermost fears about the work we're doing, or who we're doing it for.

"Why bother?" she asks, and I get it. None of us have a home, at least not like it was before the war. The whole world's gone mad with power lust. It leaves no room for the softer delicacies we once enjoyed. I look down to avoid her stare and catch sight of my hands. Covered in grease and dirt, like they always are, unless I'm running them over the stubbled skin of some soldier I'm meant to seduce, then I'm clean and flowered. The glaring contradictions in my life blind me.

"Do you think about him?" I ask her. The weight of our bodies shift as Crank starts her decent. Jazz is in the cockpit with her studying the plans we received while Specs glowers over her shoulder. There's no one around to hear our secret musings.

"Jack? All the time," she says. "I imagine a world where he never left, where I never signed up. I can see it all so clear, a life without an empty bed and blood on my hands."

Glad to know I'm not alone in my second-guessing. Where my hands carry grime, hers hold the lives she's snuffed out. As a trained assassin and our security chief, they've figured out how to exploit her talents too, no matter the nightmares it leaves her with.

"This one's different," Mouse says as she leans forward, "I can feel it in my bones."

It wakes me up, sharpens me like a knife. I'm ready for battle.

Ready for anything.

I'm a Huntsman.

We move as one, a single shadow against the perimeter, nothing more. Not a sound on the gravel rocks, as if we float about them and glide with ease. They got it wrong in the beginning. Our leaders told us to dress like men, walk like men, heavy feet and long strides to confuse the enemy. They thought our femininity made us weak.

That thinking cost lives.

We learned better.

It's the differences between us and our male counterparts that make us strong. We can do what they never hoped to. We wear the grease and grime better than they ever could. On us it's beautiful—war paint and rouge.

I wait for the guard to pause by the stairwell. My eyes dart to Mouse; she nods because she agrees. This one belongs to her. The blade slips free of her boot, catching the light once with a playful wink before she melts into the night. She's hardly a ghost as she slinks through the dark. The guard makes one guttural sound as her hand slams against his throat. The blade winks again before hiding in his belly as Mouse bears his weight to the ground.

One less Axis Nazi.

It's a quick nod before we're up the stairs, two at a time, covering space in less than ten seconds as if we were never there in the first place. I breathe once the door is clicked shut behind me. Intel says the war room is to the left then thirty feet farther, but there's no telling what we might encounter in that thirty feet.

They look to me because I'm the leader. I flick my fingers and once more we move. Lights sputter and shake as we pass, like spies transmitting our location. A sound catches my attention and I halt in a doorway, ushering my team behind me like a hen with chicks. The space is tight and I can feel Jazz breathing on my neck as I search for the disturbance. Two men, both reclined on chairs outside the door of what I suspect is the war room. Weapons lay across their laps, next gen tech with laser modifications added to the muzzle. I've heard of them but haven't seen them in action. I only saw the aftermath when Shakespeare's body came back to the hangar. Gaping holes of charred flesh, like a bullet set on fire. They aren't in their trooper clothes—the gas masks with the black bug eyes—no, these are inexperienced foot soldiers, and the war room is likely empty.

"It's all you," Jazz's whisper tickles my ear and my pulse races in response because she's right.

"I'll stay behind you," Mouse says with a squeeze to my hand. "Use your tech."

Drawing in a breath and smoothing my clammy hands over my corset, I pull the ties on my cape and let it fall into Jazz's hands. Skin is far more dangerous than iron, at least in the hands of someone who knows how to wield it. I slip on the pair of black gloves Specs designed and clench my fists into tight balls. Electricity snaps to life.

It's these steps, these moments before contact where my heart beats like I'm at a dead run, and not because I'm afraid. I'm more alive in this moment—striding toward two armed men with nothing but a black corset and a tight skirt to protect me—than I ever was on that farm in Iowa. I can say that I was forced to come here, do this, be Agent Mata Hari, but the truth is, being a Huntsman set me free to be who I should have been all along.

My last step is deliberate, loud, and awakening. They turn and see me for the first time, an apparent sacrifice for their altar of lust. But I see them as well.

Altered.

Half an arm is steel, whirring gears and dripping oil. The companion's silver face enhancements catch the low light like a crescent moon, and it's essential I don't gasp.

They yell in German. I understand, but I don't need them knowing that. Instead I tilt my head until my dark curls fall behind my shoulder and display my naked neck.

"I don't understand," I say with doe eyes. "Spechen sie Englich?"

My American accent throws them, but it's my bust that has them distracted.

"Who are you?" the taller one's voice is heavy with traces of German spit. "What are you doing here?"

I pause because only the fearful blurt out answers. And I'm not afraid.

"I'm a gift," I say, letting the words bounce against my lips with careful cadence.

"A gift?" the steel faced one asks. "A gift for who?"

"Well," I say as my smile slips across my face with the urgency of a sunset, "that *is* the question, isn't it? Because they said the General, but—" I take quite a few steps completely unimpeded until I can walk my fingers up the tall one's chest. "—here you are. Finders keepers, right boys?"

He shudders once and I smile up at him as if I know a secret. Ol' Steel Arm shifts behind me and I can feel the heat of his frame. I run my free hand over my corset, as if to smooth the fabric, but his metal hand catches mine. Gears click and jam as he deepens the pressure.

"Are you boys lonely?" I ask and drag out the weight of each word. "It's been such a long war."

"We shouldn't," the tall one says, but his eyes are telling me otherwise, wandering to every shadow I've created with my curves.

"Can't you spare a little time?" I ask, walking my fingers back up his uniform toward his face. "Trust me, it'll only take a minute."

I doubt he sees the shift in my features, but I know he sees Mouse spring up from behind Steel Arm. My right hand latches to his metal face, and then the left grips his watch. Electricity snaps as the gloves conduct their power through his shuddering frame. I hear Mouse's knife and a cry of alarm just seconds before I turn around.

Jazz grins as the men hit the floor. "You didn't save any for me. You ladies have all the fun."

I abandon the gloves. They're a one hit wonder anyway. I link my arms under the dead man's armpits. It's a struggle to move them into hiding because of the metal modifications, but we manage and pull the door shut on the violence we caused. Jazz jams her listening device against the war room door, trying multiple locations to make sure we won't be surprised. The radio at my waist crackles.

"Hari," I hear the garbled hiss of Spec's voice, "come in, Hari."

I point to the door, as if to tell Jazz to keep listening, before I walk away to find better signal. Grease mars my skin as I shift the gears at the top, adjusting the tech she's developed to maintain long distance communication.

"I'm here, Spec," I answer into the radio as I depress the lever on the side. It's a dead man's switch she found in the field. She modified the radio specifically, says it's a reminder to us of how tenuous our lives are and what we're expected to sacrifice if taken alive.

"Hari, are you alone?"

Her tone anchors my heart. There's warning beneath the structure, as if I'm in trouble, as if she knows more than I do.

"I'm alone, Specs," I answer with a quick glance over my shoulder. Jazz and Mouse are still waiting at the door. The mission beckons me.

"New intelligence. It looks like we have a double agent in the Huntsmen. Mouse may not be who we thought she was. Commander wants her brought in. Those interrogators might have been on to something all those years ago."

My blood chills at the thought. She's been at my side on every mission, the blade ready to defend my every risk. It's not possible. I can't give even the slightest credence to the thought.

"Do you have proof?" I glance back again and Jazz is motioning to me with wide eyes.

"Commander says he does. I don't know the specifics, but think about it, Hari. Think about the others."

Her words conjure up memories of the Huntsmen we've lost. Mouse was on every mission. Every death could be trailed back to a moment missed, a slip of a hand or a breath of incompetency we'd never expected from our most skilled guardian.

"I can't do this now," I say and I release the dead man's switch to end the conversation. Radio tucked back into my side satchel, I fall in behind my team.

"All clear," Jazz says with caution in her eyes, "what are orders?"

"Breech," I tell them.

There are no shadows to cling to and it leaves my palms sweaty and heart pounding in my ears. The room smells of dust and the men who plotted world domination not long ago. A center table, a desk and one window with heavy curtains haphazardly drawn. Maybe I expected more from what should be our greatest threat. Stepping to the center table, I push my fingers over the map, listening to the paper crinkle beneath my touch. Bile churns as I look at the plans. Death laid out equally in lead and red ink, deaths deemed inescapable and those not yet decided. How can they play with life like this? Evil men eager to snuff it out and stand at the top of the mountain as king.

"Fan out," I tell them. "Find the plans. This place makes me sick."

Time draining from my hourglass, I shuffle through the mess on the table. Maps make up the bulk of it, but there are also personal notes that I shove into my satchel, hopeful that they'll prove useful to others with more experience. A drawing captures my eye, and I shift it free of the chaos. The charcoal smears and blends, building shape and contours until I realize why the drawing of a face has captured me.

It's Mouse. Her silhouette.

"I've got something," Jazz calls from the far side of the room. She unrolls the plans over a desk glowing with flickering light. With a deep breath she expels the dust up into a fog of neglect. "If this is it, then we're in trouble."

I try to breathe in my courage as I take in the creation, but it stills in my chest. I can see where the name comes from. The shape of the bulb is contoured like a spindle from a spinning wheel.

"What am I looking at, Jazz?"

"Specs or Crankshaft would know better," Jazz says, "but if I'm reading it right, the blast will destroy the target at a cellular level. Commander is right. This would end the war. They could wipe us out in days."

Worse yet, if we survive, we'll have to come up with something stronger, because that's the nature of war. They created bombs, and we created long range missiles. We created enhanced vision, and they created bionic limbs for the arms and legs we'd destroyed. Each step is another one towards destruction, Science jerking mechanics along like a slave in the name of domination.

"Set the charges," I say as I draw the plans together. "It's time to go."

Mouse has been unusually quiet, watching the room as if she can feel eyes on her. She's always had that sense, a power to know what's just beyond our space. I wonder if she's altered or enhanced. I've never asked, and I've never noticed any indication until now, but Specs' warning is creeping along the perimeter of my mind and I can't push it away.

"Set them." I snap the words at her because I need to know if she'll follow orders even in a country governed by those who she used to call family.

It jars her and I watch the door while my team executes my orders.

I hold the detonator in my hand. Specs claims the signal will reach once we're beyond the walls. Impatience burns through my hand and a part of me wants to press it now, end this, put us all out of our misery. If only the charge were strong enough to end the war.

There'd be no question.

I'd press it.

To still my racing mind, I walk to the only window in the room. It strikes me odd to have a window on the interior, odd unless it's not a window at all. I brush back the dust from the pane, coughing once as it chokes in my throat. Not a window, but a portal, a viewing station for the warehouse hidden inside the building. I twist and rise up on my toes to understand what I'm seeing. Hundreds of troops stand at attention, waiting. All eyes are converged at one point. Vibrations buzz through my fingertips. A blue haze is pulsating over their faces.

"What's down there, Hari?" Mouse asks from over my shoulder.

It's too horrible, too wrong to believe and I shake my head despite the fact that I can see it's true. "Intel was wrong. We're too late."

Light increases until there is no more blue, but a white so blinding I have no choice but to shield my eyes. I expect an explosion, or a thundering vibration to shake my frame, but there's only silence.

The light is gone.

But so are the soldiers.

Replaced by heaps of ash.

The room goes pregnant with questions as I meet my team's eyes. Orders have to change, our plan is flawed. Voices spike alarm in my heart as I realize there are men entering our room. Jazz darts beneath the table. I have seconds before the door opens. I yank back the drape and flatten myself against the wall with only the heavy velvet to shelter me. In the last second, Mouse whips back the curtain and shoves her way in beside me.

"Where are the men that are supposed to stand guard?" I hear a voice ask in thick German.

There are moth bitten holes in the velvet offering me a view of the men. Three. One guard, with his gas mask and bug eyes, a general, and a lieutenant from what I can see of his uniform.

"Drinking, I'd wager," the lieutenant replies. His weapon clatters against the table and Jazz cringes beneath. "The enhancements don't subdue every human urge."

The General is non-descript, just another Nazi drone as far as I can see. No enhancements, easy to take out if I need to. The bug-eyed guard is more metal than man and it's not hard to spot the laser attachment to his modified weapon. The lieutenant is young, handsome, and familiar. I'm about to glance at Mouse for her take when her trembling hand covers her mouth to subdue a scream. With only seconds before it shatters the silence, I smash my palm over her mouth to hold the sound in. Her eyes widen with confusion, but not because of what I've done. It's because of what she's seen.

The men are moving pieces on the table, as if they're playing a game and wagering bets in a casino. I don't know how long I can keep Mouse contained before she blows like a kettle.

"Bring the car around," the lieutenant says to the guard. "The general will send the troops in tomorrow. The Allied powers will be demolished by morning."

With a click of their heels and a salute, they're gone. Spit and sweat are collecting inside my palm, but I dare not peel it back until I know we're clear. She can't breathe, but the alternative is far worse.

"Calm down," I whisper against her cheek. "I'm taking my hand away."

My only reassurance is a jerking nod, but I know Mouse and the sweat clings as I peel back. Mouse draws in a deep breath and collapses into her hands.

"We need to go," she says, "right now."

I want more answers, but we have what we came for and the charges are set. Answers will wait for the plane. Jazz pulls the plans from the desk. I keep the detonator in my grip as we exit the room. Silent feet once more, we move down the halls and make our escape the same way we came in. The night air slaps me as we ramble down the stairs. A shot rings out and I hear the siren. A bullet whizzes over my head and Jazz yelps but never stops moving. I'm not sure how far we have until we're out of range. I duck down and pull my dark cloak over my frame, melting to the shadows.

"Blow it," Jazz yells with her hand cupped over a gushing wound.

The button is hot under my thumb. I feel the tension press back. Mouse's fingers curl around the detonator as she jerks it from my hand. Instead of pressing the button, she throws it as hard as she can. I stare at her with wide eyes.

"Mouse!" I scream. "Are you out of your mind?"

"That was Jack! That was my husband!"

"He's my guy, Hari," Mouse says even while I've got her shackled in cuffs. "You can't expect me to toss that to the wind just because of his uniform."

"If his uniform is boasting a Nazi emblem, then yeah I can!" I shout back at her. "That's what you signed up for, isn't it? Wipe them out? Get your revenge?"

"What revenge? He's alive!"

"Stop," Jazz pushes off the wall of the abandoned bunker we found. "Both of you. This is crazy. How do you know it's him, Mouse?"

Mouse's face goes absolute. "I can't expect the two of you to understand, considering your special talents, but when you commit to share your life with someone, you can recognize him no matter the years. Mark my words, that was Jack."

"Our special talents?" I ask, my voice dripping with the distain I feel for her superiority complex. "Are you calling me a—"

"Hari!" Jazz stops me. "Other room, let's go."

Against my better judgment I follow her to the other side of the wall of boxes. I can't see Mouse from here and it makes my skin twitch. No mechanic or scientist yet has invented cuffs our little Mouse can't bust out of, though Crankshaft would be the most likely to succeed.

"You know we can't leave her long, so unload what's bogging your chest down, and we have to get back there," I tell Jazz.

Her eyes close, but even that has the grace of a dance. She sighs and refuses to meet my eyes. "Hari, you know I'll follow you into any fight, but that's Mouse in there, that's Nancy, and you're treating her like a criminal."

"She disobeyed orders, Jazz. Protocol is simple."

The slow shake of her head betrays her disbelief. "We've all disobeyed orders at some point. There's something more, isn't there?"

Once more that little town in Iowa is calling for me. None of this would be my lot if I'd stayed put. "Specs says the commander suspects Mouse of being a double, then Mouse hucks that detonator as far as she can and nearly gets our head blown off by the enemy. I don't know, Jazz, husband or not, something isn't adding up. But you're right, we'll sort it out when Specs gets here."

It shakes her, just as hard as the news shook me. One of our own betraying us, it's unthinkable, and yet commonplace in this new world. Who needs trust when you can make a deal with the devil and save your own hide?

"Hey! Hey! You can't do that!" Crank yells and then Mouse screams and my feet are moving before I have a chance to process what I'm hearing.

"Put her down!" Crankshaft screams.

The bunker room opens into view. Crank is yanking on Specs' metal arm, slamming a wrench against it as Specs lifts Mouse by the throat. Veins bulge from Mouse's forehead as her skin turns gray. Jazz screams.

"Specs! Release her this instant!" I shout above the chaos and then throw my body against her unmodified side. We collapse in a heap. Specs' fury turns on me, eye blazing with indignation.

"She's a double, Hari!"

"What?" Crank yells as she hears it. "Blimey! Mouse ain't a double!"

"Explain it then," Specs demands as she pulls herself to her feet. "Explain the deaths on all the missions she's been a part of. Explain why she tossed that detonator tonight."

All eyes fall on Mouse, cowering on the floor, coughing and retching as her body tries to regulate air once more. "I'm not a double," she wheezes. Blood rushes to her face as her body recovers. "But I can't kill my husband."

"Husband?" Crank is struggling to keep up. "Jack's dead."

"Not anymore," Specs says. She retrieves her papers and thrusts them at me. "New mission from the Commander. The facility must be destroyed, no matter the casualties. He's put me in charge. We move out within the hour."

"No!" Mouse screams and lunges at Specs but Crank catches her before she can do damage.

Rage burning in her eyes, Specs turns to face her. "There's nothing you can do now. Choose to live and answer for your crimes, or run inside to die with the traitor."

My team has crumbled before me but as Mouse looks to me, eyes full of despair, I know in my heart she's no traitor.

"I can see four men inside," Specs says, adjusting her frames to see through the walls. "If we subdue them, we should be able to set the new charges."

"But the blast will ignite the originals we set," Crankshaft reminds her, "then bing bang boom, it'll take out most of this quadrant, including us."

Determination glows in Specs' eyes. "Then we're a sacrifice for a cause worth dying for."

I'm all for dying if the reason is right, but Specs looks like she's lost it. I have to wonder if some screw has come loose in her modified bits and has altered her system. After all, we left Mouse tied up in the bunker and she's our best chance at surviving this breech Specs is planning. Odd to be back here again, back in the same facility, on the same night, crouched in the same hall. Feels foolhardy, but a weapon like The Spindle won't wait.

I listen to our collective breathing. The world is waiting on us—waiting outside this room, hoping we have a chance at stopping global annihilation.

"3," I start the countdown and my grip tightens on the hilt of my knife.

"2," Jazz says, making room for me to lead the charge.

"1," Specs says.

My blood chills.

The muzzle of a gun is pressed into my back.

Questions are burning through my mind. "Specs, what are you doing?" But there's no answer, only her hand on the knob as she flings it open and shoves me inside. The floor rushes toward my face. Jazz collides and we roll into a heap. Crankshaft's elbow jams into my rib cage as she scrambles to keep away from Specs' gun pointed at her head.

"Crimy Specs, what are you doing? You gone mad?" She hurls the words at her as guards pull us from the floor.

I jerk my arm free of my captor only to be captured again. "What is this, Specs?" I ask.

"Herr Rommel," Specs' isn't speaking to me, but has saluted the men behind us, "I've brought The Huntsmen as discussed."

Jazz's eyes are wide with fright. It's not the fact that Specs is speaking German, it's the fact that the Specs we know has disappeared and we're seeing her true identity for the first time.

"Very good," General Rommel says. "Take them outside."

"What do you want with us?" Jazz demands, but her question is lost in the shuffle.

"Wait," the lieutenant speaks for the first time, "one is missing. Where is your companion?"

His English is broken, despite the time I know he spent in America. I want to pull him apart, tear out his motivation and examine it before I say anything about Mouse's whereabouts.

"She's nearby, in a bunker outside the facilities. Tied up, per your instructions," Specs answers.

"Enough," General Rommel's voice silences any further conversation. "Outside."

My bug-eyed guard shoves me forward, smashing my body against the door frame before I stumble to the hall. Crank's cursing swells as she fights back. No matter how she curses or Jazz pleas, our demise is imminent. We exit the building, stumbling down the stairs. The betrayal cuts deep. The night feels empty as we stagger down the last of the stairs. It's strange to think that the moon above us is the same one that will shine on folks back in Iowa later tonight.

But by then, I'll be dead.

"Get them together!" The command sends our guards into action, shoving us until we're tight, fish in a barrel. No need to waste bullets. I stare into the bug-eyed goggles of the guard pinning me into place. Empty, hollow, void of a soul. It's no wonder these men could extinguish hundreds of them with a flick of a switch, hardly even human.

"So these are the powerful Huntsmen, yes?" General Rommel asks Specs from where she stands next to him. "I thought there might be a fight, a struggle of some kind, and here they are, common women."

He's pointing to the tears rolling down Jazz's cheeks, catching that will-be-Iowa's-moon. I don't have tears, not yet. I'm waiting. Waiting because it can't be real, Specs has to have a plan.

"Why Specs?" I ask. "Why betray us?"

"Power," Specs answers me with a grin, "I can lead this army from the front of the pack, not shoved in a dark hole where no one will see me."

"A dark hole is where snakes like you belong," Crankshaft yells before she spits in the dirt.

I'm weaseling my fingers into the back of my corset, trying to jimmy free the blade I've hidden. But the guards are taking aim. The General's finger twitches. It's too late. The betrayer stood in our midst, but Mouse was not the culprit. Every death within The Huntsmen could just as easily be traced back to Specs. Faulty radio signal, tech that failed, transmissions dropped at the wrong moment. How long had she stood in our ranks just to pick us off one by one?

The knife is pinched between my fingers, two more seconds and I could have it, but time is up. I close my eyes and watch the sunset over the hills in that small town in Iowa as I hear the gun shift and the bullets fly.

I draw in a breath, knowing it's my last. The oxygen is sweet. Bullets rattle through the air but I keep my eyes squeezed shut. My fingers tighten on the knife. Metal grates on leather as I pull it free and flip it once, catching the blade between my fingertips.

I'm not dead.

Opening my eyes, I gasp. A guard has dropped. A pool of blood grows beneath him. The other guard is aiming his gun, but not at us, at the general. Tearing the goggles and hood off, Mouse's hair falls free.

"Mouse!" Crankshaft yells as if it's too much to believe.

She's not paying attention to us. "Hands up, we're taking you in." She catches my eye and grins. "Did he really call us common women?"

"You think you're done? You think you have us?" Specs pulls a gun from her holster and levels it between my eyes. "You shoot him. I'll shoot Hari. Are you ready to sacrifice a Huntsmen?"

"You're outnumbered," Mouse tells her. "Give up, Specs."

"Three on four is hardly outnumbered."

"I agree." His voice catches me off guard as Jack sets a weapon to Spec's temple. "But two against five is a losing battle, wouldn't you say?"

Her eyes pinch shut but her hands come above her head.

"Well said, darling." Mouse's words warm the chill in the night. "Ready to go home?"

"I've been waiting on you," Jack says.

Mouse turns to Crankshaft. "Can you get us out of here?"

"You know I can," Crank says.

It's not long before we're airborne, headed back for the hangar, two criminals in tow. We circle over the top of the facility, and I swear I can still spy the faint blue glow of The Spindle. My fingers tighten around the plans we stole. No one should have this kind of power.

I give Crankshaft my command. "Light it up."

With a press of a button, she unleashes the hell storm. The whistle pierces the night, as if the facility is screaming at just the thought of what's coming. Explosions burst, vibrations rock us, but Crankshaft's white knuckle grip never wavers as she releases the full arsenal of modified weapons.

I press open the cockpit window and stare at the plans in my hand. Jazz's words filter into my mind, *We've all disobeyed orders at one point or time.* I release my grip and watch the plans unfurl and glide down to the destruction below, burning until their mystery is lost forever.

"I knew he was alive," Mouse says as we kick our feet up on the table back in the hangar, "but only recently. He was taken captive after his father died, forced to work for the enemy in order to stay alive. When he contacted me last year, I couldn't believe it, but The Commander wanted to use him as a double agent. I hoped he might be liberated by this mission, but I almost lost it when he was there in the room. Now you can see why I couldn't trigger the detonator."

"Obviously," Crankshaft agrees with her, "woulda blown one of our best assets sky high."

Jack laughs nervously. He hasn't dropped Mouse's hand since Belgium. He's the reason we had the intel about The Spindle in the first place, so it's no surprise that The Commander has offered him a spot within the 12 Huntsmen.

I had a heck of a time explaining what happened to the plans we'd taken. Blamed it on turbulence and a slippery grip. "Cryin' shame," I told the commander during debrief, just like my Granny used to say when she spilled milk. Instead of demoting me, he brought on four new huntsmen.

I look around the table, faces I know, and others that are not familiar at all. It could happen again, a betrayal and double cross. I'd be crazy to believe otherwise. But isn't that the point of being here? In this room? On this earth? Give folks a chance and see what they can do. Iowa crosses my mind and I feel the pull of home in my heart.

The transmission chirps to life. Crank dims the lights and The Commander fills the screen.

"Commander Harrison, you've had a couple days R & R. I have a mission. Are The Huntsmen ready?"

I glance at Crankshaft sitting across the table. One eyebrow juts up as a sneaky grin crosses her cheeks. Grease on my hands, fire in my heart, that's the blood of a Huntsman.

"Yes, Sir."

A self-proclaimed California country girl, **Nellie K. Neves** is an independent author, contributes to RAC Magazine, and spends most weekends crafting culinary delights. As depicted by her Lindy Johnson series, Nellie has a penchant for writing about strong female characters caught in the midst of adversity with plots known for exacting twists and turns. That is what drew her to the Brother's Grimm tale, "The Twelve Huntsmen." In her version, "As the Spindle Burns," Nellie pairs elements of the original fairytale with her interest in famous women throughout history, specifically female spies like Mati Hari. But it's best to remember, nothing is ever as it seems, especially not in love and war.

MAKE THIS WATER NO DEEPER

Blake Jessop

At the end of a dock on the Dnieper, in the shadow of the biggest hydroelectric dam in the world, the red-haired girl waited for her lover with her naked feet dangling in the water. The dam towered above her, a concrete crescent so wide it looked as if it walled off heaven. The electric lights along its crest made the reflection of the moon on the dark river seem weak and forlorn.

"You came," the red-haired girl said, a note of excitement in her voice.

"The entire German army couldn't stop me," Epov replied. He tugged at his uniform tunic to straighten it.

"Maybe you shouldn't have," the girl said playfully, and slipped her feet out of the water. She walked soundlessly to meet him, bare feet leaving damp imprints on the wood. "Aren't you afraid a rusalka might drown you or a leshy steal you away into the woods? The moon is almost full."

"We live in the age of concrete and electricity," Epov laughed. "There's no more room in the world for fairies. Look at the size of that dam! It is the greatest construction of Soviet times, and I will decide its fate."

"You are so important," the Kulak girl chirped. She clung to his uniform even though the night was not particularly cool. Not very smart, but as beautiful as a summer sunset. War, Epov noted with satisfaction, provided solace in the strangest places.

"I am. We must defend this dam from the Germans to the last man," Epov said, sweeping his arm to encompass the pier, the water, and the colossal curtain of concrete and guard towers that was the Dnieper Hydroelectric Station.

"Would you really do that?" the girl said, sounding almost as excited as afraid.

"I could be dead in a week," Epov said with a studied indifference that he only half felt. Girls liked uncaring men.

The dam spread above them like a wall between old and new, a massive reminder of the brutal perfection of the modern world. That perfection was marred somewhat by Epov's task—the Germans had crossed the border, and he couldn't see how he was to organize the defense of a target so obviously vulnerable to attack from dive bombers in the air and sappers on the ground. But he wasn't here to dwell on his problems. They could wait. Everything could wait.

"I can't believe you're not hot in this uniform," the redhead mumbled shyly, fingering the fabric. "It's real wool."

The NKVD uniform usually provoked fear or respect, which to Epov's mind were the same thing. He enjoyed both reactions equally, though this Ukrainian peasant was too dumb to recognize the uniform of the secret police. To her he was just a soldier defending the Motherland. Well and good.

"I am comfortable, *rybka*, so long as I'm with you."

"That's not what I meant," the girl said, slowly undoing the buttons. She slid the jacket from around his shoulders and put a cool hand to the bare skin at his throat. She let it linger until Epov felt heat under his collar. With a coy giggle the girl turned and walked gaily to the end of the dock. Lit in relief by the lights on the dam, she sat on the edge of the pier and slipped into the water. She did something that made the light reflecting on the surface ripple, and a moment later her simple peasant dress landed on the wood at Epov's feet with a damp slap.

"I see what you mean," Epov said, pleased at the girl's willingness, and stripped off his shirt to join her.

The water was deliciously cool and dark. The girl's pale body made a beautiful, refracted shimmer, and red hair spread around her like fronds of fiery kelp. She ducked under the surface and Epov felt the sudden tug of weeds around his feet and the slick smoothness of her skin against his. She took his hands, and her fingers found his wedding ring, twisted it for a moment.

"You're married?" she said.

"This is war," Epov replied, and lowered his mouth to hers. "She'll never know."

"No," the girl replied, pulling him deeper, her fingers gently tickling his ribs. "She won't."

When the red-haired nymph opened her eyes, summer light broke and bent in slanted green sheets down from the surface and between the waving river grasses. She yawned silently in the deep water and stretched.

Her eyes, the same emerald green as the shimmering sun, caught those of the soldier. His were deep blue, and very wide. He drew no more breath than she did, and hung in the kelp just as lightly.

Awake, she slid through the murk toward the dock. She needed her dress back, and someone would probably come to search for the soldier. There were sins in her that the abbreviated flow of the river could not wash away, but she took her chances where she could.

High on the dam, the chief engineer of the Dnieper Hydroelectric Station feels exactly the fear an NKVD uniform is supposed to produce.

"I can't find Captain Epov," Petrovsky says, "and I'm tired of your staff not lending me their full cooperation."

"We are doing our best," the engineer says in a high, nervous voice. The NKVD Major knows how to cow people like this. Only the Order of the Red Banner for Labor on the engineer's amorphous and worn-out uniform tunic prevents him from being even harsher. He doesn't really mean to be frightening, but he can't help it. Epov is probably just sleeping it off with some Kulak whore, but the Captain's absence irritates him.

"Tell me what you did to him, Comrade Shevchenko," Petrovsky says. The engineer's boyish, almost elfin face goes even whiter.

"Nothing, Comrade Major. I have nothing to do with it."

"Well, take some men down to the riverbank and find him. He's probably in the village or surveying the spillways for places to put the dynamite."

The engineer bridles.

"We must not blow the dam, Major. We can't. We've been building it for twenty years. We need the electricity to produce steel and iron to make tanks for the front, we—"

"Don't lecture me, Comrade," Petrovsky interrupts icily, "or you'll be the one on the front, building bridges for a penal battalion. We will defend the dam until the end, and failing that we will destroy it. We are all soldiers now. We all follow orders. Now go find Epov!"

The red-haired rusalka waited in the reeds. She hated the dam. The river had once been pristine, had once run free. It had been a beautiful place to drown.

She hated the water above the dam; it was too high. She hated the water down here by the lower bank where her lover had held her by her red hair under the current, but less so. The mud and reeds called to her the way wood smoke and the smell of porridge called to men.

The way Maksym had once called to her from his fishing boat. The way their unborn child had called from another world.

The nymph knew what she was, and didn't care. She had trembled as a child, when her grandmother told her stories about the Leshy that lived in the woods and would eat her if she went out at night. She had gone out at night, and the monster she found had been far more handsome. The stories meant to prevent her swimming in the river hadn't worked any better. What would a rusalka want with her? The nymphs only drowned the unfaithful, and who was more faithful than she? Who took love more seriously or swam deeper waters to see it through?

She had thought over the years, when she bothered to think at all, about what her grandmother had told her about Rusalki. The stories always seemed so unfair. Why did girls have to come back from the dead to drown the living instead of their violent husbands? Why did wives always have to carry grief and suffering forever? None of the men she drowned had ever stayed to suffer alongside her. They passed as easily into the void as leaves falling into the river, and left her by the bank to linger between the veils.

Still, she was as beautiful as she ever had been, and how many girls could say that after fifty years?

The rusalka waited, and soon an engineer and more soldiers came to look for the drowned man. They were doomed to fail, unless they stripped off their coats and weapons and dove to the bottom of the river where the current combed the weeds. There they would find him, with his eyes as wide as a trout's and twice as stupid. The thought made her smile, and her teeth glinted like pearls.

"Comrade Chief Engineer," one of the Red Army soldiers says, trying to keep his rifle clear of the murky water, "This is pointless. He's not here."

"He wasn't in the village," the engineer yells back shrilly, "and you're not going to be the ones going to the front if we don't find him!"

They search the dock and splash amidst the reeds. The green water soaks up into their clothes as surely as guilt grows on a conscience, and weighs them down just as much. The soldiers soon find an excuse to go back to the road. They light cigarettes and leave a trail of smoke behind them. The smell of the coarse Makhorka tobacco is bitter, but the engineer hardly notices it.

The dam looms like a giant concrete curtain across the sky. The engineer looks up at it, and a momentary tug of pride offsets the wetness and the fear of the Germans and the fear of Petrovsky and his uniform and what his uniform means.

"Are you looking for someone?" a small voice says. The engineer starts violently. The girl is willowy and pale. Her hair is the color of leaves turning in autumn. She picks her way lightly through the rushes. The engineer gapes at the girl's beauty, then tries to turn the expression, which must look very stupid, into a nod.

The red-haired Kulak steps in very close and takes the engineer's hand. It is a small hand, but calloused and rough. The engineer is little more than a boy. Wide blue eyes and smooth skin and a formless tunic.

"I saw a man here last night," the strange girl says, "I'll show you. What's your name?"

"Shevchenko," the engineer squeaks.

She laughs and tugs at the engineer's hand. Takes him to the bank and leads him knee-deep into the water. She takes both his hands and entwines them with hers.

"I'll show you," she says, "what you're looking for."

The young man, like every young man before him, does not resist her lips.

The kiss is so long the engineer cannot feel the river rise, and so sweet it drowns out the taste of dark water.

The rusalka sank like a caryatid tipped into the sea, and it was only then that the man began to struggle.

There was something strange in the kiss, and she felt almost sorry as she pulled him under. Lust, of course, but also longing. A quick respiration that made her wonder if the boy was a virgin; his heart was beating fast enough.

She loved this part of her half life more than any other. Loved the end that didn't end. Loved the fear in open eyes under water. It was the only moment when pain and misery left her for someone else.

She tore at the engineer's tunic and teased him with her hands, made him exhale in a rush of muted sound. She ran her cold hands under the thin cotton shirt to tickle him. Strummed her fingers along his ribs like they were the strings of a lute, then dropped them to the swell of his hips. Bubbles poured from his mouth as her hands rose to his chest to find small breasts and thin shoulders.

For a moment, their eyes joined in shock. Green foam and arctic blue.

In a surge of violent water, the engineer feels the red-haired girl release her. Something drags her to the surface to cough and choke, half-conscious and drunk with fear.

When Yulia Shevchenko opens her eyes, everything is painfully vivid. The plop of water as it clears her ears is the loudest sound she has ever heard. The leaves leaning over the river's edge are the greenest she has ever seen. She sputters and sits up.

The red-haired girl sits on the bank beside her, as still as a statue. Her pale skin has the slick look of alabaster.

"You're not an engineer at all," the nymph says, and wrings water from great sopping sheaves of red hair. Yulia Shevchenko, the woman who can't be an engineer at all, coughs some more, but her voice is only half afraid.

"I am. I oversaw the installation of the fifth generator. I have the

Order of the Red Banner for Labor!"

"You're a woman," the red-haired girl who kissed her and tried to drown her says.

"So are you," Yulia says. She can't think of anything else to say.

"Not anymore," the nymph replies.

The nymph and the engineer spoke, and neither believed the other, at first. The rusalka ought to drown the engineer for building the dam, but she has never drowned a girl, not once. The kiss was also the only one she can ever remember being earnest. Men didn't use their lips that way.

"I was looking for a man named Epov," the engineer who couldn't be an engineer said.

"With dark hair and a wedding ring? He's under the pier."

"You," the engineer said hesitantly, "drowned him?"

"That is what Rusalki do."

"There are no such things as girls who live forever and drown unfaithful men."

"There are no such things as women engineers, either," the rusalka said, and could not figure out why the girl didn't run.

"You still tried to drown me."

"I wouldn't have, if I had known you weren't a man. How was I to know?"

"I would think it's obvious," the engineer huffed, pulling unhappily at her sodden, sack-like Soviet tunic.

"Not from the way you kissed me," the rusalka said to herself, and said it out loud without meaning to.

Yulia Shevchenko knows, with the entirety of her being, that her duty as a loyal Soviet citizen is to find some way to flee and report to Major Petrovsky. He could come back here with a squadron of soldiers and their Mosin rifles. No legend could stand up to that, no matter how smooth its skin or red its hair. Instead, she sits by the river under the dam and asks questions like the shy schoolgirl she once was.

"So, are you… dead?"

"Of course I'm dead. Maksym drowned me."

Anger and disbelief start a brief shooting war on Shevchenko's face. All that comes of the struggle is a question.

"Why?"

"I was with child, so of course my father wanted him to marry me. He wasn't ready." The nymph sees the look of horror on the engineer's face. "That wasn't so uncommon, when I was born."

"When was that?"

"What year is it now?"

"Nineteen forty-one," Yulia says. Water laps at the shore and wind gently brushes the reeds. Yulia feels like it's the first time she's ever looked at them.

"A long time ago, then."

They sit still, as near and far from one another as two people can be.

"My name is Yulia. What's yours?"

"It was Maritchka, but don't think you can help me get it back. I've already drowned a few of the men who came before you, so I know how much you Russians care about the past. I could be set free from this condition if I were revenged on the men who made me this way, but who among you would even know their names?"

"They must all be dead."

"That doesn't matter. I could set myself free if I could make the river flow and wash the world clean, but how am I supposed to do that?"

"I will come back, if that would help," Yulia says, and her eyes are locked on the marsh between her knees. "Though I don't believe all this nonsense about your being a rusalka."

The girl who was once Maritchka grabbed Yulia's hands and pressed the left one violently against her breast. Her skin was cool and soft and perfect.

"What do you feel?" the rusalka asked.

"Nothing," Yulia said, stammering and blushing wildly.

"Exactly," Maritchka said, not at all sure Yulia got the point. "You've seen me, you've touched me. You should believe in me."

The engineer looked down at her hands.

"There is no such thing as a rusalka."

Hurt for the first time in what felt like centuries, the red-haired rusalka turned away and lake water flecked from her hair.

"Just because you do not know history doesn't mean it doesn't matter. Just because you dismiss it doesn't mean it didn't happen. No matter how big a dam you build the water still flows."

With that said she dove back under the water. In her wake wasn't a trace of bubbles, nor a single ripple.

In the Hydroelectric Station's control room, Petrovsky is poring over maps and design documents when he hears Shevchenko get back. A telephone sits askew on its cradle beside him, and he's breathing like a man who has been yelling. He draws breath to yell at her, but pulls up short when he raises his eyes to the chief engineer. She looks like a drowned rat.

"You look terrible, Comrade," he says dryly, "where is Epov?"

"I'm not sure," Shevchenko says distantly.

"What happened?"

"I don't know, Major."

This is a moment for Petrovsky to punish her, but he has no time. He needs her help to organize the defense of the dam. He now knows just how close the Germans are, how soon they'll be here, and just how many men the STAVKA will allow him to sacrifice to save the dam. The numbers are enough to shake even a stalwart man. Now is not the time for solving the problem of the recalcitrant engineer, and she looks as pliable as a human can, anyway.

"Get some sleep, Comrade, and report to me tomorrow."

"Yes, Major," Shevchenko says, and turns from the room.

She climbs the stairs to her tiny room in a daze. Everything is cold, muted. Nothing has color, and the concrete walls dampen her footsteps. She can't process what has happened to her, so she tries to sleep.

Maritchka touches her as soon as she closes her eyes. She invades her thoughts and won't leave her alone. She almost drowned, almost was drowned, and she can't decide in what. When she touches the spots on her ribs where Maritchka's fingers pressed, her skin tingles.

The rusalka slept as she always slept: as dreamlessly as a river in its course. In the morning she checked on Epov, smiled at the ludicrous expression on his face, and then went to sit on the end of the dock and stare at the dam. Something seemed different, like she had learned something about it in a dream that she couldn't remember awake.

The rusalka was so lost in her thoughts that when she finally heard the engineer padding shyly to stand behind her, she was as surprised as a duck hearing the sound of a gun.

"Why did you come back here without soldiers?" Maritchka asks.

For an answer, Yulia, in an agony of hesitation, wraps her arms around Maritchka. Hesitantly, at first, then desperately. As soon as she does, the water regains its murmur, and trees their green.

At first she holds on for comfort, for warmth, although Maritchka's skin is refreshingly cool. She holds on because she needs a charm to dispel loneliness and scorn utility. After a few moments, that isn't all it is. Yulia inhales the faint, mossy smell of the rusalka's neck. There is no pulse in the hollow under her chin.

"I couldn't sleep," Yulia says.

The rusalka is taller than she is, and Yulia's chin rests comfortably on Maritchka's breast bone. Her scent is the comforting kind of old, the smell of water and moss and spring along the river. Yulia forgets herself, nuzzles close enough that her lips brush the rusalka's neck. Without knowing where she finds the courage, she kisses her soft, cool skin. The rusalka starts, and Yulia's heart leaps into her throat. Maritchka's eyes go distant, but after a moment she turns her limpid green eyes downward, and gives a little shrug.

When their lips meet for the second time, Yulia finds that being drowned isn't nearly as bad as she thought.

What was most odd, for the rusalka, was that she didn't mind the dam so much as she had, once the little blue-eyed engineer had snuck her into it. It had been a long time, a very long time, since she slept between sheets. She missed the water, but found something else to immerse herself in.

The only thing she refused to do was look out the north windows at the reservoir. The broad lake made her feel sick and vulnerable, so she drew the curtains and restricted herself to the unlikely little bed, to the small warmth she hadn't known still existed.

When Yulia asked her about the high water, the rusalka found herself at a loss for words.

"Come on, now," the engineer said, "this isn't so bad."

"I'm surprised," the rusalka answered, "how warm the electric lights are."

Yulia rose and went to the window, and the rusalka found herself surprised at how strongly she felt looking at the engineer's bare back. The short hair at the nape of her neck.

Yulia raised her hands to draw aside the curtains.

"Please don't," the usalka said, "don't make the water any deeper. The world is unbalanced enough already."

For five quiet days, the world burns. Yulia reads maps during the day and drowns at night. She watches the war march closer and closer, watches Petrovsky grow more and more fearful, and she does not care.

Eventually, Maritchka can't abide the tiny shower stall anymore and tells Yulia she needs a night underwater. A childish part of Yulia assumed that whatever they were doing would free the rusalka, break her curse, but all it did was fill the tiny room with soft light. Yulia discovers that she still loves the dam, even if all it smells like is concrete and ozone and musty canvas, but it's Maritchka that makes the place come alive.

Forlorn but happy, Yulia screws on her most serious face to go to a meeting with Petrovsky. The view from the top of the dam is a stunning panorama of dawn sky and shifting forest. The town of Zaporizhia is a white-washed blot and the river snakes southward in a silver ribbon. Far off to her right there are faint columns of smoke. They can't hear the guns yet.

She makes her way through an obstacle course of munitions and men on her way to the control room. Without Maritchka, the dam is becoming dull and scentless again.

Petrovsky himself looks as feverish as she feels, but probably for different reasons. Yulia faces him with equanimity she finds surprising. She used to be afraid of him.

"I have made all the preparations you asked, Comrade Major."

"Thank you, Chief Engineer."

A silence falls between them. Yulia knows what he's thinking, and knows he doesn't have enough courage to say it. She says it for him.

"We won't be able to save the dam."

The news from the front has been catastrophic, and they both know it.

"I notice the drownings have stopped," Petrovsky says, to avoid acknowledging the truth.

"Indeed," Yulia replies, with eyes locked on the floor. "The rusalka must have had something better to do."

The Major gives a mirthless laugh.

"Well, the STAVKA have ordered us to defend the dam. To the last man. All of us."

"You want me to tell her that?"

The Major looks up.

"What?"

"Nothing, Comrade Major."

When Yulia leaves the meeting she shields her eyes against the late summer sun. High above her there's a strange drone.

She watches with detached fascination as a single German plane whines far overhead. When news of the invasion came she and her comrades had tacked up a map of Germany and brought out pushpins to mark the advance of the Red Army into the territory of the invaders. Both map and hubris had been swiftly torn down and replaced with a STAVKA aircraft recognition poster, so she knows this is a Focke-Wulf 189. A reconnaissance plane that looks oddly like a dragonfly with two tails. There isn't much time left. She hurries along the monolithic dam in a haze.

As she descends to the piers below, the air becomes clearer. She smells the musk of the riverside, hears the clear call of larks in the trees.

Maritchka is waiting for her, sitting on a low branch with her toes dangling sadly in the water. Yulia's heart quickens when she sees the rusalka. The creature smiles, and Yulia feels like she can sense the very movement of the Earth under her feet.

"The Red Army is going to fight here," Yulia says, a little out of breath and without preamble. "They want to preserve the dam no matter the cost."

Maritchka bursts into tears and throws herself into Yulia's arms. The little engineer feels a deep conflict between her joy at the embrace and the sorrow her news has caused.

The rusalka weeps, and Yulia holds her.

"I can't stand this place," she says, "I can't stand this dam and the high water and these soldiers and the dry air. Why won't the world just let me drift away in peace?"

Yulia hates, as deeply as she has ever hated, the idea of letting Maritchka go. Saying what she says takes as much courage as she has ever applied to anything. She has to lift Maritchka's head from her shoulder and her hair from her eyes.

"I have an idea, if you'll listen. I want to save us both."

"You can't save me," the rusalka says. "There is no one to take revenge on. I've tried."

"Well, I don't think it will work, but I want to try. I think the man you drowned and his comrades are wrong; there is no way to stop the invaders."

"The old river would have stopped them," Maritchka says bitterly.

"It could again," Yulia replies.

The engineer was a dreamer, a welder and a riveter. A true believer in the new way, but there was something she needed to see. Lighting cities with thousands of megawatts of power was routine; she wanted to see if she could light the whole world.

The rusalka, like all spirits, was wrong to drown men, but not completely. There was no shame in wanting to be laid to rest, no dishonor in insisting that old wrongs be made right before embarking on new ones. It hurt the rusalka to kill, but not to drown men hurt even more. Doing nothing caused the worst pain of all. On that the two of them agreed. Just because you do not know history doesn't mean you can't change it. Just because you dismiss it doesn't mean it won't happen.

Rushing with the engineer back up to the machine rooms that riddled the dam, the rusalka spoke.

"How will we destroy this monstrosity?" she asked.

"We'll plant dynamite in the spillways, then more under the water line, below the magazine they set up in the fourth generator. I can't do it; I can't breathe under water."

"I can't breathe at all," the rusalka replied, and the engineer heard both joy and love in her voice.

"We'll do it together. You never told me how to break the curse on a rusalka, how to wash away old sins, so I thought we'd try washing away every sin in the entire world."

Just before they entered the magazine, Maritchka stopped Yulia and took her hand.

"I don't want you to destroy what you love," she said.

"I don't plan to."

"Why would you do this for me?" the rusalka asked.

"Because I fear the flood less than I love you," the engineer replied.

Yulia is planting her dynamite when Petrovsky finds her. She's crouched on the grating above one of the spillways, her ears full of the roar of rushing water, so she doesn't hear the Major come. The first she knows of his presence is the cool click of his pistol against her head.

"You're a saboteur. I knew it. Why are you doing this?"

"We can't defend this dam, Major. If we flood the valley, we'll stop the Germans in their tracks."

"You'll drown us. You'll drown my officers downriver. You'll drown thousands of Kulaks."

"This is a novel time, Comrade, for you to start caring about Kulaks." Yulia feels cold in her stomach, but she isn't afraid of the pistol. The Major stares at her, appalled. They face each other above the raging man-made waterfall.

"You did it. You drowned Epov."

There's a gentle ripple of movement behind Petrovsky. A smell of moss.

"No, she didn't," the rusalka says, upending him to fall screaming into the spillway. "I did."

The rusalka enjoyed planting her dynamite. Felt giddy at the thought of tearing the world down. She didn't know how the strange red tubes worked, but she trusted the engineer.

There was an island in the river. It wasn't there when the girl Maritchka was born; only the lowering of the water when the dam was built brought it forth from the foam. The lovers huddled there to watch the world end.

"Will it be beautiful?" the rusalka asked.

"You have no idea," the engineer replied.

They wound their arms around one another, and it felt indecent to love so deeply, to feel so happy, when they were about to drown thousands, to wash the world clean.

"Do you think this will set you free?" the engineer asked.

"I don't care," the rusalka replied.

When the dam blows, Yulia's smile unlocks her lips from Maritchka's. First the spillway erupts in a column of concrete and flame so high it blots out the stars. The water ripples, and just when it seems the cataclysm might end, the underwater charges go. A wall of water rises above them, high enough to scour heaven, loud enough to drown out war itself.

Just before the water crashes over them, Yulia feels the rusalka wrap her arms around her. Hears her laughter, feels the pounding race of her heart, and the two of them are thrown heavenward in an emerald wall of foam.

Blake Jessop is a Canadian author of science fiction, fantasy and horror stories with a master's degree in creative writing from the University of Adelaide. You can read another one of his original fairy tales in "Terra! Tara! Terror!" from Third Flatiron Anthologies, or follow him on Twitter @everydayjisei.

ONE HUNDRED YEARS

Jennifer R. Donohue

We didn't know the gunsmith was a woman. It didn't matter, not to me, but it was a surprise. She was tall, broad-shouldered, with unbelievably deft hands. She was not happy to see us when we arrived, road-weary and with haunted eyes from crossing the countryside while hiding from soldiers. But we'd heard this was the way to win the war, to come to the west to a little cottage with land up against the mountains, and get a magic gun from the smith there.

The world was burning, and it seemed like a magic gun was maybe one of the only things that would fix it.

Lew was the bold one of us, the first to steal boots off of a truck, or throw a rock through a windshield, and he stood forward, stood tall, and said "We heard you were the one to come to."

"I don't know who you've been talking to," she said, looking us over. Lew. My brother Marek. Me just behind him. Artur the dog. She looked at me again, slouching in my boy's clothes even though there was really no fooling anybody, and then sighed. "Come in."

We shed our coats and hung them where she gestured. Marek gave me a brief, disapproving glance when I paused at the hearth and held my fingers out. They felt like wilted flower petals. "Really, Iga," he muttered.

"We should have Lew get us gloves next, so we have fingers left to fight with," I said, cutting and joking in equal amounts. What we wore was all we owned anymore.

We joined the resistance the day after the farm burned. Or, that's how I liked to tell it. At first, we didn't know what we would do, watching the smoke tower into the night sky, watching the sparks fly from the roof, into the hay, into the barn. We already slaughtered our pigs, thank God. I couldn't have stood it, hearing them burn, unable to help. I zipped Artur in my coat while we hid, to keep him from barking at the soldiers, running to nip at their shiny booted heels. He was a puppy then; we'd already lost so much, and saving the puppy had to be enough. It felt like so long ago but was less than a year.

And then we walked, away from the armies, away from the smoke and gunfire. The nearby town might have been taken over already, there was no way for us to tell. Our neighbors were gone, killed or conscripted, we would never know. In the forest, Lew found us and brought us to the resistance that he knew. That was part of the problem; there was more than one resistance, and they didn't all agree on the best way to do the job.

The smith fed us, ladling out soup from a huge pot on her stove. It was the kind of soup that never ended, you just added what you had to it and left it simmering. It was good, rich and warming, and when she caught me feeding a taste to Artur she frowned and found him a marrow bone that hadn't yet gone into the pot.

"The one to come to for what?" the smith asked finally, after we'd filled our bellies and gotten our color back.

Lew coughed and looked away, his cheeks reddening, and Marek scowled at him. I was the one who found my voice. "Magical guns, for the resistance."

She looked at me steadily, until I felt the hot flush in my cheeks, but I didn't waver. We had come all this way, in the cold. We couldn't lose our nerve now, it wasn't as though all of the soldiers would just give up the war and go home on their own, and the rest of the world seemed to be taking their time as well. "Magical guns," she said after a time, looking from me to each of the men. She was smiling slightly, though in derision or amusement, I couldn't tell.

"Yes," was all I could get out. But she didn't laugh, and she didn't yell. She studied the three of us, and gave a little sigh.

"You there," she said to Lew, who gave her a sidelong look like an ashamed dog. "You are a thief and I will not make you a gun, magic or otherwise." He nodded tightly. He must have considered that, on a fairytale quest such as this, he might be refused.

She turned to Marek, but his temper got the better of him and he shoved back from the table. If this had been a table of plenty, glasses and bowls would have sloshed; as it was, they only gently clinked together, empty. After the door slammed behind him, I became aware of the ticking clock in the room. The ticking clocks in the house; there were others that I couldn't see.

"I'm sorry," I said, scrambling to follow him. He wouldn't go far, I hoped. He had more sense than that, I hoped. Artur trotted along with me. Lew said something as I left, closing the door more softly behind me, but I couldn't make him out. Little explanation beyond 'the war' was needed, I thought; the war, the soldiers, the fires, the guns. And here we were for another gun.

"Go inside, you'll freeze," Marek said when he saw me. He went out in such a rush he didn't have his coat, and I held it out to him.

"I came out here so *you* wouldn't freeze." He roughly shrugged into his coat, zipped it up to his neck. There was a place just under his jaw where his beard never grew. It looked like a knife wound to those who didn't know he tripped in the toolshed when we were small.

"It was foolish, coming all this way. Of course she'll turn us down."

We stood in silence, shoulder to shoulder. Our breath came out in big cottony gusts and wreathed our heads, like when Papa and the neighbors used to smoke their pipes at the kitchen table. Mama wouldn't let them do it anywhere else in the house, to save the furniture, and our bedding. I liked the smell of pipe tobacco. It smelled homey and comforting to me, like safety. You needed time to sit down and prepare a pipe to smoke, to take care of it when you were done. Nobody in our group of the resistance smoked a pipe. Most of them were out of cigarettes, even. It was another thing Lew was supposed to get, while we were on this mission.

"We don't know she'll turn all of us down. She turned Lew down."

"And she'll find me more worthy?" Marek asked bitterly. Artur gave a soft little whine, and I put my hand on his head, opened my mouth, and closed it again. I didn't know everything my brother had done, before the war or up to now. Maybe he judged himself far more harshly than the smith would. And how would she know? Did making magic guns give you magic senses? I didn't even know what magic was, what a magic gun would mean. It was a senseless hope, like praying, or reaching a border that war hadn't touched.

"Let's just go back inside," I said after awhile. Long enough for Marek's temper and the tip of my nose to have cooled. He didn't say anything, but followed me.

Inside, Lew was smiling and the smith seemed about to. I wondered what they'd talked about. Thief or no, Lew was very charming. "Have some mead, to warm yourselves again," the smith said.

"Thank you," I said, when it seemed Marek would remain sulkily silent. "We're grateful for your hospitality." I wanted to ask again about the gun, but didn't want to hear the final no, and instead cradled the fragile hope like an egg in my hands. Tomorrow. Tomorrow we would leave, or she would say yes. Artur settled in front of the hearth again with a happy groan.

"I make it myself," she said, opening a cabinet and pulling down a bottle golden like sunshine, or like my mother's amber necklace, kept sewn into the waist of my pants. "You may have seen the hives, when you came in."

"We did! You have many hives," Lew said, and I imagined him for a moment as a honey thief, reaching in like a bear, and smiled. The hives were big and square, shut up and cloth-wrapped. I thought beekeeping must be a hopeful endeavor, not knowing from one season until the next if the hive would survive, if the bees were sleeping or dead, if the queen was a good one. But what does make a good queen bee? I didn't know; I'd only known pigs.

"I do. There used to be more people around to help me with them, and share in the results." She poured us each a small glass, with gravity. There is a special mood in sharing mead with somebody on your home, a certain intent. Maybe it was magic in itself, even as such an everyday gesture.

"Na zdrowie!" I said, lifting my glass. Cheers.

"Sto lat," said the smith. One hundred years. We all drank.

I wanted, again and again, to ask about the gun, but as the clocks ticked and the night deepened, we talked about smaller, quieter things. The dog. The bees. When the hives were opened, if they had survived, only the queens would be the same live bees as when the hives were closed. The workers only lived for six weeks, some of them living and dying entirely during the winter, and never knowing the smell of summertime, only knowing the pollen the other bees laid away, the honey, and keeping the queen warm. It made me think of the children who had been born after the war began; they did not know peace. I hoped they would know peace before they died.

When we settled to go to bed, the smith banked the fire and gave us blankets, and Lew and Marek gallantly let me take the sofa. Artur went back and forth between me and the men, then hopped up with me and curled into my belly under the blankets. I didn't know how I would sleep, with the clocks, with our unanswered question, but I slipped away quickly, warm and with a full belly. Artur's low warning growl woke me, when the smith reached down to wake me in the long dark hours of late night or early morning.

"What is it?" I asked and she shushed me.

"Please, come with me," she said quietly, calmly. She'd been so calm all along, confident, even when three strangers were on her doorstep. Even with tanks rumbling like thunder in the distance, diesel clouds smearing the sky. What would happen to her, if they came here? To us?

I did what she asked, of course, reluctantly left the warm nest of blankets and shoved my feet into boots again, pulled my coat on again. Artur started to follow, and she paused. "Will he stay?"

"If I tell him to. Artur, go sleep with Marek." He cocked his head at me in the dim light, and then paused over to settle with my brother.

Outside was very cold and very bright, the moon a lantern guiding our way towards the mountain that had loomed in the distance for the entire walk here. There was a border nearby, I remembered from the map, but into further Axis territories.

"You can't see it from here, but there's a large cross at the top of the mountain," the smith said.

"That is Giewont, right?"

"Yes. The sleeping knight." We walked longer, in the trees now, the cold ground crunching beneath our boots. We walked long enough that I thought surely there should be sign of dawn, a light in the east, the setting of the moon, but the night seemed completely still, a stopped clock. "What I am about to show you can't be told to anybody. Not your brother, not that smiling young man, not your husband when you find one."

"I won't tell," I said through stiff lips, numb from cold and sudden fear. She looked at me intently, and I noticed the laugh lines in the corners of her eyes. To have known so much laughter, and to be in the world we had now. "I promise."

"If you break this promise, what I give you tonight will turn to ashes."

"I won't," I said. She looked at me for three breaths more, and then nodded.

"Good." She stepped off of the path, and not twenty steps through the trees, there was a sheer rock face.

"I don't understand," I said, and then the mountain opened. Not like a door, and not like a parting curtain, but a little bit like both of those things. She walked, and I followed. It was warmer inside the mountain, and I thought maybe it was just because we were out if the wind, but then we came to the room with the knights, and I slapped my hands over my mouth to keep from crying out in surprise and fright.

I don't know how many of them were there, reclined on cushions, swords and suits of armor on the ground beside them, horses standing about, every last one of them breathing the sweet relaxed breaths of restful sleep. I stared at the knights, and stared at the blacksmith, as she went to one of them and picked up his sword and helmet, considered, took a gauntlet as well. The chain mail hanging from beneath the plate looked as finely wrought as my grandmother's lace.

"Take this," she said brusquely, handing me the sword. I had too many questions and not enough courage, and took it awkwardly into my arms, smelling the metal and oil and leather as I followed her back out if the cave again, away from the rocks and trees, back to her house on the edge of the village. The moon was still in the same place, and I wondered, if I drew the sword from its scabbard, if I'd be able to see my face in its blade. Such a childish, vain thought, to want to use a sword as a mirror, in a place like this, at a time like this. It was hard to know the right thoughts to have.

"What did we just do?" I asked, before she opened the door.

"Those knights have been sleeping in preparation to defend Poland. I don't know why they haven't woken up yet. Not now, and not the last time the Germans and Russians came. So. I'm tired of waiting. I will make you your gun."

"Me?" I was too loud, I knew, my voice ringing in the still night air. "But I—"

"You came asking for a magical gun for the resistance. I am making it for you." She smiled, sad, resolute. "Now go and sleep. We can talk more in the morning."

In the morning, though, breakfast was laid on the table, and the clocks ticked, but the smith was shut away behind one of the doors in the house. How did one make a gun? With heat? With hammers?

"What happened?" Marek asked. He'd woken up with Artur, so knew I'd shifted in the night.

I drank some tea to give me the time to find my voice. "She's making a gun."

"For me?" His frown was an already gathering storm.

"For me," I said so quietly that I thought he wouldn't have heard and I'd have to repeat myself, and Lew laughed loudly.

"Iga, that's amazing! You're a far better shot than I am anyway. You'll be Polish Annie Oakley."

"Who's that?" I asked.

"Nevermind his foolishness." Marek waved a hand. "She's making you a gun? She said so?"

"Yes, in middle of the night. We—" I brought myself up short. I was so close to ruining everything. It was always such a simple promise to keep, in the stories, always such a simple mistake. "We talked," I finished.

"Will she make only one? Will she make one for me too?"

"She didn't mention you, I'm sorry. I guess she would have woken you, if she was making two?" I expected him to storm out again, but instead, his frown cleared and he nodded.

"Then that's how it is," he said, and began to eat. Lew and I looked at each other across the table, and then we ate as well. Maybe Marek was relieved. He wasn't the one responsible, but he could still be proud.

"I wonder how long it takes," Lew said, stuffing more bread in his mouth.

"I hope it's fast, so she has food left," I said, elbowing him.

Lew shrugged. "She knows what she's doing."

The smith emerged from the workshop at supper. I waited, hesitated, waited through the afternoon, and then went through the pantry to prepare a meal. I wished we'd brought food to offer, meat so I could make golumpki, but there were eggs, and potatoes. Turnips. I hoped she wouldn't be angry that I cooked, but she smiled tiredly and took her seat.

"Thank you."

"You're welcome." Lew and Marek spent most of the time I was cooking outside, and were raw knuckled and their boots had brush tangled in the laces when they sat.

"We walked your fence line and repaired what we could," Marek said. "There was some deadfall that we broke up for your woodpile."

"It's a good sign, when hands left idle find their own work," the smith said.

"We've been too long idle," Marek said, and he slowly smiled. "That one gets into too much trouble." Lew grinned, shamefaced, but did not protest.

"Just like my little brother," the smith said. We all laughed, just a little, but there was nobody else at this house, had not seemed to be for a long time. Her little brother was alive or dead, safe or not, and none of us was going to ask her.

We went on like that for a week and a day. I wondered when the resistance would think we were failed or dead or captured, but nobody else mentioned it, so I didn't either. I spent a lot of time watching the pendulum on the clock in the kitchen, watching the gears grasp each other, counting the seconds like praying the rosary.

"My family made clocks," she said one evening. "My father, and my grandmother, and her mother."

"Is making guns very similar?" I asked, a little mystified.

"It came to me easily enough," she said. She seemed so tired, more and more with each passing day. I wished there was a way I could help her in the workshop, but that was a door kept closed to all of us.

"I'm all thumbs when it comes to mechanics," Lew announced cheerfully. "Marek is our man for that."

"Is that so?"

"We had a truck that wouldn't run, and a couple of our machine guns were all jammed up. Then Marek and Iga showed up and he put them to rights in just a few days. The truck took days, not the guns."

"I cleaned and oiled parts, anybody could have," Marek muttered. "Things like that need care."

"Don't let him fool you, he jury rigged a part for that truck from a different engine."

"She doesn't want to hear about the truck, Lew." But Marek's cheeks reddened just a little, and a smile glimmered in the corners of his mouth and eyes.

"There's no harm in it," the smith said. "I'll have the gun done tomorrow. You can get back to your friends then."

"Tomorrow?" I asked, putting my hands flat on the table. It was so nice here, even just waiting. With the war and everything just a dark cloud on the horizon, not a downpour we had to stand in. But of course we would leave. With a magic gun. My magic gun. My fingertips tingled just thinking about it.

"Yes."

"Is there anything I should… know? Or do?"

"There isn't any way to prepare, no," she said, with a glance like pity as she got up to clear the table. I helped, stunned to silence. Tomorrow. It was what we came for, and even after going into the mountain, seeing the sleeping knights, it didn't seem real. "You'll be all right," she said, quietly, when we reached the kitchen. Lew and Marek were talking again already, paying us no mind.

"I don't see how," I said, suddenly tearful. She paused a moment, and then set the dishes down and hugged me. I was so surprised by her embrace that I cried harder, forgetting to be polite and reserved.

When was the last time anybody hugged me to comfort me? Before our mother died.

"We never do," she murmured. I wondered who she was thinking of. Maybe just herself. It was hard to remember to think of yourself.

"Thank you," I said, once I caught my breath, once the tears stopped coming. I meant more than just that moment, but the right words wouldn't come. She nodded, though, seemed to understand me, and we finished cleaning up.

Later, I thought that surely I would have trouble sleeping. The anticipation would keep me awake until the dawn, listening to everybody's breathing, and the occasional quiet crackle of the fire. But I fell asleep, and slept as soundly as when I was a child and both of our parents were still alive, and we had never known war. Had barely known a hard farm year. I woke in the golden morning, Marek's hand gently closed on my shoulder.

"It's time," he said. I smelled the coffee, and thought Lew was uncharacteristically quiet.

"Thank you." I straightened my clothes, combed out my hair. When we first cut it all off, I thought I would miss it. But I haven't, not really. Artur wound around my feet as I walked to the table, which he hadn't done since he was very small.

The smith sat there with her coffee, with breakfast laid out, and my stomach dropped. She saw my look, though, and smiled. "It's best if you eat first," she said. "You'll likely have many hungry days before the war is done."

"Thank you," I said, though I thought it would be impossible to choke anything down. I managed some bread, some cheese. The eggs were gone, I felt bad about that. I didn't know where she got her food. I wished again that we'd had anything to bring her. We weren't even paying her for the gun, other than some dream of the war ending. Nobody had that in their pocket.

She got up and went to the workshop for a moment, and came out with a roll of fabric. I was expecting a wooden box like a treasure chest, I realized, or a holster, but why would she have either? The fabric had chickens printed on it; I had a skirt almost like it when I was a little girl. She set it in the table in front of me and it sounded like knocking on a door.

I sat for a moment, just looking at the chickens, listening to the clocks, the fire settle, Artur panting. It was like everybody else was holding their breath, like I was the only one in the room. Just me and the smith and this gun.

I reached out to unroll it, both hands, surprised at the heft, relieved. It felt like a responsibility. That, I'd expected.

I didn't know it was going to be beautiful. Silvery with gold tracing, feathered etchings on the rotor, the grip dark-polished wood like a music box, the hammer and the trigger and trigger guard seeming like fanciful filigree, not tools of war. I could see my face in the barrel, pale as though I was bathed in moonlight.

Lew was talking—I felt his voice rather than heard it—and I looked up, feeling as though I was waking all over again. The smith looked only at me, as Lew thanked her, as Marek thanked her, and I looked only at her, the gun in my hands like a baby, like an axe, like every hope and hate in the whole world.

"Sto lat," she said, and I thought of all those sleeping knights with their horses at hand, waiting under the mountain, waiting endlessly. Maybe this was how they would rise up and fight after all. One gun at a time.

"Sto lat," I said, my voice echoing in my head, in the room. One hundred years.

"Now go," she said. And we went.

It was the wrong time of day to travel as we were, ragtag and on foot, cutting across fallow fields, Artur ranging ahead and coming back. I carried the gun awkwardly inside my coat, touching the grips with my fingertips again and again. The men glanced at me, didn't say anything. We were somehow alright, unnoticed, for many miles, but at nightfall we saw sudden headlights, heard the harsh voices as we approached the road. We froze like rabbits, turned to skulk back into the night.

"Stop! Come here!"

Lew ran, Marek grabbed my arm and ran, Artur was a streak in the dusk. There was more yelling behind us, car doors, and a single shot. I stumbled, shook Marek's hand off my arm. I flapped open my coat, the gun coming into my hand like breathing, burning in my palm, and I turned as I drew, feeling like the whole world spun on me and my arm was pointing north on a compass or at twelve on a clock.

I thumbed the hammer back and the click was deafening, even with my brother yelling behind me, soldiers yelling in front of me, and my finger curled around the gleaming trigger and it seemed like I heard hoof beats as I fired the first blazing shot.

Jennifer R. Donohue is from the Jersey Shore and now lives in central New York with her husband and her Doberman, where she works at her local library and facilitates a writing workshop. She grew up with pierogies and her grandmother's Polish lullabies. Inspiration for this story came from the legend of the sleeping knights, who would one day gallop out from under the mountain and fight for Poland once more. Her work has appeared in *Escape Pod, Mythic Delirium, Truancy,* and elsewhere. Her novella *Run With the Hunted* is available in paperback and on most digital platforms. She blogs at Authorized Musings, where she shares fiction and the tribulations of the writing life, and tweets @AuthorizedMusin

THINGS FORGOTTEN ON THE CLIFFS OF AVEVIG

Wendy Nikel

Ebba grappled with the net, gripping its long, leather-bound handle as she trudged upward to the seaside cliffs. When she crested the hill, the lonely, red-roofed farmhouse behind her vanished from sight, leaving only a wisp in the sky beyond it where the village's factory churned. She let her burden fall, allowing the net to bump along on the rocky ground behind her with a *thump-thump* rhythm like a song skipping on a gramophone.

Her brother Poul would've scolded, warning her not to snag the net on the briars or dent its pole on the unforgiving stones. She'd have argued that the fleygestang wasn't that fragile, or it'd be useless for puffin-catching. It was like her: small and thin and not much to look at but stronger than it appeared.

It was still strange to have to devise both sides of their arguments herself.

The stone fleyging-seat was tucked into the cliff where no one could see her, where she could be alone with the sea and her memories, away from the farmhouse that echoed Mama's silence and the factory with its sky-darkening smoke that hung overhead, a constant reminder of the war.

This side of the island was noisy in a different manner: with crashing waves and puffins squawking their unintelligible conversations. Poul used to sit here with her, imitating their voices and pretending he understood them. As a child, Ebba had believed him. Anything had been possible then.

She extended the fleygestang as a puffin darted past, flicking her wrist to snare it in the net. It struggled and squawked as she pulled it in, as she grabbed the bird's spine and snapped its neck. Bird after bird joined the pile of limp bodies, dinner for her and Mama, plus some extras for bartering in town.

Two birds passed, swifter than the rest, and Ebba reached the net out and snared one. When she pulled it in, she found to her surprise that it wasn't a puffin at all, but a bird not often seen around these shores: a raven.

"Release me!"

Ebba nearly tumbled from her fleyging-seat in surprise. "Who are you?"

"My name is Munin, and I will grant you a feather for my release."

"A feather?" Feathers were plentiful here, though perhaps not ones as dark as his, for his were as black and shining as the machine guns Mama made down in the factory.

"Each feather contains a memory," the bird said, "any memory you choose, to relive whenever you hold it."

Ebba's heart skipped. *A memory.*

Her fingers worked quickly, expertly, without hesitation, and soon the bird was free.

"I want a memory of—"

"Ah! I know just the one." And with that, Munin stretched his wings and rose skyward, releasing a single shining feather.

As Ebba's fingers closed around it, she was there, in their farmhouse, but now it was full of warmth and laughter and life. Poul was there. It was his eighteenth birthday, just days before he signed away his future and his life, and he was dancing and singing a skjaldur, and Mama was clapping and laughing at his antics. It was the last time Ebba had seen Mama happy.

Ebba tucked the feather away, fearful of wearing out its magic. She gathered up her puffins and set out toward town.

When Ebba arrived home with their weekly rations, Mama was already in bed, her thin eyelashes fluttering and lips twitching. She hadn't left the house save for her daily shift at the factory, not even to tend the garden she'd once loved. She'd barely spoken, hadn't smiled at all in the weeks since Poul joined the war.

Ebba placed the feather on Mama's nightstand where she'd see it right away. Then, in the thick silence, Ebba crawled into bed.

Sobs cut through the stillness, and Ebba woke with a start. Moonlight through the dusty window illuminated Mama's shaking shoulders and the shimmers of tears tracing lines down her face. In the pale glow, Ebba could just make out the outline of Munin's feather, clutched to Mama's chest.

Ebba froze in horror, not even daring to breathe. What had she done? The memory was supposed to make things better, not worse, yet she hadn't heard Mama cry like that before, even when the messenger in the gravel-gray suit brought that accursed telegram, even when they buried Poul's body alongside Papa's grave.

Ebba squeezed her eyes shut and pressed her fists to her ears, dampening the sobs until they faded.

In the morning, the feather lay on the scuffed wood floor. Ebba snatched it up and laced up her boots, determined to get rid of it.

She'd take it back. She'd tie it to a stone and toss it from the cliffs so that no one could find it. She'd purge the memory, that awful memory that had made Mama cry so wretchedly. Even the aching silence was more tolerable than that pain.

Upon the worn path, the wind pressed against Ebba's back, urging her along and whistling in her ears. She clutched the feather in her gloved hands, and when she reached the highest cliff, she stumbled to her knees.

"Take it back, Munin," she called, raising the feather overhead, daring the bird to descend from the clouds like a zeppelin and retrieve it. "I don't want it anymore. I don't want Mama to be sad, and I don't want to remember if it's going to hurt so much. Take it away."

A hand reached out from behind her and touched the feather, grasping it firmly and pulling it from the sky. Ebba turned in surprise. It was Mama. Her hair was unwashed and unruly, her clothing rumpled and worn, but she was here, out on the cliffs, in her bare feet.

"I'm sorry," Mama said, her tears flowing freely down her dirt-streaked cheeks. "I'm sorry that I'd forgotten. Will you help me remember what it's like to be happy?"

Ebba flung herself forward and they embraced there on the cliff, the feather tucked between them where they both could hear Poul's singing, see his shining, happy face. They watched as he danced and smiled along with him, their shared laughter ringing in their ears and the sun breaking through the smoke to warm their tear-streaked cheeks.

And somewhere overhead, a bird called—not with the squawk of a puffin, but with the mournful cry of a raven.

Wendy Nikel is a speculative fiction author who enjoys sitting out on her back porch with a cup of coffee and watching the birds (though, no, she hasn't seen Hugin and Munin, the mythological ravens featured in this story, yet—probably because Utah is too far from Scandinavia). Her short fiction has been published by *Daily Science Fiction*, *Nature: Futures*, and is forthcoming from *Analog* and *Beneath Ceaseless Skies*. Her time travel novella series, beginning with *The Continuum*, is available from World Weaver Press. For more info, visit wendynikel.com

ABOUT THE ANTHOLOGIST

Rhonda Parrish is the editor of more than a dozen anthologies including, most recently, *Fire: Demons, Dragons and Djinns* and *Tesseracts: Nevertheless.*

In addition, Rhonda's written work has been in publications such as *Tesseracts 17: Speculating Canada from Coast to Coast* and *Imaginarium: The Best Canadian Speculative Writing* (2012 & 2015). Her YA Thriller, *Hollow*, is forthcoming (March 2020) and her website, updated regularly, is at http://www.rhondaparrish.com

MORE ANTHOLOGIES FROM RHONDA PARRISH

RHONDA PARRISH'S MAGICAL MENAGERIES

Featuring Amanda C. Davis, Angela Slatter, Andrew Bourelle, Beth Cato, C.S.E. Cooney, Dan Koboldt, Holly Schofield, Jane Yolen, Laura VanArendonk Baugh, Mike Allen, and many more.

Find these and more great short fiction anthologies at

WWW.WORLDWEAVERPRESS.COM

Also available at Amazon, Apple Books, BarnesandNoble.com, IndieBound, Kobo, and other online booksellers.

Thank you for reading!

We hope you'll leave an honest review at Amazon, Goodreads, or wherever you discuss books online.

Leaving a review helps readers like you discover great new books, and shows support for the authors who worked so hard to create these stories.

Please sign up for our newsletter for news about upcoming titles, submission opportunities, special discounts, & more.

WorldWeaverPress.com/newsletter-signup

World Weaver Press, LLC
Publishing fantasy, paranormal, and science fiction.
We believe in great storytelling.
WorldWeaverPress.com

CPSIA information can be obtained
at www.ICGtesting.com
Printed in the USA
LVHW081607090919
628854LV00016B/87/P

9 781732 254664